FRIENDS AND RIVALS

Tilly Bagshawe is the internationally bestselling author of nine previous novels. A single mother at seventeen, Tilly won a place at Cambridge University and took her baby daughter with her. She went on to enjoy a successful career in the City before becoming a writer. As a journalist, Tilly contributed regularly to the *Sunday Times, Daily Mail* and *Evening Standard* before following in the footsteps of her sister Louise and turning her hand to novels.

Tilly's first book, *Adored*, was a smash hit on both sides of the Atlantic and she hasn't looked back since. Tilly and her family divide their time between their homes in Kensington and Los Angeles and their beach house on Nantucket Island.

Also by Tilly Bagshawe

Adored
Showdown
Do Not Disturb
Flawless
Fame
Scandalous
Sidney Sheldon's Mistress of the Game
Sidney Sheldon's After the Darkness
Sidney Sheldon's Angel of the Dark

To find out more about Tilly Bagshawe and her
books, log on to www.tillybagshawe.co.uk

TILLY BAGSHAWE

Friends and Rivals

HARPER

Harper
An imprint of HarperCollins*Publishers*
77–85 Fulham Palace Road,
Hammersmith, London W6 8JB

www.harpercollins.co.uk

A Paperback Original 2012
1

Copyright © Tilly Bagshawe 2012

Tilly Bagshawe asserts the moral right to
be identified as the author of this work

A catalogue record for this book
is available from the British Library

ISBN: 978-0-00-746054-0

Set in Meridien by Palimpsest Book Production Limited,
Falkirk, Stirlingshire

Printed and bound in Great Britain by
Clays Ltd, St Ives plc

For my children:
Sefi, Zac, Theo and Summer.

ACKNOWLEDGEMENTS

With thanks to my wonderful editor, Sarah Ritherdon, and all at HarperCollins for their support, talent, hard work and willingness to move deadlines around yet another Bagshawe baby bump. To my agents Tim Glister and Luke Janklow, also to Kirsty Gordon, Claire Dippel and everyone at Janklow & Nesbit. And to my 'manny' and dear friend Vasile Cozmici, for taking such good care of my children while I write. Without you there would be no books.

Finally, huge thanks as always to my family, especially my husband, Robin, who makes my life an adventure. After sixteen years and four kids, you're still everything to me. And to think they said we'd never last . . . I love and adore you.

TB.

PART ONE

CHAPTER ONE

Catriona Charles sucked in her stomach as hard as she could and yanked on the zip of her burgundy velvet dress. It had fitted her perfectly when she'd bought it in Oxford four weeks ago, but now voluptuous folds of flesh seemed to be creeping out everywhere, like excess pastry flopping over the top of a pie dish. Tomorrow, without fail, she would go on a diet. No more Hobnobs. Or cheese. And she would cut out booze for a month. Well, perhaps not a whole month. Two weeks would probably be enough to make a difference.

'Can I help? Two hands are better than one.'

Ivan Charles, Catriona's husband of fifteen years, walked up behind her. Pulling the two sides of fabric together, he pulled the zip to the top and fastened the hook and eye.

'There.' He smiled triumphantly. 'You look gorgeous.'

He was right. With her tangle of honey-blonde hair, full, sensual lips and intelligent green eyes, not to mention a pair of breasts that many girls half her age would have given their eye teeth for, at thirty-eight Catriona Charles was still an extremely attractive woman. Admittedly two kids, a fondness for gin and tonic and cheese on toast and a loathing of physical exercise in all its forms had allowed her figure to blossom a little *too* much in recent years. It would be fair to say Catriona looked better in an evening dress than a bikini. But men had always found her Nigella-esque, just-rolled-out-of-bed look a turn-on, and couldn't understand Catriona's own insecurity about her looks.

'Really?' she sighed. 'You're sure I don't look like a lump of cookie dough squeezed into a wine bottle?'

Ivan laughed, kissing her on the back of her neck. 'Mmmm. Cookie dough and cabernet. Two of my favourite things. And here are two more.' He squeezed her breasts. 'Happy Birthday to me, eh?'

Tonight was Ivan Charles's fortieth birthday party, an event that had consumed every waking hour of his wife's time for the past three months. As co-founder and owner of Jester, a successful music management company, Ivan Charles was one of the most well-connected men in the record business. Ivan's 'friends' were so numerous they could have banded together and formed their own country. Even at Oxford, where he and Catriona had first met, and where Ivan had also met his Jester business partner, Jack Messenger, Ivan was infamous as a *bon vivant* and all-round party animal. With his model good looks (dark hair, blue eyes, toned rower's physique) and immense personal charm, he was also well known as a ladies' man. Hundreds of hearts were broken the day that Ivan Charles walked down the aisle with Catriona Farley. Though the marriage had been stormy at times, they had had two gorgeous kids together and were still going strong the better part of two decades later. Ivan Charles congratulated himself on that. Then again, Ivan Charles congratulated himself on a lot of things for which he was not, in truth, responsible. For all his wit and charisma, beneath the dazzle, Ivan Charles was a deeply arrogant man.

He's so bloody handsome still, thought Catriona, watching her husband adjust his bow tie and flick a piece of lint from the lapel of his dinner jacket. *How lucky I am to be married to him.*

Ivan looked at his vintage Omega watch, a gift from a grateful client. 'Six o'clock. Shall we have a sneaky glass of champagne before the locusts descend?'

'Are you joking?' wheezed Catriona. She could barely breathe in the dress. 'I still have all the place cards to do, the caterer's having a cow because only half the mixers got delivered and the playroom looks like a bloody bomb's hit it.'

'Who's going to be going in the playroom?' said Ivan reasonably. 'Come on, Cat. One drink.'

'Muuuuuuuuum!' A wild, animal shriek echoed along the hallway. Catriona recognized it as her twelve-year-old daughter, Rosie. 'Hector put food colouring in the shampoo bottle. My hair's gone fucking BLUE! It won't come out!'

'Don't fucking swear,' Ivan bellowed back, earning himself a reproving look from Catriona. 'What? She needs to be told. Both the children swear like bloody truck drivers.'

'I wonder why!'

'Muuuum! I need you! Now!'

Catriona rolled her eyes to heaven. It was going to be a very long night.

Jack Messenger turned his Bentley Continental off the A40 onto the single-track road marked 'Widford'. He'd first come to this part of the world in his teens, when he'd won a Rhodes Scholarship to Oxford, and it had always occupied a special place in his heart. To Jack, an American, the Cotswolds were like something out of a theme park or a Disney cartoon. The ancient churches and cottages, the crumbling dry-stone walls, the welcoming pubs and lush meadows dissected by rivers whose names conjured up a romantic, lost England: Leach, Churn, Dun, Windrush, Evenlode; all of them delighted him and inspired a sense of wonder that he'd never lost.

Since founding Jester with Ivan Charles, his best friend from those halcyon undergraduate days, Jack Messenger had lived most of his adult life in Los Angeles. Jack ran Jester's LA office, managing primarily pop acts, while Ivan oversaw the London operation. Ivan's clients were mostly classical artists, although in the last three years he'd made a concerted effort to diversify his list. Back in the early days, when they were still building the business, Jack made regular trips back to Blighty to see his old friend. With his wife, Sonya, he'd enjoyed countless boozy suppers at the Charleses' London house – Ivan and Catriona had lived in Battersea at the time. Jack remembered those evenings fondly: Catriona the ever-welcoming hostess, Ivan rattling off anecdote after anecdote until Sonya had literally collapsed with laughter at the table.

They felt a long way away now.

Sonya Messenger, Jack's adored wife, had died three years ago of breast cancer. For Jack, the laughter had died with her. After three months spent sobbing in bed, he had finally got up one morning and gone into work. The joke at Jester was that he had been at his desk ever since. The president of the United States had more downtime than Jack Messenger, whose workaholic habits were famed throughout the business; in stark contrast to those of his business partner Ivan Charles.

The conventional wisdom was that Jack and Ivan had grown apart, but in fact the two men had always been very different, the most unlikely of friends. Even as a young man,

Jack Messenger had come across as earnest and serious. His nickname at Balliol had been 'Sam Eagle' after the pompous, all-American character from *The Muppet Show*. Despite his good looks (Jack was blond and tall with long legs and a straight, almost military bearing), he had never enjoyed Ivan's success with girls, most of whom thought him arrogant and aloof. In fact, Jack was neither of these things. He was shy; something that only a few close friends, like Catriona and Ivan, fully recognized. And Sonya, of course. Jack's wife had done wonders for his confidence, coaxing out his wry sense of humour, encouraging him to be more open in public, more relaxed. Marriage suited Jack Messenger. When Sonya was alive he had flourished like a sapling in the sunshine. But her death had blighted everything. Annihilated by grief, Jack retreated further into his shell than ever. Even old friends struggled to reach him, though Catriona kept trying, inviting him on family holidays (Jack was godfather to her and Ivan's son, Hector) and to stay with them at Christmas.

Meanwhile, after a few months of genuine sympathy, Ivan started to grow tired of his partner's mood swings. 'I understand him being sad,' he complained to Catriona. 'I know how much he loved Sonya. But he's so bloody self-righteous at work, it's driving me crazy. He's always breathing down my neck about the accounts or new business or how I need to put more "face time" in at the office. It's my bloody office! And what the fuck is "face time" anyway? I ask you. Just because he uses work as a crutch doesn't give him the right to preach to the rest of us.'

In fact this was a heavily edited version of Jack's professional battles with Ivan. As Jester became more and more successful, so Ivan grew more arrogant, lazy and entitled. He often told friends that the London office 'ran itself'. The truth was that Jester's underpaid junior staff ended up carrying ninety per cent of the workload while Ivan swanned around the South of France 'networking'. And that wasn't the worst of it. Now that he was rich, Ivan had sold the villa in Battersea and bought The Rookery, an idyllic Elizabethan manor house in the Windrush Valley, complete with stables, dovecotes, peacocks and a four-hundred-year-old maze. It was Catriona's dream house, and she and the children lived there full time while Ivan commuted to a smart bachelor flat in Belgravia, where he proceeded to bed a string of Jester's young, female interns, along with a fair number of the prettier clients. Jack was livid.

'It's un-fucking-professional.'

'Nonsense,' quipped Ivan. 'I'm committed to closer client liaison, that's all. And it's important to stay on top of one's staff.'

'It's not funny,' snapped Jack. 'What about poor Catriona? She'd be heartbroken if she knew.'

Ivan's voice hardened. 'Yes, well, she doesn't know. And as long as you keep your mouth shut, there's no reason she ever should. Look,' he added, 'I love Catriona, OK? But it's complicated. She knew I wasn't a saint when she married me. There are a lot of temptations in our line of work.'

'Horseshit,' said Jack succinctly. 'I'm not banging every secretary or starlet that walks through the door in LA.'

'Well maybe you should be,' said Ivan, irritated. 'A good fuck might lighten you up a bit, you miserable sod. Just because you're gunning for a sainthood, doesn't mean the rest of us have to. If I want marriage guidance, I'll ask for it.'

That conversation had been over a year ago now. Since then, Ivan's midlife crisis, if that's what it was, seemed to have cooled. He and Jack had repaired their working relationship, but the easy friendship of old was gone for good. Catriona had invited Jack to numerous parties and events but he'd managed to wriggle out of almost all of them, using work and the long LA–London flight as an excuse. But Ivan Charles's fortieth birthday party would be the biggest music industry bash in England for almost a decade. There was no way Jack could skip it without raising serious eyebrows as to the state of the union at Jester. That was the last thing Jack wanted.

As soon as the Bentley dipped down into the valley, Jack heard the distant *thump, thump* of music drifting on the warm summer air. It was only eight o'clock, and still light, but it sounded as if the party was already in full swing. The Rookery was approached via a long, winding drive, which one entered through old, lichened stone gates. Jack had been to the house before, of course, but had forgotten how ravishing it truly was, with its formal gardens, leaded windows and wisteria-covered façade. Catriona was a natural-born homemaker, and had made it look even more magical tonight, with candles in glass pots hung from the trees, and wooden tables outside covered in a mismatched patchwork of cloths, each one sporting a jug stuffed to the brim with wild flowers.

The paddock was already heaving with cars. Jack parked his Bentley next to a filthy Land Rover and headed into the house. He hadn't got past the hallway when a very pretty, very drunk Asian girl ran up to him giggling and literally threw herself into his arms.

'I'm a damsel in distress!' she slurred. 'The zip on my dress is broken. Can you help me fix it, pleashe? Ivan says he won't.'

Something about her dress was certainly broken. It was barely bigger than a handkerchief anyway, a wisp of red silk, but what little of it there was kept slipping off the girl's tiny frame and revealing more than Jack wanted to see.

'Joyce!' Ivan's voice boomed out from the drawing-room doorway. Jack looked up to see his partner grinning like the Cheshire Cat. 'Put Mr Messenger down, darling. You're scaring him.'

The Asian girl released Jack and scurried over to Ivan, who slipped an arm around her tiny waist. Jack looked at her face more closely. Good God. It was Joyce Wu, the virtuoso violinist, one of Jester's most successful classical artists. Known for her awesome discipline and focus, Joyce Wu was still only nineteen. Her publicity pictures showed a serious young woman, usually dressed in a polo neck and long skirt, clutching a Stradivarius. It was hard to connect *that* girl to this one, drunkenly trying to cover at least one of her breasts while Ivan idly ran his fingers through her silken black hair.

'Good to see you, Jack. Can I get you a drink?' Ivan stopped a passing waiter with a tray of cocktails.

'I'll have a Diet Coke, please.'

'No you won't. It's a party,' said Ivan, thrusting something colourful and umbrella-ed into Jack's hand. Before he had a chance to protest, Jack was accosted by both the Charles children, leaping up at him and yapping like a pair of puppies. Rosie, at twelve, looked distinctly pre-teen in her 'sophisticated' Monsoon evening dress and blue-streaked hair. But Hector, her younger brother and Jack's godson, was still very much a child at eleven. Physically, he was a carbon copy of his father, dark-haired and handsome with a deliciously naughty twinkle in his eye. But in temperament, Jack had always thought of him as more like Catriona. Laid-back, gentle, sweet.

'Did you bring me a present?' he asked Jack, guilelessly.

Jack grinned. 'I might have. I guess it depends. How well behaved have you been lately? Do you deserve a present?'

'He's been bloody awful,' said Ivan, letting go of Joyce Wu and grabbing his son affectionately by the arm. 'Kicked out of St Wilfred's. Catriona's at her wits' end.'

'I got my green belt in karate, though,' said Hector cheerfully. 'Anyway, I know you've got me a present, because you always do. Is it an iPad 2?'

'If it is, I'm confiscating it,' said Ivan, shoving both his children towards the playroom where various kids were watching movies and gorging themselves on salt-and-vinegar crisps. 'Now sod off, would you? Uncle Jack has people to see.'

Ivan led Jack through the heaving drawing room, stopping every few seconds to introduce him to new clients and remind him of the names of the old ones. The room itself was beautiful in an old English sort of a way. The walls were panelled in original dark oak, worn to a rich gleam over centuries of use, and the fireplace was a vast, baronial effort in rough-hewn Cotswold stone, tall enough for a woman to stand up in without stooping. In the wintertime, huge pine logs crackled and spat in the hearth day and night. Tonight, however, the flags were swept clean and an absolutely enormous display of white flowers exploded in its centre: roses and lilies and freesias, all of them so powerfully scented that a passing bee would have fainted if it had come within a yard of them. Above the fireplace, where one might have expected to see a giant mirror or an oil painting of some illustrious ancestor, one of Catriona's photographs hung in pride of place. A brilliant amateur snapper, her specialty was portraits, but this piece was a landscape shot of the Windrush Valley in winter. To Jack it conjured up nothing so much as the forest of Narnia; a magical, snowy wonderland too strange and beautiful to be of this earth. He'd offered to buy it countless times, but neither Ivan nor Catriona would contemplate letting it go.

'Joyce Wu seemed a little unhinged earlier,' Jack whispered in Ivan's ear as they made their way towards the bar. 'Is everything OK there?'

'Joyce is fine,' said Ivan breezily. 'Better than fine actually. Polygram just made her a whopping two-album offer.'

'That's not what I meant. I meant is she coping OK with the fame, the pressure? She's still very young.'

Ivan put a hand on Jack's arm. 'Jack. She's fine. As you say, she's young. She's letting her hair down at a party, that's all. It's called having fun. You should try it some time.'

They emerged onto a stone terrace. It was twilight now, and the view of The Rookery's gardens with the meadows and river beyond was unutterably lovely. Jack sipped his cocktail and soaked up the beauty of it all. *Ivan's right. It's a party. I should try and relax.*

'Speaking of unhinged clients,' said Ivan, ' how's Kendall?'

Jack felt the tension surge back into his body. Kendall Bryce, a twenty-three-year-old pop sensation with Kim Kardashian's body and Aretha Franklin's voice, was probably Jester's most famous client. She was also Jack Messenger's personal protégée or, as he preferred to think of it, the cross he had to bear.

'Kendall is Kendall. She's difficult.'

'Is she using?' Ivan asked bluntly. Kendall Bryce's cocaine problems were as well documented as her love life. She was a good kid deep down and Jack was very fond of her. But she was insecure as all hell.

'No. I've got her doing tests weekly. She knows if she slips up again she's off our books for good. I meant to talk to you about that, actually. I need you to make sure she keeps up with the drug tests in London. Every Friday, without fail. And she's not supposed to drink either.'

'Sure,' said Ivan. But he said it with a nonchalance that made Jack profoundly uneasy. Kendall was due to perform six concerts at UK venues over the next three weeks, a thought that filled Jack with dread and relief in equal measure. Relief because it meant he got a three-week break from playing bad cop. Policing Kendall Bryce's lifestyle was becoming a full-time job. But dread because he had no control over what she might do once let off the leash.

'Jack!' Catriona Charles came running across the lawn, her face flushed with happiness, tendrils of dirty-blonde hair escaping from pins in all directions. Jack had a sudden flashback to Oxford, and Catriona tearing barefoot around the quad at Magdalen on the night of the ball. Give or take a few laughter lines around the eyes and the odd pound of extra weight, she hadn't changed. 'You made it!'

'Of course I made it. Wouldn't have missed it for the world,' lied Jack.

'We've been catching up,' said Ivan, swapping his empty glass for a full one. 'Discussing our most badly behaved clients.'

'Well, I hope you aren't going to be boring and talk business all night,' Catriona said firmly, taking Jack's hand. 'Come on. Loads of the old gang are here.'

By 'the old gang' she meant Oxford friends. Old turned out to be the operative word. For the next hour Jack found himself shaking hands and reminiscing with a series of paunchy, balding men, none of whom he'd have recognized had Catriona not told him their names. It was depressing.

'We've aged,' he said to Catriona, once he finally managed to get her alone. 'Jamie Grayson looks as old as the fucking hills.'

'Poor Jamie,' Catriona frowned. 'He's had a rough year, what with the divorce and everything. Anyway, *you* haven't aged. You and Ivan both look disgustingly young and handsome.'

Jack laughed. 'Ivan maybe. Not me. How is he, anyway? How are the two of you?'

'We're fine.' Catriona smiled, hoping it didn't look as forced as it felt. Jack was too tactful to spell it out, but she knew what *'how are the two of you?'* meant. About five years ago, she'd discovered Ivan had been having an affair with one of the girls at Jester. He'd broken it off, and seemed genuinely remorseful at the time. But then a year later, she'd caught him at it again. Since then, things had been a lot better. When Ivan was in London he called every night to say goodnight to her, and to reassure her he was alone. He'd started going to therapy, and talking to Catriona more openly about his insecurities. Turning forty, in particular, bothered him, but rather than boosting his ego with another fling, he'd started spending more time with the children, especially Hector who worshipped his father like a god.

'I think Ivan's finally growing up,' Catriona told Jack. For some reason she felt the need to expand on 'we're fine'. 'I don't mean that nastily. It's just that, you know, he's struggled with his age and the changes in our lives. But he seems more peaceful now. More content.'

'Who's more content?'

A pretty American woman in a shapeless Ali Hewson black dress sidled up to them. Jack's heart sank. 'Hello, Stella.'

Stella Bayley was the wife of Brett Bayley, lead guitarist of supergroup The Blitz. Brett and his bandmates were clients of Jack's in Los Angeles, but were currently halfway through a European tour, so Brett and Stella were temporarily based in London. Brett was thick as a plank with an ego the size of Kansas and, if the groupies were to be believed, a dick to match. His wife, oblivious to Brett's affairs but accepting of his long absences, had devoted her free time to becoming a tireless (and tiresome) eco-campaigner. Her blog, Stella's World, in which she doled out lifestyle and parenting advice to the masses, was an inexplicable hit online. Inexplicable because anyone who had actually *met* Stella Bayley knew that her entire life was run by a fleet of exhausted staff, and that she herself had about as much maternal nous as a banana skin.

'How are you liking England?' Jack asked politely. 'Are you settled in yet?'

'Settled in?' Stella gave her trademark tinkling laugh. 'If you call living out of packing cases settled in, then yeah. You know the other day, Miley comes up to me and she's like "Mommy, Mommy, can we have a picnic?" And of course it was raining outside, so I got some sheets and draped them over two of these damn cases, like a little tent, you know? And we had an *indoor picnic!* How cute is that? A little quinoa, some rice cakes and raisins made to look like smiley faces. I put it on the blog and my readers were like, Oh my God that is so *cute.* And I'm like, I *know.* I love England! I love the rain! You should hear Miley's accent. I swear she sounds like Princess Diana, doesn't she, Catriona?'

'Erm . . .' said Catriona. She had only met Miley Bayley once. As she remembered, the three-year-old barely spoke, but when she did she sounded like Mickey Mouse on helium.

Stella prattled on. 'I'm always telling my readers: having fun with your kids doesn't have to mean spending a lot of money. Brett and I are all about the simple things.' She tossed her expensively highlighted mane of blonde hair and flashed a new set of porcelain veneers in Jack's general direction. 'But anyway, enough about me. I came over to talk to Catriona about this fabulous new personal trainer I've found – Morten. He's based in Primrose Hill, but he has lots of clients in the country. Morten'll help you shed those excess pounds faster than you can say colonic irrigation. I'll give you his number.'

Eventually Stella fluttered off to share her words of wisdom with Ned Williams, a well-known tenor who lived locally and was another of Jester's clients. The look of wild-eyed panic as Stella approached was enough to make even Jack Messenger chuckle.

'Maybe I should get a trainer,' sighed Catriona, looking down at her escaping bosom and yanking up the bodice of her dress.

'And shrink the best bust in England? Don't you dare,' said Jack, kissing her on the cheek. He could have strangled Stella Bayley. 'Don't ever change, Cat. Especially not on the advice of that ridiculous woman.'

'She means well.'

'She's horrendous. You're wonderful.'

He says the nicest things, thought Catriona, watching him weave his way back into the house. She so hoped he and Ivan managed to patch things up.

Inside, Jack suddenly realized he was famished. Ignoring the dainty silver trays offering caviar blinis and mini vol-au-vents, he headed straight for the kitchen and helped himself to a large peanut-butter sandwich and two mugs of tea, ignoring the death stares from Catriona's catering staff. The Rookery kitchen was a cosy, welcoming room, dominated by a pink six-oven Aga and a gnarled old farmhouse table that looked as if it hadn't been moved for centuries. Hector and Rosie's artwork covered most of the available wall surfaces, with the remainder given over to family photographs, all taken by Cat. Hector as a baby, his chubby face smeared with chocolate cake. Rosie, aged seven, on her first pony, beaming a gap-toothed grin as she held up her 'Highly

Commended' rosette. Jack was ashamed to feel a stab of envy. He and Sonya had never had children, though they'd both wanted them. Sonya was halfway through her first round of IVF when her cancer was diagnosed, poor darling. *Am I tougher on Ivan because I'm jealous? Because he has a family and I don't?* It was an uncomfortable thought.

Pushing it from his mind, Jack went upstairs in search of a bathroom. The queue for the downstairs loo was enormous and all that Earl Grey had gone straight to his bladder. There were two sets of stairs at The Rookery: the grand, sweeping mahogany staircase that led up to the principal bedrooms and that tonight was lit by simple white candles and bedecked with yet more flowers and greenery from the garden; and the back, servants' stairs, a narrow, steeply winding passage that spat one out into a long corridor, giving on to a series of smaller, pokier rooms. Vaguely remembering there was a guest bathroom at the end of this corridor, Jack took the back stairs. Pushing open the last door, he stopped dead.

'Jesus!'

Ivan was standing at the foot of the bath with his pants around his ankles. Joyce Wu was bent over the bath, spread-eagled and moaning as he took her from behind, thrusting so hard that Joyce's tiny apple breasts quivered like twin jellies with each jerk of the hips. The young girl's eyes had a familiar, glazed look. Sure enough, when Jack glanced at the sink, a fine line of leftover white powder was clearly visible.

It took Ivan Charles a second to realize that they had been interrupted. Joyce, lost in her own world, took longer, only registering Jack's presence once Ivan stopped moving. She opened her mouth to scream, but Ivan lunged forward, covering her mouth with his hand.

'Now, now, darling. We don't need a bigger audience. One's enough.'

Shaking, Joyce grabbed her red dress off the floor and held it protectively over her naked body. Jack Messenger held open the bathroom door. 'Go home,' he said quietly.

Joyce darted into the hallway, sobbing. Ivan, meanwhile, looked distinctly unruffled. He'd pulled up his pants and was busy smoothing down his hair and removing lipstick marks from his face and collar with a damp flannel.

Jack spoke first. 'Are you out of your mind?'

'I don't know,' drawled Ivan. 'Am I?'

'Anybody could have walked in!'

'Indeed. But it had to be you who actually *did*, didn't it Jack? You're like an old housemaster, prowling the dorms looking for miscreants. And lo and behold, you found me.' He held out his hand in mock supplication. 'Go ahead, whip out your cane. I'm used to it.'

Jack's stomach turned. 'You think this is funny.'

'Well, I don't think it's tragic, let's put it that way,' Ivan shot back. 'OK, so I've been a naughty boy. But nobody knows, so there's no harm done.'

'No harm?' Jack spluttered. 'She's a client!'

'So?'

'She's a teenager!'

'Only just,' said Ivan, cleaning up the cocaine remnants before swigging from a bottle of mouthwash and spitting into the sink. 'It's my birthday. Joyce was my present. Oh for God's sake, stop looking so thunderous. It was a one-off, all right? It won't happen again. Jack. Jack!'

But Jack had stormed off down the corridor, ignoring Ivan's shouts. The servants' stairs were blocked by a kissing couple so he veered left, practically running down the grand main staircase, so eager was he to get out of there. *Bloody fool. I should never have come tonight.* So much for Ivan turning over a new leaf.

'Oh, there you are.'

Jack was so caught up in his own thoughts that he almost knocked Catriona flying.

'You're not leaving already, are you?' Her face fell. 'We haven't even had the fireworks yet. You must stay for those.'

'Sorry,' he mumbled awkwardly. 'Something's come up. I have to get back to London.'

Goddamn Ivan for implicating him in his bullshit. Now Jack was forced to stand here and lie to one of his oldest friends.

Catriona tried to be understanding. 'Oh. Well, I suppose if you have to. Anyway, before you go, I just wanted to let you know that I'll look out for Kendall when she comes over. As you know, lots of Ivan's clients come up here to stay when they're burned out or stressed or whatever. We've become quite the heartbreak hotel, haven't we?' she laughed. 'I doubt even Miss Bryce can get into too much trouble in the bright lights of Widford on a Saturday night.'

'Thank you. Really. That means a lot.' Jack looked at Catriona, then hugged her tightly, squeezing as if he might never let her go. 'You're a good woman, Catriona Charles. Ivan doesn't deserve you.'

Catriona smiled wryly. 'He probably doesn't deserve you either, Jack darling. I know he must be difficult to work with. But don't give up on him. For my sake.'

Speeding back towards London half an hour later, Jack Messenger felt as depressed as he had in months. Every time it seemed as if Ivan might finally have turned a corner and developed some scruples, he went and did something so shatteringly stupid and selfish it beggared belief.

Jack wished he *could* give up on Ivan. But after fifteen years as partners in Jester, their lives and interests were irrevocably intertwined. Being in business with Ivan Charles was like walking through life with a bomb strapped to your chest. The unpredictability, the selfishness, all wrapped up in a lethally charming package.

Come to think of it, Ivan Charles had a lot in common with the other giant headache in Jack Messenger's life. But, he reflected with relief, at least *she* was safely ensconced in his Brentwood guesthouse under the watchful eye of her twenty-four-hour sobriety coach.

Not even Kendall Bryce could get into too much trouble in those circumstances.

CHAPTER TWO

'Harder! Oh my God, what is the problem? Why do you keep stopping?'

Kendall Bryce looked over her shoulder at her red-faced sobriety coach with withering disdain. Weren't these sober health-freaks supposed to be fit? This guy screwed like a grandfather.

'My electric toothbrush makes me come faster than this. Come on, Kevin. Do it!'

Kevin Dacre closed his eyes and tried to recapture any of the sexual excitement he'd felt when Kendall Bryce, *the* Kendall Bryce, had opened the front door to him half an hour ago in nothing but a pair of Trashy Lingerie panties. Half an hour ago, Kevin was worried he might come before he got his pants off. Now, after being ordered into countless different positions, with Kendall berating him for his poor performance like a particularly ticked-off drill sergeant, all Kevin wanted was to be allowed to go home. That, and for Kendall Bryce not to tell his employer, Jack Messenger, what had happened this evening.

The worst part was that Jack had warned him, in so many

words: 'She'll try anything in the book to get you off her case. If she wants drugs or a drink she'll stop at nothing to get them. She'll probably offer to sleep with you, and let me tell you, Mr Dacre, Kendall's offers can be tough to refuse.'

'I've worked with Charlie Sheen, Mr Messenger,' Kevin had replied confidently. 'If I can keep him clean, I'm pretty confident I can handle Kendall.'

Now Kevin Dacre knew better. Nobody 'handled' Kendall Bryce. She was a force of nature, as impossible to resist as a twister or a riptide. And she had him by the balls, literally as well as metaphorically. If Messenger heard about this – if anyone heard about it – Kevin's career was finished.

At last, with a wild moan and arch of her back, Kendall climaxed. Kevin Dacre whimpered with relief. Easing himself out of her, he slumped down on the bed, exhausted.

'I'll order some pizza,' Kendall announced cheerfully. 'We can wash it down with a couple of bottles of Jack's Mouton Rothschild, and then we can go again.'

Again? Kevin started hyperventilating. 'Kendall, come on. This was fun but we both know it shouldn't have happened. And we also both know I can't let you drink.'

Kendall laughed loudly. '*Let* me? I like that. That's a good one. Besides, it was coke I went to rehab for. I'm not an alcoholic.'

'That's not the point,' said Kevin. 'You're an addict and you're in recovery. No substances means *no* substances. You know that.'

Kendall's eyes narrowed. 'All I know is that *you're* gonna break into the main house and raid Jack's wine closet for me. Because if you don't, *you* know I'm gonna pick up the phone and tell him about the great sex we just had.'

'I thought you said the sex was terrible?'

Kendall looked at him pityingly 'It was terrible, Kevin. I was trying to be kind. But you know what they say: practice makes perfect. Now, how about that drink?'

Kendall Bryce had first come to prominence in her teens as the breakout star of reality show, *Hollywood High*. Small but perfectly formed, her body had the exaggerated, pneumatic curves of a porn star. Her waist was waspishly narrow, her breasts cartoonish in both their size and gravity-defying perkiness, her butt was as high and tight as a male baller-ina's. But it was Kendall's face, a perfectly defined set of smooth planes illuminated by neon green cat's eyes, as well as her attitude, that ensured her swift rise to fame. Kendall Bryce was brattish – certainly – and spoiled; *Hollywood High* was a show about movie-industry kids, so those two attributes were prerequisites. But Kendall could also be devastatingly funny. Her pithy put-downs of contemporaries rapidly became the stuff of legend and she was embraced as a sort of young, insanely hot Joan Rivers.

What *Hollywood High* failed to show was Kendall Bryce's deep, searing insecurity, and the terrible loneliness of her home life. Kendall's father was the producer Vernon Bryce. He divorced her mother when Kendall was twelve, and since then had laid eyes on his eldest daughter a grand total of three times. Two of those occasions were court appearances, for DUI and cocaine possession respectively. The third was for Kendall's twenty-first birthday, when Vernon showed up for the cameras with a ribbon-wrapped pink Maserati complete with Ken 1 number plates, but was too busy to stay for dinner, insisting he had to rush back to his younger kids, Donny and Aiden, the twin boys he had with his new wife and whom he unashamedly adored.

Kendall's mum Lorna was a sweet, pleasant woman, but

she knew nothing about her daughter's wild lifestyle, or if she did she was too weak to do anything about it. The truth was, Lorna Bryce was afraid of Kendall. Her younger children, Holly and Joe, were both so much easier to handle. They hadn't been affected by Vernon's abandonment the way that Kendall had. That was the problem. From babyhood, Kendall Bryce had always been a daddy's girl.

Hiding her pain behind the twin masks of her extraordinary looks and her razor-sharp tongue, Kendall was determined to prove her worth to the father who had dumped her, and to the rest of the world. TV success was a start. But she wanted more than that. She wanted lasting, global superstardom. She wanted to walk on stage in packed stadiums all around the globe and hear people chanting her name.

No one was more surprised than Jack Messenger to discover that Kendall Bryce could sing. Her agent had practically laid siege to Jester's LA office on Beverly Glen until Jack agreed to see her. Reality stars releasing records was really *not* Jester's thing. Plus the Bryce girl had only just got out of jail for cocaine possession. Too much trouble by half. But Kendall's agent was so persistent that Jack relented one Friday afternoon, and gave the kid five minutes. There was an upright piano in Jack's office. He'd been an exceptional pianist in his youth and still found that playing calmed his nerves and cleared his head. He sat down and, rather meanly, started playing Christina Aguilera's *Genie in a Bottle*, an astonishingly difficult song for an untrained vocalist. Kendall Bryce didn't miss a beat. She opened her mouth and belted it out, pitch perfect and with the power and depth of a seasoned Gospel singer. Her voice ricocheted around Jack's office like a sonic boom. After fifteen years in the music business it took a lot to surprise Jack Messenger. But Kendall Bryce had done it, in about two and a half bars.

That meeting was two years ago now. Since then, under Jester's management, Kendall Bryce had gone on to become one of the best-known and biggest-selling female artists in America. But she had also had to submit her entire life to Jack Messenger's control. He'd refused to sign her unless she quit cocaine and alcohol cold turkey, and underwent regular drug testing. She had to join a gym, stop going to nightclubs unless someone from Jester accompanied her, and agree to make no comments to the press whatsoever, unless Jack had personally authorized them. The one and only time she was caught breaking one of these rules (she was photographed drunk on an unauthorized trip to the Chateau Marmont) Jack had forced her to give up the lease on her apartment and move into his guesthouse in Brentwood until her second album was in the can. Needless to say, Kendall had bucked and chafed against such draconian restraints. But she put up with them for two reasons.

One was that she knew Jack Messenger could not only get her to the top but keep her there.

The other was that she was madly, passionately and utterly hopelessly in love with him.

Jack was everything that Kendall's own father was not: decent, honest, loyal, kind and strict. He was tough on her because he cared, and though she fought against him tooth and nail, and was often so infuriated with him she wanted to cry or hit him or both, deep down she felt safe for the first time since she was eleven. Jack was also the first man who, maddeningly, appeared to be totally immune to Kendall's celebrated physical charms. Since the age of fifteen, Kendall Bryce had been used to enslaving any and all men to her will – boys at school, teachers, producers on her show. In Jack Messenger, for the first time, she encountered indifference. Her initial reaction was to assume that he was either grieving too hard for his dead wife, or secretly gay. But, especially since moving onto his property, she'd been forced to abandon both these theories. Jack had a girlfriend, Elizabeth, an attractive, professional woman in her thirties who was about as far removed from Kendall as it was possible to be: discreet, together, undemanding. In short, a grown-up. Jack was never pictured with her in public, but Elizabeth seemed unfazed by this apparent lack of commitment. Nor did she complain about the fact that he still wore his wedding ring, and spent every Saturday afternoon without fail at his wife's grave at Forest Lawn. If this was the sort of woman Jack was looking for, it was little wonder he failed to notice Kendall. But it still hurt.

As with her father, Kendall tried to get Jack's attention by acting out, in particular bedding a string of Jester's male acts to try to make him jealous. As with her father, the strategy failed miserably. In recent months things had hit an all-time low between the two of them. Consumed with longing and frustration and fury, Kendall had started drinking again. Two weeks ago she was breathalysed on Sunset and slapped with another DUI, her fourth. She was lucky to escape jail time. Jack, needless to say, was furious, refusing to allow her to fly with him to London for Ivan Charles's party, an event he knew Kendall had been hugely excited about, and forcing her to stay home with a sobriety-coach-slash-jailer instead.

One day he'll see what's right under his nose, thought Kendall, bitterly. *He'll realize he loves me; that I'm the one who can help him get over Sonya. He'll learn to love again. We'll learn together.*

Until that day, however, she wasn't about to let Jack push her around. In a week's time she'd be in London anyway, performing, and there was nothing he could do to stop her having the time of her life. Meanwhile, Kendall had no intention of joining a nunnery just to make Jack happy. Sex with her sobriety coach might not have been spectacular. But it was two fingers to Jack holier-than-thou Messenger. That alone made it worth it.

The next morning a perfect clear, blue-skied dawn broke over Los Angeles, just as Lex Abrahams was brewing his second pot of coffee on the stove. Lex rarely slept more than four or five hours a night and was always up before six. Years spent on the road as a photographer, flying from continent to continent at the whim of his famous, rock-star clients, had left him immune to jet lag and to exhaustion generally. Which was a good thing, as he now worked for Jack Whip-Cracker Messenger as Jester's in-house photographer; a dream job as long as you didn't mind insane hours, capricious artists and a pay packet that barely covered your rent and bills.

Happily, Lex didn't. Photography was his life, music his business, and Jack Messenger one of the nicest, most decent men he had ever met. All in all, Lex Abrahams considered himself one of the luckiest twenty-eight-year-olds on the planet.

Especially this morning. This morning he got to see Kendall, to show her the first images from last week's shoot for her new album cover. If Lex did say so himself, the pictures were awesome. For once in his life, he was actually going to impress Kendall Bryce. And, as Lex Abrahams knew perhaps better than anyone, that took some doing.

Pouring molasses-thick coffee into a red tin mug, into which he had heaped four spoons of sugar and a generous dash of Coffee-mate, Lex wandered out onto his patio. He loved it out here in the early mornings. It was a small space, basically just a gravel courtyard with a table, two chairs and a lone orange tree, but it was a sun-trap and it made his bijou one-bedroom apartment feel twice its actual size. At Kendall's suggestion, Lex had recently screwed a vintage mirror to the rear patio wall, to make the garden look bigger. He peered at his reflection in it now, not out of vanity but because it was there, and saw what he always saw: a stocky, slightly too short Jewish man with dark curly hair, a long but not unattractive nose, and light-blue eyes that looked as if they'd been stolen from somebody else, somebody Swedish and blond . . . a surfer, maybe. If it weren't for the eyes, Lex Abrahams would have been the most Jewish-looking Jew he knew. Ironically, given that he'd been raised in a totally non-religious household, wasn't remotely kosher, and didn't know the inside of a synagogue from a packet of peas. Still, as a photographer with a rare gift for capturing the idiosyncracies and beauty of the human face, Lex was glad he had 'a look'. Occasionally he wished it were more the sort of look that girls like Kendall Bryce swooned over. A taller, blonder, more regular-featured look. But, generally, Lex Abrahams was comfortable in his skin, a fact reflected in his never-changing wardrobe of faded Levi jeans, white T-shirt and Target flip-flops.

Kendall's pictures were on the patio table. In between sips of coffee, Lex leafed through them, trying to choose the best three for her perusal. Ever since his first job for Maroon 5, aged nineteen, Lex had learned never to give a client more than three images to choose from, especially for an album cover. Large files of JPEGs had a habit of causing major brain malfunction amongst musicians. They engendered indecision, irascibility and panic. Lex was a firm believer in physical prints laid out on a table, *one, two, three*. Of course, Kendall was a slightly different case. For all the dysfunction and imbalance of their relationship, Lex and Kendall were genuine friends.

Friends. How Lex had come to loathe that word. The truth – the tragic, pathetic, undeniable truth – was that Lex Abrahams was in love with Kendall Bryce. Of course, he had never declared his love and never would. To do so would be as futile a gesture as shouting at the TV when your team was losing, or calling up Graydon Carter and suggesting he forget about Leibovitz and hire *you* to do *Vanity Fair*'s next editorial shoot with the Obamas. Wishing it were so was one thing. Announcing your hopeless pipe dreams to the world was quite another. Kendall was as far out of Lex's league as an NFL career was out of the reach of your average high-school footballer. Friends were as much as they would ever be. He should be grateful.

But, even as a friend, Lex yearned for Kendall's approval. Deep down, part of him clung to a belief that if she truly valued him as an artist, a real talent, she might one day look past his mediocre exterior and see someone worth loving, worth being loved by.

The three photographs he plucked from the pile were unquestionably works of art, although Lex hesitated to take full credit for them. Who, after all, could make Kendall Bryce look anything other than perfect? The first two were body shots. Taken in the desert at dusk, beside a lone thorn tree, Kendall's torso and arms were twisted in a mirror image of the tree's trunk and branches. You could make out her face in profile, but the key to the image was her bare back and the billowing plumes of black hair cascading over her shoulders. The third picture was a straightforward head shot. Shot on old-fashioned film, in black and white, it captured a side of Kendall not generally glimpsed by the public. With her eyes wide and her face free of make-up, she looked young, vulnerable, emotionally naked. This was Lex's favorite, but he doubted Kendall would pick it and Jester wouldn't force the issue. Subjects rarely liked the portraits that dared to tell them the truth.

Lex walked back inside. Slipping the three prints into a fresh envelope, he carefully filed the rest and sat down to work on some editing. It would be four hours at least until Kendall was awake and up to receiving visitors, so he might as well get some work done.

By the time he next looked up, it was noon. How the hell had that happened? Quickly brushing his teeth and spritzing on some aftershave (Kendall had once mentioned that she found CK One a sexy scent, and Lex had worn it religiously ever since, to no noticeable effect), he jumped in his leased Nissan and headed towards Brentwood.

For once traffic was good. Ten minutes later, Lex turned the corner into Brentwood Park. Jack Messenger's house was on a private road, but the security guard at the gate knew Lex well and waved him through. Every time he came here, Lex was reminded of the immense financial gulf that existed between music managers and photographers. Like Jack, Lex was at the very top of his profession, one of the most well-respected snappers in the record business. As well as countless iconic album covers, he'd shot Pepsi commercials and award-winning live concert footage for bands as diverse as Aerosmith and The Dixie Chicks. But somehow the great music industry money tree failed to drop riches on Lex Abrahams' head the way it rained them down on the likes of Jack Messenger and Ivan Charles. And Kendall Bryce, of course, although nobody doubted that the artists would do well. They were the talent, the *raison d'être*.

Kendall's my *raison d être*, Lex thought idly as he pulled up outside the Messenger mansion. Jack's house was an Arts and Crafts beauty, half-timbered and covered in climbing roses and wisteria, like an English manor house. The guest-house was more open-plan, a converted barn separated from the house by a vast expanse of lawn and set back behind neatly trimmed topiary hedges. It opened directly onto the pool, which twinkled brilliant azure blue beneath the blazing midday sun as Lex walked by.

'Knock knock,' he said cheerfully, pushing open the unlocked front door. 'Kendall? I brought over some pictures from the shoot. You're gonna love—'

The words died on his lips. Kevin Dacre, the sobriety coach Jack had hired for an extortionate fee to babysit Kendall while he was in England, staggered sheepishly out of the bedroom with a towel wrapped around his hips and two empty wine glasses in his hand. Behind him a visibly hungover Kendall, in a crotch-skimming kimono robe, carried an armful of empty bottles.

'Oh, hi, Lex,' she growled, her voice hoarse from the night's excesses. 'Lex, Kevin, Kevin, Lex. Kevin was just leaving.'

The sobriety coach did at least have the decency to blush scarlet, scurrying past Lex with a pleading *I couldn't help it. Don't tell!* look in his eyes. Lex felt as if he'd been punched in the stomach. Sometimes it seemed as if Kendall was determined to sleep with every man in Los Angeles other than him. Rock stars and actors were one thing, but this dweeb wasn't even good-looking. It wasn't until the sound of Kevin's squealing tyres had died away that Lex recovered sufficiently to speak.

'Jack's gonna go ballistic. He's not kidding about kicking you off the books, you know. He'll do it if you keep pushing him.'

'Screw Jack,' said Kendall, lighting up a Marlboro red. 'Managers are a dime a dozen.'

'If you really felt that, you wouldn't be living in his guesthouse,' said Lex, grabbing the cigarette from between Kendall's fingers and stubbing it out in one of the wine glasses. 'Smoking fucks your voice. Don't be an idiot.'

Kendall pouted but didn't protest. Lex Abrahams was her best friend, one of the few people she'd allow to boss her around. Besides which, she didn't want to fall out with Lex today and risk having him spill the beans to Jack. For all her bravado, Kendall had woken up this morning feeling guilty and nervous. What if Jack got home early? She'd better replace the wine she'd stolen. And buy some mouthwash and air fresheners.

'Go take a shower,' said Lex, wishing he weren't able to smell the sex on her body. 'And open some windows up there. I'll clean up this mess.'

Kendall wrapped her arms around him. As she lifted them, the hem of her silk robe rode up, revealing two perfectly smooth peach buttocks. 'You're an angel, Lexy. I love you.'

It was all Lex could do not to weep.

An hour later, Lex dropped the car with a valet and he and Kendall walked into Joan's on third. A well-known Hollywood hangout and brunch venue, Joan's was a scene and the last place Lex would have chosen for their lunch date. But Kendall insisted, and when Kendall insisted, Kendall got.

'I'll have a big pot of coffee, cinnamon French toast and a side of bacon. And a blueberry muffin. And some frittata.'

In black Ksubi jeans, a black L'Agence T-shirt and ultra-dark Oliver Peoples shades, Kendall looked even tinier than usual. It was hard to imagine how so much food was going to fit into such a bird-like frame.

'And I'll have an egg-white omelette,' said Lex. 'Thanks.'

'Health freak,' grumbled Kendall. 'You're just showing off to make me feel bad.'

'You already feel bad.'

Kendall groaned. This was true. Her face had turned a sickening shade of pale-green, her palms were clammy and her stomach kept flipping over like one of those wind-up toys kids get in their Christmas stockings.

'You have to stop drinking, you know,' Lex said seriously. 'You can't control it.'

'I know, I know. And I will. I mean, I have. Last night was a one-off. You won't say anything to Jack, will you?'

Lex looked hurt. 'Why do you think I cleaned up your entire house? So he could catch you?'

'Thanks.' Kendall reached across the table and squeezed his hand. Through the window, a lone paparazzi snapped the moment.

'Fuck off,' snarled Lex. He knew they shouldn't have come to Joan's.

'Oh my God, that's so funny!' Kendall laughed. 'Now *US Weekly*'ll run a story saying the two of us are together. How hilarious is that?'

The food arrived and Kendall fell on it, shovelling down forkfuls of frittata and French toast like she hadn't eaten for weeks. Lex watched her, picking intermittently at his omelette.

'So,' he said, changing the subject. 'Are you ready for London?'

'Sooo ready,' mumbled Kendall through a mouthful of blueberry muffin. 'I can't wait to do those gigs, and I can't wait to meet Ivan Charles. Everyone says he's way more fun than Jack. Not that that's hard. Root-canal surgery is more fun than Jack.'

Lex was used to listening to Kendall complain about the

man who had made her a mega-star. But over the years he had also provided a shoulder to cry on while she sobbed her heart out about her unrequited love for Jack. Lex knew that Kendall's bitching was just displaced adoration. He sympathized. Unrequited love sucked.

'I'm not sure there'll be too much time for fun in your schedule,' said Lex. 'You're rehearsing every day you're not performing.'

Kendall shrugged. 'I'll make time. I wanna see Buckingham Palace and the Tower of London. And I wouldn't mind sleeping with Brett Bayley either.'

'Brett's married,' said Lex disapprovingly.

'Tell that to him,' grinned Kendall. 'How mad do you think Jack would be if Brett and I got together? We're both Jester acts, after all; both Americans in London. Our paths are bound to cross.'

'Stop being provocative,' snapped Lex. Reaching into his messenger bag, he pulled out the photographs he'd brought her. 'Take a look at these. You need to pick one for the album cover.'

'Ooooo.' Kendall leaned forward excitedly. 'Has Jack seen them?'

'Not yet.' *Jack, Jack, Jack. If only she knew how transparent she was.*

'Well, we can't use this one.' Kendall handed back the portrait shot. 'I don't look anything like myself.'

'That's exactly what you look like,' said Lex. 'The camera never lies, remember?'

'Says the man who just had a sense of humour failure about the paparazzi,' Kendall shot back. 'I look like a twelve year old with TB. That's a no.'

'You look beautiful.'

'Yada yada yada. Oh, now this I like.' She picked up one

of the thorn tree images. 'Both of these. They're sexy but classy. Like art.'

'*Like* art?' Lex sounded horrified. 'They *are* art.'

'You know what I mean,' said Kendall. 'They're arty *and* commercial. The label's gonna love them.'

'Do you love them? Lex hated himself for the tentative, hopeful tone he heard in his own voice. With other clients he was confident in his work. With Kendall, he never stopped feeling as though he was auditioning for her approval. *Pathetic.*

'I do.' Kendall beamed, leaning across the table to kiss him. 'I love them and I love you. Where would I be without you, my lovely Lex?'

Lex's heart beat so fast as she pressed her lips to his that he worried it might jump out of his chest and start throbbing away on the table. He closed his eyes, let the happiness rush through him and immediately heard the *click click click* of a camera shutter. This time it was Kendall who spun around, shaking her fist through the café window.

'He's my friend, asshole, OK? You can quote me on that. Read my lips: We are just fucking friends.'

Lex's happiness drained away like pus from a lanced boil.

One day they'll carve it on my tombstone: Just Fucking Friends.

Jack Messenger pushed open his front door with a sigh of relief. It was good to be home.

Jack didn't enjoy travelling at the best of times, and this trip to England had been particularly stressful. He'd spent the entire eleven-hour flight home unable to concentrate, or to banish the vomit-inducing image of Ivan pumping away at that teenage violinist from his mind. Poor Catriona. A midlife crisis was embarrassing enough to watch, but Cat had to live with it. Or rather, she chose to live with it. That was the part that bothered Jack the most. The fact that even after all the betrayals, all the slip-ups and lies and bullshit, Catriona Charles was still in love with her husband. She still saw the Ivan she'd fallen in love with at Oxford. Whereas for Jack, that person, his friend, was all but gone.

Dropping his suitcase on the floor, he wandered into his study. As usual it was immaculate, an oasis of calm and order in the frantic chaos of Jack Messenger's professional life. He and Ivan used to joke that running a music management business was the best on-the-job training a psychotherapist could have. As managers they were part mentor, part friend, part boss, part life coach to some of the most talented, spoiled and rampantly fucked-up individuals on the planet. Life at Jester was equal parts exhausting and rewarding, but it was never dull. Jack loved it. But he also loved leaving it behind in the evenings and retreating behind the walls of his tranquil fortress.

Sonya had designed and decorated the house, and her presence was still everywhere. Jack limited photographs of his wife to the master bedroom. He'd learned that having them around the house made some people feel uncomfortable, and prompted others to try and talk about his loss, something Jack was congenitally incapable of doing. But you couldn't pick up a cushion or switch on a lamp, without being reminded of Sonya's subtle, feminine taste, her love of colour and texture, her *warmth*. That was the one thing Jack Messenger missed most about his wife. The world was a colder place without her.

Flipping open his calendar (Jack was still a pen and paper man where possible), he groaned. He'd totally forgotten he had a dinner date with Elizabeth tonight. Elizabeth Grey was Jack's female companion of the moment. Nominally his 'girlfriend', though that wasn't a word Jack himself ever used. She was a senior exec at Paramount – smart, funny, independent and kind, as well as beautiful in the classy, understated way that Jack liked: long hair, minimal make-up, slim without being scrawny. There was absolutely nothing wrong with Elizabeth, not one complaint that Jack could level at her. Except the fact that she wasn't Sonya.

Dialling her number, Jack was relieved to get the voice-mail. 'Hi, Liz. Listen honey, I'm sorry, I'm gonna have to bail on tonight. I'm totally wiped after my trip. I'll call you tomorrow, OK? OK thanks. Sorry. Goodnight.'

He hated how awkward he sounded. Somehow he couldn't shake the feeling that dating at 40 automatically made you a jerk. Switching off his phone so Elizabeth couldn't call him back, he padded into the kitchen for a snack when something caught his eye. The door to his wine cabinet was ajar. No bottles were missing. Everything else was as it should be. But Conception, Jack's housekeeper, always locked that particular cabinet.

Kendall.

Kendall was curled up on the couch watching *Two and a Half Men* with Lex Abrahams when Jack burst in with a face like fury.

'Have you taken wine from my house while I've been gone?'

Kendall didn't look up from the screen. 'Hi, Kendall, hi, Lex. How are you? Nice to see you again,' she said sarcastically.

'Answer the question.'

'Of course not! Jesus, so what, I'm a thief now?'

'Not a thief. You replaced it,' said Jack. 'But you forgot to lock the wine closet afterwards. Where's Kevin?'

'He wasn't feeling too good,' said Kendall blithely. 'So I sent him home and called Lex to come over and save me from my deepest, darkest urges. So far it's going great.' She raised a glass of Diet Coke in Jack's direction. 'How was England?'

'Don't change the subject,' snapped Jack. 'How much did you drink?'

'It wasn't Kendall,' Lex piped up from the couch. 'It was me. I'm sorry, I, er, I had a few friends over on Friday and I needed some decent vintage stuff, so I, er, I borrowed a couple of bottles. I replaced them at the wine merchant's today. I must have forgotten to lock the, er, the closet.'

Jack sighed. He liked Lex and was an ardent admirer of his work. But when it came to Kendall, he couldn't be trusted. 'Do yourself a favour, kid. Never go into acting. You suck at it.'

'No, really . . .' Lex protested.

'Go home,' said Jack. 'Before I fire the both of you.'

Lex left. Kendall continued watching TV defiantly until Jack picked up the remote and turned it off.

'Hey! I was watching that!'

'No you weren't. Give me one reason why I shouldn't kick you off my books and out of my guesthouse right now.'

'I'll give you three,' said Kendall. 'I make you a ton of money. I'm the best female artist Jester has. And I didn't take your stupid wine.'

'You're a liar.'

Kendall tried not to show how hurt she was. Even after a long flight, in a crumpled shirt and chinos, Jack looked so insanely handsome it was torture. It was bad enough that he didn't want her. But that he should disapprove of her too was more than she could bear. The fact that she'd brought it on herself was no consolation.

'OK, fine. I was pissed at you for not taking me to Ivan's party. I should have been there.'

'You've never even met Ivan,' said Jack.

'So? I was invited.'

'And you would have gone if you hadn't proved once again that you can't be trusted. You *cannot drink*, Kendall, OK? Some people can take their liquor. Others cannot.'

He sounded exasperated because he was. Though she might not realize it, Jack was immensely fond of Kendall Bryce. He'd seen addictive personalities like hers before. They couldn't do moderation. Kendall could no more stop at one drink than stop at one breath. It was all or nothing.

'I've got to be honest with you,' he said. 'At this point I have serious reservations about letting you go to London next week.'

'Yeah, well, get over them,' snarled Kendall. 'I'm a professional. I have commitments and I meet them. I'm not about to let my fans and record company down because *you've* got an overdeveloped father complex. I'm twenty-three fucking years old, Jack!'

'Then act it. Stop behaving like a spoiled teenager. And stop letting poor Lex lie for you. Unlike you, my dear, he's no good at it. I'm going to bed. We'll discuss this further in the morning.'

After Jack had gone, Kendall went to bed and lay awake for hours, staring at the ceiling.

It's all so wrong. I'm in bed alone. He's fifty yards away, in bed alone. Why aren't we holding each other?

One day, they would be. One day, Kendall Bryce would become Kendall Messenger, and all Jack's grief and Kendall's longing and frustration would be things of the past. *It will happen. It has to happen. It's fate.*

Who knew, maybe this trip to London would be the start of a new phase in their relationship. Maybe Kendall's absence would make Jack's heart grow fonder?

Stranger things had happened.

CHAPTER THREE

Ivan Charles kept a firm grip on Joyce Wu's hips as she
bucked and moaned in pleasure. *As well she might*, thought
Ivan, who'd spent the last fifteen minutes with his head
between his teenage lover's legs, trying to bring her to climax.
Generally he wasn't much of a one for oral sex – giving it,
that is; receiving it was naturally an entirely different matter
– but he made an exception for Joyce. Partly because she
begged him to. Ivan Charles *did* enjoy a bit of begging. And
partly because her smooth, hairless Asian pussy made him
feel like he was doing a porn star, not a virtuoso violinist
from a strict Chinese family. Although that was kind of
horny, too.

Even so, fifteen minutes was enough to give anybody jaw
ache. His own orgasm already felt like a long time ago and
he'd spent the last five minutes at least thinking exclusively
about his meeting at ITV tomorrow and whether the blue
or the green Paul Smith shirt would make him look more
telegenic.

'I'm coming!' Joyce gasped, unnecessarily. Her twitching
thighs had already imparted this information forcefully to

the sides of Ivan's head. Finally she stopped moving, like an exhausted epileptic at the end of a fit, and slumped back against the chaise longue, panting. Ivan, also panting, headed to the kitchen for a much-needed glass of water.

Ivan loved his Belgravia flat. *Loved it.* The lateral, two-bedroom apartment on Eaton Gate was his own private lair, his 1,500 square foot kingdom where he could do what – and whom – he pleased. Of course, The Rookery was home and he loved that too. In Oxfordshire, with Catriona, he was grown-up Ivan, husband Ivan, daddy Ivan. The unfortunate incident that Jack had witnessed in the bathroom on the night of his birthday was an anomaly. Usually, Ivan Charles made a point of keeping his two lives, and two selves, utterly separate. Here, in London, he was Ivan the player, Ivan the music mogul. He was, as one of Jester's interns had rather brilliantly named him, after a brief but passionate affair, Ivan the Terrible. And the Eaton Gate flat was his *palais d'amour*.

Every room was filled with mementos of his triumphant career. Here, in the kitchen, two Grammys and a Brit Award gleamed proudly on a shelf above the sink. The drawing room, an elegant Georgian reception space with double-aspect sash windows and original parquet flooring, was littered with framed photographs of Ivan with music industry greats. Ivan and Burt Bacharach hugged on top of the piano, Ivan and Alfie Boe laughed on a yacht on the antique side table. On the wall above the chaise longue, where Joyce Wu lay sprawled in postcoital contentment, Ivan had a paternal arm wrapped around Charlotte Church back in her gawky teenage days.

Secretly, Ivan longed to be able to line the walls with a different kind of star. The kind of artist that Jack represented for Jester almost exclusively. He wanted to have his picture taken with Will Smith and JLS and Justin Bieber. With Katy Perry and Britney and Kendall Bryce. He wanted to be in the pop world, to be young and contemporary and relevant. Most of all, he wanted to lead Jester out of the dark ages of old school music management and into the new era of reality television, of YouTube virals and multimedia world domination. It was a terrible irony, a travesty really, that he, Ivan, who 'got' the pop scene and was excited by the brave new world of free downloads and webcam concerts, should be stuck with an overwhelmingly classical list, while Jack 'Sam Eagle' Messenger, he of the paper diaries and computer phobia and all-American family values, should represent such cutting-edge acts as The Blitz and Kendall Coke-Head Bryce. The fact that Ivan's list made more money than Jack's was insufficient consolation. Classical fans still bought albums. Pop fans downloaded (aka stole) them. But if only Jack weren't so pig-headed about Jester diversifying, into the TV world and beyond, Ivan was sure their rock and pop business would blossom exponentially. Tomorrow's meeting with ITV would be Ivan's first concrete step into these choppy waters, a step he was taking without his partner's knowledge, still less his permission. Ivan had a lot riding on it.

'Sweetheart, I hate to do it, but I'm going to have to ask you to skedaddle.' Walking back into the drawing room he passed a still-naked Joyce her clothes. 'I've got a ton of work to do this afternoon. Plus the cleaner's coming in twenty minutes. We wouldn't want her to find you here and spill the beans to the missus, would we?'

Poor Ivan, thought Joyce, pulling a lemon-yellow sundress over her head and stuffing her knickers and bra into her handbag. *Imagine being saddled with an old frump like Catriona and having to sneak around behind her back, just for the sake of the kids. He really is* such *a good father.*

'Of course not,' she said solemnly, scooping up her violin from a red brocade armchair in the corner. 'Don't worry, darling. You can count on me to be discreet.'

Ivan watched her leave, noticing for the first time how short her legs were for her body and how unsexy her walk was from behind, knock-kneed and gawky. The time had come to end things with Miss Wu. He would disengage gently, as he always did, with expensive jewellery and flowery apologies, citing family commitments for his reluctant change of heart. Ivan prided himself on the fact that not one of the clients he'd shagged then grown tired of had ever left Jester, or fired him as a manager. Women were marvellous creatures. They'd accept just about anything from a man, as long as it was done with charm, and a few choice trinkets from Asprey's.

With Joyce gone, Ivan could begin his day in earnest. Farting loudly to kick things off, a triumphant trumpet sound heralding the dawn of male freedom, he turned on Test Match special and, blasting the sound through the flat's state-of-the-art audio system, retired to the master bathroom for a shower. Afterwards, he laid out a variety of shirt and tie combos on the bed and began to give serious consideration to which made him look the most handsome. Ivan was, and had always been, terribly vain. But tomorrow's meeting at ITV genuinely merited a careful attention to his appearance. He was effectively auditioning to become one of the judges on a new talent show, an updated version of X Factor that combined both classical and popular acts. Mike Grayson, ITV's new head of programming, was flamingly gay and well known to have a soft spot for good-looking male presenters. Ivan Charles fully intended to flirt the socks off Grayson. Once he got the gig, he could begin a new charm offensive with Jack.

Holding a peach shirt and royal blue tie up to the mirror, Ivan started. *Was that a noise downstairs?* He turned off the cricket and listened. At first there was nothing. Then there it was again, a scraping, scratching sound, a bit like a . . . key! *Oh my God, Catriona!*

Frantically Ivan tore around the apartment, hiding evidence of Joyce's recent presence. Catriona never came to London – never, and certainly not unannounced. But she was the only other person with a key to the Eaton Gate flat, for 'emergencies'. This was rapidly becoming an emergency. It was too late to get rid of the fishy sex-odour that still hung in the air, but Ivan managed to pick up and throw away his used condom wrapper and lock Joyce's Rampant Rabbit vibrator in the bedroom safe before the front door finally swung open.

'Darling?' he called out hoarsely. 'Is that you? What a nice surprise.'

He heard the slam of the door and thud of a suitcase hitting the floor. Surely she wasn't thinking of staying?

But it wasn't Catriona.

Kendall Bryce looked amused to find Ivan Charles, red in the face and flustered, wearing nothing but his boxer shorts. *Well, well*, she thought, *what have we been up to?* Judging by the pervasive smell assailing her nostrils, Kendall could make an educated guess. As soon as he saw her, Ivan's colour deepened.

'How did you get in?' he stammered. 'I thought you were my wife.'

'No,' Kendall smiled knowingly. 'Luckily for you, I'd say. Kendall Bryce.' She extended a slender, diamond-encrusted hand. 'Ivan Charles, I presume.'

'I . . . I thought you were staying at the Dorchester,' said Ivan, hurriedly pulling on a pair of jeans.

'I was,' said Kendall, 'until Jack decided it was "unnecessarily extravagant". He said that Jester had an apartment here and gave me the key. I *had* thought he wanted you to keep an eye on me. But perhaps it was the other way around?'

Ivan studied her properly for the first time. She was shorter than she looked in publicity shots, not much over five foot tall, and altogether tinier. In a skintight black mini-dress that left little to the imagination, Kendall's waist was so doll-like that Ivan could have closed his hands around it. Her dark hair was pulled back in a messy bun and her stunning face looked uncharacteristically tired, with smudged purple shadows lying under each of her virulently green eyes like bruises.

'If I'm in your way, I'll happily check into the Dorchester,' she announced blithely, lighting up a cigarette without asking Ivan if he minded. 'But you'll have to tell Jailer Jack it was your idea.'

'No, no,' said Ivan. He was over his embarrassment now, and could think of few things more delightfully distracting than having this wanton girl of Jack's under his roof. 'I wasn't expecting you, that's all. Jack never said anything. Let me show you the guest room and you can settle in.'

'Actually,' said Kendall, blowing smoke in perfectly formed rings, 'what I really want right now is some food. The shit they served on the plane wasn't fit for a dog. How about you take me out to lunch?'

Ivan took Kendall to The Wolseley. As he led her to their prestigious corner table, she was suitably impressed to see Kate Winslet enjoying a salad a few feet away and Prince Harry sipping a Bloody Mary with his latest squeeze at the bar.

'Nice place,' she said casually. Despite her own fame in the US, Kendall still got star-struck, especially around people who were well known globally.

'You must have been here before,' said Ivan, ordering champagne and oysters on the half-shell for both of them.

'Uh uh.' Kendall shook her head. 'This is my first trip to London. First trip to Europe, actually. I toured Japan and the Far East last year, but other than that I've never really been abroad.'

'My goodness. A Euro-virgin,' Ivan said flirtatiously. *He's attractive*, thought Kendall. *Not as handsome as Jack, but there's a definite devilish spark there.* 'Well, we'll have to do something about that. I've got three weeks to introduce you to the delights of the Old World. Not long, but I'll do my best.'

'I bet you will,' Kendall flirted back.

'Seriously, your parents never travelled with you when you were younger? Wasn't your old man fabulously wealthy? I'm sure I remember Jack saying—'

Kendall's pretty face instantly darkened. 'My dad was never around. He probably took his new family to Europe, for all I know. But not me.'

Aware he'd touched a nerve, Ivan changed the subject. 'So you're here for the gigs, obviously. Jack sent me the scheduling for rehearsals and sound check. And you want me to organize some media appearances? I thought we could shoot for Graham Norton, and maybe Radio One Breakfast.'

Kendall inhaled an oyster and took a big slug of champagne.

'To be honest, I don't give a fuck,' she told Ivan. 'Jack's the one who keeps harping on about building my UK profile. He seems to think that breaking into the market in London will open up all the other European territories.'

'You don't agree?'

Kendall shrugged. 'What do I know? I'm just the talent, right? *I* wanted to sign with Sony, but Jack insisted I stay with Matador. He said a small label would give me more focus. So now I'm with this tiny, local LA record company with, like, zero global presence, and suddenly Jack wants me to fly all over the world and "build my profile" from scratch. Go figure.'

Ivan digested all this with interest. While Kendall perused the menu for a main course, intermittently exchanging shamelessly suggestive smiles with Prince Harry, Ivan considered the pros and cons of Jack's strategy. On the one hand, it made sense, keeping a relatively new artist like Kendall with a small label that would be guaranteed to prioritise her. Matador had a good reputation and had certainly done well by Kendall so far. On the other hand, Ivan could smell this kid's ambition through her pores. She wanted Sony because they were the biggest, and for Kendall Bryce, biggest meant best. She was impatient to make it to the next level, demanding superstardom like a screeching baby cuckoo demanding to be fed. Clearly, Jack's organic, slow-build approach to her career was frustrating her and driving a wedge between them.

Equally clearly, for all her bitching and moaning, Kendall plainly idolized Jack Messenger. In the cab on the way over to The Wolseley, she must have dropped his name into the conversation a good fifteen times. Jack thinks this, Jack says that, Jack wants the other. Ivan sensed an opportunity here. He wanted to make the move into pop, and what better way to start than with Kendall Bryce, a rising US star with ambitions in his, Ivan's, home market? But if he were going to prise her away from Jack, he would have to tread very carefully indeed.

'Listen,' he said, once Kendall had ordered a large plate

of lobster thermidor with a side of fries and Gustavo had brought them a bottle of perfectly chilled vintage Chablis, 'I want you to relax here in London and leave all the work shit to me. Try and think of it as a vacation.'

'With a couple of live performances in front of thousands of people thrown in, right?'

'Right,' grinned Ivan. 'The gigs'll be a piece of cake.'

'I hope so,' sighed Kendall, biting her lip, the first hint of anxiety she'd betrayed so far. 'I only have a few days to rehearse before the show at the Hammersmith Apollo on Thursday.'

'You'll do great. Just focus on all the fun stuff you'll be doing as soon as it's over.'

'Like what?' Kendall said morosely. 'I don't know a soul here. Jack gave me a list of friends of his I can call, but they all sound boring as fuck. I swear to God one of them was called Sister Mary Theresa. Maybe the two of us can go to matins together. Fun!'

Ivan laughed. He liked this girl.

'Look. I have to be in town tomorrow for a meeting on the Friday after your show,' he said, 'but I'll be done by four. After that I'm driving down to my country house for the weekend. Why don't you join me?'

Kendall looked doubtful. 'I don't know. Thanks for the offer, but I wouldn't want to impose on your family time. Besides, I'm not exactly what you'd call a country girl. I'm high maintenance.'

Ivan raised his glass to hers. 'So am I, my dear. So am I.'

CHAPTER FOUR

'Oh Jesus. I can't go out there. Seriously, I can't.'

Kendall hovered backstage at the Hammersmith Apollo, holding Ivan's hand so tightly she'd cut off the circulation to his fingers.

'The place is half empty. No one knows who the fuck I am over here.'

It was strange, but for some reason the smattering of vacant seats made Kendall feel infinitely more nervous than the packed stadiums she was used to back in the US. Having ten thousand people watching you was like being alone. With that size of audience, and the stage lights blinding you, there were no individuals to worry about, just a screaming, adulatory wall of noise. Here, in this gloriously old-fashioned 1930s theatre, you could look out from backstage and see individual faces. A middle-aged woman here, a pair of teenage boys there. Real people, who'd paid real money to hear *you* sing. It was terrifying.

'Everyone knows who you are,' Ivan reassured her, not entirely truthfully. 'And remember, you're here to support Adele. You think people don't know who *she* is?'

'I guess not,' said Kendall through chattering teeth.

'Exactly. The venue's sold out, with a line outside as long as your arm. It's only ten to eight. Trust me, there'll be no empty seats by the time they call you.'

He's right, Kendall told herself. *Calm down*. Pacing up and down in a skintight PVC leotard and thigh-high silver boots, a tribute to the great Ziggy Stardust, who'd performed his final concert at the Apollo back in 1973, she knew she looked the part. Adele might be a mega-star with the best voice since Aretha, but no one nailed superstar raunch like Kendall Bryce. If Jack were here he'd have expressly forbidden her outfit. 'Don't cheapen yourself,' was one of his favourite catchphrases. 'You don't have to dress like a hooker, or a poor man's Britney, to get people to buy your records.' But Jack, thankfully, wasn't here. While it was true her profile was lower in the UK, the purpose of tonight's concert was to raise it. She wasn't going to do that by dressing like Karenfrikking Carpenter.

Suddenly the lights dimmed and the low bass *boom boom boom* of Kendall's backing track began to thump around the auditorium. Ten minutes had passed already? How was that possible? She turned around to look for Ivan but he was gone. In his place were two distracted-looking sound-check guys and the four male backing dancers Kendall had been rehearsing with all week. All of them looked white as sheets, but ironically their nerves calmed Kendall's own.

'Smile, guys,' she said confidently. 'We're gonna have fun out there, right? *Right?* Because if we don't, nobody else will.'

The curtains lifted. There were a few whistles and whoops from the audience as, still in pitch darkness, Kendall and her dancers took their places. Kendall just had time to tap her headset and nod curtly to the sound engineers that her

51

mic was working properly when the lights exploded into life and the track to 'Shake It Loose', her biggest hit to date, erupted into the theatre to wild shrieks of applause.

After that it was easy. Leaping and gyrating her way through three tracks straight, belting out the lyrics that were as familiar to her now as breathing, Kendall drank in the high of the crowd's approval like a drug addict plunging the needle into her vein. Watching from backstage, Ivan was entranced. She was a different person onstage, radiating energy and excitement and *joy* like a one-woman power plant. The music was unremarkable – basic, hip-hoppy, commercial pop of the sort that hundreds of young artists were churning out all over the world. But in live perfor-mance, Kendall took it and transformed it into something unique. Her voice, her body, her angel's face, but most of all her stage presence, screamed one thing and one thing only: star. No wonder Jack was so focused on her as a client. Managing her must be like trying to hold a flame in your hand.

'Good evening, London!' Kendall shouted hoarsely after the third track, leaning on her mic stand for support and swigging from a water bottle. 'I gotta tell you, it is *wild* to be here.'

The audience cheered and wolf-whistled loudly, although at this point Ivan suspected that they would have applauded the shipping forecast if it had come out of Kendall's ridiculously sexy, rosebud mouth.

'I know you're all here to see Adele.' More applause. 'So I won't keep you in suspense too much longer. But I'm gonna perform one more track. It's from my last album, and some of you may know it. It's a little song called "Whipped".'

The most explicit track she had yet released, 'Whipped' was famous largely due to the fact that it had been banned from the airwaves in a number of US states due to its risqué lyrics. In her live routine, Kendall and her dancers hammed up the 'naughty' element, with Kendall at one point engaging in a simulated orgy with all four of her leather-clad boys. Yes, it was cheesy, but it was also sexy as all hell. The audience lapped it up like cats in a room full of cream. Even Ivan got a hard-on watching her. When Kendall finally bounced backstage, her faced flushed with adrenaline and triumph and her hair tangled wildly down her sweat-soaked back, it was all he could do not to jump on her then and there.

'What'd you think?' she panted, her green eyes gazing up into his, searching for approval. 'It was good, right? They liked me?'

'They loved you,' said Ivan truthfully. Pulling her into a bear hug, he started to laugh. 'Poor old Adele. Talk about upstaging the star! I'll bet her people are spitting blood right now.'

Despite herself, Kendall grinned. 'D'you really think so?'

'Definitely.'

'Jack would have hated all the sexual stuff,' said Kendall. 'But I think it worked, don't you?'

'Everything worked,' said Ivan. 'And if Jack can't see that, he's an idiot.'

He's an idiot anyway, for leaving you here with me.

Tonight confirmed what Ivan Charles already suspected. Kendall Bryce was more than just a pretty face. The girl had something very, very special. Something Ivan wanted, very, very badly.

Boy was he looking forward to this weekend.

'I don't understand it.' Ned Williams ran a hand through his floppy brown hair and sighed. 'How can she prefer that tosser to me? The new bloody Pavarotti indeed! Just because he's fat. Badger can do a better Don Giovanni, can't you boy?'

The scruffy springer spaniel thumped his tail loyally on The Rookery kitchen floor.

'Armando bloody Lucci, I ask you, Cat. He's a lard-arse, he's boring and he's as old as the hills.'

'He's forty, Ned.'

'Exactly. What on earth does Diana see in him?'

'Erm, well . . .' Catriona was too kind to say that perhaps Diana Grainger, Ned's ex, saw a private jet, an exquisite palazzo in Tuscany and a Tiffany diamond the size of a cobnut on her finger. Whereas Ned's idea of a romantic gesture was a day spent in the woods gathering *actual* cobnuts. Catriona had never much liked Diana. She was very beautiful, of course, but she'd always seemed to be on the lookout for what Jack Messenger referred to as a BBD – Bigger Better Deal. Apparently, in Armando Lucci, the biggest-selling tenor in the world, she'd found it. 'I expect she just wasn't ready to settle down, darling. She's only twenty-two, after all.'

Ned nodded glumly, helping himself to another industrial-sized slab of Catriona's home-made fruit cake. A broken heart did not appear to have put him off his food.

Only twenty-four himself, Ned Williams was another of Ivan's clients, one of the few who lived locally. An immensely talented tenor, Ned was still in the early stages of a promising career. He was already well known in England as a pretender to Alfie Boe's crown, and his debut CD had peaked at a respectable number six in the UK classical charts. But he was not yet in Armando Lucci's league. So far his modest success had afforded him a charming but distinctly tumble-down cottage in Swinbrook, a battered old MG sports car that was older than he was, and Badger, his wildly unkempt and poorly trained springer spaniel, which accompanied him absolutely everywhere. Handsome in a dishevelled sort of way, Ned's most striking feature was his height. At almost six foot five, he towered above other opera singers, and never seemed to quite know what to do with his ridiculously long limbs on stage – or anywhere else for that matter. Catriona adored him, but even she could have done without playing agony aunt this afternoon.

It had been a long day. Starting at eight o'clock this morning, when Rosie had announced she didn't feel very well then, seconds later, projectile-vomited Frosties right across the breakfast table, Catriona had been fighting one fire after another. In between frantic trips to the doctor's surgery in Burford and Waitrose in Witney, she'd been called in to Hector's school for the second time in a month after he'd super-glued a sleeping classmate's hair to his desk and the boy had ended up having to have a crew cut.

'Why do you *do* these things?' an exasperated Catriona asked her son on the short drive home. 'Do you want to get kicked out of St Austin's?'

'Wouldn't mind,' Hector shrugged. 'Have you told Dad?'

'Not yet.'

Catriona couldn't tell if Hector wanted Ivan to know, or dreaded it. Certainly his attention-seeking antics seemed to be aimed more at his father than at her. Now that Ivan spent so much time away in London, and increasingly took work calls and meetings even when he *was* home, he had less time than ever for the children. Rosie, at nearly thirteen, had bigger fish to fry than hanging out with her old man. But eleven-year-old Hector clearly missed his dad. Ivan knew it, and felt guilty, but as a result both he and Catriona were loath to punish the boy, and the bad behaviour got worse.

This weekend, Ivan had absolutely promised to take Hector fishing, and assured Cat that he wouldn't pick up his BlackBerry or see a single work-related person for two whole days. But at two o'clock this afternoon, he'd blithely rung home to announce that he was bringing Kendall Bryce, Jack's problem client, back with him, and could Catriona please make up the blue bedroom?

'You arse!' she shouted at him, losing her rarely seen temper. 'You promised Hector it would be just the two of you.'

'Oh, Hector won't mind,' breezed Ivan. To his astonishment, Catriona hung up on him. Then Ned had arrived, slump-shouldered and morose, and before Cat knew it was six o'clock, she hadn't even begun making supper, and the blue bedroom remained as sheet-less and towel-less as it had been four hours ago.

'Can I stay for supper?' asked Ned, through a shower of cake crumbs. 'I can't face going back to the cottage on my own. All Diana's horrible vegan food's still in the fridge.'

'Well throw it out,' said Catriona, 'and of course you can stay for supper, as long as you help me make it. Ivan's bringing someone up from London with him so we'll be six with the children. Do you know how to stuff a chicken?'

In the end, inevitably, Friday-night traffic on the M40 was grizzly and Ivan and Kendall were more than an hour late. By the time they staggered through the door at nine, Catriona and Ned had already polished off a bottle of Montepulciano and 'tested'a good half of the roast potatoes. Rosie – who'd made a miraculous recovery once she heard Ned's voice in the kitchen – and Hector had both decided they were too hungry to wait, and had polished off a family pack of Hula Hoops in front of *The Simpsons*. Despite the beautifully laid table and enticing smell of rosemary chicken wafting down the hall, the overall atmosphere that met Ivan and his young VIP guest was one of semi-drunken chaos.

'Oh, there you are,' Catriona giggled, tripping over a snoring Badger as she came out to greet them. 'We'd almost given up hope. You must be Kendall. Welcome.'

'Thanks for having me.' Kendall smiled sweetly. 'I'm sorry to gate-crash your weekend like this.'

'Not at all, we're thrilled you could come. I hear your concert was a huge success.'

Kendall smiled, gratified. 'Thanks. I'm relieved it's over, but I actually really enjoyed it. Ivan's been so supportive.'

Jack had described Catriona Charles to Kendall as some sort of goddess, as kind and funny as she was beautiful, and 'far too good' for Ivan. He'd waxed so lyrical about her, in fact, that Kendall couldn't help but feel a little bit jealous. So it was a relief to find that, while Catriona certainly did seem kind, she was actually a rather blowsy, red-faced, middle-aged woman.

Ivan kissed her on the cheek. After the hanging up incident earlier, he wasn't sure what reception he'd get, but Cat seemed to have forgiven him over the Hector thing, or was at least prepared to let bygones be bygones until they were alone. 'Shall we eat?'

Dinner was delicious. One of the few talents Jack Messenger hadn't credited Catriona with was cooking, but Kendall didn't think she'd ever tasted such succulent chicken or such melt-ingly soft sweet potatoes. But it wasn't just the food that delighted her. The Charleses' house was utterly charming, from its crumbling, wisteria-clad Cotswold stone walls to its warm and inviting shabby-chic interior. Even the dining room, often the coldest and most formal room in a house, was full of colour and life, with overflowing jugs of wild flowers plonked on the table and sideboard, mismatched floral china glinting in the candlelight and Catriona's exquisite photographs hanging on the walls instead of stuffy old oil paintings. Ivan and Catriona's children were adorable too, funny and chatty without being precocious, and the other dinner guest, Ned, seemed charming. It was exactly the sort of noisy, happy, close-knit family atmosphere that Kendall had longed for when growing up. She hadn't been sure about accepting Ivan's invitation, but now she was delighted she'd come.

'Did Cat tell you,' Ned asked Ivan, 'the record company want to talk to me about doing an album of duets?'

'Not a bad idea,' said Ivan, helping himself to the last roast potato. 'Did they have someone else in mind?'

'I think it would be a variety of people. Other tenors, maybe, or sopranos. Solo instrumentalists too. Sort of a "rising stars" thing. They mentioned Joyce Wu. She's with Jester, isn't she? Have you seen her recently?'

'Joyce? No. Not recently.'

Was it Catriona's imagination, or did Ivan seem uncomfortable all of a sudden?

'Isn't she the violinist you were telling me about?' Kendall said innocently. 'The one who left her music at the flat?'

'That's right,' Ivan said evenly. From the stiffness in his jaw, Kendall realized too late that she'd put her foot in it. Remembering the sex smell at Eaton Gate and Ivan's evident discomfiture when she'd shown up unannounced, she put two and two together.

Ivan smiled at Catriona. 'Joyce came over weeks ago to talk about renegotiating her contract. The silly girl left some sheets of one of her concert pieces behind. I haven't had a chance to return them.'

'Oh. I see.' Catriona smiled back, stamping down her creeping sense of unease as she cleared away the plates. It had been years since Ivan had last cheated on her – those days were behind them – but old anxieties took a long time to fade. Catriona's own parents had divorced bitterly when she was eight, and the thought of anything threatening her own marriage filled her with utter dread. Still, Joyce Wu was hardly more than a child. *I'm being ridiculous.*

Ned caught Kendall's eye and gave her a sympathetic smile. She seemed like a nice girl, and was certainly drop-dead gorgeous. How was she to know that Ivan Charles was a philandering prick?

'Kendall . . . er, do you like riding?' Hector asked shyly. Ivan and Catriona's eleven-year-old son had been in an almighty sulk about his father bringing a 'work person' home, until he'd laid eyes on Kendall, since when he'd barely been able to stop drooling into his chicken. Cat didn't think she'd ever seen Hector blush in his life, but he was certainly making up for it now.

'I do,' said Kendall, grateful for the change of subject. 'I used to ride all the time in Malibu when I was a kid. I adore horses.'

'Great,' Hector beamed. 'We can go for a hack tomorrow then. You can ride Sparky if you like. He's Rosie's pony but he'd be the right size for you.'

'Hey. Don't offer people *my* pony,' said Rosie on autopilot. Then, realizing she might have been rude, added to Kendall, 'You're welcome to take him, though, if you'd like. And you can borrow my riding gear too.'

'But, darling, you and Dad were going to go fishing tomorrow, remember?' said Catriona, handing out bowls of raspberries and cream. 'Right, Ivan?'

'That's right,' said Ivan dutifully. 'Looking forward to it.'

'Oh, that's OK,' said Hector, gazing at Kendall adoringly. 'It's more important to make our guest feel welcome. Dad can come riding too if he wants,' he added magnanimously. 'Although don't feel you have to, Dad. Kendall and I'll be fine on our own.'

Catriona and Ivan looked at one another and grinned. Apparently Kendall Bryce's surprise visit wasn't such a bad thing after all.

At eleven the next morning, Kendall waited with Hector and Ivan outside the stable blocks while Irene, the groom, saddled up Sparky.

It was a glorious day. A pale summer sun blazed down on the yard and the sweet, heady scent of buddleia bushes and honeysuckle filled the air, mingled with the delicious smell of horsehair and leather. To the left, across the valley, you could see the steeple of Burford's ancient medieval church. To the right the rose garden erupted in a riot of white and yellow and pink in front of the newly mown lawn, as perfectly striped as a man's bespoke shirt. Behind it, The Rookery looked even more picture-perfect than it had last night, with its elegant sash windows and flagstoned front path, flanked on either side by rows of lavender bushes, like a purple guard of honour.

Despite the beauty of her surroundings, Kendall struggled to shake off her bad mood. Jack had called at eight o'clock this morning, midnight his time. Despite herself, Kendall's heart had soared when his name flashed up on her cell phone. It wasn't like him to call so late. Was he missing her? Had he realized, finally, after dinner with another one of his thirty-something floozies, that she, Kendall, was the one he truly loved? The only one who could make him happy?

Apparently not. After a couple of perfunctory questions about her flight and whether she was settled in London, and the most cursory of congratulations on her performance supporting Adele in Hammersmith, he proceeded to lecture her on not 'overburdening' Catriona Charles.

'She's run ragged as it is, babysitting half of Ivan's acts and being everybody's shoulder to cry on.'

'I didn't ask to come down here, you know,' Kendall said stiffly. 'Ivan invited me. He thought I needed to unwind after the Apollo gig.'

'Without asking his poor wife first, I dare say,' said Jack. 'Look, it's fine you're there. Not even you can get into too much trouble in Oxfordshire.'

'Thanks a lot!'

'Just make sure you clean up after yourself and treat the place with respect, OK? It's really kind of Catriona to have you.'

Kendall liked Catriona, but she was beginning to get tired of hearing what a saint the woman was. So she had the occasional house guest. Big deal! The way Jack banged on about it you'd think she was Mother fucking Teresa. The conversation deteriorated further when Jack started lecturing her about her rehearsal schedule, and making sure she 'knuckled down' and didn't let Ivan Charles distract her. If he didn't want her spending time with Ivan, why on earth had he insisted that she stay at the Eaton Gate flat? At least Ivan knew how to enjoy himself, and didn't spend twenty hours a day chained to a desk and the other four bitching at his acts.

At last Sparky was led out into the yard, tacked up and ready to go. A barrel-chested grey with a distinctly mischievous look in his eye, he wasn't the most elegant of mounts, but Kendall vaulted onto his back in better spirits. A gallop through the English countryside was just what she needed to blow Jack Misery Messenger out of her hair.

'Ready?' said Ivan. He looked especially handsome this

morning, Kendall thought, in dark-green corduroy trousers and a tweed hunting jacket, his blue eyes sparkling happily as he chatted to his son. Whatever else Ivan might be, he was clearly a devoted father, as happy to be with Hector as the boy clearly was to be with him. Kendall thought of her own, distant father and felt an unworthy pang of envy. But Hector was too cute a kid to dislike, especially as he clearly had a thumpingly huge crush on her and was too young and naïve to know how to hide it.

'Race you to the river!' he shouted, taking off through the yard gates like a bat out of hell.

'Is he always this keen?' laughed Kendall.

'Actually no,' said Ivan, riding up beside her and casually resting a hand on her jodhpured thigh. 'It's you, sweetheart. You overexcite him.'

'You think so?'

'Definitely.' Ivan's thumb traced a languorous circle on her leg.

Kendall felt a jolt of desire run through her. It was nice to be flirted with. 'I'm sorry about last night,' she blurted. 'The Joyce Wu thing. I wasn't thinking.'

'That's all right,' drawled Ivan. 'I dare say I'll think of a way you can make it up to me.' Digging his heel into his horse's side, he cantered off after Hector before Kendall could respond.

It was a wonderful day. After two hours exploring the valley, riding through the woods towards Aston then doubling back along the Roman road towards Shipton-under-Wychwood, they stopped at a gorgeous riverside pub for a late lunch of pâté and bread, washed down with refreshing home-made lemonade. Ivan made a few work calls while Kendall and Hector played about a hundred rounds of rock paper scissors, much to Hector's delight.

Watching Kendall Bryce kidding around with his son, her dark hair wild and tangled and her face flushed after the morning's ride, Ivan decided definitively that the girl was a knockout. He knew he had to tread carefully if he was going to prise her away from Jack. Poaching Kendall as a client was the ultimate goal. Bedding her would merely be a fringe benefit, although watching her walk over to her horse, her delectable arse shrink-wrapped to perfection in spray-on white jodhpurs, he wasn't sure how long he'd be able to wait.

Back at the house, Ned Williams had brought Catriona some flowers as a thank-you for last night's dinner. Hovering in the kitchen while she made tea, he looked distracted.

Catriona said knowingly. 'If you're hoping to see Kendall, she's out riding with the boys. I'm expecting them back any minute.'

'Kendall? Don't be silly,' Ned blushed. 'I came to see you. I think I was frightfully boring about Diana last night. You must tell me to sod off occasionally, you know. I'm a big boy, I can take it.'

'In that case,' said Catriona, 'you can sod off down to the stables and wait for them. Tell Ivan to sort out the horses and bring Kendall and Hector in for some cake.'

It had struck her last night, belatedly, that Kendall Bryce might be just the distraction Ned needed to get over Diana's sudden abandonment. She was about his age, very pretty, and she seemed a sweet sort of girl, not at all the spoiled madam that Jack had warned her about at Ivan's birthday party. That is, if Hector would let poor Ned get a word in edgeways. Her son had been glued to Kendall's side like a pre-teen, hormonal limpet since the moment the girl had arrived.

'Go on,' she said kindly to Ned. 'Shoo!'

By the time Ned reached the yard, Irene already had all three horses on leading reins and was filling much-needed buckets of water. Hector, temporarily distracted from Kendall's bodaciousness by a new delivery of hay bales, was leaping happily from the top of the barn into a makeshift crash pad when Ned arrived.

'Don't let your mum see you doing that,' Ned shouted as Hector performed a dramatic commando roll onto the muddy ground. 'And by the way, it's tea time. Where's your dad and Kendall?'

Hector nodded towards the tack room. 'In there. Tell Mum I'll be there in a minute.'

Tucking in his shirt and making a token effort to smooth down his hair, Ned walked into the tack room. 'Knock knock,' he said cheerfully. 'I've been sent to inform you that tea's on the . . . table.'

The smile died on his lips. Ivan had Kendall pinned against the wall. They weren't kissing, but his knee was pressed into her groin and his distinctly predatory face was less than an inch from hers. As soon as he heard Ned, Ivan stepped back, and did his best to act as if nothing had happened. 'Jolly good,' he grinned. 'I'm famished. I'll see you in there, shall I?'

Ned didn't move as Ivan brushed past him. He was still looking at Kendall. Her dark-blue shirt was unbuttoned just low enough to show a hint of cleavage and was coming untucked from her tight white riding breeches. She looked tousled, sexy, and more than a little guilty.

'Oh, come on,' she said to Ned. 'Don't give me the evil eye. It was just a bit of harmless flirting. Nothing happened.'

'It would have, though, wouldn't it? If I hadn't come in.'

'Of course not,' Kendall said brusquely. She always got defensive when she knew she was in the wrong. 'Ivan's a colleague.'

'Ivan's a shit,' said Ned bluntly. 'And Catriona—'

'Oh, yes, I know, I know, she's marvellous and he doesn't deserve her. I've heard it all before.'

Ned frowned. Last night he'd got the impression of Kendall as a sweet, funny girl. A little vain, perhaps, but certainly not an out-and-out bitch. He was disappointed.

Registering the emotion on his face, Kendall shot back, 'If he's such a shit, and you're so loyal to his wife, why do you let him represent you? Isn't that a bit hypocritical?'

'I'm not sleeping with him,' said Ned.

'Nor am I!'

'Not yet.' Turning on his heel, Ned left Kendall standing there.

Lex Abrahams was fast asleep when the phone rang.

After a gruelling, insanely long day's shooting out in Palm Desert (Enrique Iglesias had seen the shots Lex had done of Kendall Bryce last month and decided he wanted a similar look for his own new album), Lex got back to LA to a mountain of editing and paperwork and hadn't collapsed into bed until after three.

Glancing groggily at his bedside clock now, he saw it was ten o'clock. No doubt the call was from Jack Messenger, dumping another ten tons of work into Lex's in-tray. There was a reason Lex Abrahams had agreed to work for Jester, but right now he couldn't for the life of him remember what it was.

He picked up the receiver. 'Hello?'

'What's wrong with your voice?' Kendall asked accusingly. 'You sound like you've been gargling with sandpaper.'

Lex cleared his throat, wishing he didn't feel so stupidly elated to hear from her. 'Late night.'

'Partying? Lucky you.'

'Working actually. How are you? How's England?'

'It sucks.' Without drawing breath, she proceeded to moan about everything from having her Dorchester reservation cancelled, to her show and rehearsal schedule, to Ivan Charles's 'holier than thou' clients presuming to try to tell her how to live her life. 'As if I don't get enough of that shit from Jack. How is he, by the way?'

Lex could hear how much effort she put into trying to keep her tone casual.

'Jack's fine, Kendall.'

'D'you think he's missing me a little bit?'

'It's only been a few days, honey,' Lex said kindly. 'How's Ivan Charles? Is he as disgraceful as everyone says?'

'Actually, he's a good guy,' said Kendall. 'He's fun. Good-looking too.' Lex suppressed a pang of jealousy. 'That's probably why Jack hates him.'

'I wouldn't say he hates him,' Lex yawned, stretching out his arms like a cat. 'More like disapproves.'

'I miss you, Lexy,' Kendall said suddenly, her voice taking on the needy, little-girlish quality it often did when she was bored or in need of attention. 'I wish you could have come with me. Can't you ask Jack to fly you out?'

Lex felt his stomach flip over like a pancake. Deep down he knew she didn't really want him there. Or, if she did, it certainly wasn't in the way he wanted her. But every time Kendall threw him a straw of hope, he clutched at it like an idiot. If she had any idea how much he missed her, how constantly she filled his thoughts, she wouldn't say these things and torture him. At least he hoped she wouldn't. For all her many faults, Lex didn't think of Kendall as deliberately cruel.

'Sorry,' he sighed. 'I've got three albums and a ton of editing to do before you get back. I'll be lucky if Jack gives me five minutes off to go to the bathroom. Anyway, you're only there a few weeks. You should try and make the most of London while you can.'

At The Rookery, upstairs in the blue guest bedroom, Kendall gazed glumly out of the window. It had been a lovely day today, exhilarating and flirtatious and fun, until Ned Williams had come along and given her a guilt trip. Sometimes she felt as if Lex Abrahams was the only person in the world who was unconditionally on her side. If only he were a bit more attractive, and a lot richer, he'd make a perfect husband.

Well, almost perfect.

There would only ever be one Jack Messenger.

CHAPTER FIVE

Jack Messenger leaned back in his two-thousand-dollar ergonomic Therapod office chair and felt a warm rush of satisfaction.

He always enjoyed coming to work. Jester's offices at the top of Beverly Glen, near Mulholland Drive, had some of the most spectacular views in Los Angeles. Jack's corner office was almost all window. In one direction lay the shimmering blue Pacific with Catalina Island in the distance. In the other, the jutting skyscrapers of downtown LA were framed by a ring of perfect, snow-capped mountains, encircling the city like benevolent giants. It was hard to get depressed in Jack's home city; in a space so flooded with light, so energized with sunshine and blue skies and astonishing natural beauty. Between the constant light and the equally constant flow of work, Jester was a place where Jack came to forget the pain of his home life. It worked.

Today he was in even better spirits than usual. In front of him on the desk were Lex Abraham's album cover shots of Kendall. Even by Lex's usual high standards, they were exceptional, exactly the sort of haunting, slightly unexpected images that drew the eye and translated into bumper sales. With visual media stimulation everywhere, it was becoming both harder and more important to grab an audience's attention, to stand out in an ever-growing, ever more visually dazzling market. But Lex had done it, and he'd done it with understatement. Of course, Kendall was an unusually beautiful girl, even by the standards of an industry where exceptional beauty was considered the norm. But Lex's shots had transcended her looks, conveying an innocence and intelligence and depth not typically associated with Kendall Bryce. Matador, her record company, were gonna love it.

Lex's pictures weren't the only reason for Jack's good mood. It was two weeks since Kendall had left for England, and she wasn't due back for another week. Her first gig had gone well, and the trip, miraculously, had been scandal-free, so far – a personal best for Miss Bryce. With Kendall out of his hair for the best part of a month, Jack finally felt able to relax at home and his productivity at work had shot up too. Brett Bayley and Kendall Bryce between them took up more of Jack's time and energy than the rest of his client list combined. Like Kendall, Brett had on-off addiction problems (and on-on stupidity problems), especially when it came to dealing with the media and/or keeping it in his pants. But Brett's band, The Blitz, were also in London on the first leg of their European tour. To have both his 'problem children' away at the same time almost felt like being on vacation. Jack hadn't realized how stressed he was with the pair of them till Kendall had gone too and he'd finally had a chance to breathe.

Which wasn't to say he didn't miss her. To this day Jack didn't know what it was that drew him to Kendall. On the surface she was everything he disliked in a woman:

vain, selfish, attention-seeking, capricious. But there was a need in her that Jack responded to, a need for a father and for a friend, a true friend who didn't blow smoke up her ass like the rest of her rich, spoiled Beverly Hills crowd. Since Sonya died, there'd been a void in Jack's life that was more than just romantic. He hadn't only lost his wife, he'd lost his family, his future, his reason to care. In some strange, undefined way, Kendall had filled that void. Not romantically, of course. As sexy as she was, Jack needed a relationship with Kendall Bryce like he needed a hole in the head. But, emotionally, Kendall mattered to Jack at a time when he'd feared that no one would ever matter to him again. In a bizarre way, taking care of her was a relief.

There were other things too. Kendall was powered by fear the way that a car was powered by gasoline. Jack Messenger understood fear. Beneath Kendall's bravado and bullshit lurked a sweet, smart, funny girl with a good heart. Jack wanted more for that girl than career success. He wanted her to be happy, which was one of the reasons he'd kept her at Matador for so long, rather than let her swim with the sharks at one of the big global record companies. Eventually she would have to make the move to the big league. But Jack was in no rush to hurry her out of her safe little cocoon.

The intercom on Jack's desk buzzed into life.

'It's Kendall for you. Line one.'

Jack's smile broadened. *Speak of the devil.* 'OK, put her on.'

Back at the Eaton Gate apartment, Kendall stumbled around the kitchen opening and closing drawers with one hand, while the other kept precarious hold on the neck of a bottle of Moët. Ivan's phone was wedged between her shoulder and ear, playing Jester's hold music. Beverly, Jack's Rottweiler of a secretary, was 'checking' whether the great man was available to speak to her, and Kendall had decided to multi-task while she waited.

'I can't find a fucking corkscrew,' she called out to Ivan drunkenly. 'Your fucking kitchen's fucking dishorganished.'

Ivan, who'd drunk the best part of a bottle of Chablis himself at their celebration lunch, but who at twice Kendall's body weight was doing a better job of holding his drink, walked in to a deafening clatter of cutlery. Kendall had upended the entire top drawer onto the tiled floor. Dressed only in a pair of knickers and a T-shirt – she'd stripped off as soon as they got back from Boisdale's, declaring herself 'boiling' in her Hudson jeans, and Ivan's flat 'a fucking oven' – she seemed to be attempting to search through the drawer's contents with her bare foot.

'You don't need a corkscrew, angel,' said Ivan, relieving her of the Moët and expertly de-corking it with the softest of pops. 'It's champagne.'

'Ooooohhhh. Oops,' said Kendall.

'Now go and sit down next door and I'll get you a glass, before you totally trash the place. Who are you calling?' Ivan glanced at the phone.

'Jack.' Kendall hiccuped loudly, then collapsed into giggles.

Ivan's eyebrow shot up. 'Really? I'm not sure that's the best idea.'

'Courshe it is. Jack has to be the firsht to know. He'll be happy for me, you'll shee. He lovesh me really.'

Ivan didn't know whether Jack loved Kendall or not. But he'd have been willing to put good money on him *not* being happy about today's events.

The reason Kendall was so drunk was that she and Ivan

had only just returned from a long, celebratory lunch. They were celebrating for two reasons. The first was that ITV had called last night and confirmed Ivan's appointment as a judge on *Talent Quest*, their newest reality talent show. And the second was that at eleven o'clock this morning, Kendall had signed a huge, two-album deal with Polydor's Fascination Records. Fascination were already huge in the UK, representing the likes of Cheryl Cole and Take That, but their big focus was on signing more big-name US acts, acts whose profile was still building and who were prepared to deal exclusively with the label. Kendall Bryce fitted the bill perfectly.

Financially there was no doubt it was a terrific deal. Not only would Polydor buy Kendall out of her remaining contract with Matador, they were more than tripling her upfront money, and had committed a huge sum to promotion of her albums and at least one live tour. It also fitted well with Jack's strategy of broadening Kendall's appeal internationally, and particularly in the crucial UK market. The problem was that Ivan had made the deal. And he had done so without consulting Jack.

Ensconced on Ivan's suede couch, with a fresh glass of Moët in her hand, Kendall waited impatiently for Jack to come on the line. Perhaps she was a *little* tipsy. The grandfather clock in the corner was swaying from side to side like a metronome, and the swaying didn't seem to stop when she closed her eyes. But if she couldn't let her hair down today, when could she? Jack would be so proud when he heard about her deal. Perhaps now he'd finally believe that she was capable of great things? She was determined to show him she was mature enough to make good decisions, and that all the time and effort and money he'd invested in her had been worth it. Only once he stopped seeing her as a problem, a burden, would he be able to see her as a woman. *The* woman. *His* woman.

Coming to England had changed Kendall's thinking about a lot of things. She'd agreed to move into Jack's guesthouse because it meant being near him and seeing him every day, but she realized now that had been a mistake. She'd become too commonplace in Jack's mind, too familiar, a part of the furniture. They needed some distance.

Plus the trip itself had been far more enjoyable than Kendall had ever imagined. Her first gig, at the Apollo, had been a blast, and had received gratifyingly glowing reviews. Meanwhile, Ivan had put together a media tour that had her racing from rehearsals to TV studios to radio stations twenty-four seven, but he managed to make the gruelling days feel like fun. That was the thing with Ivan. With his sharp, caustic sense of humour, his flirting and his love of a good party – and of mischief-making in general, he was more like a naughty frat boy than a management company chaperone. Kendall loved Jack deeply and totally. But being with Ivan made her realize how dull her life in LA had become. Jack was still in mourning. He was depressed. It wasn't until she got away that Kendall realized that his sadness was contagious.

'Hey, kiddo! How's it going over there? I hear you killed at the Apollo.'

Kendall felt awash with happiness. She couldn't remember the last time she'd heard such enthusiasm in Jack's voice. Absence really had made his heart grow fonder.

'Yeah, it was great,' she gushed. 'The *Evening Shtandard* said I sounded like Aretha Franklin.'

Jack went silent. When he spoke again, all the warmth had drained from his voice. 'Have you been drinking?'

Kendall was about to deny it when a loud hiccup gave her

away. She giggled. 'Jusht a little bit. But I had a very good reason. You are talking to the new, frontline act for . . .' She made a *boom boom boom boom* noise like a drum roll: 'Fascination Records!'

She waited for Jack to respond. He didn't. Holding the handset away from her ear, Kendall looked at the swirling keypad curiously. Had she accidentally pressed mute?

'Are you there?' she said eventually. 'I think I losht him,' she called to Ivan.

'I'm here.' Jack's voice was icy cold now. It began to dawn on Kendall that all was not well. 'I sincerely hope you're joking.'

'Why would I joke about a thing like that?' Kendall asked, defensively. 'I thought you'd be pleased. Aren't you going to ask me how much it's for?'

'No,' said Jack. 'Because whatever damn fool agreement you've made, you're gonna unmake. You are under contract with Matador.'

'Not any more I'm not.' Kendall felt her anger rising. 'Polydor are buying me out.' Why could Jack never, ever give her the benefit of the doubt? He was against this deal before he even knew what it was.

'I assume Ivan's behind this. Is he with you?'

'Ivan was kind enough to set up the meeting. But it was my—'

'Is he with you?' Jack interrupted tersely.

'Yesh. We're at the flat,' said Kendall.

'Put him on.'

Ivan, who'd been hovering in the kitchen doorway listening to the conversation, smiled encouragingly at Kendall. 'He'll calm down,' he reassured her in a stage whisper, before taking the handset. 'Jack. It's Ivan. How are you, mate? Your protégée here told you the good

74

news? As of today, she's officially Jester's highest-paid client.'

Jack exploded. 'What the fuck are you playing at?'

'I'm not playing at anything,' Ivan said smoothly. 'I'm doing my job. Getting the best deal possible for Jester's clients.'

'Kendall's *my* client!' Jack roared. 'I sent her to you for a few weeks to do a handful of concerts. And you go and blow up her record deal?'

'Don't be so melodramatic,' breezed Ivan. 'Nothing's been "blown up". Matador are getting their money. Kendall's moving on to bigger and better things, that's all. It happens all the time. Besides, you were the one who wanted her to raise her profile over here.'

'I didn't want her to move to a British fucking label!'

'Why not? They've got The Jonas Brothers and Miley Cyrus.'

'Yeah, as side deals! Not as their primary label.'

'Which is exactly why they wanted Kendall. She'll be the first big US act they've signed exclusively, and they've paid handsomely for the privilege. It's a forty-million-dollar deal, Jack. If you'd pull your head out of your arse for five minutes, you'd realize this is a good thing.'

Ivan rolled his eyes at Kendall, who was looking increasingly tense and miserable on the couch. Whatever happened, he must not let Jack talk her out of this. This morning's paperwork would take weeks or even months to finalize. If Kendall wasn't committed, the whole thing would unravel, and any hopes Ivan had of making the move across to the pop market would be dead in the water.

'You know, if you *really* cared about Kendall, you'd be happy for her,' he said slyly. 'Forgive me for saying so, but you seem mightily concerned about your own, personal interests here.'

Jack started yelling so loudly that Ivan had to hold the phone away from his ear. As a result, Kendall heard everything.

'Kendall's a child,' he roared. 'She's spoiled and short-sighted and completely emotionally immature.'

Kendall blushed scarlet. Was that really what Jack thought of her?

'She has no idea of the kind of risk she's taking, walking away from a US record deal at such an early point in her career. She's an addict, Ivan. She's unstable and needy and she's simply not ready for the kind of pressured environment you're throwing her into.'

Ivan responded, fixing his eyes on Kendall as he spoke.

'I disagree. I've found the young lady to be smart, savvy and very much in control of her own career decisions. I made the introduction at Fascination. But it was Kendall herself who's been driving this thing.'

'Bullshit,' said Jack, again loudly enough for Kendall to hear. 'Kendall's no more capable of driving a deal than she is of staying off the booze. I should know. I've been wiping the girl's nose for the last two years. She's a walking disaster.'

Suddenly sober, Kendall got up and snatched the phone back from Ivan.

'You listen to me, you smug asshole. You're not my father, and you're not my boss. You're my manager. Which means that *you* work for *me*. I'm not going to be held back in my career just because your nose is out of joint that I finally made a decision without you. And it was a good decision.'

'It was a terrible decision,' said Jack, deadpan. 'Let me speak to Ivan.'

'No!' said Kendall. She was angry, but she also felt close to tears. She was pleased about the money, of course she was, but what she wanted more than anything was Jack's approval. She hated herself for wanting it, and she hated him more for not giving it. '*I'm* the client. You can damn well talk to me.'

Jack hung up.

'I don't believe it,' Kendall spluttered. 'Of all the arrogant—'

Ivan's mobile rang. 'Let's talk about this calmly, OK?' Cupping his hand over his mouth, Ivan walked back into the kitchen and pulled the door closed. 'We're supposed to be a team, Jack. Team Jester.'

'A team?' If it hadn't been so outrageously hypocritical it might have been funny. 'You got my client to sign a deal behind my back!'

'Our client,' corrected Ivan. 'They're all our clients, remember?'

This was one of Jack's favourite catchphrases back in the old days. He wasn't amused to have it used against him.

'And it wasn't done behind your back. It was an opportunity; it came up very quickly, and Kendall wanted to take it.'

'You should have called me.'

'It was the middle of the night in LA. I took an executive decision, as your partner. I genuinely thought it was what you wanted.'

Jack let out a mirthless laugh. These days, Ivan was about as 'genuine' as a plastic Rolex.

'You know, sometimes I really think you're intent on holding Jester's European business back.'

'That's crap,' said Jack robustly.

'Is it? Then why are you so against me diversifying and pursuing our interests in reality television?'

'Because they're not "our" interests, they're yours,' said Jack. 'You want to take time out from the clients to become a TV personality.' He injected these last two words with as much disdain as humanly possible. Ivan, who'd been about to casually drop his ITV offer into the conversation – Kendall's deal probably made this his best opportunity to 'bury' any other bad news – suddenly thought better of it.

'And this bullshit with Kendall is all about you too,' Jack ranted on. 'You want to move into pop and you're using her to give you a foot in the door. She may be too naïve to see through you, but I'm sure as hell not. I trusted you.'

'No you didn't,' said Ivan bitterly. 'You haven't trusted me for years. Just because I don't always see things exactly the way you do. Seriously, Jack, who died and made you God?'

In his light-filled office in Beverly Glen, Jack felt his fingers tighten around the phone. How he wished it was Ivan Charles's neck. For Ivan to pull a stunt like this was bad enough. But to try to turn it around, as if it were somehow *his* – Jack's – fault . . . The whole thing was beyond ridiculous. On the other hand, today's confrontation had been a long time coming. Perhaps it was no bad thing finally to air their grievances openly? As a partnership, Jester couldn't go on like this.

'Kendall Bryce is my client,' Jack said evenly. 'I will decide what deals she signs and when. I want you to call Polydor and back out.'

Ivan laughed. 'Come on, Jack. You know I can't do that.'

'Sure you can. Tell them Kendall's had a change of heart.'

Ivan paused for a moment, then said, 'But she hasn't had a change of heart, has she? She wants this Jack. It's *you* who's out of step here.'

'Either you undo this deal and send Kendall back to LA,' Jack said slowly, 'or I leave Jester.'

Back in London, Ivan leaned against the kitchen sink for

support. Jack Messenger, leave Jester? Would he really go through with it?

The idea had some advantages, of course, not least among them that Ivan would no longer have to work with Mr Saintly himself, or be hamstrung in his TV and other ambitions by Jack's stubbornly old-fashioned approach to the business. On the other hand, Ivan had built the London business by being able to promise his clients global reach. If losing Jack meant losing the LA office, he would struggle to attract new talent, and might even lose some of the clients he now had.

If . . .

But what if I didn't lose the LA business? I prised Kendall Bryce away from Jack easily enough, and she's in love with the guy. I already have a good relationship with The Blitz. What if I convinced them all to stick with Jester? To stick with me? My star's on the rise, after all. Talent Quest*'s going to make me a household name.*

Buoyed up by the twin successes of the last twenty-four hours and the adrenaline of his fight with Jack, not to mention well over a bottle of good red wine, Ivan felt emboldened.

'If Kendall wants to stick with Polydor, I'll stand by her.' He chose his words carefully. 'And if you elect not to manage her at that point, then I will. Beyond that, what happens is up to you.'

A few minutes later, Ivan opened the kitchen door and walked back into the living room looking shell-shocked.

'What happened?' All Kendall's earlier defiance was gone. She looked small and anxious curled up on the sofa, like a child who'd just overheard her parents arguing. 'Did he back down?'

'Not exactly,' said Ivan. 'He quit.'

Kendall's jaw dropped. 'Quit? What do you mean? That's not possible. Jester means everything to Jack. It's his life.'

'He gave me an ultimatum,' said Ivan. 'Either I get you out of the Polydor deal and send you home, or he'd leave the business.'

Kendall tried to process this, her eyes welling up with tears. 'You mean . . . this is my fault?'

'No, angel, of course it isn't your fault. Your fault for what?' Ivan sat down and put his arm around her. She was drunk and emotional, but she looked so fucking adorable in her knickers and T-shirt, with smudged mascara streaking over her high cheekbones, he felt a familiar stirring of desire. 'For signing a record-breaking deal? For making a real splash in London, like Jack asked you to? I know you're fond of him. But I'm afraid Messenger's being a stubborn arse. This is a power thing between him and me. You just happened to get caught in the middle of it.'

Nuzzled against his chest, inhaling the protective warmth of his body, Kendall suddenly felt strangely close to Ivan. For years she'd wanted Jack to hold her like this, to hold her at all, but he was as cold towards her physically as a statue. She had Lex, of course – Lex was an amazing hugger – and scores of lovers. But none of them felt as safe and strong and solid as Ivan Charles did at this moment. Ivan was handsome and funny and powerful and smart. He'd done more for her career in the last two weeks than Jack had done since he signed her. Equally importantly, he was fun to be around. With Ivan, life was unpredictable and exciting. With Jack it was boring and claustrophobic and . . . *disappointing.* The years of unrequited love had worn her down. Before she knew what she was doing, Kendall found herself reaching up and clasping her hands around Ivan's neck. It was Kendall who made the first move, but Ivan responded instantly, kissing her full on the mouth with a force and passion that took her breath away.

'Are you sure you want to do this?' His hands caressed her thighs as he whispered in her ear, his warm breath tickling her neck.

'You mean the deal?' she whispered back. 'Or *this*?'

'Both.' Ivan's hands were beneath her T-shirt now, fumbling with the strap of her Elle Macpherson bra. 'If you go back to Matador and Jack,' he planted a slow, lingering kiss on her collarbone, 'everything could go back to the way it was.'

Kendall closed her eyes. Ivan's hands and mouth and body felt wonderful. Wrong but wonderful. She forced herself to think about Jack. If she did this deal she would never go back to his guesthouse. Would she even go back to LA? She wasn't sure. Either way, Jack Messenger would no longer be her manager. *He won't be my friend either. Or anything more than a friend.*

But then she remembered the things she'd heard him say to Ivan. *'She's spoiled . . . emotionally immature . . . a walking disaster.'* With friends like that, did she really need enemies? Maybe Jack needed to lose her – really lose her – to realize she was something worth having?

Or maybe not. Either way, Kendall wasn't about to walk away from forty million dollars just to massage Jack's ego. Not when there were so many more appealing things to massage. Reaching down, she tentatively touched the bulge in Ivan's jeans. It was enormous and hard as a bullet. For a second she thought about Catriona, and about Ned Williams in the stables at The Rookery, giving her the third degree. But only for a second. Clearly Ivan made a habit of extramarital flings. One more was hardly going to make a difference.

'I don't want things to go back to how they were,' she murmured, unbuckling his belt. 'I want London. And Fascination. And you.'

It was all Ivan Charles could do not to punch the air in triumph.

CHAPTER SIX

The next morning, Catriona Charles came down to breakfast to find Miley Bayley, the three-year-old daughter of The Blitz's lead singer Brett Bayley and his wife Stella, drawing on the walls in indelible marker.

'Stella!' she said, horrified, removing the pen from the little girl's clutches to a cacophony of spoilt wails. 'Look what Miley's doing. It's everywhere.'

'Hmm?' Stella Bayley looked up absently. Sitting in the middle of Catriona's kitchen floor in the lotus position, her lithe, perfectly toned limbs folded over one another effortlessly, like bent pipe cleaners, she was clearly in a world of her own. 'Oh, sorry, sweetie. I was meditating. Nothing gets through to me when I'm in the zone.' She turned her attention to her whining daughter. 'Hey, baybeeeee,' she crooned. 'Whassamatter? Did you get scared, Miley-Moo?' Scooping the child up into her arms, she turned back to Catriona. 'We try never to raise our voices to her,' she said chidingly. 'Brett and I are big believers in peaceful parenting.'

Catriona bit her lip and counted to ten. What had possessed her to say yes when Stella invited herself down for the weekend? She was a well-meaning girl at heart, and Catriona felt sorry for her, trying to create an illusion of the perfect family life while married to the vain, philandering Brett Bayley. Stuck at home with Miley while her husband gallivanted around Europe on tour with his band must be a lonely life. But, even so, having Stella as a house guest was tough work. She wouldn't eat anything that wasn't organic and cruelty-free and purified to within an inch of its life. She would only sleep in east-facing bedrooms – something to do with energy flow – and was terribly keen on 'healing' people by laying her hands on their heads. Rosie and Hector both found this hilarious, but the poor dogs were really quite frightened by it. Old Mr Carruthers, the gardener, had threatened to give in his notice last time if Catriona's American friend didn't leave him and his tomato plants well alone. But worst of all was the little girl. Catriona felt guilty actively disliking a child of three. But Miley was without doubt the most whingeing, overindulged, obnoxious brat she had ever encountered, the spitting image of her famous father, and obviously destined to be just as much trouble.

'I'll pay to get it repainted,' said Stella, sensing that Catriona had perhaps been pushed too far this time. 'But you mustn't yell at Miley.'

'I didn't yell at Miley, Stella. I merely pointed out that she was defacing my walls and took away the pen.'

'The problem is she's so creative,' sighed Stella, smothering her daughter with kisses. 'Gifted children often struggle with boundaries. Don't they, Miley-Moo?'

'What the bloody hell happened in here?'

Ivan's voice made both women jump. Standing in the doorway with his overnight case in his hand, he looked tired, unshaven, and distinctly grumpy.

'Darling!' Catriona's face lit up. Ivan almost never came

home early. 'I wasn't expecting you till tonight. How lovely you're here.'

But Ivan evidently wasn't feeling lovely. He'd forgotten Stella Bayley was down for the weekend, and was irritated to find her hanging around in his kitchen with her snotty toddler glued to her hip. 'Who the hell scrawled shit all over my walls?'

Sensing a drama brewing, Miley secured her own starring role by bursting into noisy tears.

'It seems Miley had a little accident with one of our permanent markers,' explained Catriona.

'Jesus Christ,' Ivan turned on Stella. 'Can't you fucking control her?'

'How dare you curse in front of my child!' Stella shot back. 'What's the matter with you?' Sweeping past him, a sobbing Miley in her arms, she stormed out of the room. 'We'll be upstairs in our room if anyone wants us,' she called over her shoulder to Catriona. 'Packing.'

Catriona sat down at the table with her head in her hands. Suddenly she wanted nothing more than an aspirin and to crawl back to bed. 'That wasn't very diplomatic, darling,' she said to Ivan. 'You'd better go and apologize.'

'Apologize? Look at this shit.' He pointed to Miley's artistic efforts, which extended right around the base of one wall and halfway up the side of another. 'We only redecorated at Christmas. What the hell are they doing here again anyway?'

'You knew they were coming,' Catriona said wearily. 'Brett's away again and—'

'I don't care. Seriously, this place is turning into a fucking doss house. We never get a weekend to ourselves.'

Lovingly, Catriona reached out and stroked his cheek. He would have to apologize to Stella. They couldn't have the wife of one of Jester's biggest clients storming out of the house in high dudgeon. But secretly she was pleased that Ivan wanted more family time. It was what she wanted too, more than anything.

'I came home early to talk to you,' said Ivan. 'A lot of stuff's happened at work. It's been an exhausting bloody week, you've no idea.'

'I'll put some coffee on and make breakfast,' said Catriona, kissing him. Her week had been exhausting too, taxiing the children around from one engagement to another, filling in Ivan's horrifically late tax returns and cooking for an apparently endless stream of house guests. Saying no had never been her strong suit. 'You go up and smooth things over with Stella. Then we can talk.'

'Do I have to?' Ivan scowled. But he knew she was right. If ever there was a time to stay on the right side of Jester's big clients, this was it. In the coming weeks, Ivan and Jack would be battling to the death over each other's acts. Losing his temper with Stella Bayley was hardly the best start to Ivan's charm offensive. 'OK.' He kissed his wife back. 'Sorry for being such a grump. I'd like a bacon sandwich please, extra crispy. With ketchup.'

Catriona laughed. Grumpy or not, life was always much more fun when Ivan was around.

Half an hour later, having eaten humble pie and cooed grovellingly over the ghastly Miley, Ivan had mollified Stella Bayley sufficiently to be allowed to breakfast alone with his wife.

'Alone time is so important in a love relationship,' Stella said earnestly, 'especially when you have kids. It's a real hot topic on my blog: keeping the flame alive.'

Having spent the last twenty-four hours in bed with Kendall Bryce, indulging in a sexual marathon the likes of which he hadn't attempted since his own early twenties, the only flame Ivan was interested in was the one beneath the frying pan cooking his bacon. But he did want to talk to Cat. He needed her advice about this business with Jack and Jester, and her approval of him taking the *Talent Quest* job. After fifteen years of marriage, he relied on Catriona's opinion heavily. She was the only person on earth Ivan fully trusted, and it was a relief to be able to confide in her.

After two bites of his delicious sandwich and a gulp of Earl Grey tea, he got straight to the point.

'Jack and I have had a row.'

Catriona frowned. 'Another one? What's it about this time? Honestly, I do wish the two of you would work it out. You've been partners for so many years, and friends for even longer.'

'Yeah, well, not any more. He says he's leaving Jester.'

'Don't be ridiculous!' said Cat. But one look at Ivan's face told her he wasn't joking. 'You actually think he means it?'

Ivan shrugged. 'It looks that way.'

'But why? And leaving to do what?'

Ivan gave her an edited précis of his heated phone conversation with Jack, including heavily biased accounts of Kendall's new deal with Polydor and his own offer from ITV.

'Jack's jealous,' he concluded, 'pure and simple. He's ticked off because I was the one who brokered Kendall's deal, even though we're both getting paid on it. And he's scared shitless of me taking Jester into the twenty-first century. I swear to God, he'd have all our acts putting out albums on vinyl if he thought he could get away with it.'

'Hmmm. I'm not sure,' said Catriona. 'There must be more to it than that.' The Jack Messenger she knew was the last person likely to be motivated by petty jealousy. She could imagine Jack to be more old-fashioned in his outlook than Ivan. He was in life, so why not in business? But to break up Jester, such a wildly successful business, over such differences seemed to be a gross overreaction.

'I think you should talk to him,' she said at last, thoughtfully sipping her own tea. 'Or I can if you like. Don't forget, he's still grieving over Sonya. People in depression often don't make the most rational decisions. I dare say he's already regretting what he said.'

Ivan pushed his chair back from the table sullenly. 'Why do you always take his side?'

Catriona's eyes widened. 'What do you mean? I'm not taking his side.'

'Well, you could have fooled me. I thought at least *you'd* be pleased about the *Talent Quest* thing. It's a huge opportunity for me, you know.'

'I *am* pleased,' Catriona insisted. 'I told you I was pleased. I just think that Jack—'

'Jack's a stubborn bloody fool!' Ivan said petulantly. 'He's arrogant and self-righteous and I'm tired of having him looking down his oh-so-moral nose at me. Why shouldn't I take a job in television? I mean, what the fuck is so wrong with that? Jack talks about it like I'm selling my soul to the devil.'

'But surely you can talk it through?' persisted Catriona. 'After all these years.'

'I don't want to talk it through,' said Ivan. 'Kendall Bryce is pissed off with Jack for treating her like a child and, you know what, I know how she feels. Nothing I ever do is good enough for him. I'm not the one who's walking away from the partnership, Cat. Jack is. So it would be nice to think that my own bloody wife supported me, and wasn't only concerned about Jack's sodding feelings.'

'Ivan, I do support you. I always support you.' Reaching across the table, she grabbed his hand and looked him in the eye, willing him to believe her.

She's still got the most beautiful eyes, thought Ivan. He knew he was being childish about Jack, that what had happened between them was at least half his fault. But it still made him jealous and angry hearing Catriona defend him. Ivan might betray his wife's love, but that didn't mean he didn't need it, and her approval. They were like two sides of the same coin.

He entwined his fingers with hers and squeezed them tight.

'Let's go to bed.'

'Now?' Catriona giggled. 'It's ten o'clock in the morning!'

'So?'

'I thought you were exhausted.'

Ivan grinned. 'I've rallied. Just don't say another word to me about Jack Bloody Messenger.'

'I won't,' said Catriona. And she didn't. Upstairs, Ivan bolted the bedroom door, peeled off her dressing gown and pyjamas, and was out of his own clothes in seconds. Somehow having just come from Kendall's bed made being here with his wife even more exciting. Catriona's body was the exact opposite of Kendall's – soft and warm and overflowing, like diving into a mound of soft pillows. If fucking Kendall was a workout, making love to Cat was like the massage afterwards: comforting and familiar and deeply pleasurable.

For her part, Catriona could barely conceal her delight. She and Ivan had a healthy sex life, but she couldn't remember the last time they'd sneaked off like this for a quickie, especially in the middle of the morning. God knows what the children and Stella were up to. It all felt so illicit and joyful. *Life affirming*, as Stella would have said.

'Oh, by the way,' said Ivan afterwards as she lay in his arms, 'Kendall Bryce's going to be staying on at Eaton Gate for a while until she finds a permanent place in London. I hope that's OK with you. She got caught in the middle of all this nonsense with Jack and I think she's still feeling a bit fragile.'

'Of course,' said Catriona. 'You should have brought her down here. She's a sweet girl and Rosie and Hector both adore her. Especially Hector. I think he has a bit of a crush actually. It's sweet.'

Ivan kissed her on the forehead. 'No. We have to start ring-fencing our family time a bit more. I can deal with clients during the week, but weekends here are for us.'

A flicker of guilt, trying to make itself felt in Ivan's chest, was quickly extinguished. What Catriona didn't know wouldn't hurt her. As long as he kept his two worlds separate and compartmentalized, everything would work out just fine.

Jared Crane looked across the desk at his client and frowned.

He was not happy.

Jared Crane was the senior partner at Crane and Farrelly, one of the top corporate law partnerships in Beverly Hills. Wealthy, successful people paid Jared Crane an astronomical amount of money, by the hour, for legal advice. Having paid the money, it seemed to Jared only right and proper that they should then *take* the advice he had given them.

The client sitting opposite him today had a reputation for stubbornness. But he also had a reputation for caution, intelligence and good sense, which was what made today's events even more distressing. The document he was about to sign was one that Jared Crane had drawn up for him, against Jared's advice and at the client's own absolute insistence. Jared Crane had told him in no uncertain terms that signing it was not in his best interests. But yet here Jack Messenger sat, directly across the desk from Jared, with a silver Mont Blanc pen in his hand and a look of grimly determined stupidity on his handsome face.

'Where do I sign?'

'Penultimate page. At the bottom. But, Jack, I wish you'd reconsider. Or at least cool off for a few days before I send Ivan his copy. Once he signs, it's done, and can't be undone.'

Jack dashed off a signature and handed his lawyer the document. 'It's already done, Jared. I can't work with him any more.'

'Fine, but you do understand it's *you* who's walking away from the Jester name. You're effectively giving Ivan Charles the brand – a brand you've spent your entire professional life building.'

Jack shrugged. 'It's just a name. I don't mean to sound arrogant, but clients are loyal to me, not to Jester. I'll start a new company and carry on as before.'

It does sound arrogant, thought Jared Crane, *or at least foolhardy*. Brand names were important in any business, but especially in music, and they couldn't be replaced overnight. In his enthusiasm for a fresh start, Jack Messenger was giving up his rights in something very valuable. And not to a friend, but to a man in whose interests it was to try and destroy him professionally.

'Have you called your clients and discussed it with them?'

'Not yet,' said Jack.

'Don't you think you should?'

Jack frowned. He knew Jared Crane was looking out for his interests, but his mind was made up. 'With respect, Jared, I know how to handle my clients. The one thing artists hate is uncertainty. Once I've formally split with Ivan, I'll let people know where things stand. Day to day, nothing will change for most of them.'

Jared Crane watched Jack Messenger leave his office with a spring in his step, satisfied with the morning's business. Jared hoped his own pessimism was unfounded and that things would work out all right for his client. Until today, he'd never put Jack Messenger down as impulsive, still less a fool.

He buzzed his secretary with a heavy heart. 'Linda, I have a document here I need you to FedEx. Uh huh. Express delivery to London.'

'Hey, Brett, it's for you. Ivan Charles.'

Reluctantly Brett Bayley put down the lap-dancer and picked up the phone. His hotel room at the Georges V in Paris was littered with empty champagne bottles and wraps of coke, the remnants of which dusted the top of the coffee table like snow. So far The Blitz were enjoying the French leg of their tour immensely.

'Whassup, man?'

'Good morning, Brett. Has Jack called you?' Ivan's voice was low and rich, like slowly pouring honey.

'Jack Messenger? No. Why would he?'

'Well,' Ivan cleared his throat, 'he's decided to leave the company and set up on his own.'

'*What?*'

'He didn't even bother to call you?' Ivan sounded surprised.

'No,' Brett frowned. 'He didn't. This is the first we've heard of it. I guess I should call him.'

'That's up to you,' said Ivan casually. 'I'm just calling to let you know how much we at Jester value The Blitz as clients. I hope you'll consider staying with us.'

Brett hesitated. 'I don't know, man. Jack's been with us from the beginning, you know? We kind of owe him.'

'Do you think so?' said Ivan. 'Well, I must say that's very generous of you. I'd have said that he owes you, after a decade of skimming twenty per cent off your top line.'

Brett had never really thought of it like this. 'I guess he could have called us at least.'

'Indeed,' purred Ivan. 'I should probably also mention that now that I'm running Jester, we're going to be halving our commission for our top-tier acts.'

The lap-dancer was massaging Brett's shoulders, her huge silicone breasts pressed against his back like beach balls. He struggled to concentrate. 'Halving it, you say?'

'Uh huh. Ten per cent.'

Brett Bayley was no Einstein. But a ten per cent commission rate was unheard-of in the music business. It would mean millions of extra dollars in his pocket every year. And, after all, he *did* have a wife and kid to think about now.

'No pressure,' said Ivan. 'Have a think about it.'

Lex Abrahams sat at the bar at Cecconi's on Melrose indulging in some surreptitious star-spotting. Out on the patio, Simon Cowell was holding court amongst a bunch of artists and record-company execs, including Gwen Stefani and David Alaia, the new head of Sony. Inside, Jennifer Aniston and a mystery man were huddled at a corner table, and Kobe Bryant, the Lakers hero, was enjoying a quiet dinner with his latest girlfriend, a Croatian model with legs like a giraffe and the brain power to match. As a music biz photographer, and longtime West Hollywood resident, Lex spent half his life amongst celebrities, but he was ashamed to admit he still experienced a small thrill when a beautiful actress or a brilliant sportsman sat down next to him. It was part of the buzz of living in LA and, although few people admitted to feeling it, it was one of the main reasons that celebrity hang-outs like Cecconi's were fully booked all year round. It always made Lex laugh when pretty girls claimed they came here for the food. It was like saying you went to Hyde for the music, or the Chateau Marmont for the views.

'Can I get you another margarita?'

The girl behind the bar reminded him of Kendall. She had the same glossy dark hair and angular cheekbones. Lex had successfully not thought about Kendall for an entire ten minutes, but now his mind wandered back to her. He'd only had one phone call from her since she arrived in London, which he assumed meant she was enjoying herself. As a general rule, Kendall only ever called him when she needed something – usually a shoulder to cry on about Jack. She'd be back in a few days and Lex was frightened by how violently he was longing to see her again.

He smiled at the barmaid. 'Sure. Why not?'

Jack was late, and Lex had nothing much else to do. Having worked on back-to-back shoots for the last six weeks, he now found himself with the rare luxury of a few days off. He'd been thinking about driving down to La Jolla for a well-earned mini-break when Jack Messenger called asking to meet for a drink. He'd sounded excited on the phone, as if he had good news he wanted to share.

When Jack finally arrived, weaving his way through the tables towards the bar, Lex noticed how many female heads turned to look at him. Even in a restaurant full of famous, attractive men, Jack Messenger stood out from the crowd. Lex put it down to the fact that, unlike almost everybody else here, Jack genuinely didn't care what sort of an impression he made. LA was crawling with good-looking men, but very few of them were so self-contained, so entirely without vanity. Jack Messenger didn't play it cool. He *was* cool. Big difference.

'Sorry. Crazy day.' Sitting down next to Lex he ordered a gin and tonic and a charcuterie plate from the bar. 'Have you eaten already?'

'Yes,' lied Lex, who couldn't afford Cecconi's prices. He'd mop up the alcohol with a big bowl of pasta when he got home. So what's this all about? I'm intrigued.'

Jack took a deep breath. 'I'm leaving Jester.'

His eyes sparkled with excitement. Lex wasn't sure how to respond.

'Wow,' he said eventually. 'That's big news. Where are you going?'

'I'm not going anywhere. I'm staying right here.'

Lex looked puzzled. Had he had one margarita too many? 'You mean you're retiring?'

'Noooo.' Jack laughed. 'Jesus, thanks a lot. I'm not that old. I'm splitting with Ivan, that's all. It's been a long time coming and I think it's gonna be better for both of us. I'll set up shop here in LA, and we'll gradually regrow a European business. Ivan can reinvent himself as a reality star, or whatever the hell it is he thinks he does these days.'

Lex processed this information. He'd worked for Jester on and off for the last five years, and in all that time he had only met Ivan Charles twice. Nevertheless, he'd made a big impression. By far the more flamboyant of the two founding partners, it was Ivan who people most associated with the name Jester. Jack was the quiet, powerful engine that kept them going, but Ivan Charles was the face of the company.

'What does Kendall think about all this?'

For the first time, Jack's expression darkened. 'It was Kendall who started this whole ball rolling,' he said bitterly. 'Not that I'm complaining. The way I see it, she did me a favour.'

He told Lex the whole story, how Kendall had reneged on her US record deal and signed with a British label behind his back. 'She called me, drunk out of her mind. When I challenged her about it, she refused to call the thing off – or rather, Ivan refused on her behalf. No question he's leading her by the nose on this thing. So Kendall's with Polydor and I'm washing my hands of the both of them.'

Lex didn't try to hide his shock. Not just that Kendall had taken such a huge step without even telling him; but that Jack would actually go so far as to cut her loose.

'You can't be serious. You're going to stop managing Kendall?'

'I'm perfectly serious. I'm prepared to manage Kendall, but only on my terms, which she refused.'

'But Jack—'

'Look, if Kendall wants to piss her career away in Europe in exchange for the first big cheque she's offered, that's up to her,' Jack snapped. 'She'll see through Ivan soon enough. When she does, I dare say she'll come crawling back.'

Lex flattered himself that he knew Kendall Bryce better than anyone. She and Jack were as stubborn and bull-headed as each other. It would be a cold day in hell before Kendall 'crawled' back to anyone. The pair of them were proud to a fault.

'If you want to call it quits as well, I understand,' Jack said sulkily. 'Entirely your call. I know you and Kendall are close.'

'Don't be ridiculous,' said Lex. 'Of course I'll keep working with you.' He considered Jack Messenger a friend but, far more pertinently, he relied on him for a solid sixty-five per cent of his income. It was typical of Jack's unconscious arrogance that this simple economic fact had never occurred to him. 'It's very sudden, that's all. Quitting Jester and dropping Kendall, all on the strength of one argument. You don't think you're overreacting?'

Jack's frown deepened. He did not think he was overreacting, and he was tired of everyone telling him he was. So far the only person who'd been unconditionally supportive was Elizabeth, his on-again off-again girlfriend. Liz thought that breaking out on his own was an 'awesome idea'. Jack put this down to the fact that she had seen first-hand how much stress Ivan Charles's antics had caused him over the past year, and what a daily nightmare it had been babysitting Kendall Bryce. It didn't occur to him that Elizabeth Grey was hopelessly in love with him and would probably have said anything she knew he wanted to hear.

Lex Abrahams was braver. 'What if it doesn't stop with Kendall?' he asked Jack, who had downed his G&T and already ordered a second. 'What if Ivan's already out there now, trying to secure Jester's other big acts?'

'I can't see him doing that.' Jack sounded supremely unconcerned. 'He has his list, which I have no intention of going after, and I have mine. It's in the clients' interests to make a clean break.'

'Maybe, but since when did Ivan Charles put the clients' interests above his own? He could be on the phone right now, making promises to half your acts. Either way, you ought to call people, man. Let them know what's going on, reassure them. Have you spoken to Brett Bayley?'

'No,' said Jack, irritated. 'Why would I?'

'Because he's in London right now, on Ivan's home turf, and because The Blitz are your most lucrative act?' offered

Lex. 'Kendall told me Brett's wife spends a lot of time with Ivan's wife. That could be dangerous.'

'Nonsense,' said Jack dismissively. 'I've managed The Blitz since they were a bunch of high-school kids. I'm like a father to those boys. Brett Bayley's not going anywhere. Besides,' he added, worryingly from Lex's perspective, 'anyone who wants to go should go. I'm not interested in representing people who don't want me as their manager. If Kendall thinks Ivan can do a better job than I have, then good luck to her. I won't be begging anyone to stay.'

An hour later, Lex drove the few blocks back to his apartment in a state of high anxiety. He knew Jack Messenger to be a smart businessman. He had founded Jester, after all, and must comfortably be worth tens of millions of dollars. But this latest decision seemed totally out of character: risky, impetuous, the sort of thing that Kendall might do.

Kendall. It still hadn't fully sunk in. Had she really traded in Matador for a niche European record label, and Jack for his charismatic partner? It all seemed so unlikely. And what did it mean? Was she going to stay in England now? To move there permanently? Surely she wouldn't actually relocate to another continent without telling him. Lex needed to believe he meant more to Kendall than that. Jack might be ready to wash his hands of the troublesome Miss Bryce, but then he had the luxury of not being in love with her.

I'll call her, get to the bottom of it. There must be two sides to this story. Once I know what she's thinking, I'm sure I can get her to see sense.

Kendall woke alone in Ivan Charles's bed. It was only six a.m., but there was no chance of getting back to sleep. Light was already chinking through the blinds in the Eaton Gate flat, and a particularly noisy removal van had inconsiderately decided to start unloading right beneath the master bedroom window.

Kendall officially still had her own room down the hall, but in the ten days since she and Ivan had become lovers, she hadn't spent a night there. She felt surprisingly lonely when Ivan disappeared to Oxfordshire. It was a comfort to sleep on sheets that still bore the scent of him, and Kendall felt in need of comfort.

In the immediate, euphoric aftermath of her Fascination deal, and the unexpected thrill of beginning a new affair, she'd spared little thought for the long-term implications of her epic row with Jack. Now, as the days passed with no sign of bridge-building on either side, the true enormity of what she'd done was starting to sink in. The entire focus of her career and life had now shifted to London, a city she still barely knew and where she was living out of two suit-cases. Ivan had made it all seem so fun. It *was* fun when he was with her, as if the rest of her life, the boring part full of ties and responsibilities and angry record-company execs, faded into a distant dream and only the thrilling present was real. But as soon as Ivan was physically gone, be it to work or home to his wife and family, Kendall felt like what she was: a stranger, alone and friendless in a foreign city. Forty-million-dollar deals were all very well, but she needed a life. The one she had right now revolved wholly and frighteningly around Ivan Charles, a man she had only met for the first time less than a month ago.

Reaching for her cell phone on the bedside table, she turned it on and checked for new messages. There were six, all from LA, but none of them from Jack. Five were business-related and one was from her mother, who had clearly forgotten Kendall was travelling and sounded irritated that she hadn't stopped by the house since the spring. Depressed, Kendall was just about to switch the handset off when to her astonishment it rang. *Number Withheld*. It could be Ivan, from a payphone, although perhaps that was unlikely at this time in the morning. Or Jack, pleading with her to come back . . .

'Hello?'

'I just had dinner with Jack. What the hell's going on? Why didn't you call me?'

The sound of Lex's voice burst Kendall's hope-bubble like a pin in a birthday balloon.

'Oh, hi, Lex,' she sighed. 'I meant to call you but it's been totally crazy. Ivan's got me on an insane publicity schedule. I've hardly had a minute to myself.'

'So it's true, then? You have dropped Jack for Ivan.'

Kendall bit her lip hard. Was that what Jack was telling people? That *she* had dumped *him*?

'Are you out of your mind?' Lex asked accusingly. 'After all Jack's done for you?'

'OK, just hold on a minute,' said Kendall. 'First of all, Jack dropped me, not the other way around.'

'After you signed a deal without discussing it with him!'

'Discussing? With Jack? Come on, Lex, you know the man. Jack doesn't *discuss* things with me. He orders me around like a child, and I'm sick of it.'

'Kendall, you should have told him.'

'Well maybe I would have if he ever called me,' Kendall shot back, stung because she knew deep down that Lex was right. 'Did he tell you what a great deal it is? I bet he didn't.' She filled Lex in on the numbers. He had to admit they were eye-popping and that Jack *had* failed to mention them.

'Would you walk away from that kind of money just to keep Jack sweet?'

'No,' said Lex, 'I wouldn't. But I wouldn't stab him in the back either. And I wouldn't ignore his advice. Yes, it's a lot of money, but it means turning your back on the US market, or at least shifting your focus at a crucial point in your career. Jack thinks that's a mistake.'

'Oh, bullcrap,' said Kendall. 'Jack's just pissed because for once in his life he's not in control. Ivan brokered the deal and Jack can't stand it. He doesn't care about my *interests*.'

'How can you say that?' Lex sounded genuinely shocked. 'You know he cares. My God, Kendall, I don't think you realize how serious this is. Jack's leaving Jester over this. He's breaking up the company.'

Kendall shrugged. 'That's his decision. Look, it's not my fault if Jack's decided to throw all his toys out of the crib. Ivan says he's always had a spoiled, immature streak.'

Lex laughed bitterly. 'Yeah, well, Ivan would know.'

'What's that supposed to mean?' Kendall went on the defensive.

'It means he's a Machiavellian, self-centred jerk,' said Lex. 'If you don't know that now, you soon will.'

'You barely even know him,' said Kendall.

'Nor do you.'

A frosty silence settled between them. Lex broke it first.

'And what about me? When were you planning on telling me that you weren't coming back? Or was I supposed to read the press release like everybody else?'

Kendall had never heard him so bitter before. For some reason it made her want to cry.

'I was going to tell you.'

'When?'

'I don't know. Soon. It was a sudden thing for me too, you know. It's not like I planned it.'

There was so much Lex wanted to say. When he'd dialled

Kendall's number he had a hundred and one reasons on the tip of his tongue why she should come home, why she should make things up with Jack and convince him to stay at Jester and put this whole, crazy episode behind them. But now Lex realized there was only one *real* reason he wanted her home. It was the same reason he had for calling, and for feeling betrayed that he'd heard Kendall's big news from someone else, and not from her. And it was the one reason he could never, ever tell her.

I love you.

Please don't leave me.

Out loud he said coldly, 'All right then. Well . . . good luck,' and hung up.

Thousands of miles away, alone in Ivan Charles's bed, Kendall Bryce, Fascination Records' newest mega-star, burst into tears.

CHAPTER SEVEN

Over the next three months, shockwaves from Jester's sudden, unexpected implosion reverberated through the music industry. Although Ivan and Jack's inner circle had known for some time that all was not well between them, to the business at large it was a shock to learn just how bitter and toxic their relationship had become.

More shocking still was how quickly, and catastrophically, Jack Messenger's career nosedived. Jack had started this war but, for reasons nobody fully understood – perhaps out of some misplaced sense of gentlemanly conduct – he seemed intent on walking onto the battlefield unarmed and undefended. Ivan Charles was not so naïve. From day one he saw the break-up of the Jester partnership for what it was – a fight to the death – and set about annihilating his former partner. Without hesitation he called every one of Jack's acts, offering them vast financial inducements to remain with Jester, as well as slathering on the charm. Jack was a brilliant manager, but he had never understood as Ivan did the cavernous depths of insecurity that fuelled most artists. Ivan validated and praised and gushed and ego-massaged until his jaw ached. Jack couldn't bring himself to do it, and it was a reticence that cost him dearly. While Jack adopted a 'business-as-usual' approach up in Beverly Glen, Ivan spent entire days on the phone, like Jerry Maguire, relentlessly lobbying and cajoling for business. He flew to Paris to schmooze The Blitz and to New York to sign a new deal with Jason Kray, a young man Jack had been grooming to become the next Michael Bublé. He relentlessly leaned on all his contacts in the press, making sure that Kendall's face was everywhere and that her picture never appeared without Jester's name being mentioned. Meanwhile, as final preparations began for the launch of *Talent Quest*, Ivan's own face and name began to become well known, at least in England. ITV and the production company, House of Cards, set up an endless stream of interviews for Ivan. He made sure to talk about Jester and his famous acts in all of them. If the show was a success, and especially if it was syndicated globally, the new Jester would be clinging firmly to its coat-tails.

For Catriona Charles it was a period of mixed emotions. On the one hand she was delighted for Ivan, of course. She hadn't seen him this energized since Jester's early days. In the first week or two after Jack left, Ivan had been terribly anxious, but the business now seemed to be going from strength to strength. Kendall Bryce, who had always struck Catriona as a sweet girl, not to mention incredibly beautiful and talented, was an almost overnight sensation. Bursting onto the British pop scene like a supernova, with her debut British single going straight in at number three and advertisers clamouring to work with her, Kendall had put Ivan firmly and instantly on the map as a pop manager. Much as Catriona loved Ned Williams and Ivan's other, classical acts, she could see that managing Kendall had catapulted her husband into a bigger, infinitely more glamorous world.

It wasn't a world that particularly appealed to Catriona. But Ivan loved it, and she was thrilled to see him so happy.

But there was a price to pay for Ivan's success. Despite his expressed desire to spend more time at home, and especially to focus on Hector, Ivan was travelling almost constantly. Catriona didn't think she had ever known him work so hard. If he wasn't at the TV studios, rehearsing – the pilot of *Talent Quest* was going out live, to an estimated audience of twelve million – he was promoting the show, or locked in a recording studio with Kendall, or flitting around the globe signing more and more acts to the 'new' Jester. In the last month alone, he'd had to double the size of Jester's London workforce and move offices to an ugly but much larger space in Hammersmith, just to keep pace with demand. Meanwhile the demands of his family took second place, and Catriona found herself effectively a single parent. She tried not to mind for herself. Things would calm down with Ivan's work eventually. But she did feel sorry for the children, especially Hector, whose behaviour was on a downward slide again and who clearly resented his father's long absences.

And finally there was Jack. Though she did her best to hide it from Ivan, Catriona couldn't help but feel guilty about her old friend, especially as all of Ivan's current success seemed to have been bought at poor Jack's expense.

'It's not my fault if his clients don't have confidence in him,' Ivan protested. 'I'm not putting a gun to anyone's head.'

'But you are undercutting him,' Catriona pointed out meekly.

'I'm offering a competitive rate, darling. There's nothing to stop Jack doing the same.'

All of which might be true. But it still made Catriona feel

uncomfortable, watching Kendall Bryce on television telling interviewers how much she owed to Ivan and how happy she was in England. It was only back in the summer that Jack had cornered Catriona at Ivan's party and asked her to keep an eye on Kendall. How could he see Kendall's defection as anything other than a betrayal?

A week before Christmas, Catriona sat at the kitchen table at The Rookery, mindlessly peeling potatoes. Tonight at seven o'clock the first *Talent Quest* was finally going to air. Ivan was up in London, the show was going out live; though Catriona had offered to go with him, he preferred to do it alone.

'I'm so bloody nervous as it is, I'll fall to pieces completely if I know you're there,' he told her this morning. Standing in the bathroom, his face seaweed green, the poor thing looked as if he were off to face a firing squad. 'Is this hair dye too obvious? I feel like the roots are almost orange.'

'It's fine darling, very natural,' lied Catriona. Ever since he'd turned forty, Ivan had started obsessing about the signs of ageing, from the grey streaks at his temples to the faint fan of lines etched at the corners of his eyes. Since he'd been offered the television job, his anxiety about his looks had got exponentially worse. Catriona couldn't understand it. In her eyes, Ivan was much more handsome now than he had been in his twenties. She was the one who was going to seed. But like all her husband's foibles, she treated this one with kindness and equanimity, and did her best to bolster his confidence.

In the end, Ivan's hands were shaking so much that Catriona had had to shave him, otherwise he'd have appeared on screen looking as though he'd just staggered out of Sweeney Todd's. 'You and the kids watch it here, and make sure you Sky+ it.'

'Of course,' Catriona said loyally. She'd have to ask Rosie to show her how the Sky+ worked again. Last time Ivan had asked her to record *Entourage*, she'd somehow ended up with six episodes of *Ben & Holly* instead. 'Call us as soon as it's over, won't you?'

Ivan kissed her on the cheek. 'I promise.'

That was nine hours ago. It was six o'clock now, an hour till kick-off, and Catriona was starting to feel unpleasantly nervous herself. Outside, the afternoon's thin dusting of snow had turned into a full dump. Through the kitchen window, Catriona watched the fat, soft flakes fall in silent succession, illuminated by a brightly full winter moon. She loved all the seasons in Swinbrook, but winter was probably her favourite. The crisp blue skies and snowy river bank never failed to lift her spirits, but it was also wonderfully comforting to come in from the cold to The Rookery's roaring log fires, or to brew up a saucepan of home-made mulled wine on the always hot Aga. Of course, the downside of the cold weather was the irresistible urge to eat biscuits and mince pies and buttery mashed potatoes and all other varieties of warming comfort food. When Ivan was around, Cat made more of an effort to restrain her appetite. But left to her own devices, and particularly when Hector or Rosie were playing her up, she found it nigh on impossible not to go for the extra spoonful of brandy butter. She spent her life wrapped up in baggy sweaters anyway, like Nanook of the North. It wasn't as if anyone was going to actually *see* her expanding stomach, or the embarrassing red lines left by the waistband of her favourite elasticated tweed skirt.

Tonight, however, Catriona was too nervous to eat. She was only peeling the stupid potatoes for something to do, and because the alternative was going upstairs to try and reason with a sulky Hector, who was refusing to come and watch his father's television debut. ('Why should I care about Dad's things? He never gives a shit about mine.') The boy was getting more like a teenager by the day. Or comforting Rosie, who'd taken to her bed this morning in a paroxysm of grief because Ned Williams had announced he was abandoning his Widford cottage for Christmas and jetting off to Mustique instead.

'Mustique!' Rosie spat out the word in disgust. 'It sounds like a bloody deodorant.'

'Please don't swear, darling.'

'Why would he want to go to Mustique when he could be here with us in Burford? It doesn't make any sense. And what about poor old Badger? I bet he pines to death. Dogs do that, you know. Then Ned'll be sorry. How can he be so *selfish?*'

After an entire afternoon of the children's histrionics, Catriona had given up and retreated downstairs. But as soon as she was alone, she found her own nerves began in earnest. Just thinking about poor Ivan going green in the Green Room – was that why they called them Green Rooms, because everyone felt so ill before they went on air? – was enough to turn her stomach in sympathy. *Please, please let him be good. Let the show be a success.*

Having taken the edge off with two large gin and tonics, Catriona poured herself a third for luck and went through into the drawing room to find the TV already on. Rosie had apparently tired of sobbing Ned's name into her pillow and decided to watch her father's television debut after all. Coiled up on the sofa with a big bowl of Quality Street, she looked happy as a clam. *Oh, the resilience of youth*, thought Catriona.

'It's still the adverts.' Rosie scooched over to make room for her mother. 'Should I go and get Hector?'

'No, leave him,' said Cat. 'There's no point forcing it. He

can watch the recording later. Oh my God, it is recording, isn't it? Daddy'll kill me if I muck it up.'

'Yeeees, Mum.' Rosie rolled her eyes wearily. Catriona's technological incompetence was legendary. 'Ooo, oo, oo, it's starting!'

'Good evening ladies and gentlemen and welcome tooooo . . . *TALENT QUEST*!'

As the voiceover boomed out, the camera zoomed around a cheering studio audience. There were strobe lights everywhere and clouds of dry ice from which the show's presenter, a generic blonde called Isabella James, emerged in a gold-sequined minidress. A cantilevered stage lifted her upwards, the cameras trained firmly on her lithe, gazelle-like legs, while a six-piece live band played the show's theme tune to rapturous applause.

It's very old-fashioned, thought Catriona. *Almost like a seventies game show.*

'Cool!' Rosie breathed rapturously. 'I love the smoke.'

Isabella James rattled off her script from the autocue, briefly outlining the show's premise – to find the best vocal talent from all sides of the spectrum, pitting classical against pop and jazz against opera – before introducing the judges.

First up was Stacey Harlow, lead singer of Heavenly, a hugely successful girl band. A natural performer, Stacey smiled and waved at the camera, as relaxed as if she were posing for a family photograph. Next was Richard Bay, a handsome American in his early thirties, better known for his string of celebrity girlfriends – Cameron Diaz, Scarlett Johansson and Amanda Seyfried to name a few – than for the fact that he had written and produced two of the most successful Broadway musicals of recent years. And finally Ivan, whom Isabella James introduced as 'Britain's top music manager and the man who brought you the sensational Kendall Bryce.'

The audience applause was clearly Ivan's cue to acknowledge the camera with a nod and a smile. Instead he stared straight ahead, jaw rigid, beads of sweat clearly visible on his forehead. Catriona winced.

'What's wrong with Daddy?' asked Rosie. 'He looks awfully strange.'

Some heavy-handed make-up girl had gone overboard with the foundation, possibly in an attempt to hide Ivan's nerves-induced pallor. The result was a ghastly, orange, waxen look that made him look ten years older – a plastic George Hamilton melting beneath the studio lights.

Isabella James sashayed down to the judging panel. 'So, Ivan,' she said chirpily, 'how do you feel about meeting *Talent Quest*'s very first live contestants? Are you confident we're going to unearth the recording stars of the future?'

The camera closed in on Ivan's face. For a few awful seconds he said nothing, frozen like a rabbit in the headlights. Then, at a nudge from Stacey Harlow, he belatedly looked up at the autocue.

'Very confident Isabel . . . er, sorry, Isabella. The standard in the audition rounds was extreme. Er . . . Extremely. Extremely high. I'm sure our quest will be a success.'

You could have cut the awkwardness in the studio with a knife. Poor Ivan! Catriona couldn't bear it. Not only had he fluffed his lines, but his voice sounded terrible, a flat, lifeless monotone. Ivan was a brilliant speaker, a natural raconteur. It was as if the camera had reached inside him and sucked out all his charisma, replacing her bright, brilliant husband with a wooden puppet.

She prayed he'd warm up as the show got under way, but if anything things got worse. The acts were mediocre, with the exception of one eleven-year-old choirboy who sang 'Pie Jesu' quite beautifully and without any accompaniment. But while the other judges joked with the contestants and bantered easily with the presenter, Ivan continued to parrot his lines lifelessly, his body and manner both as stiff as a corpse.

When it was over, Rosie stretched out her legs, scattering Quality Street wrappers all over the carpet. 'I thought that boy was brilliant, didn't you?'

'Yes,' said Catriona. 'Wonderful.'

Perhaps the rest of the show's viewers had also been too focused on the competitors to notice Ivan's lacklustre judging performance? She did hope so. *Things probably seem worse to me because I'm his wife.*

'What the fuck was that? Late-onset fucking autism?'

Don Peters, *Talent Quest*'s executive producer, didn't pull his punches when he saw Ivan after the show.

'I know I wasn't great,' admitted Ivan, disconnecting his mic. Following Don into his office, he felt like a naughty schoolboy. 'But it was my first live show.'

'Not great? It was crap, Ivan. It was a fucking embarrassment.'

'Oh, come on. I wasn't *that* bad.'

'You reckon?' snarled Don Peters. 'You wanna see the tape?'

Ivan didn't want to see the tape. He wanted to go home, crawl under the covers and hide for the next six months. The irony was that he'd always assumed television would be so easy. Surely any monkey could stand up and read a few lines off a screen. He was so used to being around artists, performers who loved the stage and revelled in it like a drug, it hadn't occurred to him that he might actually find a live audience intimidating. Nothing had prepared him for the stage fright he'd felt tonight: the sweating palms, racing heart and dry mouth that had crippled his performance. He'd made a fool of himself in front of twelve million people.

'Look, I'm sorry, all right? I don't know what happened. I'll get it together next week, I promise.'

'You'd fucking better,' Don Peters growled. 'You're not irreplaceable, you know.'

Twenty minutes later, alone at last in the back of a cab on the Embankment, Ivan finally allowed the full horror of what had happened tonight to sink in. Humiliation swept over him like a hot flush. Grimly he turned on his phone to find three messages from Catriona. In none of them did she say in so many words how awful he'd been, but the concern in her voice made it pretty obvious. Not that he needed any confirmation. He knew it was a disaster. *A total fucking disaster.*

Suddenly he wished he were going home to The Rookery tonight and Catriona's quiet understanding, and not to Eaton Gate and Kendall's insatiable physical and emotional demands. The problem was that, after a few short months together, Ivan had fallen hard for Kendall Bryce. In the beginning, it had been the thrill of 'stealing' Kendall from Jack that had fuelled his attraction. That and Kendall's youth, fame and ridiculously sensual body, so pneumatically proportioned it must have been dreamed up by a teenage boy and willed into glorious, erotic life. But as time went on, Kendall became more than a mere sexual distraction. She was so vital and ambitious and *young*. Being with her made Ivan feel all of those things too. As much as she exhausted him, both in bed and with her chronic, almost manic neediness, Kendall also energized him in a way he hadn't felt since leaving Oxford. Back then Ivan had felt invincible, immortal, ready to take on the music business and the world and make his mark. But recently, with the creeping onset of middle age, that life force had begun to drain away, like sap oozing out of a slowly dying tree. Catriona, dear, gentle Catriona, was content to grow older with him. But Ivan wasn't ready to go gently into that good night. He still raged against the dying of the light, and Kendall Bryce raged with him. She had brought him back to life.

There was, of course, a price to pay for this rebirth. His relationship with Kendall was a constant performance, sexual, professional and emotional. He could never be himself with her, or show weakness the way he could with Catriona. Nor did Kendall soft-soap her responses. She found Ivan's insecurities boring and had no interest whatsoever in easing the pressures of his working life. On the contrary, Ivan was there to make *her* life easier, not just as her lover but as her manager. Like most artists she was insecure about her career and talents. She expected constant reassurance, and when she didn't get it was liable to act out, flying into alcohol-fuelled rages that left Ivan feeling drained and help-less. Most of all, though, he feared losing her sexually. Everywhere Kendall went, men swarmed around her like hungry locusts. Used to being the strayer in his relationship, Ivan had no idea how to handle the jealousy that over-whelmed him whenever Kendall was away from him. Which was at least every other weekend, as well as for week-long stretches during the school holidays. Ivan knew he was neglecting Catriona and the kids, particularly Hector, and he did feel guilty about it. But between the demands of his blossoming career, his family and his difficult young mistress, he felt increasingly like a butterfly having its wings pulled off, which wasn't a pleasant sensation.

The cab rounded the corner of Sloane Square, still busy with Saturday-night revellers. It was only ten o'clock, although to Ivan it felt much later. Wearily, he paid the driver and opened the front door of the flat.

'Kendall?'

'In here!' Her voice barely reached him over the noise of the hairdryer. Walking into the bedroom he found her stark naked, bent over at the waist, drying her long hair upside down. Ivan felt his dick harden instantly. Walking over, he slipped a hand between her legs.

'Did you miss me?'

'Hmmm?' Kendall turned off the hairdryer and turned around to face him. Her face was flushed from the heat and from hanging upside down and her half-dry hair fell tousled to her shoulders. Ivan didn't think he'd ever seen a vision so desirable.

'I said, did you miss me?' he growled, grabbing her bare bottom with one hand and fondling her left breast with the other.

'Not really.' Kendall's eyes flashed with a potent combination of mischief and lust. The truth was that, beneath the bravado, she was far more insecure in Ivan's affections than he would ever have imagined. But she'd learned long ago that the only way to hold a powerful man's interest was to keep him on his toes. Unlike Jack Messenger, Ivan Charles was naturally jealous. He was also turned on by drama; in this respect at least, he was with the right woman. 'How did it go?'

Irritated, Ivan released her. 'You know how it went. You saw it. It was a bloody disaster.'

'Actually, I didn't see it,' said Kendall, switching the hairdryer back on.

'What do you mean you didn't see it?' said Ivan, unplugging the dryer at the wall.

Now it was Kendall's turn to be irritated.

'I mean, I didn't see it. What part of that are you failing to understand, exactly?'

'It was the pilot show, for fuck's sake,' Ivan exploded. 'It was a big deal for me. And you couldn't even be bothered to switch on the TV?'

'Jesus,' Kendall rolled her eyes. 'My girlfriend Lisa called from LA, OK? So I was on the phone with her for, like, an hour. And then I had to wash my hair.'

'Wash your *hair?*'

'Yeah. It was dirty. Seriously, I don't see what the big deal is.'

She reached down to turn the hairdryer on again, but Ivan grabbed her wrist. He knew she was doing it deliberately, taunting him, feigning a lack of interest just to elicit a reaction. But he couldn't help himself. Tonight had been one of the worst nights in his life. The least he expected from his mistress was a little support.

'How would *you* feel if I didn't show up to one of your concerts? Or I didn't watch your performances on the talk shows? After Graham Norton, I sat and listened to you for hours while you analysed every fucking question he asked you. Remember that?'

'That was different,' said Kendall. 'You're my manager. It's your job to care about my career. Last time I checked, I don't take fifteen per cent off *your* top line.'

'This has nothing to do with money,' said Ivan as she wrenched her hand free. 'It has to do with you being a spoiled, self-centred little madam.'

'Yeah, well,' Kendall shrugged. 'Maybe I'm tired of listening to your midlife crisis, did you ever think of that? What do you want me to tell you, anyway, Ivan? If you think you did a bad job tonight, chances are you did. Maybe you're not cut out for television. Jack may have been an arrogant ass at times, but at least he always put his clients' careers before his own. Maybe you should try doing the same.'

'You bitch,' said Ivan. Kendall's hypocrisy was breathtaking.

'Call me what you like,' she shot back. 'But if you're looking for an ego-masseuse, I suggest you try your wife.' Pushing past him she began pulling clothes out of the closet. Some she flung into a Burberry overnight bag, others she pulled on over her still-damp limbs.

'What are you doing?' asked Ivan, whose head was starting to ache. Fighting with Kendall was fine as long as it resulted in make-up sex at the end.

'What does it look like? I'm leaving.'

'Don't be so melodramatic,' said Ivan, reaching for the bag, but Kendall was too quick for him, sweeping it up off the bed and heading for the door.

'I'll be at The Dorchester when you're ready to apologize.'

'*Me* apologize?'

'And I'm charging the room to your Centurion Card,' Kendall added over her shoulder, slamming the front door of the flat behind her with an almighty, violent bang.

Ivan clutched his temples. To his immense annoyance, he still had the remnants of a hard-on. What the hell was he doing, risking his marriage and draining his energy on an affair with this infuriating, intoxicating, hell-cat of a girl? Joyce Wu had never given him this sort of trouble. No one had ever given him this sort of trouble.

Wearily, he poured himself a double Laphroaig, downed it, then poured himself another. Tomorrow morning he would drive down to the country. At least he could be sure of a little tea and sympathy from Catriona, and it would be good to spend some time with the children. A trip to the toy shop in Carterton would smooth things over with Hector, and dear little Rosie, God bless her, adored her daddy whatever he did.

Maybe I will break things off with Kendall, he brooded darkly. Although he knew the moment he ended it she would hook up with someone else, a thought so unbearable it had him reaching for the bottle again. At least he would let her stew in her own juices at The Dorchester for a day or two. *If she thinks I'm rushing over there to grovel at her feet, she's got another think coming.*

Ivan was woken the next morning by the telephone. At least, he thought it was a telephone. It may have been an air-raid siren, or a fire alarm, or an electric drill boring its way merrily through his cranium. Whatever it was, it was deeply unpleasant, considerably increasing both the throbbing in his head and the wave of nausea that overtook him as soon as he sat up.

'Hello?'

No answer. Ivan looked perplexed, then realized he was holding an electric alarm clock to his ear. Dropping it with a curse, he got out of bed and scrambled under a pile of clothes on the floor until he unearthed the house phone.

'Yes?' he barked. 'Who is this?'

'Ivan, it's me, Mike. Have you seen the papers?'

Mike Marston-Gilley was Ivan's agent. Ever since he'd begun thinking about branching into reality TV, Ivan had discussed the idea with Mike M-G, an old school friend with a reputation as something of a star-maker on the British small screen. It was Mike who'd landed him the *Talent Quest* gig. No doubt he was calling to begin the grim business of post-morteming last night's disastrous first show. Which was his job, of course, and had to be done. But not before Ivan had got up, thrown up and downed a vat of coffee and a plateful of bacon sandwiches.

'I haven't seen anything,' groaned Ivan. 'I just woke up.'

'Riiight.' Mike hesitated. He was a kind, polite man, but Ivan could tell at once from his tone that the news wasn't good.

'The reviews are awful, I take it,' he said, sitting down as the hammering in his head intensified. 'Who was the worst, the *Mail*? Bloody Melanie Phillips has always had it in for me. Or was it *The Times*? That smug twat Adrian Gill's been trying to get his own TV show for years. God preserve us from jealous critics, eh?'

There was a long silence on the end of the phone. Finally Mike Marston-Gilley said, 'Ivan, this isn't about *Talent Quest*.'

'It isn't? Then what's it about?'

Mike let out the sort of sigh that no one ever wants to hear from their agent.

'You'd better sit down.'

CHAPTER EIGHT

Ned Williams arrived at the Burford Newsagent's just as it was opening. It was bitterly cold outside and still dark, but Ned's face glowed hot and red after his early morning run. At his feet a snow-bedraggled Badger panted forlornly. Rosie Charles was quite wrong about Badger pining to death when Ned left for Mustique. Had the poor mutt known he was in line for three weeks of lie-ins by the Aga, he would have thrown his hairy head back and howled for joy. Much as he loved his owner, Ned's latest fitness-jag was definitely beginning to pall.

'Ran all the way here, did you?' Mrs Chapman, the newsagent, winked conspiratorially, a grin lighting up her fat, gossip's face. 'After this, I suppose?'

She handed Ned a copy of the *Mail on Sunday*. He was about to say no, that he frankly wouldn't wipe his arse on the *Mail* and was rather hoping for the *Sunday Times* as usual, when he saw the front-page headline. And picture. Reaching into his pocket he pulled a wodge of notes out of his pocket.

'It's only a pound,' said Mrs Chapman.

'I know,' said Ned, pressing the notes into her clammy hand. 'I'll take every copy you've got.'

'Every copy?' The old woman laughed. 'How're you going to carry them, my lovely? That dog going to drag them home on a sledge, is he?'

'Just get them off the shelves, all right?' said Ned. 'I'll run home for the car. Is it all right if I leave Badger with you? I think he could do with a bowl of water.'

Half an hour later, Ned was driving his battered old MG along the back road to Swinbrook. Badger lay sleeping on the back seat, surrounded by a vast pile of newspapers. It was an impulse decision, buying out Burford News, and probably a stupid one. The locals would get hold of the story soon enough. Ivan Charles was one of their own, after all. Ned had probably bought Catriona no more than an hour or so of respite from the inevitable public humiliation. But an hour was better than nothing.

In the kitchen at The Rookery, Catriona was frying bacon and tomatoes for her and Rosie's breakfast. It was only half past seven, but Rosie had been up since six, mucking out her beloved Sparky, and Catriona had barely slept worrying about Ivan. He'd been so upset last night, he hadn't even felt up to talking on the phone, which was really unlike him. She felt particularly bad that he'd had to go back to the Eaton Gate flat and make small talk with Kendall Bryce. She was a nice enough girl, but really, after months in England, Catriona didn't see why she couldn't have found her own place to live. Poor Ivan couldn't be expected to play host for ever.

Desperate to call him, Catriona restrained herself, distracting herself instead by cooking breakfast while Rosie waxed lyrical about her pony and how he really needed a new set of fleece blankets now that the snow had settled in. Cat was reaching up behind the Aga for pepper when a knock on the kitchen window nearly made her jump out of her skin.

'Ned! Good gracious, you frightened the life out of me.'

'Ned? He's here?' Rosie gasped. 'Oh my God oh my God oh my God.'

Catriona tried to open the window, but a thick shelf of snow had sealed it closed like glue. Ned made a gesture to indicate that he would go to the back door, giving Rosie time to tear back upstairs like a banshee and beautify herself before he saw her.

'Just don't let him leave, Mummy, OK? Make sure he's still here when I come down.'

A few moments later, a flushed, visibly anxious Ned appeared in the kitchen doorway. He had a newspaper under his arm and a semi-comatose Badger at his heels.

'Are you all right?' Catriona asked him. Even by Ned's erratic standards, this was early for an unannounced house call. 'Would you like some tea?'

'No, thanks. Well, yes, but . . . I'll make it. You'd better sit down. Are the children still asleep?'

'Hector is. Rosie's probably emptying half of my make-up bag onto her face and drowning herself in Miss Dior. All for your benefit, I hope you realize. You can't go before she comes downstairs again, by the way.' She started to laugh, but something in Ned's eyes made her stop. 'What's all this about?'

Grimly, he handed her the newspaper. 'It's Ivan.'

Catriona stared at the front page for a long time but said nothing. Slowly she sank down into a chair.

'I'm so sorry,' said Ned. 'But I thought it would be better coming from me than . . . Well, someone else. Has he called?'

Still mute, Catriona shook her head.

'What about the media?'

At that very instant, the phone rang. Ned leaped on it instantly. 'Hello? No, she's not here. At her sister's, I think, I'm not sure. I'm a friend. No, I don't know when she's going to be back. Look, just bugger off all right?' He hung up, then disconnected the phone at the wall. Later he'd have to pull out all the others. Bloody Ivan. The bastard ought to be shot.

The front page of the paper was a grainy but nonetheless clearly recognizable picture of Ivan Charles kissing Kendall Bryce in a London restaurant. 'TV Judge Beds Bryce!' ran the headline, with a subheading promising readers 'more intimate pics' on pages four, five, six and seven. Like a zombie, Catriona turned the pages. For the first time, pain broke through the shock on her face. A series of shots, all taken with a zoom lens through an open window, showed Ivan and Kendall partially dressed and locked in a series of passionate clinches. They were standing up, but the body language (not to mention the fact that Kendall was topless in two of the pictures) made it clear the embraces were a prelude to sex. What hurt most was that the shots had clearly been taken at Eaton Gate.

That's our flat, thought Catriona. *That's our bedroom.* Her hands began to shake.

'Did you have any idea?' asked Ned.

Catriona shook her head. 'I knew she was staying there. But she's only a baby. I never thought . . . She's been here, you know. To The Rookery. Twice.'

'I know,' said Ned, who remembered walking in on Kendall and Ivan in the stable block last summer. 'I met her, remember?'

'She seemed like such a sweet girl. The children adored

122

her. Especially Hector. Oh God.' Catriona looked up, stricken. 'What am I going to tell the children?'

'Nothing,' said Ned. 'They don't need to know. Unless you're going to leave him, of course. Are you?'

'No,' said Catriona automatically. 'We've been together for twenty years. You don't just throw that away over one mistake.'

Ned felt like pointing out that this affair with Kendall wasn't 'one mistake', but the latest in a long line of calculating, selfish decisions by a remorseless adulterer with a major Peter Pan complex. But he bit his tongue. He was here to listen, not preach.

'But the children will still find out,' Catriona went on. 'If they were toddlers we might have been able to get away with it, but at this age they're bound to hear malicious gossip at school. Especially with Ivan all over the telly every bloody Saturday night. How *could* he?'

'Hi, Ned.' Rosie reappeared, sashaying into the kitchen in a pair of tight Top Shop jeans and her mother's brand-new, horrendously expensive Brora sweater. Her cheeks glowed with blusher like a painted doll's, and she appeared to have applied her mascara with a trowel. When she hugged Ned, he practically choked on a waft of perfume and hairspray. 'You're here early. Have you changed your mind about Mustique?' she asked hopefully

'Er, no,' said Ned. 'I'm off on Wednesday. I just popped in to see your mum.'

Catriona hastily closed the paper and folded the front page picture out of sight. An awkward silence descended, and for an awful moment Catriona thought that Rosie might sense something was wrong and force the truth out of them. Instead she disengaged herself from Ned, pouted disapprovingly and began making herself some toast.

'What about poor Badger?' she grumbled, getting the honey jar out of the larder and attacking it with a spoon on her way to the table. 'Dogs can actually pine to death when their owners abandon them, you know.'

'Ned's not abandoning Badger, darling,' said Catriona automatically. 'He's going on holiday.' It felt strange to be having a normal conversation with her daughter about Ned Williams when a hand grenade had just exploded so spectacularly into her life. Why hadn't Ivan called her? Where was he now? In the flat, with *her*, with Kendall? Suddenly she felt sick.

Ned turned to Rosie. 'Actually,' he said, 'I was going to ask you if you'd consider taking care of him for me while I'm gone.' Sensing Catriona's shift in mood, he wanted to get rid of Rosie and give them a chance to talk. 'I'd feel much better if I knew Badger was really happy, and he would be with you.'

'Me?' Rosie flushed with pleasure. 'You'd really trust me with him?'

'Of course. He adores you. He's out in the hall now, having a drink. Why don't you go and break the good news to him, show him where he'll be sleeping, that sort of thing. Dogs like to have a good sniff around before they move in.'

Rosie skipped off delightedly, forgetting her toast and slamming the door behind her.

'Thanks,' Catriona said weakly. 'Do you think I should call Ivan?'

'Absolutely not,' said Ned. 'This is his mess. Let him call you.'

'I can't just sit here and do nothing.'

Gently, Ned took the paper from her and threw it in the bin. 'Go and have a shower. Get dressed. I'll make you some breakfast and hang around until Ivan gets back.'

'Thanks.' Catriona's eyes welled with tears. Ned's kindness was more than she could bear.

'Oh, and Catriona?' he said as she got up from the table 'Don't forget to unplug all the phones.'

Kendall woke up late in her suite at The Dorchester, but she didn't feel rested. She'd had terrible dreams. In the last one she was walking through a beautiful forest when a fire swept through the trees out of nowhere, engulfing her in flames. She ran, tearing her legs on thorns, choking on smoke, but when she finally emerged from the forest to safety, she found she was standing on the edge of a cliff. For a moment her heart soared when she saw Jack standing on the other side, arms wide. *Jump and I'll catch you*, he seemed to say. But then she did jump, and he turned away, and she fell deeper and deeper into the abyss, with Ivan's voice echoing in her ears all the while '*Bitch . . . Bitch . . . Bitch.*'

She woke up panting, fists clenched, adrenaline pumping unpleasantly through her veins. After the initial relief of realizing it was just a dream, and she was not in fact plummeting towards certain death, depressing reality set in. Last night's fight with Ivan. That's why she was waking up in a hotel room. It was a fine line between keeping Ivan on his toes and pushing him away completely, and Kendall was frightened she might have crossed it this time.

Not that he hadn't deserved it. Ever since *Talent Quest* had become a reality, Ivan had spent more time worrying about his nascent television stardom and less time focusing on Kendall's album, her first with Fascination and a critical turning point in her career. She'd risked a lot, leaving Jack and Los Angeles and Matador and putting all her eggs in Ivan and Jester's basket. The least Ivan could do was to give her the attention she not only deserved but needed. Why should she be expected to sit at home like the little wife, glued to his stupid TV show? Jack wouldn't have needed that kind of validation. Then again, Jack wouldn't have been sleeping with her in the first place. He couldn't even cheat on a dead wife, never mind a living one.

Jack.

It had been several months since Kendall's defection broke up the Jester partnership and put an abrupt end to her and Jack's professional relationship. Any hopes she might have had back then of her absence making Jack's heart grow fonder had long since withered on the vine. She'd heard nothing from him. Not a word of congratulation when she released her first UK single, nor when she made *Rolling Stone*'s 'Ones to Watch' cover back in October. Lex was pissed at her too, but at least he still emailed every few weeks. Kendall always asked after Jack in her replies. She missed him, she missed them both. But Lex pointedly never responded to these enquiries, other than with a curt 'He's fine.'

Career-wise, it was no secret that Jack Messenger was far from fine. That he'd lost, if not everything, then certainly the bulk of his clients when he'd walked away from Jester. Kendall longed to talk to him about it. Not to apologize exactly – she still felt she was right to take the Polydor deal – but at least to explain that she had never intended to destroy Jester, or to hurt Jack professionally. But that bridge had not so much been burned as incinerated. There could be no way back, no leap across the cliff.

Which left her with Ivan. Ivan could be vain, self-centred and insecure, all traits which irritated Kendall, perhaps because she recognized them in herself. But when he let go of his anxieties, he was still terrific fun: rude, witty and unpredictable in a way that made life exciting. Sexually he was dynamite – they were dynamite together. He told Kendall that he and Catriona no longer slept together, that they hadn't for years and, despite it being the ultimate cliché, Kendall was inclined to believe him. Certainly his hunger for her, his wild, toxic need, was a strong indication that something pretty fundamental must be missing in his marriage. And yet, increasingly, Kendall felt threatened by Catriona Charles. When Ivan went home to Oxfordshire for the weekends, he returned to London refreshed, calmer, visibly happy. Kendall, on the other hand, spent weekends in a frenzy of activity – shopping, clubbing, having lunch with Stella Bayley and her coterie of Primrose Hill celebrity friends, snapped everywhere she went by the ubiquitous paparazzi. But invariably by Sunday evening she felt depressed, anxious and deeply lonely. When Ivan came home she would pick a fight with him, and they would end up having wild, intense, make-up sex. By Monday things had settled back to 'normal'. But Kendall was left with a deep fear of Ivan abandoning her, going back to his kind, comfortable, country wife and leaving her to fend for herself in London. She couldn't let that happen.

After a long, hot shower and a room service breakfast of poached eggs, granary toast and a positively ambrosial fruit compote, Kendall felt considerably better. She would check out later this morning, return to the flat and make things up with Ivan. Perhaps she'd stop by La Perla on Sloane Street on the way and pick up something tiny and lacy and provocative to help seal the deal.

The phone rang. The room phone. *No one knows I'm here except Ivan. He's calling to apologize, to make the first move.* Feeling hugely relieved, Kendall took a few seconds to compose herself, then picked up.

'Hello?' Her voice was deliberately languid and sleepy. She wouldn't want him to think she'd been up for hours, worrying.

'Was it you?'

There was nothing apologetic in Ivan's tone. It was cold and accusatory.

'Was it me, what?'

'Don't act like you don't know what I'm talking about. Did you leak the story to the *Mail on Sunday*? We're all over the front page, and a six-page fucking spread inside. I've just got off the phone to Catriona. She's in pieces.'

Kendall took a moment to digest what he was telling her.

'A tabloid's running a story about our relationship. Is that what you mean?'

'Yes, that's what I mean,' snapped Ivan. 'Someone must have tipped them off and it sure as hell wasn't me.'

'Well it wasn't me either!' she said indignantly. 'For God's sake, calm down. Where are you now?'

'Where do you think I am?' said Ivan. 'I'm in the car on the bloody M40 trying to get home. There are reporters camped outside my front fucking gates. Poor Catriona's under siege in there.'

'I see,' Kendall said coolly. 'Poor Catriona, eh? And what about poor me? Who's going to help me deal with the reporters? Have you even called Sasha yet?'

Sasha Dale was Kendall's newly appointed publicist. Five foot one, blonde and with an angel's face, Sasha had the mind of a sewer rat and the hide of a rhinoceros. Stories like this were her bread and butter. She would know how to handle the situation.

'Are you kidding me?' said Ivan. 'My marriage is about to implode and you're worried about your image?'

'Well one of us needs to be,' Kendall shot back. 'About

both our images. Even if you don't give a shit as my boyfriend about the entire country branding me a home-wrecker, as my manager it is your *fucking job* to care!' She was properly angry now. 'How dare you put this all on me? It's not my fault your wife is upset, it's yours. No one forced you to fuck me, Ivan.'

'Don't talk like that,' said Ivan, wincing at the harshness of her language. 'It's ugly.'

'Yeah, well, sometimes the truth is ugly. But clearly that's all I am to you. A fuck. A cheap, disposable fuck.'

'That's not true.' Ivan sighed heavily. His head throbbed horrendously and sweat soaked through his shirt. This was unquestionably the worst morning of his life. 'Look, I'm sorry I accused you, OK?'

Kendall said nothing.

'Calling Sasha's a good idea,' Ivan went on. 'You should do that, and stay where you are for now, lay low. It may take me a few days to smooth things over at home with Cat, but I'll call you as soon as I can.'

'No,' said Kendall.

The traffic slowed. Ivan's Jaguar eased to a halt behind an articulated lorry.

'What do you mean, "no"?'

'I mean I'm not going to sit around and wait for you to figure out a way to have your cake and eat it. Either you get back to London by seven tonight, prepared to tell the world we're together. Or I'll be on the nine o'clock flight back to LA.'

Kendall was almost as shocked to hear the words coming out of her mouth as Ivan was. She hadn't intended to give him an ultimatum. Apart from anything else, the practical problems of her upping sticks and leaving – the most imme-diate of which was that she was expected in a recording studio in Shepherd's Bush tomorrow morning to start laying down the rest of her Polydor album – were overwhelming. She could always go and crash with Lex for a few weeks, but then what? Her contract required that she spend at least eight months of the year in the UK. Besides, she didn't need a publicist to tell her that the one thing sure to make her look like the guilty party in the media was running away. If she wanted the British public to buy her records, she had to stay and fight her corner.

But she'd been overcome by the emotion of the moment. Listening to Ivan's concern for his wife, versus his knee-jerk rage against her, Kendall had a sudden, terrifying glimpse of the future. If she let him go to Catriona now, if she didn't take control of events, she would lose him. Certainly as her lover, and in all probability as her manager too. She had to take action, to threaten something so drastic, so unexpected, that it would force his hand. She had to make Ivan feel the same gut-wrenching fear that she felt. It was self-defence.

'Kendall, be reasonable,' said Ivan, whose hands were starting to slip off the wheel with nervous sweat. 'I have a family. You knew that. I have kids.'

'I'm not asking you to leave your kids.' Kendall struggled to keep the tremor out of her own voice.

'But you're asking me to leave my wife.'

'No, Ivan. I'm just telling you that if you go back to your wife tonight and throw me under a bus, I won't be here waiting. I'm telling you you have to choose. The choice you make is entirely up to you.'

She hung up and sank down on the bed, shaking.

What have I done? What the hell have I done?

Then she pulled herself together and picked up the phone again. 'Sasha? Yeah, hi, it's me, Kendall. I guess we should talk.'

*   *   *

Catriona Charles sat down on the dog-eared sofa in the library, then got up and walked across the room, then walked back and sat down again. Ivan was on his way, he'd be here any minute, and she literally had no idea what to do with herself. It was as if, in a few short hours, everything had changed, so that even her own body felt unfamiliar, awkward and out of place.

Ned Williams, God bless him, had taken the children ice-skating in Oxford. A couple of reporters were already hanging around outside The Rookery's gates as they drove off, but Ned texted Cat to say that he'd told Hector and Rosie they were there about *Talent Quest* and neither of the kids had questioned him. Of course, they'd have to know eventually, probably before tomorrow. But Ned was right. This was Ivan's mess. He could bloody well tell them.

He'd called about an hour ago, and to Catriona's great shame all her intentions to remain calm and dignified had flown out of the window. He hadn't got any further than 'I'm so sorry, Cat,' and she'd started sobbing and howling like a wounded animal, screaming at him that he was a dirty old man and that the children would never forgive him. He'd tried to tell her it was nothing, a fling, but every word was like a needle in her eyeball and in the end Catriona had simply turned off her mobile, unable to stomach any more.

There had been affairs before, and they'd hurt, but not like this. Catriona knew Kendall. She liked her. Had liked her. Seeing the pictures hadn't helped, of course. As long as she lived she would never get those images out of her mind. But it was more than that. Things had been so good lately between her and Ivan, so close and loving, almost like the old days. Yes, there were tensions with his work and the children. But Cat had genuinely believed he'd grown out of the womanizing, that all this nonsense was behind them. *What a fool I was*, she thought bitterly. *A trusting fool.*

At last Ivan's Jaguar pulled into the drive, spraying gravel in an arc into the snowy lavender bushes. Cat smoothed down her skirt and fiddled with her hair. She felt ridiculously nervous all of a sudden, as if she were the one who'd done something wrong. The front door opened and closed. 'Catriona?'

'In here.'

Her voice sounded strange and strangled. Ivan walked into the library and saw at once the turmoil of emotions playing across her face. Hurt, pain, anger, fear, confusion. In a long brown tweed skirt and mismatched yellow sweater, with her pale face stained and bloated from crying, she was not looking her best. But there was a poignancy to her unattractiveness that somehow made the encounter even harder. It was impossible not to pity her, and not to hate himself for reducing her to this sad, dishevelled state.

'I'm sorry,' he said again. 'I know it's hopelessly inadequate but I don't know what else to say.'

'There's nothing else to say,' said Catriona. She sat back down on the sofa. Ivan joined her, tentatively reaching for her hand. She let him take it, but felt nothing inside. Numb. As if the hand didn't belong to her. For a long while neither of them spoke. Then Ivan said, 'Where are the children?'

'Out. With Ned.'

Irrationally the mention of Ned's name made Ivan bristle. 'Where?'

'Oxford. They'll be back soon, I expect.'

'Do they . . . have you told them anything?'

Catriona shook her head. 'You'll have to tell them, Ivan. It's all a complete nightmare. Can you imagine the stick they're going to get at school?'

'I know. I'm sorry.'

'We might have to move them. Or, at the very least, take some time away as a family. A month abroad, maybe, until the worst of the storm dies down.'

Ivan withdrew his hand awkwardly. 'I can't leave England, Cat. Not now. I'm under contract to ITV and I'm up to my neck with Jester—'

'Screw IT bloody V!' Catriona recoiled, furious. 'And screw your precious career! This is not about you, Ivan. It's about *us*, our family, our marriage. I assume you've told Kendall it's over? Because I swear to God, if I find one sniff of that child in our flat or anywhere else around this family, I'll . . .'

She stopped short. Ivan had stood up and walked over to the window. He had his back to her, but something about his body language, the oppressed hunch of the shoulders, the bowed head, made the hairs on her arms stand on end.

'You *have* ended it, haven't you?'

Slowly, painfully slowly, Ivan turned around. He couldn't meet Catriona's eye. 'It's not that easy,' he mumbled.

Catriona felt as though she was having an out-of-body experience. Was this really happening? When she spoke, her voice sounded distant, almost detached.

'Why not? On the phone you said . . . you said it was just a fling.'

'It is. It was.' Ivan looked desperately to left and right, as if searching for an answer. 'I didn't intend any of this to happen, Cat. It just snowballed and . . . I don't know.'

'Are you in love with her?'

Ivan forced himself to look at her. 'She makes me feel young,' he said helplessly.

Catriona let out a short, joyless laugh. 'Oh. And I make you feel old, I suppose?'

'It's not you,' said Ivan miserably. 'None of this is about you, Cat. It just happened. One minute I felt like everything was slipping away from me. Like the best of my life was all behind me. Don't you ever feel like that?'

'No,' said Cat truthfully, 'I don't.'

'Of course you don't,' Ivan smiled. 'You've always been more confident than me. More mature. It's why you're such a good mother.'

'Please,' said Catriona. 'Stop.'

'But I need more. I can't help it, I just do. Kendall's reawakened something in me, my ambition, my lust for life. It's hard to explain.'

For a moment Catriona just stared at him. She knew him so well, his strengths and weaknesses, faults and kindnesses. In so many ways he was still a little boy. But rightly or wrongly, she loved him.

'And what about us?' she asked him.

Ivan glanced out of the window, searching for escape. He couldn't answer that question. There was no answer to that question. But instead of divine inspiration, he heard the ominous rumble of Ned Williams's car.

'The children,' said Catriona mindlessly.

Seconds later they burst into the house, brandishing bruised knees and elbows and talking over one another about their ice-skating prowess. Ned nodded briefly at Ivan and made himself scarce. He didn't dare look at Catriona, who seemed oddly frozen on the sofa, as if someone had pointed a remote at her and pressed pause.

'We saw your programme last night. You were very good,' said Rosie loyally, wrapping her arms around Ivan's waist.

Hector hung back in the doorway, trying not to show how pleased he was that his dad was home. 'So, how long are you staying this time? Just for a night?' His chin jutted

134

out defiantly, daring Ivan to contradict him. But it was Catriona who spoke.

'Daddy's going away for a while,' she said dully. 'He just came home to get some things.'

The look on Hector's face could have stripped paint off a wall from fifty paces. Without a word he turned on his heel and stomped off to his room. Rosie looked more confused.

'What do you mean, "going away"? Going away where? When will you be back, Daddy?'

Ivan tried to speak but the words stuck in his throat. At last he managed a stammered, 'I'll see you soon, Rosie, OK?' and bolted out to his car, driving guiltily away like a thief in the night.

'I thought you said he came to get some things?' Rosie looked at her mother. Catriona was staring straight ahead, unmoving, almost catatonic. Something was clearly very wrong. 'Mummy?'

Cat looked up as if seeing her daughter for the first time.

'Your father's met someone else,' she said quietly. She wished there were a way to soften the blow, but she knew from experiencing her own parents' divorce that honesty was the only policy. 'He's in love with her.'

Rosie's eyes widened in disbelief. 'Who? Who's Daddy in love with?'

Catriona sighed, defeated. 'Kendall Bryce.'

Speeding along the A40 towards Woodstock, Ivan gazed at the road ahead in a daze. This morning, everything had been fine, everything had been normal. He was married, he was seeing Kendall, and the two compartments of his life co-existed in what looked with hindsight like perfect harmony. But now that was all gone. Kendall had put a gun to his head and told him to jump, and he'd jumped. All he

135

could think about was the look on Hector's face as he turned away from him. *What have I done?*

He was still in shock when his mobile rang.

'Cat?'

'I'm surprised you're answering your phone, you old dog.' Don Peters, *Talent Quest*'s producer, sounded in an inordinately good mood. 'Kendall Bryce, eh? That's nice work if you can get it.'

When Ivan had last spoken to Don, he'd been spitting teeth after Ivan's first-night fiasco on the judging panel. Had that really only been last night? It felt like a lifetime ago.

'Don. Look, if you've called to talk about the reviews, I'd really appreciate it if we could do the post-mortem tomorrow. This shit with Kendall . . . I'm really buried right now.'

'Fuck the reviews,' said Don Peters jovially. 'I wouldn't wipe my arse on a stupid review. I'm calling about our ratings. Have you seen them?'

'No,' said Ivan. 'Funnily enough I've been busy with other things today.'

'Fourteen million! Fourteen fucking million' said Don triumphantly. 'That's only three million short of the *X Factor* final. We are a massive, fuck-off hit, Ivan. Even if you were a car crash.'

'Thanks a lot!'

'Hey, take it as a compliment. People slow down to watch car crashes. We keep up those figures and we're all gonna be rich as Croesus. Now, listen, what's happening with you and Kendall? Are you an item or what? I need to make some sort of a statement on behalf of the show. The public like to know these things.'

Ivan blinked and rubbed his eyes. This was all happening so fast. From live TV disaster to ratings triumph, from a tabloid exposé to officially coming out as a couple with a girl half his age. In the past, for every big change in his life, he'd had Catriona by his side to support and guide him. But now, for the biggest change of all, she was the one person he couldn't talk to. With every mile he put between them, every mile he drove closer to London and to Kendall, twenty years of love and friendship slipped further and further from his grip. It was terrifying, but exciting at the same time.

We'll be as rich as Croesus.

You and Kendall.

Nice work if you can get it.

The line from Macbeth popped unexpectedly into his head. *'I am in blood/Stepped in so far that, should I wade no more,/Returning were as tedious as go o'er.'*

Or, more prosaically: *It's too late now.*

'Yes,' he said. 'We're an item. I'm on my way back to her now. But, listen, Don, I still need to talk to my children. My wife and I . . . this is all very new. I'd rather you didn't go giving statements before the dust has settled. I haven't even seen Kendall yet, since the story broke.'

'Fair enough,' said Don. 'We'll give a standard "don't comment on the personal lives of our judges" line. But it's good news for us. People love a good romantic melodrama. I'll eat my hat if our numbers aren't through the roof next week. So cheer up, eh? Every cloud has a silver lining.'

Above Ivan's head, the heavy black snow clouds were indeed clearing, and as he drove through the white cliffs that marked the Oxfordshire border, a chink of bright-blue sky appeared before him, like an arrow pointing the way to a brighter future.

There was nothing for it now but to look forward.

It was time to move on.

CHAPTER NINE

Jack Messenger turned up the steep, craggy path above Will Rogers Park in Pacific Palisades and turned his iPod up to full volume. He was listening to a download of a new indie band from Detroit, the inexplicably named Land of the Greeks. As yet unsigned, but doing well on YouTube, the three geeky teenage boys had a gift for uplifting, soaring melodies that Jack hadn't heard in a long time. There was something nostalgic about their sound, which ironically was what made it fresh. Jack made a mental note to call them once he got back to the office.

Not that he was in any hurry to return to Beverly Glen, or even home to what had once been his sanctuary in Brentwood. Since news reached the US about Kendall Bryce's affair with Ivan Charles, Jack had found himself living in a hideous goldfish bowl. Suddenly the story of Kendall's defection to a British label and the break-up of Jester, which had aroused little interest in the American press at the time, was a big deal. Jack's phone was ringing off the hook with reporters wanting 'his side of the story' on the music business scandal *du jour*. Ironically, Kendall's profile was now higher than ever,

Stateside, as a result of her affair with her much older, married manager. Worse, Ivan, who until now had been completely unknown outside the UK, was being feted on *E!* and in the trashier US tabloids as 'Dastardly British Hottie Ivan Charles', and even as 'The new Simon Cowell'. It made Jack wince to think how delighted that comparison must make his former friend and partner.

And, of course, while the public on both sides of the Atlantic settled back with their TV dinners to enjoy the latest instalment of the Kendall/Ivan soap opera, back in the real world the anguished repercussions of the affair continued to cause untold suffering. Last week Jack had had a particularly harrowing call with Catriona, who at times seemed to be almost on the verge of a breakdown.

'Hector's been suspended from school again,' she told him, her voice ragged with strain. 'His headmaster's tried to be understanding, but he says Hector can't come back unless he starts seeing a behavioural therapist three times a week.'

'What does Hector say about that?' asked Jack. 'It might not be a bad idea.'

'Hector told me to fuck off. He said if anyone needs a therapist it's me because I'm clearly going mad. I think he might be right. Yesterday I put washing-up liquid into a chicken casserole instead of red wine vinegar. There were soap bubbles everywhere.' She broke down in sobs. 'He's so angry with me, Jack. Before it was all directed at his father, but now he seems to think I must have pushed Ivan away.'

'That's nonsense,' Jack said firmly. 'He's just a kid, Cat. He doesn't mean it.'

'Doesn't he?'

'No. And nor, I suspect, does Ivan. This thing with Kendall is an infatuation, a classic midlife crisis. He'll be back eventually, believe me, like the proverbial bad penny.'

'I don't think so,' sobbed Catriona. 'Not this time. Rosie went to visit him in London last weekend and she said he seemed "really well and happy". They went to the Hard Rock Café. Ivan bought Rosie a knickerbocker glory that apparently cost eighteen pounds. Eighteen pounds on a pudding!' She started laughing, then crying again, apologizing all the while as if any of this were her fault.

Jack felt terrible. It crossed his mind that he was at least partially to blame for this nightmare. If he hadn't sent Kendall to England in the first place, if he hadn't suggested she stay at the Jester flat, if he hadn't overreacted about her Polydor deal and played so pathetically into Ivan's hands, perhaps none of this would have happened.

He knew now that he'd made a titanic mistake in walking away from Jester. That he should have listened to everyone who had urged him to look before he leaped: Jared, Elizabeth, Lex Abrahams. He had allowed his anger and foolish, stubborn pride to rule his head. It was humbling to have to acknowledge just how easy it had been for Ivan to walk off into the sunset with his acts, effectively stealing the business lock, stock and barrel from under his nose. The final insult was losing The Blitz. Brett Bayley had broken the news as if it were nothing, a minor irritation.

'Stella's so happy in London, man. This blog of hers is really taking off. It just feels like the right time to make a move, you know?'

It was bullshit, of course. Ivan had called all Jack's clients behind his back, undercutting him with the lure of a ten per cent commission. Brett Bayley was sticking with Jester for one reason and one reason only, and it had nothing to do with his wife's stupid blog. Jack could have said as much to Brett. That he and his band had been penniless kids when Jack took them on and that without him they wouldn't *have* a career. But he was too proud to stoop to such a conversation. If The Blitz wanted Ivan Charles to manage them, then so be it. Jack Messenger wasn't in the business of pleading. The problem was that, if things continued the way they had been, Jack wasn't in any business at all.

The path forked left and plunged sharply down into the canyon. The muscles in Jack's calves ached, and he could feel himself starting to tire. The Land of the Greeks song had finished now, and to Jack's irritation his iPod shuffled onto one of Kendall's early releases, a light, poppy track called 'As I Am' that showcased her powerful vocals. Since she'd left, Jack had nursed his anger towards Kendall like a precious child. He knew that the moment he let it go, he would have to admit to himself how much he missed her, how empty the Brentwood house felt without her dramas and tantrums, her raucous, infectious laugh and her lust for life. Kendall had unwittingly helped him in this effort by running off with Ivan, something Jack found so morally and physically repugnant it made him nauseous just to think about it.

He stopped, angrily yanking his headphones out of his ears and taking a swig from his water bottle. It was time to head home, shower, and kick himself out of this funk. Then he would drive over to Lex Abrahams' place and have a serious talk about the future of the business. Since Jack had broken up with Elizabeth last month, Lex had become his closest confidant. Other than Sonya, of course, whom he still turned to nightly in his prayers and dreams. It scared him to think that the young photographer was probably the only person left in the music industry that he trusted. One thing you could say for career catastrophes: you find out who your friends are.

* * *

141

Kendall stretched out her long legs on the Green Room couch and reached for another packet of salt and vinegar crisps, her third.

'You'll ruin your figure,' said Isabella James archly. Do you know how much sodium there is in those things?'

Kendall gave *Talent Quest*'s presenter a dismissive glance and returned to her Walker's. She could tell instantly that Isabella didn't like her. Blonde, bland, minor league TV presenters usually didn't. Used to having all the male attention to themselves, the Isabella James's of this world didn't take kindly to having the likes of Kendall Bryce swanning in and upstaging them. If Kendall had been a one-off guest performer, it might have been different. But as Ivan's girlfriend, both Isabella and Stacey Harlow, Ivan's fellow judge and the other *Talent Quest* 'hottie', knew that Kendall Bryce could well become a semi-permanent fixture on what they saw as *their* show. They resented her for it hugely.

'Seriously,' said Isabella. 'You don't want to get heartburn while you're performing.'

'I'll worry about my performance. You worry about your mung beans,' said Kendall scornfully, nodding towards the über-healthy, macrobiotic veg pot that Isabella was picking at like a miserable bird. 'You know, those things make you fart like a bastard,' she added cruelly, enjoying the titters from the runners, all of whom were delighted to see the up-herself Miss James taken down a peg or two.

'Kendall, sweetheart, you're on in five.' Don Peters stuck his smiling, bald head round the Green Room door. 'Do you mind coming to door three for a final sound check?'

'Not at all,' said Kendall, licking her fingers and deliberately dropping the half-eaten packet of crisps on the table in front of Isabella. The fact that *Talent Quest*'s producer, and Ivan's nominal boss, was being so obsequious towards her had no doubt increased Isabella and Stacey's hostility, but Kendall didn't care. She wasn't here to make friends. She was here to build her brand with Ivan as a couple. Already a star at the height of her solo career, Kendall knew that, together, she and Ivan could become far more than the sum of their parts, a marketing man's wet dream. She had her sights set on commercials and endorsement deals, and Ivan's TV platform would be a huge help with that. When Don Peters suggested that she do a live performance on *Talent Quest*, Kendall had practically bitten his hand off. She was already enjoying herself hugely.

Already seated at the judges' panel, waiting for the live taping to begin, Ivan also felt confident. Earlier he'd watched, gratified, as his fellow judge Richard Bay, a well-known lothario almost ten years Ivan's junior, had crashed and burned in his attempts to flirt with Kendall. Richard's chat-up lines might have worked on Scarlett Johansson, but Kendall appeared gloriously aloof to his charms, announcing in front of the entire production team that she was 'crazy in love' with Ivan, and telling Richard that the two of them had 'better sex than you could even imagine'. When the cameras finally started rolling and Kendall marched onstage in a clinging white silk dress to rapturous applause from the studio audience and started swaying sensuously to 'Shake It Loose', Ivan felt like the luckiest man in the world.

Needless to say, Kendall aced the song, but the real performance was to come. With a fake smile plastered on her Barbie-doll face, Isabella James walked over to Kendall for the on-camera congratulations.

'Kendall Bryce, ladies and gentlemen!' she shouted to the audience, grabbing Kendall's right hand and raising it in triumph. 'What a performance, eh? Amazing. Judges, what did you think of that?'

Stacey Harlow and Richard Bay clapped and smiled duti-fully. Ivan made a big show of standing up and blowing kisses at Kendall. Breaking free from Isabella in an 'unscripted moment', Kendall skipped over to where the panel was sitting, leaned down to give camera two a provocative glimpse of her ample cleavage, and proceeded to kiss her famous boyfriend lingeringly on the lips. The entire audience went wild.

Watching the screen in the Green Room, Don Peters offered a small prayer of thanks. Hiring Ivan Charles had been a risk, a risk that in *Talent Quest*'s early days, Don had seriously regretted taking. But now, since Ivan had shacked up with Kendall, his star was rising so fast it was blinding. Even better, Brit-pop's new golden couple were dragging the show up with them. Tonight's ratings were bound to be off the charts, and 'that kiss' would be splashed all over every gossip magazine and tabloid come tomorrow morning.

Don Peters was a happy man.

Back in LA, Jack was driving his Mercedes convertible along the well-worn route from Brentwood to West Hollywood – San Vicente, Wilshire Boulevard, Beverly, Doheny – drinking in the sunlight and flower-filled gardens like a humming bird gorging on nectar. Even in early February, Los Angeles could produce some sparkling, blue-skied days that made you glad to be alive. Today was one such day.

Fuck Ivan Charles. Fuck Kendall Bryce. Fuck Brett ungrateful Bayley. Jack was free of all of them, free to start again. It was time to start looking on that as an opportunity, time to rise from the ashes of Jester into a bright and hopeful future. Jack knew that Lex had been down too since the busi-ness dried up, and it was clear the boy was missing Kendall. He never said anything, but there was a tiredness in his face and a deadness in his eyes that hadn't been there before she left. Lex had actually taken a few weeks off work over the holidays, very unusually for him. Jack hadn't seen him since, but he hoped the break would have done him good.

Turning left into Lex's street, Jack pulled in outside the condo. He noticed that the mailbox was stuffed to bursting, and when he walked up to the front door all the shades were drawn and the inside lights switched off. Perhaps Lex was still away? He rang the bell. No answer. He tried again, still nothing, and was starting to walk away when he heard the door being unlatched. It opened a crack and a pale, unshaven face groggily appeared, blinking against the sunlight like a mole.

'Jack. Whadda you doing here?' Lex's voice was heavily slurred and the stench of alcohol on his breath made Jack reel. 'You di'n' call. You shoulda called.'

Pushing the door properly open, Jack walked past him into the apartment. He hadn't seen such squalor since his own student days. Weeks'-worth of old takeaway boxes were strewn all over the furniture and floor in various stages of mouldy decay. The TV was on low, some Spanish language show about DIY that Lex clearly wasn't watching but apparently hadn't had the energy to switch off, and beer cans, candy wrappers and every other conceivable kind of rubbish flowed out of the trash baskets like water from a fountain. The smell was quite astonishingly awful.

'What's going on?' asked Jack, ignoring Lex's protests and lifting the blinds, opening windows to let in some desperately needed fresh air. 'Are you sick? Did somebody die?'

'No and noooooooo,' said Lex, ill-advisedly attempting a sort of standing pirouette and ending up collapsed on the litter-covered couch in a fit of giggles. 'I am fit as a fucking fiddle. Happy as a clam. I am in the pink!'

He reached for a half-full glass of liquid on the coffee table but Jack was too quick for him, snatching it up and sniffing it with distaste.

'Tequila? It's eleven o'clock in the morning, Lex.'

Lex shrugged. 'That makes it seven p.m. in England. I'm toasting Kendall in shpirit.' He threw his arms out wide. 'To you and Ivan the Terrible. May you live long and prosper!'

'Is that what this is all about?' asked Jack, throwing the half-drunk cocktail down the sink, along with what was left in the bottle, and hunting through the drawers for bin liners. 'Kendall?'

'I love her,' said Lex morosely, and with more than a touch of drunken melodrama. 'She'sh the only woman I'll ever love.'

'Baloney,' said Jack robustly. 'There's more than one woman for everyone.'

'There wasn't for you,' said Lex, with more insight than his inebriated state might have suggested him capable of.

'That's different,' said Jack gruffly. 'Besides, you aren't really in love with Kendall. You only want her because she's unattainable.'

'Funny,' said Lex. 'Thatsh exactly what I used to say to her about you.'

'*Me?*' Jack looked at him astonished. 'What do I have to do with it? Kendall was never romantically interested in me.'

Lex laughed, but it was a laugh without warmth or humour. 'You know, for a smart guy, you can be a real moron sometimes.'

Had he not been drunk, he would never have spoken to Jack like that. They were friends, yes, but Jack Messenger was very much Lex's boss, and Lex had always treated him with a degree of deference and respect. Now, however, his guard was down, and the truth came tumbling out like lava from a freshly erupted volcano.

'Kendall's always been in love with you. Crazy in love with you. The whole world knows it but you.'

'That's ridiculous,' blustered Jack.

'Yeah well, love is ridiculous. Just look at me! Pining away here for a girl who barely knows I exist. Kendall only signed the deal with Polydor to impress you, to show you she could make a success of things on her own, that she was mature enough to be dating you.'

Jack shook his head. This was a truly horrible thought; too horrible to entertain even for a moment. 'You're wrong.'

'I'm not wrong. I *know* Kendall, Jack. You think you know her but you don't. She's been in love with you for years. All those guys she slept with, dragged back to the guesthouse for sex . . . they were all meant to make you jealous, to get your attention. This affair with Ivan is the same damn thing. She doesn't want that guy. It's all for your benefit.'

Angrily, Jack started scooping up pizza boxes off the floor and stuffing them into the trash bag. If there was any truth to what Lex was saying, he didn't want to know about it. But there wasn't any truth to it. He'd have noticed, surely, if Kendall had had those sorts of feelings for him? She'd have said something, done something. No, Lex was seeing things through a double of haze of alcohol and his own infatuation with Kendall. He wasn't rational.

'Take a shower,' he ordered, not unkindly, 'and a couple of Alka-Seltzer if you have them. I'll clean up the worst of this shit and then I'm taking you out for brunch.'

Lex groaned. 'I can't, man. My head. I need to sleep.'

'Uh uh,' said Jack. 'You've been sleeping too long. Perhaps we both have. You have twenty minutes to get washed and dressed or I swear to God I'll drag you into that bathroom and do it myself.'

Forty minutes later, Lex sat green and shivering at a corner table in the News Café on Robertson, slowly chewing a slice of plain brown toast and sipping black coffee. He appreciated that Jack was trying to help him, but the brusque military manner, combined with his insistence on eating a mountainous stack of pancakes and syrup washed down with some vile, green-looking juice right in front of him was failing to lift Lex's spirits.

'Feel better?' Jack took another long swig of the sick-juice. 'Are you sure you don't want any bacon? A good fry-up always helps me when I'm hung over.'

'I'm not hung over,' grumbled Lex. 'I'm still drunk.'

In fact, the shower had sobered him up considerably, although his head still ached violently from the booze and unaccustomed sunlight. Since he'd seen the first TV report on Kendall's affair with Ivan Charles, Lex had barely left the apartment. His so-called Christmas vacation had consisted of crawling under the duvet with a month-long supply of spirits, locking his door, and hoping for the waves of pain to go away. Just the thought of that middle-aged letch looking at her, never mind touching her, making love to her, made Lex's stomach heave. If he'd had work to do, if he'd been busy like he was this time last year, he might have forced himself to get it together, to put one foot in front of the other. But with his main employer, Jack, caught up in his own troubles, there was nothing and no one to save him from sliding into the abyss. If Kendall had been gone before, she was really gone now. Lost to him for ever.

'Still drunk, eh? Well that's no good,' said Jack, with relentless good cheer. 'I don't want a drunk for a partner.'

For the first time, Lex tuned out of his own misery and glanced up. 'What do you mean, "partner"?'

Jack's grin broadened. 'I mean,' he said, 'that we're going to set up a new agency. The two of us, together. As partners. It'll be a fresh start.'

Lex almost choked on his toast. 'That's . . . wow. I don't know what to say. That's incredibly generous of you, but I really don't have the resources . . . I couldn't put any money in.'

Jack waved a hand dismissively. 'Of course not. I'll fund the thing, and I'll be senior partner. You'd bring your talent and work like a dog. How does twenty per cent equity sound?'

To his intense embarrassment, Lex worried he might be about to cry. The only thing worse than a drunk was an emotional drunk, but Jack's kindness was so unexpected, and what he was offering was such a lifeline, it was difficult not to tear up.

'What, you want more?' Jack joked.

'No! No, no, no. God no. I'm just . . . why would you give away twenty per cent of your business?'

'I'm not giving it away,' said Jack. 'Believe me, I expect you to earn it. You won't just be taking images any more. You'll be actively finding and managing new acts.'

'I'm a photographer, Jack, not a manager.'

'You're both. Think about how much hand-holding you did with Kendall, how much she leaned on you, relied on your advice. And not just with Kendall. I've seen the way you work with scores of Jester's clients. You build a rapport with them, part-friend, part-mentor, part-therapist. That's managing. You're so natural at it, you don't even know you're doing it.'

Lex took a long slug of bitter coffee and winced. There

was some truth to what Jack was saying, and of course it was flattering. But did he really have what it took to co-run a music-management company? After what Jack had been through with Ivan, Lex didn't want to let him down. 'There's more to it than that, though, isn't there?' he said.

'Of course there is. There's the business side: the deal-making, the schmoozing record companies and PR people, all the endless organization of tours and publicity. But that's what I'm good at. Ivan was always better with clients, with the touchy-feely stuff,' he added, a trace of bitterness creeping into his voice. 'At first I thought that was my mistake, letting my partner get closer to the clients than I was. But after a while I realized, I just picked the wrong partner. I need to work with someone I can trust. I trust you, Lex.'

'Thanks,' said Lex quietly. 'That means a lot.'

'So, are you in?' Jack held out his hand.

For the first time in a long time, Lex smiled. 'I'm in,' he said, shaking Jack's hand.

'Great,' said Jack. 'We're going to be huge!' Then, with a look of malice that Lex had never seen on his face before, he added darkly 'And we're going to bury Ivan Charles.'

PART TWO

CHAPTER TEN

Los Angeles, one year later . . .

Lex walked out onto the master bedroom balcony and gazed out across the garden to the shimmering Pacific. A ruby-red sun was just beginning its slow descent into the horizon, bleeding a magnificent trail of pink and orange, purple and ochre into the deep blue ocean. Lex had bought the Malibu house last year and moved in six months ago, but he still had to pinch himself when he woke up every morning. Was this peaceful slice of paradise really his, with its flat, manicured lawn, its lemon and orange trees and beds full of ginger and acacia flowers, its spectacular views? It wasn't a grand house. In fact, it had been built as a farmstead back in the thirties, when Big Rock Drive and the whole of Malibu Canyon was still a working agricultural area. But with its five bedrooms, charming white-wooden interiors, farmhouse kitchen and now a fully kitted-out basement darkroom, it was a world away from the cramped, rented apartment in West Hollywood that had been Lex's home for the previous seven years. He still found it hard to believe just how much his life had changed in such a short space of time. And he owed it all to Jack Messenger.

Well, perhaps that wasn't strictly true. Yes, it was Jack who had founded JSM (Jack Sonya Management) and who had brought Lex in as a partner. But the new agency's phenomenal success, their rapid growth from a standing start to becoming one of the industry's major players, had been at least fifty per cent down to Lex's energy, drive and almost superhuman work ethic. That and the fact that artists, all sorts of artists, just wanted to work with him.

Lex and Jack were the 'nice guys' in a business full of sharks. As it turned out there was a real gap in the market for a management firm based on decency and integrity, and JSM's reputation quickly grew. For every Brett Bayley, willing to sell his soul for a cut-price management commission, there were ten bands who were sick of managers treating them like a commodity, bands prepared to pay *over* the odds for personal, tailored service they could trust.

Building the business had been a crazy learning curve for Lex, utterly exhausting but also great fun. When they weren't scuttling back and forth between accountants and lawyers and PR firms in LA, Lex and Jack were on the road, touring the country looking for new acts to sign. It was an old-fashioned way to do business to say the least, showing up at small, live venues, following word-of-mouth recommendations or Facebook buzz, trying to unearth real, grassroots talent. And, of course, they saw a lot of mediocre acts, from Missouri to Michigan, as well as talented musicians who, with the best will in the world, just weren't commercially marketable prospects. But they also found some nuggets of pure gold. After more than fifteen years in the business, Jack was adamant that he wanted to build the agency on new acts, unknowns, rather than poaching established performers from rivals. In fact, they ended up with a client list that was a mix of both, not because they actively approached famous, big-name artists, but because those artists started approaching them.

It was a small list – JSM represented a total of twenty-five acts, half of whom would probably take years before they started making serious money – and in some ways a limited one. They had no classical artists, no folk, no rap. With the exception of two male country vocalists and one female rock band, they were exclusively focused on pop. Their two highest-profile stars were Martina Munoz, a young, very commercial Hispanic singer with a huge following in Latin America, but who was still trying to 'break' the international market; and Frankie B, a well-known old-school soul singer and songwriter, who'd had a glittering early career then sunk without trace as he battled crack addiction in his thirties, ultimately winding up in a Georgia jail. There he got clean and found God, and when he got out laid down a few tracks of a new soul-slash-gospel album that were so good Jack actually cried when he heard them. With Jack's support, encouragement, and canny and relentless salesmanship, helped by the raw, iconic pictures Lex took to promote the new album, *Saved*, Frankie B staged one of the most spectacular comebacks the industry had ever seen.

It was *Saved* that had bought Lex this house. But he owed the album more than that. While shooting the cover in an LA suburb last spring , he'd met a funny, sassy and altogether gorgeous make-up artist by the name of Leila Browne. Lex and Leila had been dating ever since, and everyone agreed Leila had brought a peace and contentment to his life, a stability that he'd never really had before. Finally, and it had taken a long, long time, Kendall Bryce was out of his system. They were still in loose touch, an email every few months. In some ways Lex still missed her, but he didn't miss the turmoil she had brought to his life, and he no longer felt pain to see her on screen or read about her, or when her name popped up in his in-box. It was as if he had woken from a dream. His heart, his life were his own again. And it was a good life now, full of hope and promise for the future.

'Come inside, honey.' Leila's voice drifted out through the bathroom window. 'I need some help with my zipper.'

Lex wandered back inside. Tonight was a big night for Lex and JSM. Frankie B had been nominated for a Grammy for Best Album, and the agency were throwing a lavish party in his honour at The Four Seasons, for which Lex and Leila were now getting ready. In reality, *Saved* had little hope of winning. Frankie was up against the likes of Justin Timberlake and Madonna. But to be nominated at all was a huge achievement, not just for Frankie but for the agency, and it would further boost the record's already sensational sales.

In the master bathroom, Leila stood with her back to him, but he could see her smiling, freckled face in the mirror. Tall and athletic, with light-brown hair to her shoulders and a pretty, open face, Leila was the quintessential girl next door. Attractive rather than sexy, as a make-up artist she knew how to make the most of her glowing skin and wholesome good looks. With only a light dusting of peach blush and some rich black mascara, she'd brought her whole face to life. The strapless, pale-pink Vera Wang gown she was wearing accentuated her height and slender arms. Lex dutifully yanked up the zipper to the top, between her shoulder blades, and fastened the hook and eye.

'How do I look?' She spun round to face him.

'Gorgeous,' he said, truthfully. He didn't feel the wild stirrings of passion with Leila that he'd felt around Kendall, but he didn't miss them. Leila was sweet and kind and calm, a graceful steady ocean liner to Kendall's raucous, supercharged speedboat.

'I hope so,' said Leila, "cause I can hardly breathe in the damn thing. You should get dressed, you know. The boss can't be late for his own party.'

Lex laughed. He never would be able to think of himself as 'the boss' of JSM, or even one of the bosses. Jack was the boss. He was just the lucky bastard who got to tag along for the ride.

Tucked away behind tall green hedges on Doheny Boulevard, The Four Seasons Hotel is a Beverly Hills icon. With its European architecture and interiors, surrounded by lush tropical gardens, it exudes an aura of peaceful luxury, a sanctuary of elegant rooms and sun-filled terraces just a mile from the bustling heart of Rodeo Drive. Less flashy than the Roosevelt or the Mondrian, and less stuffy than The Peninsula or even The Beverly Hills Hotel, The Four Seasons boasts a quiet exclusivity that's a world away from the rock-'n'-roll excesses of the nearby Chateau Marmont, the usual venue of choice for music industry parties, particularly in the run-up to the Grammys.

It was no accident that Jack Messenger had chosen The Four Seasons rooftop pool bar as the venue for tonight's celebration. Back in the bad old days, Frankie B had partied with the best of them up at the Chateau. But the new sober, spiritual Frankie had had to be persuaded to attend a party at all, particularly as the guest of honour. It was only after Lex convinced him that the celebration was in recognition of the album and everyone who had worked so hard on its success that Frankie relented. Lex hadn't added that the PR would be vitally important to JSM, that they had to leverage

Saved's Grammy nod for all it was worth while it was still fresh in people's minds, and while their other acts still stood to benefit by association.

Lex and Leila arrived bang on time at seven-thirty. Jack was already there, along with his new assistant Sandra, a whirling dervish of efficiency and organization who held JSM together day to day, checking table plans and guest lists, making sure the waiters knew who was teetotal and who wasn't, who was Jewish or vegan or only ate raw food (this was Hollywood, after all), and generally making sure the scene was set for a smooth, flawless event. In a fabulously cut Armani tuxedo and simple white shirt, Jack looked even more handsome than usual. The only embellishment to his outfit was a pair of antique lapis cufflinks, a first anniversary gift from his wife Sonya. Every time he turned his wrist or lifted his arm in greeting, they flashed the same dazzling blue as his eyes. Lex, who was neither vain nor envious by nature, admired his partner's effortless good looks as an art lover might admire a painting. In all the months they'd travelled together, he'd never known Jack to bring a girl back to his hotel room; even in LA, his dating was low-key to the point of invisibility, as well as determinedly casual. Since calling it off with Elizabeth, Jack had rarely seen the same woman more than twice. Watching him now, greeting the first of the arriving guests, Lex wondered how long his friend would keep up his self-imposed monasticism. Jack was too young to spend the rest of his life alone.

Not that he seemed unhappy generally. Jack loved his work and was as consumed by building JSM as Lex was. If he still harboured dark thoughts of vengeance towards Ivan Charles, he no longer spoke about them, seemingly content to focus on his own agency's success and future. Even so, watching the women steal desiring glances at Jack while *he* stood hand in hand with Leila, Lex couldn't help but feel sad that his friend was so determined to live the remainder of his life a bachelor.

'Hey you two.' Jack greeted Lex and Leila warmly as more of JSM's acts and plus ones streamed out onto the roof garden. 'Looks like it's gonna be a good turnout.'

Martina Munoz had already arrived in a show-stopping silver Dolce & Gabbana minidress, and was chatting animatedly to J Lo by the poolside. Land of the Greeks' lead singer, Ben Braemar, a dead ringer for a teenage Jesse Eisenberg, was wandering around with his mouth open, making no attempt to hide his awe at being surrounded by so many famous names. The Greeks had been one of the first acts Jack had signed to the newly established JSM, and they were already making a big splash on the indie scene. Their first deal wasn't huge, but their debut album had won enormous critical acclaim. In a couple of years, as long as they kept their noses clean and continued producing that quality of work, all three of the boys would be millionaires many times over. As always at Grammy events, a smattering of actresses and Hollywood stars mingled with the musos. Kate Hudson was laughing loudly at a joke told by her ex-husband, Chris Robinson of The Black Crowes, and Jamie Foxx was aggressively chatting up one of the prettier waitresses as she tried to weave through the crowd with her champagne tray. As well as the publicly well-known faces, Lex spied a number of industry powerbrokers, including two record-company chairmen, Jay Monroe, head of the most powerful PR agency in Hollywood, and a smattering of big hitters from the networks, including the legendary Bob Greenblatt from NBC, who was here with a record-producer friend.

Lex took a deep breath and hurled himself into the

throng, glad-handing and smiling his way through the VIPs and ordinary guests alike. Despite being the designated 'people person' in the JSM partnership, Lex had a lot less experience of these events than Jack, and he still felt awkward and faintly ridiculous chatting up the heads of record companies. This time a year ago he had been a penniless photographer. Surely none of these people could possibly take him seriously as an agent? But he did his duty, playing the part as best he could, while Leila swapped make-up tips with J Lo.

The sit-down dinner was supposed to start at eight-thirty, but by eight-forty-five the guest of honour had still not arrived.

'Where's Frankie?' Lex cornered Jack at the bar, refilling Jay Monroe's glass. 'He hasn't chickened out, has he?'

'No,' said Jack, automatically smiling as an LA news photographer approached with a camera. 'He called me from the car; he's on his way. I guess some old habits really do die hard. Frankie used to show up days late for meetings in the old days, looped out of his mind. By his standards, he's early.'

Eventually the man himself showed up, looking diffident in a white Zegna suit at least two sizes too big for him and a matching trilby with the word 'JESUS' embossed in gold lettering around the brim. Flashbulbs popped dutifully as he posed with Jack and Lex, the head of his new record company, various other JSM acts and a posse of senior execs from MTV. After that it was dinner, a delicious smorgasbord of dishes prepared by The Four Seasons' Michelin-starred chef and his team, followed by a toast to *Saved*, and a short-but-sweet speech by Jack Messenger.

'We're here to celebrate Frankie B's remarkable achieve-ment with his wonderful comeback album,' he began.

'Frankie is a personal friend. We all know this success has been hard earned, and I can't think of anyone working in this business today who deserves the recognition of a Grammy nomination more than he does.'

Wild applause. Frankie, smiling now, stood up and thanked the Lord.

'But Frankie's is not the only comeback we're giving thanks for tonight. Two years ago, as most of you know, I was down and out in this business.'

Lex wondered nervously where Jack was going with this. One of Hollywood's few taboos was failure, even past failure. Alluding to it, especially at an event like this, was the equivalent of talking about divorce statistics at a wedding, or farting in the middle of the national anthem. Happily, Jack quickly got back on-message.

'In the past eighteen months, I'm proud to say that JSM has enjoyed success beyond all of our expectations. I happen to believe this is because we represent the best names in the business today.' He name-checked a few, to a ripple of applause. 'And because of the efforts of my partner and friend, the talented Mr Lex Abrahams.' More applause, this time led enthusiastically by Leila.

'Tonight marks the beginning of a new phase in the life of JSM, a phase that I believe will see us rise to even greater heights of achievement, both commercially and artistically as an agency. As the great Frank Sinatra once said, "The best revenge is massive success." Tonight is the beginning of a journey that will see us achieve that success.'

The last words: *and our revenge*, were left unsaid. But as Jack Messenger raised his glass, Lex caught the look of fierce determination beneath his perfect smile. The media lapped Jack up as music's Mr Nice Guy, and in many ways he was. But there was a toughness there too, a desire not just to win but to beat Ivan Charles and Jester, to leave his enemies trailing in JSM's dust.

'To *Saved*!' said Jack. 'To JSM.'

And to vengeance, thought Lex. Clasping Leila's hand, he wished he didn't feel quite so uneasy.

CHAPTER ELEVEN

Catriona Charles sat at the Victorian mahogany desk in her tiny study and looked critically at the photographs in front of her. As portraits, they were distinctly average. The first little boy had a sullen, spoiled look on his face completely at odds with the cute head cocked to one side pose and whimsically clutched teddy bear. The three-year-old girl from Oxford looked fat. (Then again, she *was* fat; there was only so much one could achieve, even with clever lighting.) And her elder sister's forced smile made her look as if she were in the early stages of rigor mortis.

If she did the sittings again in her own studio, Catriona was sure she could do better. But then she'd end up out of pocket and, as Ned Williams kept telling her, this *was* supposed to be a business. Grimly she placed each of the shots in separate brown envelopes, scribbled the parents' names on the front and sealed them. She couldn't afford artistic integrity, at least not this month.

Sighing, she looked out of the window into the cobbled passageway below. Known in Oxfordshire as 'twittens', these narrow, hidden paths that wound between medieval workers' cottages were a feature of the backstreets of Burford. Catriona loved them, almost as much as she loved the narrow strips of cottage garden planted along their edges, crammed to bursting with old English flowers like pink hollyhocks, weeping white dog roses and imperial purple foxgloves. It had been a wrench leaving The Rookery. According to Ivan and the divorce lawyers, selling the house in Widford was a financial necessity, and at the time Catriona had been too emotionally and physically wrecked to argue with them. But as time passed she'd grown very fond of her new village house, a modest four-bedroom Georgian home, originally built for the town doctor. Part of what she liked about it was that it was *her* house. Having married so young, and given up work as soon as Rosie was born, Catriona had never owned property of her own before. It was a nice feeling, a secure feeling. These days Catriona Charles didn't get too many of those.

There were days when being divorced from Ivan still felt like a shock. When she would wake up with a strange, sinking feeling, as if something were wrong or lost or missing but she couldn't remember what it was. And then it would hit her. The marriage to which she'd devoted her entire adult life and which, despite its flaws and rocky patches, she had truly believed would last a lifetime, was over.

The pain was still there, but what had begun as sharp, unbearable agony had faded into a dull, constant ache of loss and regret. A lot of that was down to the house. With its small, unruly walled garden, crumbling sash windows, and ugly, early Eighties decor, it was crying out for some love and attention. Catriona, who desperately needed a project to distract her from the pain, devoted every spare minute – when she wasn't running around after the children or scrambling around for money to pay last winter's oil bill

– to restoring the property room by room and inch by inch, transforming it into her own, idyllic safe haven. First she ripped up the depressing green carpets to reveal exquisite three-hundred-year-old flagstones. With the help of Ned Williams's trusty sledgehammer, she and Hector had had one of their happiest days in years, knocking through plasterboard to unearth no less than five original Georgian fireplaces. After that there were wooden boards to be sanded, wallpaper to be stripped and walls painted in off-white and grey and cheerful duck-egg blue, light fixtures and furniture to be picked up from local country-house auctions and antiques markets. And finally, once spring arrived, there was the joy of getting to grips with the garden, clearing weeds and pruning back creepers, planting a few of her own favourites like Sweet Williams and scented stocks, and digging out a miniature kitchen garden that she filled with herbs and artichokes and tomato plants, each one a symbol of new life and hope for the future.

But if Catriona's new home brought her pleasure, most of her day-to-day life was still a huge struggle. Ivan's TV show, *Talent Quest*, was now in its second series and phenomenally successful. The first season, in which Ivan had managed to transform himself from a wooden, awkward figure of fun to an acerbically funny judge who both appalled and delighted the British public, had already made him a household name. This year, thanks to his championing of an adorably shy young contestant from Yorkshire by the name of Ava Bentley, Ivan was more popular than ever. Ava was the nation's new sweetheart, and Ivan revelled in his role as her mentor. But, despite *Talent Quest*'s soaring ratings, Ivan continued to claim he was 'tapped out' financially, and his maintenance payments to Catriona, such as they were, had become increasingly erratic. The problem appeared to lie with Jester. The agency's acts continued to thrive, but Ivan seemed to have established a fee structure so low it had landed the business in an acute cash-flow crisis. With *Talent Quest* taking up so much of his time, and with Jack Messenger and the LA office gone, Ivan had had to take on more and more staff, so his overheads were rising just as Jester's income took a dip. Or something like that. In any event, short of taking him to court, something for which Catriona had neither the resources nor the energy, there was nothing she could do but cut back herself and attempt, for the first time in her life, to earn an income of her own.

It was one of the mother's at Rosie's school who'd suggested the photography business, after seeing some shots of Catriona's in the school magazine. 'You could start with my children. I'll pay you a hundred quid plus expenses for a decent portrait of them all together, looking half-human. If you can pull that off with my three terrors, believe me, you'll be beating off new business with a stick.'

While that hadn't quite turned out to be true, Catriona was gratified and amazed to discover that there really was a market for what she had always enjoyed as a hobby. So far she was only making pin money, paying for the weekly shop at Morrisons and the children's after-school clubs. But if she really organized herself, took out an ad in the local paper, put fliers up in surrounding villages and local schools, she was sure she could turn the thing into a proper going concern.

The problem, besides her ongoing battle with artistic integrity, was time. Officially Ivan was supposed to have the children every other weekend and for at least a few weeks in the school holidays. In reality, his work schedule meant that he could take Rosie for a night once a month at best – Hector still refused point-blank to see his father – and the last two holidays had been a write-off. Rosie had gone with Ivan and Kendall to Cape Town last New Year and apparently had a great time. But with Hector still at home, and his behaviour wildly erratic and attention-seeking, this was no break for Catriona.

Hector's evident unhappiness, and her own utter inability to get through to him, frequently brought Catriona to the brink of despair. She'd gained weight, largely due to a hefty reliance on gin and tonic in the evenings after another long day of battles with her son. His private school, St Austin's, had finally thrown in the towel a year ago and kicked him out. Since then, he'd burned his way through two more establishments before Ivan decided enough was enough, he wasn't throwing good money after bad and the boy could damn well go to the local comprehensive. For a few wonderful weeks, this worked well. Hector seemed to enjoy the relative freedom of Burford High. But eventually it dawned on Catriona that the spring in his step wasn't because he was revelling in choosing his upcoming GCSE courses, but because he wasn't going to school at all but hopping off the bus at the top of the high street and hitching lifts into Witney, where he spent the majority of his afternoons hanging around McDonald's or watching matinees at the Odeon.

In a rare show of parental solidarity, Ivan had actually torn himself away from his fabulous new life in London and driven down to Burford to confront the boy with Catriona, face to face. It was the first time Catriona had seen Ivan in more than six months, a prospect that frankly terrified her, but she put her own anxieties aside for Hector's sake and made a titanic effort to appear normal and relaxed in Ivan's company. Unfortunately, the meeting was a disaster. Despite both parents' best efforts it descended into a screaming match, with Hector hurling abuse at Ivan and Catriona help-less to placate either of them, or even get a word in edge-ways. Poor Rosie had been terribly upset, and that night Catriona leaned more heavily on her green bottled therapist, Dr Gordon's, than ever, waking up the next morning with a hangover that could have raised the dead.

Now, picking up her three brown envelopes she went downstairs, grabbing her handbag from the kitchen table, and ventured out into the village. It was a sunny, early June day, not yet really hot but with all the promise of summer hanging heavy in the honeysuckled air. As usual, the steep hill of Burford High Street was busy with traffic, but the village still looked ravishing with its mellow stone terraces, spectacular Gothic church and ancient stone bridges crossing the rippling Windrush. Catriona stopped at the post office first, stamping the sub-par portraits and slipping them into the scarlet pillar box with a guilty conscience. To cheer herself up she crossed the road to Huffkins tea shop, treating herself to an enormous slice of carrot cake and picking up two sugar mice for Rosie and Hector, a childish treat that both of them still secretly loved to find on their pillows. Leaving the tea shop, having successfully replaced one guilt with another (had she really just wolfed down all that cake?), she was startled to discover her mobile ringing. She only kept it on so that the children or even Ivan could reach her in an emergency. After a long marriage spent mostly at home raising children, followed by a divorce from a much more glamorous and high-profile husband, Catriona had learned quickly and brutally just how few real friends she had left. Days, even weeks, could pass without her phone ringing at all. When it did, more often than not it was some stranger trying to sell her something.

Perhaps it was a client, someone wanting to give her a

new commission? She kept forgetting she was a business-woman now. Brightening, she put on her capable, professional voice. 'Hello? Catriona Charles speaking?'

'Good afternoon, Mrs Charles. This is PC Scott of Oxford Police. It's about your son, Hector.'

Catriona froze. Oh God. He'd been killed. He'd been hit by a car or a train or . . . she clutched at a dry-stone wall for support.

'He's been arrested and charged with vandalism and breaching the peace.'

Relief flooded through Catriona's body, swiftly followed by anger. Bloody stupid child! What did he hope to gain by this nonsense?

'I see.'

'You can come down and pick him up if you like. Otherwise we can keep him overnight in the cells. Either way, he'll have to appear before the magistrates' court tomorrow morning at eleven.'

Suddenly Catriona felt overwhelmingly tired. She knew she ought to ask what he had done exactly, where it had happened and why. But she hadn't the energy to put any of it into words.

Taking her silence for shock, PC Scott continued kindly, 'As a juvenile and a first offence, they'll let him off with a caution. But if you want to give him a scare, you might want to let him sweat it out with us for the night. Take him home after court in the morning.'

A million thoughts raced through Catriona's mind, the most unpleasant of which was that she was going to have to tell Ivan, who would no doubt blame her for not being firm enough with Hector, even though it was clearly his abandonment that had pushed the boy off the deep end in the first place. Hector was still only thirteen, and a young thirteen at that. The thought of him spending the night in jail, alone and frightened, tugged at all her maternal heart strings. At the same time, she knew that the more she rode to his rescue, the more he'd keep screwing up.

At last she said, 'Thank you, PC Scott. He can stay there for the night. I'll see him at court in the morning.'

Then she hung up, pressed her hands to her eyes, and burst into tears.

Ivan leaned in close to his dressing-room mirror, intently studying the results of his latest round of Botox injections. The crow's feet around his eyes were gratifyingly absent, and the deep grooves that ran down from the corners of his nose to either side of his lips looked noticeably fainter. It was a good result, but ever since a snide television critic in the *Evening Standard* had described him as 'the waxen-faced Mr Charles', Ivan had become anxious to the point of paranoia about his looks.

Even Kendall had learned not to tease him about the fillers, or the fortnightly trips to John Frieda to get his hair dye touched up.

'It's part of the job in television,' he insisted defensively. 'Showing up with grey hair would be considered grossly unprofessional. I wouldn't bother otherwise.'

Bitchy reviews aside, the reality was that Ivan did look good. Terrified of looking like an old man next to his beautiful young girlfriend, he worked out obsessively and was far more cautious about his diet than he had ever been with Catriona. Sometimes – often, if he were honest – he missed the carefree, calorie-filled family suppers of the old days. Cat's sticky toffee pudding with homemade butterscotch sauce still haunted his dreams on a regular basis. But his new life required energy, and energy, at his age, required discipline.

There were days when his levels of exhaustion actually scared him. Apart from the gruelling business of being a key player in a hit TV show, he still had an immense workload at Jester, which was losing money at an alarming rate. No matter how many new agents he hired, some at extortionate salaries, the big clients still wanted Ivan's personal attention. And none more so than Kendall, who was almost as demanding professionally as she was in bed. Only last night, bucking and writhing on top of him, frantically in pursuit of her third orgasm of the night, she suddenly stopped and began grilling him on the marketing campaign for her second UK album. Her first release, *Girl Reborn*, had performed solidly but had not been the spectacular, ball-out-of-the-park smash that both she and Polydor had been hoping for. Kendall blamed this roundly on poor marketing, which she in turn blamed on Ivan.

'You'd better not take your eye off the ball this time,' she warned him, arching her back and clenching her muscles around Ivan's already wilting dick. How the hell was he supposed to maintain a hard-on while she nagged him mid-shag? He felt like an old horse being ridden into the glue factory. 'I'm tired of hearing about bloody *Talent Quest*. You're supposed to be *my* manager, and *my* boyfriend. This album should be your number one priority. Ivan? Are you listening to me? What the hell happened to your erection?'

Secretly, Ivan had started turning to Viagra to help him keep up with Kendall's needs. Not that sleeping with her was any kind of chore. Sex, in fact, just got better and better, a drug he needed every bit as badly as she did. But if the spirit was willing, the forty-two-year-old flesh was weak. Between the stress of his home and work lives, as well as the lingering guilt over Catriona and the children, especially Hector, he felt as if he were being pulled apart. Piled on top of all that was the financial pressure of running two households, paying school fees and maintenance, and trying to keep pace with Kendall's wildly profligate spending. He'd wanted fame and excitement and he'd got them. But once the adrenaline rush faded, Ivan felt more tired than he ever had in his life.

A runner put her head round the door. She was a pretty girl, blonde and slim with pert apple breasts that jiggled deliciously underneath her white T-shirt. She couldn't have been much more than eighteen. *A few years ago*, Ivan thought, *I'd have had a crack at that.* Now just the thought of more sex made him want to crawl under a duvet in a dark room and go to sleep for a year.

'Ava's about to go on. Do you want to come and watch?'

Ivan brightened. 'Absolutely.'

Ava Bentley, a sweet, slightly chubby seventeen-year-old from Rosedale Abbey in Yorkshire, had become Ivan's lifeline, his golden ticket. The most talked-about contestant of the show so far, Ava had won the nation's heart with her natural, infectious laugh, her unaffected good humour and, of course, her sensational voice. If Ivan played his cards right – and he intended to – Ava would be Jester's Messiah, the voice of an angel that would lead his ailing business out of the wilderness and back into the light.

Slipping into the back of sound stage one, where the remaining contestants were in the midst of a last-minute run-through of their songs for tonight's show, Ivan smiled paternally at his favorite *Talent Quest* mentee. This week's theme was 'jazz greats' and Ava was performing Etta James's famous 'At Last'. Seeing Ivan, she waved at him sweetly mid-song, like a primary-school child spotting its mother in the audience of the nativity play.

'Ava, love, keep your focus,' John the voice coach shouted encouragingly. 'Eyes front, remember. Camera one.'

'Sorry.' Ivan smiled sheepishly. 'Just forget I'm here.'

Ava finished the track, her high, pure voice lending the song a breathless, innocent quality quite different to the soulful Etta James and Beyoncé versions. Skipping over to Ivan in a knee-length floral dress, she looked even younger than her seventeen years, her face flushed with happiness and excitement.

'Was I all right?' she asked nervously, in the broad Yorkshire accent that the whole of Britain had come to know and love. 'I felt like the last verse was a bit wobbly.'

'You were perfect,' said Ivan. 'Seriously. Don't change a thing, my darling. Are your mum and dad here yet?'

Ava looked around. 'Somewhere. They're dead excited about our dinner tonight. My dad said the restaurant you've booked is well posh.'

Ivan laughed. 'Tell your dad he can get used to posh restaurants from now on. Only the best for Britain's newest singing superstar.'

Both Ava and her parents were simple people who trusted Ivan implicitly. It had been no mean feat to secure Ava's loyalty to him, personally, rather than to *Talent Quest*, and to tie her rising fortunes inexorably to his own. Tonight's after-show dinner was the latest step in his relentless wooing of the Bentleys. But he wasn't out of the woods yet.

'Stop it,' Ava giggled. 'I haven't won it yet, you know. Some of the others are dead good, especially Michael.'

'Michael? Who's Michael?' Ivan teased.

The reality was that he didn't, in fact, *want* Ava to win the ITV competition. If she actually won the show, and right now she was Ladbrokes' odds-on favourite, she would be contractually bound to release her first album with Sony, under the terms of the deal Don Peters had made back when *Talent Quest* launched. Peters' own management company, Phoenix, would take charge of the winner's career.

If Ava came in second or third, however, legally she would be free to sign with whomever she chose, and on whatever terms. If Ivan was going to poach her for Jester, (and get her clueless parents to sign away fifty per cent of her earnings up front), he had to navigate his way through a minefield. First, he had to make sure Ava did well enough on the show to keep her profile high in the press, but not so well that she won. Secondly, he had to convince her and her parents to agree to Jester's terms, which meant shielding them from *any* other influences within the business who could have told them how extortionate and exploitative Ivan's proposal actually was. And thirdly, if he pulled it off, he had to figure out a way to smooth things over with Don Peters sufficiently to be allowed to keep his job on the show. Legally, runners-up were free to cut their own deals. But amongst show insiders, the absolute assumption was that Don Peters, as *Talent Quest*'s creator, had first dibs on all contestants, especially the budding media stars like Ava. After the first series, all seven finalists had signed up with Phoenix. Stealing Ava Bentley from under Don Peters' nose was going to ruffle more than a few feathers.

If Ivan got that far.

Meanwhile, unfortunately, it wasn't as if Ava Bentley was his only priority. During the week he squeezed as many hours as he could into Jester, doing his best to lift the flagging morale of the Mayfair office. Brett Bayley had been bugging him for weeks to sit down with The Blitz's record company and thrash out a new deal. Ivan had hoped to schedule that for tonight – one less monkey on his back – but dinner with the Bentleys had to take precedence. He also badly wanted to check in on Kendall. She was bored and restless between albums, something which worried Ivan immensely. It was when *he'd* been bored and restless that he'd cheated on Catriona. The thought of Kendall so much as looking at another man was enough to make his palms sweat and his heart tighten painfully in his chest. But, as usual, there wasn't enough time for everything.

'Oh look, they're bringing the audience in. Hadn't you better go and get ready?' said Ava.

Ivan glanced at the stream of great unwashed pouring down the aisles and into their seats. The warm-up man would be here in a minute, delivering the same lame gags he used before every show. Sometimes Ivan hated the monotony of television.

'I guess we both should,' he said, kissing Ava on the cheek. 'Break a leg.'

As she walked away, Ivan's BlackBerry buzzed in his shirt pocket. His heart leaped for a moment – if Kendall was calling him, it meant she wasn't in bed with someone else – then sank when Catriona's name flashed up on the screen. Guiltily, he pressed 'ignore'. Whatever it was, it would have to wait. He simply didn't have time for an argument about bounced maintenance cheques right now.

Earlier that day, at lunch in Notting Hill, Kendall had sat opposite Stella Bayley at Tom's Deli on Westbourne Grove, doing her best to look interested.

'It is soooo important not to rush the developmental stages. That's one of the things I really do struggle with in this country. Like, Miley's five now, and she has a phenom-enal EQ, but have you tried finding a school that promotes freedom of expression and spiritual growth in London?'

Kendall hadn't.

'I mean, seriously, good luck. They'd rather stuff the kids full of alphabet and math and, like, facts – at *five years old*. Don't they realize the personality is still so malleable with these kids? They need to *play*, to explore this crazy world of ours through their own senses. It's like, no one outside of America has even heard of kinesthetic learning.' Stella let out an exasperated sigh and sipped her carrot juice. 'It's all I'm talking about on my blog.'

Under normal circumstances, Kendall would never have sought out a friendship with Stella. Before she came to London, she'd even had a vague idea of sleeping with her husband, Brett. (Admittedly that was before Kendall had *met* Brett Bayley. The man was so thick he was positively primeval and had all the erotic allure of Shrek. That was one notch on the bedpost she could live without.) But a combination of loneliness, and the fact that Stella provided an oblique window into the 'other' sides of Ivan's life – she was still friends with his ex-wife, Catriona – drew Kendall into an unlikely bond with the blogger queen. Beneath all the earth-mother bullshit, Stella was also kind. Unlike everybody else, she hadn't rushed to judgement over Kendall and Ivan's affair, and had always been willing to lend a neutral ear about the relationship. With Jack cutting her off completely, and Lex, her former rock, making no secret of his disapproval, Kendall was grateful for Stella's support.

'What are your plans for the summer?' Kendall changed the subject, taking a bite of her own delicious goat's cheese and red onion tart. 'Will Brett be home?'

'Yes!' Stella's make-up-free face lit up in a perfect white smile. 'I'm so excited.' As ever, Kendall felt guilty that everybody knew about Brett's womanizing but his wife. Stella's devotion was so blind it was almost superhuman. 'We've taken a house in Malibu, actually. I'm really looking forward to spending some time back home. I think Miley needs to reconnect with her roots.'

Miley's not the only one, thought Kendall sadly. With a new, crucial album to finish and promote, there was no way she could take a real vacation before Christmas. She missed LA like a physical pain sometimes. The beaches, the sunshine, the food; shopping on Robertson; partying at Hyde. She missed Jack too. With Ivan she'd discovered an intensity and a passion different to anything she'd known before. But there was an innocence to her long, unrequited love for Jack, a purity to those feelings that she was scared she would never experience again. Clearly Jack didn't love her. He didn't even like her. But there was a part of Kendall that would always love him. The thought that she might never see him again made her terribly sad.

The one person she really wanted to talk to about all this was Lex. He'd always been her shoulder to cry on, and he and Jack were partners now. Perhaps, over the past year and a half, Jack had softened towards her? Really, the least Lex could do was to let her know, but apparently he was too busy with his boring make-up artist girlfriend to make time for his old friends.

Kendall had followed JSM's rise with mixed feelings. She told herself she was happy for her old friends and, on one level, she was. But she couldn't shake the irrational feeling that she'd somehow been cheated of something. That she, Kendall, should have been a part of JSM's brave new world. Intellectually she realized that it was she who'd burned the bridges, she who had left them. But, emotionally, she felt abandoned.

'I miss LA,' she told Stella wistfully. 'I wish you could pack me in your suitcase.'

'Aw, honey,' Stella squeezed her hand. 'I couldn't do that. Ivan would be lost without you.'

Kendall frowned. 'I doubt it. He's so caught up with this chick Ava from the show.'

'The little fat girl?' said Stella, not unkindly. In Stella Bayley's world of the mung bean, anyone with a BMI over sixteen was 'fat'. 'Oh my God, she is so cute. Have you seen her?'

'How can you not see her?' grumbled Kendall 'She's everywhere. Like poison ivy.'

Stella laughed. 'Come on, she's only a kid. And you gotta admit her voice is awesome.'

Kendall didn't think she had to admit any such thing. To her ears, Ava Bentley sounded like a five-year-old on helium. Kate Bush meets Alvin and the Chipmunks. She stabbed angrily at a piece of tart, glaring at her food in glum silence.

'Did you see the pictures of JSM's party for Land of the Greeks' new album? ' Stella asked brightly, thinking a change of subject back to LA gossip might cheer Kendall up. 'Jack Messenger looked gorgeous. He doesn't age, that man.'

Kendall felt a sharp stabbing pain in her stomach.

'I'd love to get him to spill his diet secrets on my blog, but ever since Brett decided to stay with Jester, we're *personae non gratae* on that front.' She sighed. 'Understandably, I guess. Anyway, half the world was at that party.'

'Really?' Kendall feigned disinterest.

'Sure, Katy Perry, Will-I-Am . . . . . . who else was there? Steven Tyler. That Martina kid everyone's raving about. There were some great shots of your friend Lex too, looking quite the big shot. His girlfriend seems really pretty.'

Kendall laughed dismissively. 'Please. Leila? She's so fucking hearty. She looks like my Phys Ed teacher from seventh grade. I'll bet she has enough armpit hair to weave a Kazak rug.'

Stella Bayley eyed her friend contemplatively. 'Is something wrong, Kendall? I might be off beam here. But I seem to be picking up a lot of anger.'

Kendall pushed her plate away, not hungry all of a sudden. 'Sorry,' she said. 'I guess I am in kind of a funk.'

'Maybe you and Ivan should get away for a couple of days? Have some fun. Brett stayed at Babington House with the band a couple of weeks ago; he said they had an amazing time.'

I'll bet they did, thought Kendall.

'He came home full of the joys of spring.'

Perhaps it wasn't such a bad idea. Not a vacation as such, neither of them had time for that, but a couple of days to enjoy each other's company. Whether it was Ivan's fault or her own, there *had* been too much bickering between them lately. When they first got together, all they ever did was laugh. It felt like a long time ago.

'You know what?' said Kendall brightening, 'I'm gonna do it. I'm gonna book us in for next week and surprise him.'

After leaving Stella, and calling Babington House to book the Coach House for the following Thursday and Friday nights, Kendall spent the rest of the afternoon merrily flexing Ivan's platinum AmEx. She bought a thousand pounds' worth of lingerie at Agent Provocateur, a divine pair of sky-high Jonathan Kelsey stilettos in shocking pink – not exactly country-house-hotel attire, but they looked great with her new purple crotchless knickers and peekaboo bra – and treated herself to a facial, mani-pedi and a full Hollywood bikini wax at Bliss, emerging billiard-ball smooth onto Sloane Avenue just as the sun began to set.

It was a glorious summer's evening in West London, with happy groups of people spilling out of the pubs onto pavements, drinking and laughing and enjoying the unaccustomed warmth. Kendall decided to walk home.

Since Jester sold the Eaton Gate flat, she and Ivan had been renting a riverside apartment on Cheyne Walk. The views were spectacular, almost as eye-watering as the monthly rental bills, but Kendall had fallen in love with the place and no amount of cajoling by Ivan could persuade her to consider somewhere less extortionate. Besides, what was the point of being a pop star with a multi-million-dollar record deal if you couldn't at least live where you wanted to?

By the time she got home and took the creaky old 1930s elevator up to the top floor, the sun had finished its descent and a magical, iridescent blue twilight covered the sleepy river like a blanket. For the first time in weeks, Kendall felt genuinely happy. This trip away would mark a new start for her and Ivan. She would return refreshed, energized and ready to pour her heart and soul into finishing her new album. Everything would be all right.

The art-deco clock above the fireplace said nine o'clock. Ivan would have left the *Talent Quest* studio by now and be on his way to dinner with Ava Bentley and her family. The thought of Ava prompted a brief flicker of displeasure, but Kendall pushed it aside. Ivan had assured her he wouldn't be late, and she could use the time to have a long, luxurious bubble bath and change into her new, thigh-skimming Agent Provocateur kimono. When Ivan caught a glimpse of her powdered, silky-smooth pussy beneath the cerise silk, all thoughts of Ava would fly out of his head in an instant.

As it turned out, his timing was perfect. Kendall had just tied her kimono belt, lowered the lights and put a sexy Hotel Costes track on the sound system when the front door opened.

'Hey.' Ivan smiled triumphantly. 'Dinner with the Bentleys was amazing. They're totally on board with signing Ava to Jester. They were eating out of my hand.'

'That's wonderful, darling.'

For the first time, Ivan noticed Kendall's sexy get-up, the lights and music. His smile broadened into a grin. 'You look incredible,' he said, kissing her and trying not to think about how much the slip of silk nothing she was wearing might have cost, or how much other loot she might have bought. When Kendall shopped, she rarely did things by halves. Still, it was a long time since she'd made this sort of an effort.

'You haven't seen the half of it,' she whispered, guiding his hand down between her legs. At the touch of her bare skin, Ivan instantly hardened, pulling her to him with a possessive groan of arousal. Christ she was sexy.

'I've booked us a little trip away,' said Kendall, burrowing herself into his chest. 'I'm sorry I've been a bitch these last few weeks. I really want us to try and—'

Ivan's mobile rang loudly, cutting her off.

'It's Catriona,' he grimaced.

'Leave it,' whispered Kendall, reaching for the zip on his fly. 'Please.'

Ivan hesitated, then reluctantly pulled away. 'I can't,' he said. 'I've been ignoring her calls all day. It might be the kids.' Turning his back on Kendall, he walked into the kitchen. 'Hello? Cat? What's up?'

Kendall clenched her fists and closed her eyes, trying to contain the anger welling up inside her. Why, *why*, did his ex-wife always come first? He'd closed the kitchen door, but she could still hear him apologizing, appeasing, trying to calm Catriona down. *It's me he should be apologizing to*, thought Kendall bitterly, pouring herself a large vodka and tonic from the drinks tray.

By the time Ivan emerged from the kitchen, a full forty minutes later, Kendall was three sheets to the wind, her face settled into its more familiar sullen scowl. Ivan looked as if someone had just lowered the weight of the world onto his shoulders.

'It's Hector,' he said bleakly. 'The stupid boy's gone and got himself arrested.'

Kendall yawned dramatically and poured herself another drink. 'Uh huh.'

'Apparently he went into Oxford, bought a spray can of paint and wrote, "Ivan Charles is a sad wanker" on the walls of the Bodleian.'

'At least he's observant,' commented Kendall said wryly, but there was no warmth or affection behind the joke.

'He's up before the magistrates in the morning,' Ivan ploughed on. 'I offered to go down there and stay a few days, but Cat told me I wasn't welcome. That it was my fault Hector was so screwed up in the first place, and that if I showed up at court, the press would be all over the story and make the whole thing ten times worse.'

'She's right,' said Kendall. 'Besides, you're not even free to go. I already told you, I've booked us on a mini-break, remember?'

'This is a bit more important than a fucking holiday,' said Ivan, somewhat tactlessly. 'This is my family.'

'Oh really. And what the hell am I, may I ask? A cheese sandwich? Fuck you, Ivan.'

Kendall got up unsteadily, weaving her way towards the corridor.

'Kendall. Come on. I didn't mean it like that. He's my son, that's all. It's not easy being told I'm not wanted at my own son's court hearing.' Ivan reached out a hand to stop her going but she shrugged him angrily away.

'You can sleep in the fucking spare room,' she shouted over her shoulder, staggering into the bedroom and slamming the door shut behind her.

Ivan considered going in after her. That was clearly what he was supposed to do. But the thought of another hour's drunken arguing followed by gruelling make-up sex was more than he could bear. He was also genuinely distressed about Hector and felt awful for having taken the best part of a day to return Catriona's calls. The poor thing must have been out of her mind with worry.

Too tired even to feel depressed, he went into the spare bedroom and flopped down on the bed, fully clothed. Seconds later, he was asleep.

He was woken by bright sunlight from a chink in the curtains falling across his face. The bedside clock said 9.15 a.m. He'd been asleep for nine hours, the longest unbroken stretch he'd had in months, and felt groggy and heavy limbed. Slowly, the events of last night reasserted themselves. The triumphant dinner with Ava Bentley's family, Kendall's sexiness, the news about Hector and Kendall's subsequent tantrum.

Last night he'd been too exhausted to deal with her. This morning he was too angry. What the hell did she want from him, anyway? He loved her, he bloody worshipped the girl, but his thirteen-year-old son had just spent the night in a jail cell and all Kendall wanted to talk about was mini-breaks.

The master bedroom door was still firmly closed when Ivan went for his shower, and remained so while he dressed and put a pot of coffee on to brew. Firing up his MacBook he sent six emails, one to Don Peters, one to the office manager at Jester, three to clients with whom he had meetings scheduled, and one to Ava, warning them all that he had a 'family crisis' to deal with today so his schedule might be a bit out of whack. Even if he wasn't wanted in person, he reasoned, Cat might want his help dealing with lawyers over the phone or paying any fines Hector might have racked up through his stupidity. Having pressed send, and eaten two slices of Marmite toast washed down with strong Colombian roast, he was about to leave a note for Kendall and head out the door when he relented. A note looked a bit cold, especially after such a big fight. He should talk to her. Steeling himself for rejection, he knocked on the bedroom door.

'Kendall? Baby?'

No answer.

'Come on, Kendall, we need to talk. I have to go to work in a minute and I don't want to leave things like this.'

Still nothing. He tried the door, expecting to find it locked, but it opened to reveal a room flooded with sunlight. Propped up against the pillows was an envelope. Ivan opened it and read the single-line note inside.

'Gone back to LA. Don't call. K.'

CHAPTER TWELVE

Kendall felt a rush of excitement and happiness as her plane touched down at LAX. When she'd walked out of the Cheyne Walk apartment at the crack of dawn this morning, she hadn't known herself whether she'd actually have the balls to go through with it. Flouncing off to The Dorchester was one thing, but disappearing to LA, running out not just on Ivan, but on her Polydor work commitments, was a big step. But here she was, gazing out of the window at palm trees and traffic through a shimmering heat haze, as if she'd never been away.

Over the course of the eleven-hour flight, in between sleeping off her hangover and gorging herself on warm milk and cookies, Kendall had rationalized her decision. It was an impromptu vacation, that was all. She didn't intend to stay long, just long enough to shake Ivan out of his complacency and help crystallize his thinking as to who was the priority in his life: Ava Bentley, his ex-wife or her. If Polydor kicked up a fuss about it, she could always tell them she was going into the recording studio here, or working on her vocals with her old coach, Maria Atavista, a legend in the industry.

It wasn't as if she had any live dates she was missing, and none of the PR stuff for the next two weeks could be considered crucial.

Obviously last night's showdown with Ivan had been the catalyst. But her conversation with Stella Bayley had also brought it home to her just how much she was missing the States. It was the little things she missed most – Access Hollywood at seven o'clock, Maroon 5 on the car radio, In-N-Out Burgers and Cheetos and real mac and cheese, the processed stuff that glowed the same neon yellow as SpongeBob Square Pants. Her life in London was luxurious and privileged and exclusive, but Kendall had never taken to British culture the way that Stella had. She still felt like a rarefied fish out of water.

At Immigration, when the officer smiled and said, 'Welcome home', it was all Kendall could do not to kiss him. Picking up her Louis Vuitton case, she sailed through Customs on a wave of happiness and went straight to the Olympic Cars desk, where she picked up her pre-reserved Aston Martin V12. The car was gleaming black with a cream interior and mocha coffee trim, and just sitting behind the wheel made Kendall feel like a million dollars, the conquering heroine returning in glory after two long years of battle. Even the inevitable 405 traffic couldn't dampen her spirits. Crawling towards Beverly Hills, listening to Ryan Seacrest on *Kiss*, she drank in every moment, every sight and sound of the city and the life she'd left behind.

She deliberately hadn't booked a hotel. She figured she'd surprise everyone at home and show up unannounced – bearing gifts, of course. Her first stop was Neiman Marcus in Beverly Hills to pick up something teenage and cool for Holly and Joe, her younger half-siblings, and a suitably statement-like designer purse for her mom. If there was one thing guaranteed to soften Lorna Bryce's heart, it was a Balenciaga tote although, come to think of it, she probably had the entire fall collection by now. Not without a pang of guilt, Kendall tried to work out how old the twins would be by now. Seventeen? Eighteen? Although she'd called occasionally and sent Christmas gifts, she hadn't actually laid eyes on either of them for over two years.

After three hours of shopping, and a stop for a mouth-watering Pinkberry frozen yoghurt, where she was gratify-ingly snapped by at least four paparazzi, jet lag finally began to catch up with her. Driving the short route to her mother's house on North Canon Drive, Kendall found herself fanta-sizing about her childhood bed, sinking into those soft pillows surrounded by all her old soft toys. It was all she could do to keep her eyes open, but at last she came to the familiar cedar-wood gates and typed in the old code.

Nothing happened. For one awful, sinking moment it occurred to Kendall that Lorna might have moved house. *Surely she wouldn't do a thing like that without telling me?* But then the familiar, gravelly voice of Pepe, the groundsman, crackled over the intercom.

'Can I help you?'

'Pepe, it's me, Kendall. There's something wrong with the gate, the pass-code's not working.'

There was a short silence. Then the gravelly voice said, 'Wind down your window please. Look at the camera.'

'What?' said Kendall, irritated. Pepe didn't remember her fucking voice? But she did as she was asked, removing her sunglasses to stare up at the swivelling CCTV above the gate. A few seconds later, it dutifully swung open and Kendall drove into the paved forecourt.

OK, so it wasn't quite the warm welcome for the prodigal daughter returned that she'd been hoping for. None of the staff rushed out to greet her, and the boy who appeared to help her with her suitcase was new. But she refused to allow her spirits to be dampened. Clutching her beautifully wrapped peace offerings, she rang the bell.

'Miss Kendall!' The tiny Mexican housemaid looked suitably shocked. *At least Elena remembers me.* 'What are you doing here?'

'Just visiting,' said Kendall. 'It was a spur-of-the-moment thing. Where's Mom?'

At that moment Lorna Bryce emerged from the kitchen. The first thing Kendall thought was how much she'd aged. The peach Juicy sweatpants and Stella McCartney vest that had long been her casual uniform looked ridiculous on her now, clothes for a much younger woman. Despite the Botox and highlights, Lorna's face was mottled with sun-damage and the skin on her forearms wrapped the bones like crêpe paper. It hit Kendall like a punch in the stomach that her mother would not be around for ever, that this latest time apart had been too long.

'Kendall. Why didn't you call?' Lorna's tone was neither hostile nor gushing. It was polite, friendly even, but it certainly wasn't the flood of emotion Kendall had been expecting. 'When did you get in?'

'A few hours ago.' Kendall stepped forward and hugged her mom, but the gesture felt stiff and awkward. 'Where are the twins? I bought some gorgeous Sass & Bide jeans for Holly and a limited edition Tony Hawk T-shirt for Joe. He is still into skateboarding, isn't he?'

Lorna's kind face tightened. 'No, Kendall. He's not. I don't think he's been on a board since he was sixteen. The twins turn twenty this winter.'

'Oh, well. I guess he can always return it,' blustered Kendall. 'Is he home?'

Lorna rolled her eyes. 'No! Joe lives in New York now. He went out there to college last year and he's working at a midtown attorney's for the summer. Holly's in Sudan building schools with World Vision. If you ever read my emails, you'd know all this.'

'I read your emails, Mom,' lied Kendall, putting her presents down guiltily on the hall table. 'I have a very hectic life, that's all. I can't keep track of everybody, all the time.'

'Why don't I put some coffee on?' said Lorna, trying to be conciliatory. 'You can fill me in on all your news.'

'Actually, Mom,' said Kendall, 'I'm really beat after my flight. I thought I might just go to my room and crash. We can catch up over dinner, just the two of us.'

Lorna's face clouded over. 'Oh, honey, I can't. I'm actually leaving tonight for Napa. Bob's taking me on a tour of all the vineyards. We've got reservations at Auberge de Soleil,' she added with a smile.

'Who's Bob?' asked Kendall.

'Bob. Bob Lieberman? We've been dating since last summer.'

'Oh,' said Kendall, trying to picture the mystery man who could be sexually attracted to her mother. 'Well, can't you cancel? I might only have a few days. I could be gone by the time you get back.'

Lorna took both of her daughter's hands in hers. 'Kendall, honey. You've been gone for a long time. I'm happy to see you. I wish you'd called. But I can't just drop my entire life because you suddenly got a break in your schedule.'

Kendall managed a smile. 'Of course not, Mom. I'm sorry. I've been excited to see you, that's all. London's so far away.'

'You're welcome to stay here if you'd like,' Lorna added. 'I've been using your old room for storage, my shoes were getting way out of control, but the blue guest suite is all made up.'

'That's OK,' said Kendall, surprised to find herself close to tears. There was no way she could sleep in this house alone, and in a room that wasn't even hers. She felt as though she'd been erased. 'I'll get a hotel.'

An hour later, walking into her premier one-bedroom suite at the Chateau Marmont, Kendall flopped back on the bed, exhausted. She knew she was being unreasonable. Why should her mother cancel her plans at the last minute? She was the one who'd walked out, after all, with barely a backwards glance at the family she'd left behind. She didn't even know that her brother was away at college, or that her sister was saving the world in Africa. London and Ivan and her new, whirlwind life had swallowed her whole. What did she expect?

But it still hurt.

For the first time since she landed, she switched on her phone, checking for texts or missed calls from Ivan. There was nothing. A creeping fear began to steal over her. Had she made a terrible mistake by leaving? What if Ivan went back to Catriona, with her motherly calm and her smoothly run household and unconditional, unquestioning love? He wouldn't, would he? Kendall still didn't know whether *she* loved Ivan, whether the desire and attachment she felt for him could be called love. But she did know that the idea of him leaving filled her with abject panic.

He's the one who should be bloody panicking, she thought angrily, forcing her fears aside. Besides, she'd come here to get away from Ivan, to reconnect with her American roots and that was what she intended to do. Propped up wearily against the pillows, she scrolled through the contacts on her US phone, searching for a friend to call, but realized she was out of touch with almost all of them. Her father was in there under Bryce (Vernon), but it would be a cold day in hell before Kendall punched out those digits. Jack was there too, with a string of emails and numbers as long as her arm: Jack New York, Jack Home, Jack Euro Cell, Jack e-fax, Jack new cell. Seeing the numbers, Kendall found herself welling up again. *I must be more tired than I thought.* Finally she stopped at the one name she should have called first. Whatever the petty spats between them since she left LA, Lex Abrahams was still her best friend.

Dialling the number, she found herself feeling unaccountably nervous. After three rings, the familiar voice picked up.

'Kendall. Is that you?'

He hadn't erased her number. That was surely a good sign. 'Yeah, it's me.'

'Where are you? Are you in the States?'

There was noise in the background, people laughing and talking.

'Actually, I'm right here in LA.' Kendall had to half shout to make herself heard. 'I'm just checked into the Chateau. Kind of a last-minute thing.'

There were a few seconds of silence. Then Lex said, 'Is everything OK?'

No, everything isn't OK. I'm lonely. To her immense embarrassment, the tears she'd been holding in all evening suddenly burst forth and began pouring down her cheeks. She wiped them frantically on the bedspread, desperate that Lex shouldn't hear how upset she was.

'Everything's fine. Really great, actually. Why don't you come pick me up in an hour and I'll fill you in over dinner.'

'I have plans tonight,' said Lex matter-of-factly.

'Oh.' Back in her day, Lex *never* had dinner plans. Or, at least, he never had plans that he wasn't prepared to cancel at a moment's notice from Kendall.

'Tomorrow then.'

'To be honest, Kendall, it's kind of a crazy week for me. I can meet you for lunch tomorrow, how's that? Polo Lounge at one?'

'Sounds perfect,' said Kendall in a cheery voice, smothering her disappointment like a mother stifling her child's cries. 'See you there.'

As soon as she hung up, the dark cloud descended. Everyone had forgotten her. No one cared. Even Lex, her Lex, was doing her a favour by squeezing her in for lunch. Utterly deflated, and too tired even to take a shower, Kendall turned off the lights, slipped fully clothed beneath the covers, and fell instantly into a deep, deep sleep.

The next morning she awoke late in much better spirits. After coffee and French toast on her private terrace overlooking the pool, she slipped into a flirty Dolce & Gabbana sundress and sparkly Jimmy Choo flats and called down to valet for her car. As soon as she hung up, her publicist called.

'Kendall. What the fuck's going on?' As usual, Sasha Dale cut to the chase. The diminutive dynamo was not given to small talk, or indeed to pleasantries of any kind.

'Nothing. I needed to get away, that's all. I'm on vacation. How did you find me here?'

'Vacation?' Sasha echoed scornfully, not bothering to answer Kendall's question. 'You're gonna have to give me something better than that. Are you and Ivan splitting?'

'No! Absolutely not.'

'Great. So we'll leak it that you *are*, then set up some more drama around that, something that lends itself to a pictorial. We'll make it look like you're having a fling with someone out there, then you and Ivan can romantically get back together. Who can we set up as a new love interest?'

'No one!' said Kendall.

'There must be someone. It doesn't have to be real. Just a friend who we can make look like something more.'

Kendall had started out on a reality show, so she understood the concept of a scripted romance, and how to pull one off. But the whole idea was pretty distasteful.

'What about Lex Abrahams?' asked Sasha bluntly. 'You two are close, aren't you?'

'Yeees,' said Kendall tentatively. 'Sort of.' How the hell did Sasha Dale know that? 'I'm about to meet him for lunch actually. But there's no way he'd go for it.'

'Why not?'

'Because it's tacky as hell!' said Kendall. 'And because he has a girlfriend. The kind of story you're talking about could seriously screw things up for them.'

'Even better,' said Sasha, without a trace of irony. 'More drama. I love it.'

'Look, I wouldn't do that to Lex and that's final.' Kendall was getting irritated. 'I'm still with Ivan, I'm on vacation, and if you can't make a story out of that, then too bad.'

She hung up feeling stressed and anxious, but the short drive along Sunset to the Beverly Hills Hotel was enough to lift anybody's mood. Baking, broiling sunshine, of the kind you just didn't ever seem to get in Northern Europe, flooded the car till Kendall could feel her forearms starting to bronze. A light breeze blew back her hair in classic movie-star style, and every time the traffic slowed she was aware of people staring, trying to figure out whether it really was her or not. By the time she strutted into The Polo Lounge and across the patio to Lex's table, Kendall radiated confidence like a stadium floodlight.

'Hey! Hello, stranger.'

The Lex who stood up to greet her was unrecognizable

as the scruffy, slightly downtrodden photographer Kendall once knew. His face was still the same, with its long aquiline nose and the blue eyes that seemed to have made their way into his swarthy features by accident. But in all other ways he looked totally different: older, mature and brimming with a quiet confidence of his own. His unruly nest of curly dark hair had been cropped close, and his scruffy baggies and T-shirt replaced with a pair of preppy Ralph Lauren shorts and a pale-blue polo shirt that worked wonderfully against his tanned, coffee-brown skin. He wore a simple but expensive vintage Omega watch in rose gold, and a classic pair of Ray-Ban aviators lay casually discarded on the white table-cloth. When he kissed Kendall on the cheek, he smelled of expensive aftershave.

Success suits him, thought Kendall. 'You look terrific,' she beamed, genuinely delighted.

'So do you,' said Lex. 'But then you always did.'

They sat down and stared at one another for a few moments, neither of them quite knowing what to say. While Lex might look confident, and had even felt it on the way over here, now that he was actually sitting opposite Kendall in the flesh, his stomach had started doing unpleasant back flips and his palms were slick with sweat. He'd forgotten just how beautiful she was. It was surreal, otherworldly, and horribly disconcerting. As if no time had gone by, he found himself fighting the urge to reach out and touch her, and when she spoke his eyes were drawn mesmerically to her full, unbearably sensual lips.

'So what brings you to LA out of the blue?' he asked, determinedly keeping his voice casual.

'Nothing really,' Kendall shrugged. 'I had an unexpected break in my schedule. It's just a vacation.'

'You're visiting your family, I guess,' said Lex.

'Sure,' said Kendall tightly, pushing the pain of yesterday's failed reunion out of her mind. 'Here and there, you know. I have a ton of people to see.'

Lex ordered the linguine vongole and a chopped salad. Kendall, still full from her French toast, plumped for tuna tartare. In an effort to impress Lex, she eschewed the white wine she so desperately wanted and ordered an iced tea instead. Lex did the same.

'Ivan not with you?' he asked casually.

'No. He had to work,' said Kendall, defensively. 'We're not joined at the hip, you know.'

'But you're still together?' *Pathetic*, thought Lex. *Why the hell did you ask her that?* But the words were out of his mouth before he even knew he'd thought them.

'Of course,' said Kendall. 'We're very happy and madly in love. Ivan's completely changed my life.'

'That's great,' Lex lied. 'I'm happy for you.'

Another awkward silence was broken by the arrival of the food. Kendall longed to talk to Lex properly, to have a real conversation about her life and feelings, the way they used to do. But this new Lex was so slick, so together, so distant, at least from her, she was too scared to tell him the truth.

'How about you?' she said eventually, scooping up a succulent forkful of lemony fish and avocado. 'Are you still with what's-her-name?'

'Leila,' Lex frowned. 'Yes, I am. She's great. JSM takes up ninety per cent of my time, but I'm lucky to have a partner who's so tolerant.'

A partner? Kendall's lip curled involuntarily. 'I'd love to meet her,' she said, without enthusiasm.

'Well you're about to,' said Lex. 'She's gonna swing by for dessert. She was curious to meet you too.'

Kendall could have screamed. It was bad enough Lex only

meeting her for lunch. But to invite his bloody dull-as-ditchwater girlfriend along, without even asking her? That was really too much. Grabbing a passing waiter by the elbow she said, 'You know what? I changed my mind. I'd like a large glass of Cabernet Sauvignon please.'

'Speak of the devil.' Lex's face lit up as he pushed back his chair. 'Here she is now. Hey, honey, you're early.' Reaching out both hands, he kissed the tall, brown-haired girl on the lips. Under the tablecloth, Kendall dug her nails painfully into her palms.

'I know,' laughed Leila. 'The shoot finished early – never happens, right? And then I actually got good traffic in Beverly Hills. Must be my lucky day.' She stretched out a hand to Kendall. 'Hi, I'm Leila. I've heard so much about you.'

'Really?' The chill in Kendall's voice could have frozen molten lava. She waited for Leila to sit down, then pointedly turned her attention straight back to Lex. 'So how's business? I hear great things about JSM.'

'It's amazing.' Reaching over, Lex idly massaged the back of Leila's neck. He was glad she was here. Her presence seemed to have broken the spell that Kendall had cast over him, bringing him back to reality and safety. 'I'm very lucky.'

'It has nothing to do with luck,' Leila jumped in loyally. 'You deserve it. You've worked your butt off building that company.'

'I'll bet you have,' said Kendall, still looking solely at Lex. 'Jack always was a great one for cracking the whip. How is he?'

'Fine.' Lex's face closed down, giving nothing away. 'Fine' could have meant anything from 'about to marry a supermodel' to 'dying of cancer'. The message was clear: Kendall no longer had a right to know.

Unfortunately, no one had sent Leila the memo. Either

missing the tension between Lex and Kendall, or choosing to ignore it, she started chattering away about what a committed partner Jack was, and how close he and Lex had become since they started JSM together.

'And he's been absolutely darling to me, so welcoming right from day one, hasn't he, Lex? I thought it was so sweet he named the company after his wife. We just wish he would find someone new to settle down with. All he does is work, but if anyone deserves to be as happy as we are, it's Jack.'

This was too much for Kendall. Turning on Leila waspishly she said, 'Obviously you don't know Jack very well. He'll never marry again.'

'Well, maybe not yet.'

'Not ever. He's never gotten over Sonya's death because he's never wanted to. Jack clings to his grief, it's just the way it is.'

Leila's face darkened. She'd heard that Kendall had a bitchy streak, but this was a really horrid thing to say, especially after the kick in the teeth Kendall had already given Jack by defecting to Ivan. She waited for Lex to say something, but he seemed engrossed by the remnants of his chopped salad, so she spoke up herself.

'Well I think you're wrong,' she said defiantly. 'These things take time, but I'm sure Jack will marry again eventually. At least he's starting to get out more. After Ivan stabbed him in the back and stole all Jester's clients, he barely set foot out of the house for a year. Did he, Lex?'

'It was a tough time,' admitted Lex. 'For all of us.'

'More self-pity,' sniffed Kendall. 'Jack had nobody to blame for Jester's break-up but himself. I should know. I was there.'

This wasn't what she felt, but Lex's girlfriend's pretensions to closeness with Jack were too irritating to be suffered in silence. Maybe she'd been too quick to reject Sasha Dale's idea of a staged Lex fauxmance? It would serve Lady Muck Leila right if she *did* lose her precious boyfriend. Who the hell did she think she was to preach to her, Kendall, about Jack Messenger's feelings?

The waiter arrived before Leila had time to think of a suitably cutting riposte.

'Can I tempt anybody with dessert?'

Three grim heads shook in unison.

'Just the cheque, please,' said Lex. He tried to ask Kendall a couple of small-talk-type questions about her new album and Ivan's reality show, but neither of their hearts were in it and it was a relief when the bill arrived.

As they walked back into the lobby together and made their frosty goodbyes, Leila couldn't resist one last dig. 'I'll give Jack your regards, shall I? Lex and I are having dinner with him tonight at The Brentwood.'

The knife was well aimed and it pierced Kendall clean through the heart, but she was damned if she was going to show it.

'Do,' she said, slipping on her sunglasses and flicking back her glossy mane of hair, almost hitting Leila in the eye. With a final peck on the cheek for Lex, she hopped into her flashy sports car and roared away.

Leila turned to Lex. 'How on *earth* were you ever friends with that creature? She's vile.'

But instead of agreeing with her, Lex lost his rarely seen temper. 'Why the hell did you have to keep banging on about Jack?' he shouted. 'You were only supposed to stop in and say "hi".'

He marched off to the valet, leaving Leila gazing after him, open-mouthed.

*   *   *

Jack held the candle up next to the menu and struggled to make out the specials. There was mood lighting and then there was The Brentwood, a West-side favourite so dimly lit it was like trying to feel your way around in a mine shaft. Perhaps the gloom was designed for privacy, so that the industry insiders who dined here could enjoy their Dungeness crab cakes without being gaped at and hassled by the hoi polloi. Or perhaps it was an attempt to make the fat, over-dressed divorcees at the bar look less unattractive. Either way, it was giving Jack eyestrain. Why on earth had he agreed to come out tonight?

Lex and Leila had obviously invited him out of pity. They were nice kids, but Jack wished they'd turn their compassionate attentions on someone else and leave him to stay home with a good bottle of claret and his boxset of *24* DVDs. The truth was, even when Sonya had been alive, Jack hadn't been much of a one for dining out. As a manager, he had to socialize constantly for work. On the rare chances he got to switch off, all he wanted to do was bolt the front door, turn on the TV and shut the world out.

'Here, take this.' Leila pulled a pen-light out of her purse and handed it to him. 'I use it to do close-up make-up work, but it's a neat little gizmo.'

Jack flicked it on. The tiny bulb spewed light over the menu like a supernova, making it instantly legible. He laughed. 'That's cool. I have to get one of those.'

While he scrolled through the entrées, Lex said quietly, 'So, you'll never guess who I saw for lunch today.'

'Who *we* saw,' Leila corrected him.

'Who?' asked Jack, not really interested.

'Kendall.'

Jack's head shot up as if he had whiplash. 'Kendall's in

LA?' The idea seemed to upset him, or at least to throw him off his stride. 'Did you know she was coming?'

'No,' said Lex. 'I don't think she knew. She said it was a last-minute thing.'

'Is Ivan with her?'

'No.' Both Lex and Leila noticed Jack's shoulders visibly relax at this answer. 'I got the sense that maybe all wasn't well back in London. But we didn't have a chance to get into it.'

Jack felt as if the floor beneath his chair had been replaced by a spinning plate. He had horribly mixed emotions about Kendall, from anger to nostalgic affection and everything in between. He certainly didn't want to see her. He wasn't ready for that. But at the same time, the fact that she was in LA and had seen Lex but not him bothered him more than it should have.

'Was she apologetic? About what happened with Jester. Did she seem regretful?'

Leila choked on her breadstick, but after a sharp look from Lex, said nothing.

'She asked after you,' said Lex diplomatically.

'Hmm.' Jack returned to his menu, the subject apparently closed, but throughout dinner it was clear his mind was racing. Lex talked about the Grammys and the deal he'd just cut for one of JSM's clients, a jazz singer from New Orleans, with Sony. Jack nodded and smiled at the appropriate moments, but when he got up to go to the bathroom, Leila said, 'I don't think he heard a word you said, honey.'

Lex agreed. 'This Kendall thing really floored him. I thought about not saying anything, but I don't like the idea of keeping secrets and . . . oh my God.'

'What?' Leila followed his gaze. Standing just inside the door, with two girlfriends from her old, pre-Jack partying days, was Kendall. In skin-tight black leather pants, spiked boots and a Rick Owens distressed denim jacket, she looked fiercely sexy. Everything from her body language, to the slashes of black rock-chick eyeliner ringing her amber eyes, seemed to be a challenge. *Try not to look at me. Try not to want me. I dare you.*

'She knew we were going to be here!' Leila said furiously. 'She's stalking you.'

'She's stalking someone,' said Lex bitterly, 'but it isn't me.'

'Well you needn't sound so disappointed about it,' said Leila, who hadn't forgotten Lex's outburst of temper at The Polo Lounge earlier. She didn't know what hold Kendall Bryce had over her normally considerate boyfriend, but she didn't like it. 'And for goodness' sake, stop staring. She'll see us.'

'Too late,' said Lex. Whispering something to her girl-friends, Kendall headed over. Every head in the restaurant turned to stare as she glided up to Lex's table.

'Hey, guys.' She smiled disingenuously. 'This is so weird, running into you again.'

'No it isn't,' said Leila, all pretence at politeness now abandoned. 'I mentioned at lunch that we'd be here tonight. You came here deliberately.'

'Believe it or not,' said Kendall witheringly, 'just because Lex hangs off your every word doesn't mean the rest of us do. I never heard you say anything. This happens to be one of my favourite restaurants. I always eat here when I'm in town.'

'Yeah, right,' sneered Leila.

Before Lex could say anything, Jack arrived back from the bathroom, looking as if he'd seen a ghost. Even Kendall seemed to blanch, although it was hard to make out anything clearly in the candlelit gloom.

'How are you?' Jack asked stiffly. He made no move to hug her or kiss her hello.

'I'm great, thanks,' said Kendall.

There was that defiance again, thought Lex, the chin jutting forward and upwards, shoulders thrown back. *What's she trying to prove?*

'How are you?'

'Thriving, thank you. JSM's going gangbusters. Lex and I are having the time of our lives,' said Jack, sitting back down at the table but pointedly not offering Kendall a seat. To Leila's intense annoyance, Lex grabbed a free chair from a neighbouring table and rectified this state of affairs.

'I can't stay long,' Kendall muttered gratefully. 'I'm here with some friends.'

'Don't let us keep you,' said Leila, earning herself a withering glare.

Jack went on. 'Of course it helps working with a partner I can trust,' he said snidely. 'Speaking of which, how *is* Ivan? Is the world of reality television all he dreamed it would be?'

You could have scooped up the sarcasm and eaten it with a spoon. Kendall was hurt. After two years she'd hoped for more forgiveness from Jack, or at least for the bitterness to feel less raw. She also wanted him to ask about her, not Ivan. But she kept her game face on.

'*Talent Quest*'s a huge hit, as I'm sure you know,' she said coolly.

'Yes, I've seen a few episodes,' said Jack. 'Some of the contestants are extremely gifted. I wouldn't mind signing Ava Bentley myself.' Kendall winced inwardly at the mention of Ava's name. 'But the judging panel are an embarrassment.'

'Nothing embarrassing about their salaries,' snapped Kendall. 'It was absolutely the right move for Ivan to go into television. I think his only regret is that he was held back for so long.'

'Guys . . .' said Lex, trying to make peace, but it was no good. Jack's fire was up now. There could be no turning back.

'Yes, I can see he's made it a priority over management,' said Jack, leaning forward on his elbows. 'Your last album's sales are a pretty strong indicator of that. As are Jester's profits. Still, as long as you're both happy.'

'We are,' Kendall shot back. 'Blissfully. There's nothing like tripling your income and having really great sex to put a smile on your face. You should try it some time, Jack. You too, Lex.'

'You bitch!' shouted Leila. 'Who the hell do you think you are?'

Kendall stood up. Lex noticed her hands were shaking. 'You know, it's a shame, Jack,' she said. 'You've changed. You're not the man I remember.'

For a moment Jack looked genuinely wounded. Then he said quietly, 'We've all changed, Kendall. Good luck.'

Back at the bar with her friends a few minutes later, Kendall watched Jack leave, alone, without so much as a glance in her direction. All of a sudden she was twelve years old again, watching her father, Vernon, walking out of the house, as cool as a cucumber, while her mum lay collapsed and sobbing on the front step. 'Don't make a fool of yourself, Lorna.' Those had been his last words as a member of Kendall's family. He hadn't even glanced back at his stricken daughter, so eager was he to move on and begin his new life.

A stony-faced Leila followed a few minutes later, followed by a distressed-looking Lex.

'He doesn't mean it, you know,' Lex whispered kindly to

Kendall on his way out. 'Take care of yourself.' Then he, too, was gone.

Leila drove Lex's Range Rover back to Malibu, staring resolutely at the road ahead. She was angry, understandably so, but what bothered Lex more were the tears brimming in her eyes and threatening to spill out at any moment.

'I'm sorry,' he said lamely.

'For what?' asked Leila. 'For sticking up for her after her atrocious display of spite at lunch? Or for *not* sticking up for me when she said I was shit in bed tonight?'

'She didn't exactly say that.'

'You see? There you go again! Defending her. Putting her first. As if she's ever, *ever* put you first.'

Lex sat in guilty silence. It was so incredibly unlike Leila to go off the deep end, he knew he must have pushed her there. There was also the uncomfortable fact that everything she said about him and Kendall was true. True and embarrassing. He didn't *want* to be that person, the schmuck who always put Kendall first. Not any more. But at the same time he couldn't help but feel sorry for her. Her loneliness was palpable, and her anguish over Jack. There was more to her than the spoiled bitch that Leila saw. Still, it was no excuse.

'Are you in love with her?'

Leila had pulled over to ask the question. To Lex's horror, she was crying properly now.

He took her hand. 'No.' At that moment he didn't know whether that was the truth or not, but it was the only answer he could give.

'And what about me? Are you in love with me?'

'You know I love you,' Lex answered carefully. 'Look, I know I was a jerk today, Leila, and I'm sorry. I'm sorry I hurt you.'

Leila looked him in the eye. 'If you're really sorry, promise me you won't see Kendall again while she's here.'

Lex hesitated. He thought about the look on Kendall's face when he left just now, the desolation beneath the put-on smiles. Those girls she was with weren't friends. They wouldn't support her. All they cared about was being vicariously associated with fame and money. But if he turned his back on her, they were all Kendall would be left with.

Then he thought about Leila, all the happiness she'd brought him, the love, the unwavering loyalty and support. He knew he had no choice.

'OK,' he said. 'If it means that much to you, I promise. I won't see her again.'

The next five days were hell on earth for Kendall. The morning after her disastrous run-in with Jack, she received a furious email from her record company, swiftly followed by numerous phone calls, all demanding that she return to the UK immediately or consider herself in breach of contract.

Kendall was pretty sure this was bullshit. Polydor didn't own her, and she was entitled to take some personal time. In normal circumstances she would have had her manager calm the waters, but as Ivan still hadn't made any contact with her whatsoever, she was damned if she was going to be the first one to call. So she picked up the phone to Lex (he was a manager now, after all, and ought to have some advice as to how to handle this sort of hysteria), only to be told that his stupid-ass girlfriend had forbidden him to have any more contact with her.

'Are you serious?' Kendall exploded down the phone. 'You let your girlfriend choose your friends?'

'It's not like that,' said Lex.

'How is it not like that? Jesus, Lexy, I'm sorry but you need to grow a pair.'

'You're not sorry,' Lex snapped. 'That's your problem, Kendall, you're never sorry for anything. I don't suppose it occurred to you that the reason Leila's so upset with you is that you were unforgivably rude yesterday?'

Kendall hung up – she didn't have time for this crap. The phone rang immediately. Evidently the chief executive of Polydor viewed her abscondment as serious enough to warrant a personal call from the top. Halfway through his diatribe, Kendall shouted into the receiver, 'Listen, asshole, my dad's got cancer, OK? So quit giving me a hard time and back the fuck off,' and hung up feeling mildly satisfied. By the time anyone figured out that Vernon Bryce was actually in rude health, Kendall would be back in the studio and all this drama would be over.

The irony was, she would happily have flown back to London on the next plane. There could be no disguising it now, her trip to LA had been a disaster. Her family were too busy to see her, Jack was clearly nowhere near forgiveness, and now even Lex was giving her the cold shoulder. The thought of spending the next however-many-days in the company of acquaintances and hangers-on was an even lonelier prospect than being by herself. But she couldn't go back to Ivan with her tail between her legs, not having made such a grand, dramatic gesture. If she did that, whatever tenuous hold she still had over him would unravel completely. It would only be a matter of time till she and Ivan were history. She *had* to get him to crack first.

A day passed, then another, then another. No one called. Kendall's initial relief when the record company stopped hassling her was soon replaced by panic. What if they were quiet because they were figuring out a way to sue, to try to claw back their advances? Most worrying of all, though, was Ivan's continued radio silence. Had he left her? Moved out of the Chelsea flat? She scoured the Internet for recent pictures or reports about him since she'd been away, looking for clues as to his state of mind. But other than a few fluff pieces about his bond with Ava Bentley, and a single shot of him looking relaxed walking into the *Talent Quest* studios, Starbucks in hand, she had nothing to go on. At least he was in London and not holed up in the countryside with his wife. But he certainly didn't seem to be missing her.

After five days cooling her heels at the Chateau, with shopping and spa trips the only thing to break the monotony of her days, Kendall finally snapped. She couldn't live in this limbo for ever. She had to do something. With a sinking heart, she dialled Sasha Dale's number.

'Ah, the prodigal daughter.' Kendall's publicist couldn't hide her delight. 'I was wondering when you'd call. You're in a hole and you want out of it, right? OK, kid. Get a pen. Here's what you're gonna do . . .'

Lex was at Gold's Gym on Venice beach, working out with Gunther, his personal trainer, when he got the call.

'Kendall, calm down.' He held the phone away from his ear, trying to catch some words between the deafening sobs. 'I can barely make out what you're saying.'

'My chest!' Kendall wailed hysterically. 'Lex, I need you. There's something wrong with my . . . I think I'm having a heart attack!'

Lex sat up and pressed the phone back to his ear. 'Have you taken anything?'

There was silence on the other end of the line.

'Kendall! What have you taken?'

Her voice came back, frail and pitiful, like a little girl's. 'I need you, Lex. I think I'm dying.'

Lex could hear her gasping for breath and felt his own heart rate shoot through the roof. 'It's OK, sweetheart. You're not dying. Are you at the hotel?'

Kendall whimpered her assent. She told Lex her room number.

'Just stay where you are,' said Lex. 'I'm on my way.'

'Anything I can do?' asked Gunther as his client sprinted back to his car.

'Yeah,' Lex called over his shoulder. 'Call nine-one-one. Tell them it's a suspected overdose, twenty-five-year-old woman. She's at the Chateau Marmont, suite two-seventeen.'

All the way back to Hollywood, weaving in and out of traffic like a madman, Lex wrestled with his guilt. He should never have abandoned Kendall. He saw how vulnerable she was last week, how close to the edge, but he'd let Leila talk him into walking away. If something serious had happened, he would never forgive himself.

The drive was torture, like one of those dreams when someone's chasing you and you're trying to run for your life but your legs are mired in treacle. The traffic seemed slower than ever, and none of the usual rat-runs or short-cuts worked. It took him almost forty minutes to reach the hotel and another ten to convince the staff to let him see Kendall.

'I was the one who called the ambulance, OK? She begged me to come to her. Please. I have information the doctors need to know.'

When he finally got to Kendall's room, the scene was remarkably calm. Kendall was lying back in bed, with a paramedic at either side, breathing slowly in and out of a paper bag. She looked pale and tiny and frightened, but not like a woman at death's door.

'Are you Lex?' one of the paramedics asked.

Lex nodded.

'Good,' the man smiled. 'She's been asking for you.'

'What happened? I've been driving like a maniac. I . . . I thought she'd OD'd.'

'You did the right thing to call us,' said the paramedic, reassuringly. 'But she's fine. There are no drugs in her system.'

'Then what?'

'She's been having a panic attack. Very unpleasant, but not physically dangerous. Panic attack sufferers often experience acute chest pains. The symptoms are similar to cardiac arrest, so you can't take any chances.'

Lex paused a moment to let the full import of what the doctor was saying sink in. He sat down on the end of Kendall's bed, dizzy with relief.

'You'll be OK now, honey,' the other paramedic said. Having checked that her blood pressure and pulse were normal, he began packing up his things.

'If you need us again, you can call any time,' said his colleague. 'Don't be embarrassed.'

Kendall looked up from the paper bag and smiled weakly. 'Thanks,' she said. 'Sorry for all the trouble.'

When she and Lex were alone, she asked timidly, 'I guess you're mad at me too. I'm sorry. I didn't know who else to call.'

'I'm not mad.' Scooching up to the top of the bed he laid a hand her forehead. 'And it's me who should be sorry. What brought all this on?'

'I don't know.' She bit her lower lip. 'The thought of going back to London, I guess. Oh, Lex! I've made such a mess of everything.'

She started to cry. Instinctively, Lex put his arms around

her. Kendall pressed her body against him. Lex could feel the soft, pillowy swell of her breasts beneath her T-shirt and smell the sweet coconut lotion on her skin. A wave of pure physical longing swept over him, so violent he felt like crying himself. Instead he held Kendall as long as she wanted, then listened while she sank back on the pillows and poured out her heart to him about London, her homesickness, problems with Ivan and fears that she'd made a terrible mistake in her career.

'It was so much money,' she sobbed. 'And Ivan seemed so sure it was the right move. But now he's caught up with *Talent Quest*, and if my next album doesn't break every record in the book, there's no way Polydor will renew my contract. But of course, they're barely promoting it because they took such a bath on the first disc. You know how it is.'

Lex nodded sagely. Very few record labels these days stuck with their artists for the long haul.

'I'd quit and pay back the money if I could,' sniffed Kendall, 'but it's too late. No one in the US will touch me now.'

'I'm sure that's not true,' said Lex soothingly. 'You burned some bridges, but at the end of the day it's talent that matters. It's your voice.'

'You really think so?' Kendall brightened for a moment. Then she looked at him and said softly, 'Why are you so good to me, Lex?' Reaching up she stroked his cheek, slowly tracing a finger along the line of his lips.

Every nerve, every sinew in Lex's body buzzed into life. He'd wanted her so badly, and for so long, he hardly dared believe this was real.

'What do you want from me, Kendall?' he whispered.

In reply she sat up and pressed her lips to his. It was a

gentle kiss, more tender than passionate. Closing his eyes, Lex allowed the pleasure of it to sweep through him in a few seconds of purest joy. But as Kendall finally pulled away and lay back again, smiling, he found he felt not happy but profoundly uneasy. As if he were somehow being played for a fool.

'Will you stay with me today?' asked Kendall. 'We haven't talked properly in so long, Lex.'

'I don't know.' Lex hesitated. Quite apart from his work commitments, Leila might call at any minute. How the hell was he supposed to explain the fact that he was holed up at the Chateau with Kendall. 'I have to get back to the office at some point.'

'At least stay for lunch.' The desperation in Kendall's voice was painful. Whichever way he turned, Lex felt guilty. 'You can order room service and we'll have it on the terrace. *Please*, Lex. Just lunch.'

'OK,' he said, earning himself another kiss from Kendall as she bounded off the bed and into the bathroom. For a girl who thought she was dying an hour and a half ago, she seemed to have made a quite miraculous recovery.

Lex dialled down for two Cobb salads and a fruit plate. He would have a quick bite with Kendall, make sure she was OK, then drive straight to the office. Tonight, after work, he'd explain everything to Leila. Well, perhaps not *everything*. But enough for her to see that this was an emergency, something unexpected that he'd been forced to respond to in the heat of the moment.

When Kendall emerged onto the balcony, the moment got considerably hotter. She'd showered, but instead of dressing, had slipped into a barely there, shocking-pink La Perla silk robe. Beneath it Lex could clearly see the lace trim on her matching pink bra, and when she sat down and crossed her legs got more than a flash of her smooth, brown inner thighs.

'Ooo, salad,' she gushed, attacking her plate with gusto. 'My favourite.'

Lex, whose mouth seemed unaccountably to have turned to sandpaper, said nothing. After a few moments, Kendall reached across the table and took his hand. 'Is something the matter? I don't bite, you know.'

'I'm fine,' he said. 'Just . . . thinking.'

Pushing back her chair, Kendall walked barefoot to the other side of the tiny table and climbed up onto his lap. 'About what? You can tell me. We're friends, aren't we?'

'Of course we're friends,' stammered Lex. He could feel his erection growing beneath Kendall's bare legs and was sure she must be able to feel it too. As intoxicating as it was to touch her and have her in his arms, there was something jarring about her sudden need for physical contact. 'But this is . . . more than friendly. Wouldn't you say?'

Kendall threw back her head and laughed, which made her robe slip open even further. 'You're so coy! Funny, after all these years I never would have had you down as the prudish type. Aren't you attracted to me?'

'You know I am,' said Lex almost angrily. 'But I'm with someone. You know that too.'

'Only if you want to be,' said Kendall, leaning in to kiss him again. Just as she moved, something caught Lex's eye. On an opposite balcony, a few floors above them, a man was watching them. Too late Lex saw his Canon camera, its zoom lens pointed right at their table.

He sprang to his feet. 'Hey! HEY!' he yelled, pointing at the balcony. 'What the hell are you doing?' Unperturbed, the paparazzo kept snapping. Lex grabbed Kendall by the arm and dragged her back into the bedroom, drawing the curtains behind him.

'What the fuck is going on?' he demanded.

'Nothing,' Kendall said innocently. 'What do you mean?'

'The photographer,' said Lex, exasperated. 'You know what those pictures are gonna look like. They're gonna look like we're having an . . .' The words died on his lips as the penny dropped. 'Oh my God.' He backed away from her. 'You set this up, didn't you?'

'Set what up?' said Kendall.

'That's why you were all over me!' Lex warmed to his theme. 'Why you wanted to eat on the balcony. So the paparazzi you tipped off could get a good, clean shot. You staged this whole thing.'

Kendall pouted, belting her robe defensively around her waist. 'Don't be ridiculous. Paparazzi are part of my life, they always have been. You know that. Why would I *want* somebody to take pictures of you and me together?'

'I have no idea,' shouted Lex, who wasn't buying Kendall's butter-wouldn't-melt routine for a second. 'Maybe you want to screw things up for me and Leila. Or maybe you want to make Jack jealous.'

'I couldn't care less about Jack!' blurted Kendall hotly.

'All I know is you used me, and frankly, I don't give a shit why. I don't deserve that, Kendall. I came over here because I thought you were dying.'

'I thought so too!' insisted Kendall. But for the first time a hint of a blush had appeared on her cheeks and her eyes flickered with guilt.

'Bullshit,' said Lex. He looked at her with such loathing, such disgust, she couldn't help but feel ashamed. 'What kind of sociopath fakes a heart attack just so they can set up some bogus pictures? You make me sick.'

Lex strode furiously to the door. Kendall stood by the bed looking small and fragile, but Lex felt no sympathy. He'd always known she could be selfish and manipulative. But he'd never imagined she could be so calculatingly cruel, especially not to him. He felt as if someone had plunged a knife into his chest.

He hesitated in the doorway. 'Whoever it is whose attention you're trying to get, I hope it was worth it. Because you just lost a friend.'

Kendall said nothing, just stood and watched as the door slammed shut behind him.

Two days later, curled up under a blanket in the upper-class cabin of Virgin Atlantic Flight Twenty-Three to London, Kendall found it difficult to sleep. The pictures of her with Lex had been published on *TMZ* and Perez Hilton's website within hours, and by yesterday morning the story of her 'affair' was global news.

Sasha Dale, naturally, was delighted. Even better, Ivan had called her, frantically begging her to come home. 'I know I've pushed you away, Kendall. But I promise you'll be my number one priority if you come back to me.'

'What about Ava? And your "family commitments"?' The last two words dripped with sarcasm.

'I'll do whatever it takes to make it work,' pleaded Ivan. 'I need you, Kendall. I need you in my life and I need you in my bed. And I know deep down you need me too.'

'You'll have to pull your finger out with Polydor,' said Kendall. 'They're pissed as hell with me for coming out here. I need a manager who can defend me. A manager who actually gives a shit about my career.'

'I do give a shit,' said Ivan. 'When you get back here, I'll prove it. You're gonna be the biggest thing since Lady Gaga.'

As a strategy, the Lex pictures couldn't have gone better. Ivan had cracked. She was going home. But Kendall felt hideously guilty. The shame and sadness, knowing she'd betrayed Lex in the most manipulative and awful of ways, sat heavily in the pit of her stomach like a rock. She tried to tell herself that Lex would be OK. The ghastly Leila would doubtless forgive him. At the end of the day he hadn't actually *done* anything with Kendall, other than have lunch. He'd be able to explain and repair the relationship. But Kendall and Lex's friendship was damaged beyond repair, and for this she knew she had only herself to blame. The look of disgust on Lex's face as he left her hotel room would stay imprinted on Kendall's memory for a long, long time.

Still, she told herself, perhaps it was time to move on? As hard as it had been, this trip to LA had taught Kendall a lot of things. It had taught her you could never go back. The days when Jack Messenger had been her world and Lex Abrahams her rock were gone now, gone for ever. So was her close relationship with her mother and siblings. Kendall had made her choices and carved out her own path. Her only option now was to walk it.

Pulling the blanket more tightly around her shoulders, she slipped in her earplugs and pulled on her eye mask. Eventually she fell into a fitful sleep.

CHAPTER THIRTEEN

St Peter's Church in Upper Slaughter is widely considered one of the most beautiful in the Cotswolds. Built in the twelfth century of the same crumbling, lichened-grey stone that built the surrounding cottages and manor house, its small interior is packed with treasures from the past. Medieval tombs of knights and their ladies, brass memorials to local landowners or benefactors, some dating back to the 1300s yet all beautifully preserved. From the hand-carved, ivory lectern to the 700-year-old bell tower with its swinging ropes hanging down like rainbow-tipped bulrushes, everything about St Peter's spoke of the care and love of countless generations of villagers.

Walking down the nave with her Nikon camera slung around her neck, Catriona Charles was bowled over by the beauty of the place, the palpable sense of peace that hung in the air like incense. Unfortunately she was also bowled over by a chronic hangover, the kind that made it difficult to move or even breathe without succumbing to hideous nausea.

Needless to say, as she knocked back an endless stream

of gin and tonics last night, she'd completely forgotten about today's assignment to photograph the church for the parish's 900-year celebrations. When Reverend Timson had telephoned her at nine o'clock this morning to ask her to bring some extra lighting, Catriona answered the phone with a brusque, 'Whoever you are, piss off', then had to pretend it was a wrong number when the reverend called back later.

I must stop drinking, she thought glumly as she struggled to fix a temporary spotlight onto one of the stone saints above the side chapel. They didn't call gin 'mothers' ruin' for nothing. If she carried on at this rate, she'd ruin her business, such as it was. She'd already ruined her figure. This morning, staggering out of the shower, she'd counted four rolls of fat – *four* – on her belly, and been utterly horrified by the cellulite wasteland that was her arse. Her thighs looked like a pair of barrage balloons stuffed with lumpy porridge, and the hairy, formless calves underneath them weren't much better. A few more months and she'd have 'cankles', a condition Catriona only knew about from reading Rosie's old copies of *Heat* magazine, something else she needed to give up.

Her one consolation was that it was September at last, which meant a legitimate return to gardening cords and baggy, shapeless sweaters that hid a multitude of sins. Thank God the summer was finally over. What a nightmare it had been. As so often these days, it had been Hector who'd got the ball rolling with his arrest in Oxford back in June. Catriona's hope that a night in the cells might provide the short, sharp shock her thirteen-year-old son so badly needed proved to be ill-founded. She'd turned up at the magistrates' court to find a cheerily unrepentant Hector delighting in the flurry of media attention he'd caused by writing 'IVAN CHARLES IS A SAD WANKER' on the hallowed walls of Oxford's most beautiful medieval library.

'The *Daily Mail* said they'd pay me two hundred quid to talk about what a crap father Dad is,' Hector told Catriona happily as they drove home after his 'official warning'. 'I'm going to ring up the *Sun* and see if they'll give me more.'

'You're going to do no such thing,' said Catriona furiously. 'And any money you do have, saved or otherwise, I'm confiscating until I know you can be trusted with it.'

'You can't do that! That's stealing,' said Hector. 'That's against the law.'

'Oh, an expert on the law, are we now? And what do you call vandalism and fighting with a police officer, may I ask? *You're* the one who's just been had up in court, Hector. Never mind Dad's behaviour, what about yours? You're turning into a yob.'

'Yeah, well, it's better than turning into a lush,' Hector shot back. 'You only want my money so you can spend it on booze.'

Catriona had kept her cool and driven home in silence, sending Hector up to his room and ignoring his bellows of protest as she seized his PlayStation, Nintendo DS and two packets of Benson & Hedges from his sock drawer. 'You've made life miserable for everybody else,' she said firmly. 'Now you can bloody well see what it feels like.'

By supper time a grudging ceasefire had been reached between them, and Hector agreed to join his mother and sister for shepherd's pie and summer pudding. Unfortunately Ivan picked this exact moment to call and 'see how things were going'. Grabbing the phone, Hector had literally screamed at his father never, ever to contact him again and poor Rosie had fled the kitchen in tears.

Undeterred, Ivan had called back repeatedly over the next few days, offering whatever support he could to Hector and, when Hector wouldn't speak to him, to Cat. Clearly he felt helpless, being so far away, and stung by his son's rejection.

Catriona almost felt sorry for him. It was the first time since the divorce that she'd seen Ivan make any real effort to try and put things right with Hector, and she'd allowed herself to hope that perhaps a breakthrough might ultimately be possible. But then bloody Kendall Bryce went and got herself pictured romping with an old flame in LA, and Ivan scuttled back to her like a spider to its hole, dropping the kids yet again like two hot potatoes. They were back to square one.

From that point on, the summer went from bad to worse. Ivan and Kendall, reunited and very publicly back in love, were never out of the papers. Being force-fed a diet of Kendall's perfect, pert, twenty-five-year old body, draped over Ivan in a series of barely-there bikinis, didn't do wonders for Catriona's self-esteem. In August, Rosie had joined the two of them in St Tropez and Cat had to endure coverage of Kendall in the same minuscule bikinis, bonding with her daughter. Even that might have been bearable, had Hector gone too and given her a few weeks' precious peace, but of course he'd stayed at home in Burford, polishing up his bid for a place in the 2012 Olympic sulking squad. Was it really any wonder that Catriona had turned to drink?

'Ah, there you are, my dear, marvellous, marvellous.' Reverend Timson, a nervous mouse of a man with a bald pate so shiny you could see your face in it and delicate, veiny hands that jumped around like a puppet's whenever he spoke, scurried up to Catriona. 'How are things coming along? Are you almost finished with the pictures?'

'Er . . . not quite,' said Catriona, who had yet to take a single shot. Everything took longer through her hangover fog, and she had to sit down every few minutes and put her head between her knees so as not to be sick.

'Righto,' said the reverend, apparently not hearing her negative response. 'Marvellous. Because I was going to ask you if you'd pop over to the almshouses with me afterwards and take some portrait shots of the ladies who do the flowers? They're terribly kind, our flower ladies, and I know they'd want to be a part of St Nicholas's nine hundredth, you know. Nine hundredth! Goodness gracious. It's a long time, isn't it, eh? A long time.'

Not as long a time as this job is going to take me if you don't bugger off and let me get on with it, thought Catriona uncharitably. Reverend Timson's ceaseless chatter was like having a tiny woodpecker lodged inside her skull. She would cheerfully have sold her soul for two Alka-Seltzers and a soft bed.

'I'll probably need another hour in the church at least,' she mumbled apologetically. 'The exterior shots shouldn't take as long. But it's worth getting it . . . right.' At the last word, she covered her mouth with her hand. The nausea had come out of nowhere, but she was suddenly very afraid she might throw up all over the tomb of the Delaney family.

'Are you quite all right, my dear?' asked the vicar. 'You don't look terribly well.'

'I'm fine,' said Catriona, darting for the door. 'I just need to get a . . . tripod . . . from the car.'

Two hours later, Catriona drove home feeling lower than she had in weeks. Being sick in the bushes beside her car was beyond shaming. She was sure the flower ladies must have smelled it on her breath, or picked up what a state she was in from her matted, sweaty hair and generally dishevelled appearance. How could she come to such a beautiful, sacred place on such a glorious day and stagger around like a drunken teenager?

Back home, she was relieved to find that both the children were out. Running upstairs to the bathroom, she was sick again. Then she stripped off her clothes and plunged under a cold shower, gasping for breath as the icy jets stung her skin back to life. She cleaned her teeth twice, put on a clean T-shirt and baggy sweatpants, and finally downed the Alka-Seltzer she'd been dreaming of all day before collapsing on the bed. Grabbing last month's *Red* magazine, she turned to the advertisement in the back she'd noticed a few weeks ago and, with a shaking hand, dialled the number.

'Hello? Is that the women's alcohol helpline?'

'Mum? What are you doing?'

Catriona dropped the phone like a lump of hot coal. Rosie, looking flushed and happy in grass-stained jodhpurs and a Ned Williams UK Tour T-shirt, stood hovering in the doorway.

'I thought you had a job today?'

'I did,' said Catriona, feeling faint with relief that Rosie hadn't heard who she was calling. 'I just got back. How was school?'

'Fine. Oh, the school secretary from Burford High rang again. Hector didn't show up to class today. Surprise, surprise.'

Catriona sighed. 'OK.' Closing her eyes, she lay back on the pillow. She truly didn't have the energy for another battle with Hector today. Perhaps it was time to give up on school, stop his allowance money and make him get a Saturday job?

'You look tired, Mum,' said Rosie, drawing the bedroom curtains. 'Have a rest. I'll come and wake you up at suppertime. I'm sure Hector'll be back by then.'

Ivan sat in the editing booth, headphones over his ears, nodding encouragement at Kendall. Not that she needed it. Standing barefoot in the studio, looking tiny in her favourite Hudson jeans and a plain white T-shirt, with her hair pulled back off her face in a messy bun, she was belting out the title track of her soon-to-be-released album *Flame* as if she were singing live at the O2. Even after all this time, it astonished Ivan to hear that deep, powerful voice surging out of Kendall's doll-like frame. If this album bombed, it wouldn't be for lack of vocal talent.

But it wouldn't bomb. With the dark days of the summer and last year's lacklustre sales behind them, Ivan had moved mountains to prove to Kendall that she was his priority, and to Polydor that if they wanted to see a return on their forty-million-dollar investment, they needed to start thinking strategically about promotion. With all twelve of the album tracks now laid down, and four singles chosen, the only production work left to do was the remixes. Ivan had come up with the inspired idea of a duet with Ava Bentley.

'It's perfect,' he told Kendall. 'You have the brand and the international profile. She's fresh, with a big likeability factor. Plus *Talent Quest* has over twelve million viewers. If even a fraction of those buy the duet single, it'll have a major knock-on effect for your overall album sales. And the press'll be insane.'

Slightly to his surprise, given Kendall's furious jealousy and resentment about Ava all year, she hadn't needed much persuasion. 'It's a good idea,' she told him. 'Just as long as you don't turn into Ava's babysitter when we come to promote it. You're *my* manager, not hers.'

To his even greater surprise, when Ivan sneaked a terrified Ava into the Soho Recording Studios after *Talent Quest* rehearsals wrapped – contestants were strictly forbidden to make any recordings or enter into any commercial deals until the show was over – Kendall actually seemed to like her, wrapping an arm around the teenager's quaking shoulders as she led her to the mic, patiently waiting for Ava to get her confidence back after each fluffed cue or missed note.

'She's sweet,' Kendall told Ivan during a snack break, once Ava had disappeared to the loo. 'I think she's kinda star-struck.'

'Why wouldn't she be?' said Ivan, slipping a hand beneath Kendall's T-shirt and up her bare back. 'You're already a legend. When this album drops you're gonna be even bigger. Right now, Ava's just a kid from Yorkshire.'

While Kendall finished her vocals on the other side of the glass, Ava came and sat with Ivan in the mixing booth. 'I took another packet of crisps from the kitchen,' she said shyly. 'I hope that's all right.' In a floor-length white cotton skirt from Matalan and a flowery, long-sleeved Miss Selfridge blouse, she looked far younger than her seventeen years, and as timid as a little vole.

'Of course it's all right,' said Ivan. 'You must be starving.'

He'd whisked her away from the ITV studios so fast there'd been no time for lunch. It was a bold move, bringing Ava here to record with Kendall, but if anyone had seen them, Ivan figured he could easily cover his tracks. He'd brought Ava along as a friend, to watch Kendall at work. It wasn't as if a deal had been signed for these duets, or any money had changed hands. No one need know that the two girls had actually sung together.

'She's amazing, isn't she?' said Ava, gazing at Kendall through the glass.

'She is,' said Ivan, truthfully. Since Kendall's return from LA in a blaze of publicity, things had been going better between them. Sexually the relationship had been great before, but Kendall's 'dalliance' with Lex had reawakened Ivan's jealousy, and now their love life was more explosive than ever. Between recording sessions, Ivan had taken her away on the mini-break she'd been angling for for months, stocking up on an array of lavishly inventive sex toys in

Soho the day before. For forty-eight hours, he and Kendall had remained locked in their suite at the Hampshire Four Seasons while Ivan filmed them indulging in every sexual fantasy either of them could imagine. When they'd finally staggered down to breakfast on day three, dishevelled and flushed and still reeking of sex, families seated nearby glared disapprovingly and ushered their children to the other side of the restaurant.

Things were better on the home front too. Kendall, less tense now that Ivan had wangled a decent publicity and promotion spend out of Polydor for her new album, agreed to go down to St Tropez with Rosie for a few days in the summer. She combined the trip with work, promoting her album *Flame* on NRJ, the local radio station and recording an interview for Canal Plus. But she also made a real effort to connect with Rosie, taking her on endless shopping and beach trips, forcing Ivan to let her try the jet skis, much to Ivan's paternal panic and Rosie's teenage delight. For the first time, Ivan began to imagine the possibility of a proper future with Kendall. Perhaps somewhere between all the tours and promotion and parties and TV shows, they could forge a real life together?

There were still plenty of obstacles to such a scenario, not least of them Hector, whose fury after Ivan and Kendall got back together in June seemed to have grown exponentially. It had reached the point where he refused to speak to his sister for more than a month, just because Rosie had committed the crime of going on holiday with her father. As good as things were with Kendall, Ivan still felt immense guilt about the divorce. When he thought about Hector as a little boy, how sweet and loving he'd been, Ivan's adoring shadow, it brought tears to his eyes. If Ivan ever married Kendall, that little boy would be lost to him for ever.

A car arrived to pick up Ava and take her back to the hotel where she and the other *Talent Quest* contestants were staying. Kendall finished the last tweaks to her vocals and slipped off her headphones, smiling at Ivan for approval.

'Brilliant,' he mouthed through the glass then, looking at his watch, added, 'drink?'

They had dinner with Polydor's CEO tonight at Zuma. If he were lucky, and Kendall's good mood held, Ivan just about had time to loosen her up with a couple of vodkas then take her back home for some sex beforehand. The thought of Kendall's beautiful, full round breasts filling his hands, and her back arching with pleasure as he fucked her from behind, pushed all other thoughts out of Ivan's mind. It was time to go.

Rosie woke her mother at seven o'clock for supper. Hector still wasn't home.

'He probably went over to Harry's to play Warcraft,' said Rosie, scooping deliciously stodgy pasta in cheese sauce onto Catriona's plate. 'Maybe he ate there.'

'Maybe,' said Catriona. She'd reached the point in her hangover where she felt ravenously hungry, and gratefully wolfed down two helpings of Rosie's pasta before she thought much more about it. It was only as she cleared away and began loading the dishwasher that she thought perhaps she ought to call Harry's mother over in Little Barrington.

'Hector? No, he hasn't been here. Harry did mention he wasn't at school, though.'

At this point it surprised Catriona that Hector's friends still felt his truancy worth mentioning. It would be bigger news if Hector *had* been at school. Still, it was unlike him not to come home in the afternoons, led by his stomach if nothing else, and a desire to spend as much time as possible locked in his room, glued to Facebook. If he did have plans, he always called.

She tried his mobile, but it was switched off. This in itself wasn't unusual. He was always forgetting to charge the thing and running out of batteries. Even so, Catriona felt uneasy. She called more of his friends, working her way down the school contact list, her anxiety growing with each conversation. No, they hadn't seen Hector. No, he hadn't mentioned any particular plans tonight. Eventually it emerged that none of the Burford High kids had even seen him at the bus stop that morning, or smoking outside the gates before school. It was as if he'd walked out of the house that morning and vanished.

At 9.15 p.m., feeling slightly foolish but not sure what else to do, Catriona called the police. 'He didn't go to school this morning, and nobody's seen him since he left the house.' The sergeant on the other end of the line was sympathetic and reassuring. Thirteen-year-olds did this sort of thing a lot. He might be in the cinema somewhere with his phone off, or at an arcade. Chances are he'll walk in the door in an hour or so, wondering what all the fuss is about.

Catriona hung up and tried to relax, turning on an old episode of *NCIS* to watch with Rosie. But she couldn't concentrate, and at ten o'clock went up to Hector's room, hoping to find some sort of clue as to his whereabouts.

As usual the bedroom was a tip, clothes everywhere. Dirty football boots had shed clumps of mud all over the carpet and bed, and drawers were left hanging open, like gaping mouths appalled at the squalor in which teenage boys choose to live. Catriona glanced over at Hector's desk, piled high with empty crisp wrappers and half-eaten crusts of sandwiches. She tried switching on his computer, but didn't know the password. Maybe Rosie would know it?

Pulling open a drawer, she found a scrunched-up piece of paper with a list scrawled on it in biro.

'Shorts, T-shirt, Nintendo, charger, trainers . . .'

It's a packing list, thought Catriona. *But why would he be packing?* Then she saw the last three items and her blood ran cold. 'Cash (mum office?). Present for J. Passport.'

Passport? Catriona ran to her office, heart pounding, and opened the drawer on her dresser where she kept the family passports and important documents. *Please don't let it be gone. Please, please don't let it be gone.*

Ivan scooped Kendall up into his arms and carried her into the bedroom.

'You were amazing tonight,' he whispered, laying her down on the bed and climbing on top of her, peeling down the shoulder straps of her dress.

'You think so?' giggled Kendall, her pupils already dilating with desire at the prospect of what was to come. The quickie they'd had before dinner had been rough and exciting. Ivan had taken her on the living-room floor, using a small vibrator in her ass at the same time as he fucked her, giving Kendall a terrifically intense orgasm. She could hardly wait for round two.

'Wait there,' he whispered, springing up and darting out of the room. Kendall lay back and wriggled out of her dress, wondering which toys or props he was going to fetch for her this time. Still in her knickers and bra – she wanted to leave him something to take off – she started to touch herself, building her excitement but being careful not to let herself get too close to the edge. Ivan would be furious if she came without him.

After five minutes, she was starting to feel furious herself. Where *was* he? Just when she was about to get up and go and find him and drag him back to bed, Ivan came back in looking ashen.

'It's Hector,' he said dully.

'Again?' asked Kendall. But it wasn't a hostile question. She could see the misery on Ivan's face. 'What's he done now?'

'He's gone missing. Run away, I don't know. He's taken his passport and a few hundred quid in cash,' said Ivan. 'The police are at the house now. They've got people out looking for him.'

Kendall walked over and put her arms around him. She knew that Hector's hostility towards her was a sticking point in her and Ivan's relationship. If she proved herself sensitive and mature now, perhaps that would change. 'Try not to worry too much,' she said gently. 'I'm sure they'll find him. Lots of teenagers do this sort of thing. I'll bet you anything Catriona gets a phone call as soon as the money runs out.'

'I'll have to go down there in the morning,' he said bleakly. 'Talk to the police. Check on Rosie.' He almost said 'and Cat', but wisely thought better of it.

'Of course,' said Kendall, hugging him. 'I'll come with you if you like.'

Ivan hugged her back tightly, grateful that for once she wasn't making a scene. 'Thanks, sweetheart, but I should go alone. It's a family thing. Besides,' he added hastily, watching Kendall's face fall, 'there's always a chance Hector might show up here. Someone should hold the fort, just in case.'

They both knew that there was zero chance of Hector turning up on his father's doorstep. And that if, by some miracle, he did, one glimpse of Kendall would be enough to send him running for the hills. Kendall's own theory was that half the reason the boy played up was to force his parents back together. With every Hector-induced crisis, Ivan was sucked back into the vortex of his old life, back to Catriona, while Kendall was the one left abandoned.

In the past, the strategy had worked perfectly. Indeed, last time she and Ivan had almost broken up over it. But this time Kendall bit her tongue. *I refuse to be outsmarted by a thirteen-year-old boy. I will keep my cool and wait for the storm to pass.*

'OK,' she said, kissing Ivan on the lips and leading him back to bed. 'I understand. But do try and get some sleep now, darling. There's nothing you can do tonight. And you never know, he may even have turned up by morning.'

Hector didn't turn up by morning. Or the next morning. Or the next.

Inevitably the press got wind of the story that Ivan Charles's troubled teenage son had been reported missing, and soon Hector's picture was appearing on the front page of national newspapers. Catriona's house in Burford morphed into Piccadilly Circus, with friends and neighbours and parents from the school all 'dropping in' to see what they could do to help. Ned Williams was an almost constant presence, much to Ivan's annoyance, but there was little he could do if Catriona wanted him there. Even more unnerving from Ivan's point of view were the daily calls from Jack Messenger, checking in on Cat and for updates on Hector. It hadn't occurred to Ivan that Catriona might have kept in touch with Jack after the divorce, still less that the two of them could become close. He wanted to scream at everyone to get out of his house and to leave his bloody wife alone. Except that it wasn't his house, and Catriona wasn't his wife, all of which added to his already sky-high stress levels.

Meanwhile, the police's early sanguine optimism about

Hector's likely return had gradually been replaced by a much more sober concern for his wellbeing. Airports, ports and train stations had all been on high alert for over seventy-two hours now, but no one had seen the boy since a CCTV camera picked up a grainy image of what looked to be Hector near a bus stop in Oxford early on Tuesday morning. Meanwhile, the police began to focus their suspicions on the mystery 'J' for whom Hector had intended to buy a present before he disappeared, trawling his computer for any friends or contacts whose names began with that initial and interviewing every Jenny, Jason and Jim at Burford High. The worst moment for Catriona came when Detective Inspector Rathers, the officer in charge of the case, suggested that 'J' might not be a real friend at all, but an older man who had groomed Hector on Facebook using an assumed identity.

'Often these kids think they're going to meet a girl, or a mate their own age, but the truth is they have no idea who set up half these profiles or what their motives might be.'

Catriona slumped down on a kitchen chair. Ivan rested a comforting hand on her shoulder and asked bluntly, 'And what might their motives be? Sexual? Violent?'

'Sometimes,' said DI Rathers seriously. 'In your case we should consider the possibility that there might be a financial motive involved. Although, if that were the case and someone had snatched your son, we'd have expected a kidnapper to have revealed their demands by now. Of course, all this is just speculation, Mrs Charles,' he added. Poor Catriona looked as if she might be about to faint at any moment. 'He could just as easily have gone to meet up with a girl; the two of them might have panicked because of all the media coverage and decided to lie low.'

On Friday afternoon, after a perfunctory call to Kendall,

Ivan dropped Rosie off at a friend's house for the weekend. The Burford house was a zoo, with police tramping up and down the stairs day and night and photographers hanging from every nearby tree or rooftop. It didn't make sense for Rosie to live cooped up there like a prisoner, and both Ivan and Cat struggled to control their anxiety around her.

'Promise you'll call me if you hear anything, Daddy. Anything at all, even bad news.' As Rosie got out of the car, her eyes filled with tears.

'I promise,' said Ivan, kissing her. 'And there won't be any bad news. You know your brother, he's the proverbial bad penny. He'll turn up.'

'Do you think . . . do you think me making friends with Kendall in the summer might have been the last straw?' Rosie asked, her lower lip wobbling with emotion. 'He was different after I came back from France. So angry.'

'No,' said Ivan firmly. 'You had nothing to do with this, Rose. Nothing. It's me he's angry with, not you.'

As always on his rare trips to Oxfordshire, Ivan was booked in at Burford House, a cosy, family-run hotel in a charming Tudor building on the high street. He drove back there now to shower and change before walking over to Catriona's for supper and their first totally private chat in four days.

He found Catriona in the kitchen, sitting at the table staring blankly at the wall. In front of her were a bowl of potatoes that she'd begun to peel, then forgotten about, overwhelmed by desperate thoughts about her son.

'I'll do that,' said Ivan quietly, sitting down next to her. Catriona looked up, startled. She hadn't even recognized that he'd come in. 'Any news since I've been gone?'

She shook her head. 'Nothing.'

For a while they sat together in silence, Ivan peeling, Catriona staring numbly ahead. Eventually Catriona spoke.

'DI Rathers was asking me more questions this afternoon, about the morning Hector left and the evening before. He said that anything I remembered, anything I could tell them about Hector's state of mind might be vitally important.' She started to cry. 'But I couldn't tell them anything, Ivan. I was so blotto the night before, I doubt I'd have noticed if Hector had come home with a sub-machine-gun under his arm. And the morning he left, I was out cold. I didn't even . . . I didn't even say goodbye to him.'

Ivan got up and pulled her to her feet, hugging her tightly. He felt the tears stinging his own eyes. 'Cat, you have to stop this. Wherever Hector went, he'd been planning it for days, maybe even weeks. You having a few drinks had nothing to do with it.'

'It wasn't a few drinks,' Cat sobbed. 'I was blind drunk, Ivan. What if I never see him again?'

'You will see him again,' Ivan looked at her sternly. 'They're going to find him, darling. Look at me. They are *going* to find him.'

Catriona looked at Ivan through a haze of tears. It was amazing how he could be so strong in some things, and so weak in others. She realized, slightly to her own surprise, that she was glad he was here.

He started to stroke her hair, the way a father might pet a child. 'Why don't I stay here tonight? In the guest room, obviously. I don't like leaving you here alone.'

'I'm used to being alone,' said Cat, not to make him feel guilty but because it was the truth. 'Besides, I don't suppose Kendall would be too pleased about it.'

'Kendall understands,' said Ivan brusquely. He did not want to think about Kendall. Even hearing Catriona say her name felt wrong and uncomfortable. Here, in this house with his wife, the woman he'd spent half his life with,

Kendall didn't exist. None of his life in London existed. 'Anyway it's not just for you, it's for me too. I don't want to be alone. Not tonight.'

He moved closer. For one terrifying, thrilling moment, Catriona thought he might be about to kiss her. *Did she want him to?* Before she had an answer to the question he backed away almost shyly and sat back down at the table. 'Only if you feel comfortable, of course,' he mumbled, picking up another potato and staring at it intently, avoiding eye contact. 'I wouldn't want to impose.'

Catriona smiled. It was a long time since she'd seen this side to Ivan. The kindness, but also the neediness, the lost little boy wanting his mother. 'You're not imposing. Of course you can stay.'

It was a bittersweet evening. Catriona fried up some mince, onions, garlic and home-grown tomatoes and made a delicious scratch shepherd's pie. While she was cooking, Ivan set the table, pouring a glass of red wine for himself and a Diet Coke for Catriona at her request, and chatting about anything and everything other than Hector. Old friends, anecdotes from their Oxford days that had both of them alternately laughing and gasping with horror at what complete idiots they'd been back then. It felt good to be distracted. But every few minutes the laughter would stop, and one or other of them would fall silent, their minds drawn inexorably back to Hector and the hideous uncertainties of the present.

In the end, after supper, Ivan suggested getting out some of the old photo albums and looking at pictures of Hector and Rosie as babies. 'Are you mad?' said Catriona. 'I'm barely holding it together as it is.' But to her surprise she found flipping through the pages immensely calming. Anything to push out the image of Hector locked up in some paedophile's cellar somewhere, or lying cold and dead in a ditch.

At eleven o'clock, leaving Cat with the pictures, Ivan went into the kitchen to make them both some hot chocolate. Opening the larder, he found shelves stuffed with chef's ingredients, herbs and spices and an endless bottled array of pickles and chutneys and jams, as well as the usual staples of family life: Coco Pops, Hobnobs, giant multipacks of Mini Cheddars, Hector's favourite. He thought about his and Kendall's kitchen in Cheyne Walk, with its unused chrome appliances and bare cupboards. All they had in the fridge was champagne and Kendall's Essie nail polish. All of a sudden he felt unbearably lonely.

Sloshing milk into a Le Creuset pan and sticking it on the hot ring of the Aga to boil, he filled two mugs with chocolate powder and looked around the room. It was smaller and far less grand than the kitchen at The Rookery, but Cat had managed to make it bright and homely, as warm and welcoming as a womb. Photographs of the children and examples of their childhood artwork were everywhere, as well as some of Catriona's own more recent work. A jug of fading peonies littered petals onto the scratched farmhouse table, and jaunty, mismatched china in a rainbow of colours hung from hooks on the ceiling above Ivan's head. *Hector must have been mad to want to run away from here*, thought Ivan. *I must have been mad.*

Through the half-open door he watched Catriona, poring lovingly over the pictures of their children. She'd gained some weight and looked a mess in an old, holey brown cardigan, with her tangled hair sticking out at all angles, the result of running her hands through it so many times. But there was still something luminous about her. Her flushed, youthful skin, soulful blue eyes, but most of all the immense kindness and warmth that seemed to seep out of her pores like sap oozing from a tree. It struck Ivan then like a bolt from the blue.

I still love her.

'Ivan!' She spun around suddenly. 'The milk! It's boiling over, I can hear it.'

'Oh! Shit.' Ivan grabbed the pan, scalding his wrist with bubbling white liquid. 'Fuck!'

Just then the phone rang. Ivan and Catriona stared at each other for a second in panic – at eleven at night, this wasn't a social call – then Catriona literally dived on the receiver.

'Hello?'

'Cat. How are you?' Jack Messenger's voice seemed to come from another world. Languid, happy, relaxed.

It wasn't the police, calling to say they'd found a body.

It wasn't Hector, calling to say he was coming home.

Relief and despair landed a double punch to Catriona's stomach so violent she had to sit down. 'Jack. Hi.' She shook her head at Ivan, who had a face like fury. *What the fuck was Messenger doing calling at this time of night? How selfish could he possibly be?* 'I'm OK,' lied Catriona. 'I was just going to bed.'

'Well before you do,' said Jack, 'I have someone here who'd like to talk to you.'

There was a crackle on the end of the line. Then Catriona heard the most wonderful, miraculous two words in the world. 'Hello, Mum.'

CHAPTER FOURTEEN

'Oh my God. Oh my GOD. Oh my actual GOD!'

Hector Charles turned fully around to stare at the gold hot-pants-wearing blonde twins rollerblading past him on the Santa Monica bike path. Unfortunately he himself was on a bike at the time and came within a hair's breadth of ploughing into a young mother jogging with her stroller.

'Moron!' yelled the mother. 'Look where you're going!'

Jack Messenger pulled his godson aside. 'They're not worth getting killed for, you know,' he grinned.

'You wouldn't say that if you lived in Burford,' sighed Hector. 'This place is amazing. I'm never going home.'

The relief Jack felt when Hector had turned up on his doorstep six days ago was hard to describe. He'd spoken to Catriona almost every day since the boy had gone missing, and though he'd always been supportive and encouraging, privately he'd begun to think that perhaps the worst really *had* happened. So when the familiar freckled, dirty, mischievous face appeared on his front porch, a little older than when Jack had last seen him but otherwise not much changed, he'd been too overjoyed even to be angry.

He had, however, insisted that Hector call his parents immediately. 'You do realize they've been out of their minds with worry?'

'Mum has, you mean,' said Hector bitterly.

'They both have,' said Jack firmly. Much as he hated Ivan, he knew from Cat just how torn up he was about Hector's disappearance. 'And Rosie. You've had half the British police force out looking for you, you know. Your face is on an Interpol alert.'

'Cool,' said Hector. It struck Jack what a young thirteen-year-old he was. Almost as if his development had been arrested at age eleven, the year his father walked out.

'It's not "cool",' said Jack. 'You paid for that plane ticket with Ned Williams's credit card, which you *stole*.'

'I didn't steal it. I borrowed it,' said Hector breezily. 'Anyway, Ned won't mind. He's famous, he's got loads of money. He didn't even notice I'd used the card, did he?'

This was true, although Jack suspected it owed more to Ned Williams's scatterbrained lifestyle than his groaning bank balance.

'Call it what you like,' he said firmly, 'it's still fraud. And what about the cash you nicked from your mother's purse?'

'What about it?' said Hector defiantly.

His conversation with Catriona was emotional. When Ivan came on the line, Hector vehemently refused to talk to him, then ended up screaming that he refused to come back to England while his father was still living with 'that bitch' and stormed off into Jack's garden to roll a cigarette.

'Give him time,' Jack told Catriona when she came back on the line. 'He's welcome to stay with me for a while until he gets his head together. I'll put him to work at JSM, making the tea or something.'

Ivan had been all for dragging the boy onto the next

plane by the scruff of his neck to begin his long round of apologies: to his family, to the police who'd wasted valuable time looking for him, to his school. 'He needs to learn that actions have consequences. Besides, things are bad enough between Hector and me without bloody Jack sitting on his shoulder pouring poison into his ear, telling him what a shit I am.'

'Jack wouldn't do that,' said Catriona. 'He loves Hector.' She wasn't wild on the idea of Hector staying on in LA either. So they'd agreed a compromise. Hector could spend a few days with Jack, then Catriona would fly out alone, talk to him, and bring him back.

That had been almost a week ago. Catriona's plane was due to land at three o'clock tomorrow afternoon, and though Hector was looking forward to seeing her, he was still adamant that he wasn't going to go back to England.

'How about lunch at Johnny Rockets?' he asked his godfather. 'It'll be like the condemned men's last meal, before Mum shows up and makes me eat disgusting healthy stuff.'

'Sorry, mate,' said Jack. 'I've got to stop by the office. I thought we could go out this evening, though. Land of the Greeks are performing at The Viper Room. I could take you backstage afterwards, meet the guys. Of course, if you've already made other plans . . .'

'No!' Hector interrupted hastily. 'No, no, no. I'd love to go.'

A rock concert! At The Viper Room! With backstage passes!

It was official. Jack Messenger was the coolest godfather in the world.

On a busy stretch of the Sunset Strip in West Hollywood, the iconic all-black façade of The Viper Room sat perched like a sleepy crow in the moonlight.

Despite having a music manager for a father, Hector Charles had never been anywhere remotely so cool in his short life. Following Jack into the hallowed, triangular auditorium where River Phoenix famously died of an overdose on Halloween night in 1993, the boy's eyes were on stalks.

'You wanna hear a cool story?' Jack asked him, strolling behind the closed bar and helping himself to two Diet Cokes.

Hector nodded enthusiastically.

'You know who Adam Duritz is?'

'Sure. Lead singer of Counting Crows.'

'Exactly. After their first album came out, Adam got so sick of the fame and the pressure, he came and worked here as a barman. For six months. Isn't that wild?'

'Totally,' said Hector, who was rapidly becoming au fait with LA speak.

A geeky twenty-something, in skinny jeans and a faded Labatt's beer T-shirt, tapped Jack on the shoulder. 'Hey, man. How's it going? Is there a long line out on Sunset yet?'

'Ben, hi. Yeah, looks like we're gonna be standing room only. This is my godson, Hector, by the way. He wanted to come and see you guys play.'

'Hey, Hector. You wanna come backstage, meet the guys? I'll bet Jesse'll let you have a go on his guitar if you're nice to him.'

'You're . . . you're Ben Braemar,' Hector stammered.

'Last time I checked,' laughed Ben, winking at Jack and ushering an ecstatic Hector through the 'Artists Only' door.

Thirty minutes later, Hector and Jack watched from the front row as the Greeks powered through their short, eight-song set. Jack was gratified by how much the group had grown in confidence as live performers since he'd first signed them, but without straining at the choke lead to play ever bigger, more commercial venues. The boys from Detroit had no desire to stray from their indie roots, which made them both exciting to brand and market and a dream to manage versus the fame-hungry, bubble-gum pop acts that had long been Jack's bread and butter.

Shaking his floppy hair to the deafening *boom, boom* of Lionel Scree on the drums, at one with the sweating, pulsing, universally black-clad fans behind him, Hector Charles was like a boy transformed. Jack didn't need to ask him how he felt. The kid was clearly having the time of his life.

Later, on the short drive west back to Brentwood, he barely drew breath about how 'awesome' it all was. 'Jesse showed me how to do three chords, and then he and Lionel were playing rock paper scissors and they started fighting with each other, not really serious you know, just fooling around, and they were rolling on the floor laughing and it was *so* cool. And then Ben told them to grow up and they all signed my back in indelible marker, look.' He lifted up his T-shirt proudly. 'Can you take a photo later, in case it fades before I have to leave? I seriously wish I didn't have to leave.'

Jack smiled. 'You wanna be in a rock band now, huh? Don't tell your mother I encouraged you.'

'Oh no,' said Hector. 'I could never be in a band. I'm crap at music. But I'd love to do what you do. You know. Schmooze.'

Jack burst out laughing. 'Is that what you think I do for a living? Schmooze?'

Hector shrugged. 'Kind of. Yeah.'

If you're anything like your father, thought Jack, *you'll make a world-class schmoozer.*

What on earth would poor Catriona do then?

* * *

At tea time the next day, Catriona walked through LAX feeling as nervous as a teenager on her first date. Which was perfectly ridiculous, of course. By rights it was Hector who ought to feel nervous, not to mention contrite, at the prospect of seeing her. What could be more pathetic than being afraid of confronting your own child?

It didn't help that she was here, on foreign turf. She tried to remember the last time she'd been to America. It must have been for a Jester thing. Oh yes, one of Ivan's classical acts, a tenor, had done a live show in Madison Square Gardens and Ivan had dragged her along. That must have been over a decade ago, back when he still wanted her to travel with him. *Back when I was slim and pretty and young*, she thought sadly. Although actually, coming through customs at LAX made her feel rather better on the weight front. She'd expected LA to be crawling with improbably proportioned Barbie-doll women with stuck-on silicone tits and hair extensions. In fact, although she'd spotted a few of those, most people seemed to be quite enormously fat, especially the women her age. Europeans looked down on Americans for their obesity, but it seemed to Catriona that Americans had got fatness right. None of the hefty ladies in front of her in the queue looked remotely embarrassed about their extra pounds. Most were married to similarly vast men, and they all seemed perfectly happy, chattering away, the wives reapplying their lipstick with as much confidence as Marilyn Monroe. *Not like me, skulking around like a sad old sack of potatoes*, thought Catriona.

'Cat!'

Jack Messenger's was the first face she saw when she emerged into the Arrivals hall. He looked blond and tanned, a little more lined around the eyes than the last time she'd seen him, but still preposterously handsome in that awkward, professorial way of his.

'Hi, Jack, darling.' She hugged him, then pulled back, suddenly realising that her breath was probably off after eleven hours on an aeroplane. 'I can't tell you how sorry I am for all this trouble.'

'What trouble?' beamed Jack. She'd forgotten what an incredible smile he had. Since Sonya died she'd seen it so rarely, but when he turned it on it was like a lighthouse beacon. 'Your son is an absolute riot. I haven't had so much fun in years.'

Catriona tried to equate the sullen, embittered teenager she'd lived with for the past two years with the word 'fun' and failed utterly.

'*And* I get to see you, here in LA of all places. How many years have I been trying to drag you out here, huh? The way I see it, Hector did me a favour.'

'How is he?' Cat asked warily. 'Is he waiting at home?'

'No, he's out. I thought you and I should talk privately before he got back. I'll fill you in in the car.'

They drove to Jack's home, Catriona fighting back her tiredness to focus on what Jack was telling her. Not that any of it was news. Hector resented Ivan and in particular his relationship with Kendall. He felt his father had been 'stolen' from him, and was angry because he felt powerless to stop the break-up of his family. 'A lot of the anger and acting out he projects onto you is really aimed at himself. He feels like he's a disappointment.'

'Well he is, when he pulls stunts like this,' said Catriona, exasperated.

Jack reached over and put a comforting hand on her knee. 'I know you've been through hell. But I don't think he's trying to hurt you. This stuff with Ivan is complicated. Part of him still looks up to his father hugely, but there's a resentment there. Like 'how come Dad's so successful; how come he gets the career and the fame and the money and the beautiful girl, and I get nothing?' At least some of Hector's obsessive hatred of Kendall is down to straightforward sexual jealousy, in my opinion. The kid fancies her, and he hates himself for it.'

Catriona winced as if someone had just squirted lemon juice in her eyes. Jack was probably right, but it was hardly the most tactful thing to say, to her of all people. If Kendall was 'the beautiful girl', what did that make her? Then again, Jack had never been one for soft-soaping things. In many ways his honesty was part of his charm.

At last they pulled in to the driveway. Catriona gasped with pleasure. 'Oh, Jack, it's gorgeous. It's not what I imagined at all. Just look at the *garden!* It's almost like the countryside.'

'Sonya designed the garden,' he smiled proudly. 'The house is all her too. You'll see when you get inside. I'm just the lucky bastard who gets to live here.'

The house was indeed stunning, and very feminine, with all its white wood and light and soft, floral accents. As for the guest room where Catriona would be sleeping, it was like something out of a fairytale, complete with its own wisteria-covered terrace and a wildly romantic four-poster bed. Throwing open the French windows, she was entranced to see a bright orange and blue hummingbird hovering over a honeysuckle flower.

'Oh, Jack,' she sighed, drinking in the sunlight and the deep lapis blue of the sky. 'This is heaven. No wonder Hector wants to stay.'

Jack left her to unpack. Cat hung her meagre collection of baggy, shapeless clothes in the closet and lay back on the bed for a moment's rest.

When she woke it was dark. The windows were still open, and there was a distinct chill in the air. For a second she felt completely disoriented, with no idea where she was. Then the shadowy forms of the room reasserted themselves and she remembered. *Jack. LA. Hector.*

She came downstairs to the sound of whoops and yells coming from the sitting room. Jack and Hector both had their backs to her and were leaping around in front of the television screen, waving their arms around like a couple of lunatics.

'No way! You jammy git,' said Hector, elbowing his godfather to one side. 'I can't believe you made that jump.'

'Watch and learn, kid,' said Jack. 'Watch and learn.'

'What on earth are you doing?'

Catriona's voice made them both spin around.

'PlayStation Kinect,' said Hector, a huge smile plastered across his face. 'It's awesome. It's like Wii but way better. D'you want to play?'

'Me? Oh no. No no no. I'm not . . . no.'

'Come on,' said Jack, taking her hand and pulling her over. 'You can take my spot. I'm too good for him anyway.'

'As if!' snorted Hector.

'You use your body as the controller,' explained Jack. 'The icon on the screen will follow your movements.'

'What's an icon?'

Hector rolled his eyes. 'It's the little man on the screen, Mummy. You're that guy, on the raft on the right. I'm the guy on the left. You're racing me down the rapids and trying to stay afloat, OK? Go!'

The next thing Catriona knew, she too was hopping around as if she had St Vitus's dance, and flailing her arms like a deranged air-traffic controller. But within a few minutes she found her embarrassment fading. Hector was

244

right. This *was* fun. Best of all, it was fun he was willing to share with her, fun they were having together. A few minutes here, in Jack's house, had brought them closer together than two years of begging and pleading at home.

After the game, the three of them had supper together. Catriona had already agreed with Jack not to bring up the question of her and Hector's return tonight, or to read him the riot act about his sudden disappearance. As a result it was a pleasant evening, the first pleasant evening that Catriona had spent with her son in a very long time.

After Hector went to bed, she and Jack sat outside on the verandah for a drink. Jack cut to the chase. 'I think you should consider letting him stay here. At least for a few months.'

Catriona shook her head. 'I can't. It's a very generous offer, Jack, but it's not practical.'

'Why not?'

'Because! He has school back home—'

'Which he never shows up for.'

'True, but he's only thirteen, he can't just drop out.'

'We do have schools in the States, you know,' Jack chuckled. 'We're not all walking around in loincloths and living in caves.'

'I couldn't possibly afford to educate him here,' said Catriona. 'Ivan would have to pay and it'll be a cold day in hell before that happens. If he even knew I was having this conversation with you, he'd hit the roof.'

For the first time all evening, Jack's face darkened. 'Why do you still care what Ivan thinks? He left. You're the one who's still here, picking up the pieces.'

'He's still Hector's father,' Catriona sighed.

'Only in name,' said Jack.

By the moonlight, Catriona could see the bitterness in

Jack's face. Ivan had hurt him too. No wonder he empathized so much with Hector. Her own feelings about Ivan were more confused now than at any time since the early days of their divorce. In the days after Hector's disappearance, Ivan had been her rock, the one person who truly understood what she was going through. Although he'd gone back to Kendall and to London, and she'd flown out here, Catriona felt certain that something had changed between them. That a connection she thought had died had somehow been re-established, a new bond had begun to spring forth from the ashes of the old. Of course, part of her still agreed with Jack, that Ivan had forfeited his right to decide the children's future. But another part feared cutting him out completely.

'Anyway, it's not just about Ivan,' she said eventually. 'Actions are supposed to have consequences. This evening was all very nice, but what sort of message does it send to Hector if he gets to run away like that and instead of being punished, he's rewarded?'

'I'm not saying there shouldn't be consequences,' said Jack. 'If he comes to work for me at JSM he'll be working like a dog, believe me – he won't know what's hit him. I just think that being here is helping him. I think it could help you too.'

'Me?'

'Sure. You need a break, Cat. When was the last time you had a real holiday?'

'A long time ago,' she admitted. 'But I can't just up sticks and leave. For one thing there's Rosie.'

'You said yourself Rosie's staying with friends for a bit," said Jack. Look, I'm not talking about for ever. Just a couple of weeks, for you and Hector to reconnect, away from Burford and Ivan and all the stresses of home.'

Gazing out across Jack's beautiful, moonlit garden,

sipping an ice-cold gin and tonic (another slip, but it had been a long, stressful day), it suddenly felt like a wonderful idea. Why *not* stay for a week or two? What harm could it do, other than irritating Ivan? And Jack was right, she had to start making her own decisions and putting herself first.

'All right,' she said. 'I'll stay. Just for a little while. I'll call Rosie's friend's parents in the morning and let them know.'

She was touched by how delighted this seemed to make Jack. It occurred to her, belatedly, that perhaps he, too, was lonely. That he might welcome the company of an old friend as much as she did.

Catriona went to bed that night excited and with a renewed sense of hope for the future. The last two weeks had been a living hell, but perhaps the old saying was right, and it really was darkest before the dawn?

Los Angeles was a revelation for Catriona. Rarely had her preconceptions about a place been so wrong. She'd imagined a sprawling, urban metropolis, clogged with pollution and gangs and glittering with the sort of vulgar fakery that always made her feel depressed. Instead she found a place bursting with natural beauty, from the white sand beaches and hidden coves of Malibu, to the wild craggy canyons that looked like the sets of an old-fashioned Western, to the suburban gardens bursting with ginger flowers and lemon trees and roses and lavender and agapanthus, a glorious riot of colour and scent.

Catriona had never been much of a sun-worshipper. Beach holidays bored her, and if she didn't wear a big hat and slather on icing-thick layers of factor 50, she had a hideous tendency to turn as pink as a rare lamb chop. But the constant sunshine in Los Angeles also meant constant light, and she had to admit she found that uplifting. Like walking out each morning into a bath of happiness.

There were other advantages too. Hector, who was temporarily working at JSM as Lex Abrahams's bag carrier, among many other things, was like a boy transformed. Not once did Catriona hear him complain about the fourteen-hour days, or the minimum-wage pay. He practically skipped into the car with Jack every morning, heading for the Sunset Plaza offices despite the fact that he often didn't make it home till after ten and was usually so tired he barely had the energy to make himself a peanut-butter sandwich before collapsing into bed. Having never shown the slightest interest in the music business growing up, he drank it in now like a bee gorging itself on nectar, cease-lessly rabbiting on about Frankie B and Martina Munoz and the rumour that Willow and Jaden Smith might be thinking of moving to JSM from their long-term manage-ment company.

'It would be a serious coup to get the Smith kids,' Hector told his mother earnestly. 'JSM really needs to develop a younger demographic.'

'A month ago he couldn't spell "demographic",' Catriona told Jack, relating the story over dinner at Nagao, a sushi joint in Brentwood.

'I doubt he can spell it now,' laughed Jack. 'But it's great that he's enthused about it. Kids need an interest, a focus. It keeps them out of trouble.'

'Oh really?' Catriona raised an eyebrow teasingly. 'That's your conclusion, is it, after all your long years of parenting?'

'Sorry,' Jack smiled, passing Catriona a delicious crab-and-salmon no-rice roll smothered in roe. 'I'm teaching my grandmother to suck fish eggs.'

It had been such a delight spending time with Jack. In a few days, Catriona would have to go home, and was shocked by how sad the thought of leaving him made her. They'd agreed that Hector would stay on for another month hanging out at JSM, then come back to England to repeat Year Nine. If he worked hard, kept out of trouble and did well in his exams, he could come back to Los Angeles the following summer and perhaps even get a job on Maria Munoz's US tour.

Suddenly depressed by the thought of her imminent departure, Catriona ordered a third glass of red wine. Jack put his hand over hers. 'Feel free to tell me to fuck off and mind my own business,' he said. 'But don't you think you've had enough?'

'Oh.' Catriona withdrew her hand, embarrassed. 'Yes, probably. Why, have I been slurring my words or something?' She giggled nervously.

'No,' said Jack. 'But I've noticed you drink a lot more than you used to. And it worries me that you do it because you're sad.'

It was such a perceptive comment, and so kindly and gently delivered, that Catriona found herself on the brink of tears. 'No wonder you think I'm a drunk,' she laughed, dabbing at her eyes with a napkin. 'I'm so bloody overemotional.'

'I don't think you're a drunk,' said Jack. 'I never said that.'

'Well, I am,' said Catriona. She told him about the day that Hector went missing, how she'd been so far gone she hadn't made it out of bed that morning. 'Imagine if something really *had* happened to him? I'd never have forgiven myself. Sometimes I look in the mirror and I hate what I've become. A sad, fat, middle-aged lush. No wonder Ivan left me.'

Jack took both her hands. 'That is one fucked-up mirror.

When *I* look at you I see an amazing, strong, loving mother. Not to mention a very sexy woman.'

Catriona blushed. 'Sexy? Ha! I don't think so.'

'I do,' said Jack, deadly seriously. 'You've never had any idea how beautiful you are.'

For a few seconds, a crackle of sexual tension hung in the air between them. Catriona had always thought Jack madly good-looking – you couldn't not; but she'd only ever known him with Ivan and had never viewed him as anything other than a friend.

'I suspect that's another reason you drink,' said Jack. 'Insecurity. Believe it or not, Kendall's the same.'

Catriona snatched her hands away. 'My God, Jack. I don't want to talk about Kendall, OK? If it weren't for that girl, none of this would have happened. She destroyed my marriage.'

'You don't really believe that, do you?' said Jack. 'It was Ivan who destroyed your marriage, Cat. He's the one who seduced Kendall, not the other way around.'

'How do you know that?' Catriona said hotly.

'Because I know Kendall. Yes, she can be selfish and sexually impetuous and all of that. But she was just a kid when she came to England, a kid who wanted to hit back at *me*. She didn't stand a chance against a shrewd manipulator like Ivan.'

Catriona said nothing. It was easier to blame Kendall than to blame Ivan. Less painful. Why was Jack trying to take that one small comfort away from her?

'You know at Ivan's fortieth birthday party, at The Rookery? I walked in on him and Joyce Wu in the bathroom.'

'At his party?' Catriona shook his head. 'No, no, that's not possible. I was there. Ivan was actually very sweet to me that night, I remember.'

'Cat, I was there. He was fucking that girl over a bathtub. She was only nineteen, for goodness' sake. And you know what? After I caught him, he didn't even care. He practically laughed in my face when I challenged him about it.'

Tears poured down Catriona's cheeks. Even after all this time, what Jack was telling her was like a knife in the heart, the wound as fresh and raw as if it had happened yesterday. 'Why didn't you tell me at the time?'

'Come on,' said Jack. 'How could I?'

'Well, why are you telling me now then?' she shouted at him. 'I don't understand. Why are you trying to hurt me?'

Other diners had turned to look at them. What had begun as a quiet dinner had rapidly taken a turn for the dramatic. Jack did his best to calm things down. 'I'm not trying to hurt you. I want you to see Ivan for what he was, what he is, so that maybe you won't feel so much loss. You know, after Sonya died, I started drinking a lot. At one point it got really bad. I was easily finishing two bottles of red on my own every night, on top of spirits at lunch.'

'So what stopped you?' sniffed Catriona.

'She did. Sonya did. I thought about her looking down at me, how sad and disappointed she'd be . . . That and the fact I felt like crap.'

Catriona risked a small smile.

'You're a beautiful woman, Cat, inside and out. Don't let Ivan, or some false image of Ivan that was never even true in the first place, ruin the rest of your life.'

Sensing a lull in hostilities, the waitress brought over Catriona's red wine.

'I changed my mind,' she said. 'I'm happy to pay for it but I'm not going to drink it. Just a green tea, please. And the check.'

'I'm paying,' said Jack.

'No you're not. I am. It's the least I owe you after tonight. After everything.'

She leaned forward to kiss him on the cheek, but somehow, intentionally or otherwise, Jack moved his head and their lips ended up meeting. Catriona froze, like a deer in the headlights, waiting for Jack to jerk away. But instead he reached a hand around the back of her neck and kissed her. It was more tender than passionate, but it was so unexpected, and it had been so long since Catriona had been kissed by anyone, she felt a rush of longing shoot down her body from her heart to her groin. When Jack finally pulled away she was speechless, gasping for air like a fish in a net.

'Let's go home,' said Jack.

When they got back to the Brentwood house, Lex Abrahams was in the kitchen, contemplatively sipping a hot chocolate with Hector.

'What are you doing here?' Jack looked at his watch. 'Isn't Leila expecting you?'

'I drove Hector home,' said Lex. 'And no, actually, she's not expecting me. We broke up.'

Jack's eyes widened. 'What? When?'

'Last night,' said Lex. He sounded dispirited rather than heartbroken. Catriona, who'd only met Lex once before years ago and whose mental image was of the tired, dark-haired boy being mauled by Kendall Bryce in the newspaper pictures, thought he looked remarkably handsome in a white T-shirt and vintage leather jacket from American Classics. Far better looking in the flesh than he was in the *Daily Mail*.

'Isn't that kinda sudden?' asked Jack.

'Women,' said Hector knowingly, taking a slug of his own hot chocolate. 'They're so unpredictable.'

Lex laughed. He'd grown fond of his eager-beaver assistant in the last two weeks. Hector had inherited all his father's social skills, humour and *joie de vivre*, but none of Ivan's legendary ego. He was fun to have around.

'Not really,' he told Jack. 'It's been coming for a while. There's no big drama; it was a mutual thing. We just knew we weren't going to get married so at a certain point it didn't make sense to go on.'

Jack frowned. He wasn't buying this version of the story, and couldn't help but feel that the bomb Kendall had lobbed into Lex and Leila's relationship back in June must have had something to do with it. But now wasn't the time to go into it. 'You know Catriona Charles, Hector's mother?'

'Sure.' Lex shook her hand. 'How are you enjoying LA?'

'It's been wonderful, thanks,' said Catriona. 'A real breath of fresh air.'

Lex noticed that she looked at Jack when she said this and that he returned the look with a warm smile. *Now that would be something,* he thought, *if those two got together.*

'Oh, Jack, by the way Lisa Marie came round earlier,' said Hector. 'She said you left these at her place and she's looking forward to seeing you Saturday night.' He handed Jack a pair of jade cufflinks.

Jack snatched up the cufflinks, blushing furiously. 'OK, thanks.'

'You're dating Lisa Marie?' Lex nudged his partner in the ribs. 'You old dog! You never said anything.'

'There's nothing to say,' muttered Jack.

'Who's Lisa Marie?' asked Catriona, wishing that she didn't care so much about the answer.

'Oh my God, Mum, she's *gorgeous,*' said Hector. 'She's the new senior account manager at JSM and she looks exactly like Jennifer Garner, except less wholesome and a bit more, you know, slutty.'

'Hector!' said Catriona, Lex and Jack in unison.

'Well, she does,' muttered Hector. 'Are you really shagging her, Uncle Jack?'

Lex laughed loudly. Poor Jack looked as if he wanted the floor to open up and swallow him. 'I think you'd better get upstairs, buddy, before you find yourself out of a job. And a home. Go on, scram.'

A few minutes later, Lex left too, before Jack could quiz him any more about Leila. Catriona faked a yawn. She wasn't remotely tired, her mind and body were both racing, but she needed to be on her own. 'I think I'll head up too.'

'Are you sure?' Jack looked disappointed. 'I could make us hot chocolates too. Or a chamomile tea?'

He's so handsome, thought Catriona. *And lovely and kind.* It would be terrifyingly easy to fall in love with him.

'No thanks,' she said, forcing herself to be sensible. 'I'm honestly shattered. I'll see you in the morning.' Turning her back on him, she traipsed up the wide wooden stairs to bed.

Alone in the kitchen, Jack realized with a sinking heart how empty the house was going to feel when she left. A few weeks later Hector would be gone too. *They're Ivan's family, not mine.* The thought filled him with a bitterness that was very close to hate. JSM were already more profitable than Jester, and going from strength to strength, but he was still nowhere near exacting the vengeance he longed for and that consumed him day and night. Perhaps the time had come to walk into the lion's den? To take the fight to Ivan on his own home turf and destroy his business, the way that Ivan had so callously set about destroying Jack's?

Upstairs, in her princess-and-the-pea four-poster, Catriona stared at the ceiling, her mind whirring like a Magimix. The kiss with Jack earlier already felt like a dream, but perhaps no more so than this entire trip to LA. *He's with Lisa Marie, the gorgeous account manager. That's reality. He probably only kissed me out of pity.*

Her thoughts turned to Ivan, how close they'd suddenly become in the days after Hector disappeared. Would any of that closeness still be there when she returned? Did she want it to be, after everything he'd put her through?

She fell asleep dreaming of Joyce Wu and Jack Messenger's lips and the Windrush Valley, calling her home.

CHAPTER FIFTEEN

Kendall Bryce sat down on the squashy red sofa in the Vivement Dimanche studio and smiled dazzlingly at the host. In a close-fitting white Chloé trouser suit, teamed with a black silk Gucci shirt and sky-high Zanotti platforms, she looked sexy, chic and radiantly confident. The bright lights of the TV studio and the rapturous applause of the audience brought her to life like the first rays of spring sunshine rousing a hibernating animal. From backstage, Ivan watched her with a combination of nerves and pride as she laughed and joked coquettishly with Pascal Dubonnet, the handsome presenter of France's most-watched chat show.

'Tell us about *Flame*,' Dubonnet was asking. 'There's been so much secrecy about this album. Is that because you've taken your sound in a different direction?'

'In some ways,' said Kendall, crossing her legs to give Dubonnet and camera one a better view of her spectacular cleavage. 'Hopefully you'll get a sense from the track I'm going to perform today, "Liar, Liar".'

'Now is this the song you've released free on iTunes as a "teaser", before the album's release next week?'

'That's right.'

'So tell me, Kendall, do you like to tease?'

And they were off, flirting and exchanging banter like old friends, their 'chemistry' delighting the audience and Ivan in equal measure. *She's such a fucking pro*, he thought proudly. He knew how scared she was about tonight's show. So much rested on this album's success, for both of them, and Kendall's French, though fluent, was rusty. But as ever, when the pressure was really on, she hit the ball out of the park. Ten million viewers, most of them music buyers, would be glued to their screens right now, eating out of Kendall's perfectly manicured hands.

Ivan reached into the pocket of his Paul Smith jacket, pulled out a Xanax and swallowed it. His doctor had warned him that he couldn't go on living his life at this pitch of stress, good advice if only he'd had some suggestions as to how, exactly, Ivan was supposed to reduce the pressure. Hector's disappearance had shaken Ivan to his core. The few days he'd spent in Burford with Catriona had been awful and wonderful at the same time, but they'd destabilized him, offering him a glimpse of the calmer, more peaceful life he'd once had and might perhaps have again, if only he could somehow find his way back there. Then Hector had turned up, and relief and joy had swiftly turned to anger as Jack Messenger stepped into the picture, setting himself up as some sort of alternative father figure and even luring Catriona into his meddlesome net.

Unfortunately, or perhaps fortunately, Ivan had had little time to brood on Jack's insidiously worming his way into his family. With *Flame* just weeks from official release, and *Talent Quest* still having six episodes to run before the season finale, he was sucked immediately back into a ceaseless vortex of work. The maths was simple. *Flame* had to shift at least 200,000 copies in the European market within a month of its release, or Polydor would drop Kendall from its books. Cheryl Cole's last album had struggled to top 170,000 domestically, so those numbers were a big ask.

Meanwhile the situation with Ava Bentley was becoming like walking a tightrope through a minefield. In between promotional commitments with Kendall and his *Talent Quest* duties, Ivan had somehow found time to spirit Ava into a privately rented recording studio and lay down some new material by Ingrid Michaelson, one of the best pop writers in the business and known for her discretion. The plan, based on a handshake agreement with Ava's father, Dave, was for Ava to pull out of the *Talent Quest* competition due to ill-health, thus releasing her from her ITV contract. During her 'recuperation' in a private location, Jester would officially sign her as a client, and Ivan would broker a behind-the-scenes deal for her first two albums, based on the already recorded material, including her duet with Kendall. By tying Ava's star and Kendall's together, he hoped to have enough leverage at Polydor to extract killer deals for both girls.

Still, until he had Dave Bentley signed on the dotted line, he was jumpy. Ava's spurious illness would be fraud, pure and simple, if it were discovered, and though Ivan had left no paper or email trail that could link him to the plot, the recordings he'd made with Ava were hard evidence of his intent to break the terms of his own contract with *Talent Quest*.

Meanwhile, things with Jester went from bad to worse. Over the summer, the last vestiges of Ivan's classical list had all deserted to other managers, and the grumblings of dissent from his remaining clients were beginning to grow deafening. Ivan had been pulled in too many different directions for a long time, but he was starting to feel like Stretch Armstrong on a mission impossible. He'd already had to go back to the bank twice for bridge loans, until the Kendall and Ava deals came good. But if some serious money didn't hit Jester's corporate account by Christmas, there was a real chance Ivan would have to file for bankruptcy.

Kendall's interview finished and she gave her first live performance of 'Liar, Liar', an upbeat, pop-dance number with a distinctly Britney feel, to an ecstatically enthusiastic audience. Afterwards Ivan took her for dinner at Lapérouse on Quai des Grands Augustins.

With its rich-red velvet chairs, gilt walls and ornate crystal chandeliers, Lapérouse was not so much romantic as decadently sensual, and every forkful of food was an orgasm in itself.

'Did you really think it went well?' Kendall asked, spearing a butter-drenched snail with a miniature silver fork and sucking on it greedily. Her creamy white breasts had all but escaped from the black silk prison of her blouse. Ivan gazed at them lustfully.

'You were spectacular, darling. If "Liar, Liar" doesn't go straight in at number one in France, I'll eat my chapeau.'

'Aren't you hungry?' Kendall asked, massacring what was left of the escargots.

'Only for you,' growled Ivan.

It was true. When he was with Catriona he felt safe and comfortable, and he missed the easy friendship and understanding of their marriage. At those times, Kendall felt like an irrelevance. But when he was actually with Kendall, his desire was so crushing, so total, it was as if nothing else existed. He worried constantly that she didn't want him as much as he wanted her, and felt he had to prove himself in bed against other men. Though she never spoke about him any more, Ivan remained consumed with jealousy about Jack. The idea that, in Kendall's mind, he, Ivan, was somehow second best filled him impotent fury.

'*L'addition, s'il vous plaît.*' He signalled to the waiter.

'What? Why?' said Kendall, wiping a smear of melted butter from her lips. 'We only just got here. I wanted dessert.'

'You'll get dessert,' said Ivan, grabbing her hand across the table and running his tongue hungrily along her wrist. 'And so will I.'

'Keep up, slow coach. Poor Badger should have had his feed an hour ago.'

Ned Williams called back over his shoulder to Catriona, who was struggling up the hill behind him, pink-cheeked and panting.

'Bugger Badger,' she shouted back robustly. Surely it wasn't normal to feel *this* bad after a mere two-mile jog? She'd called Ned this morning in hopes that a running partner might spur her on to greater things and make her too embarrassed to give up and collapse in a heap on the grass at the first sign of a stitch, like she usually did. The strategy had worked, but at a price. Sweat streamed down her face and back and ran in a hot, salty river between her bouncing breasts. The 'extra-firm' sports bra she'd bought at Debenhams in Oxford last week turned out to be no match for Catriona's 36F assets, which she was sure must be getting saggier with each stride. Meanwhile, her ribcage wheezed like a broken concertina, pain pounded through her legs and feet, and her mouth and throat were as dry as sandpaper.

On the plus side, she'd already lost ten pounds since she returned from LA last month, and was determined to drop at least another twenty. Inspired by Jack's pep talk, she'd given up the booze. Not a drop had passed her lips in forty days. *Like Jesus in the desert,* she thought, before realizing it wasn't actually the best analogy. Our Lord had probably never broken his grandmother's prized Doulton vase while staggering around the living room drunkenly trying to copy the moves on *Got to Dance.* Still, forty days without a drink was an achievement, and Catriona was proud of herself, especially once she began to notice the effect on her body. Apart from the weight loss, her skin was better, her eyes clearer and her energy levels back up to their pre-divorce best. For the first time in years, she began to see in the mirror the vestiges of the 'beautiful woman' Jack described her as. A couple of times she even thought she'd caught Ned looking at her in a less-than-totally-platonic manner, although she quickly laughed off her own vanity. *Fat or thin, I'm still almost old enough to be his mother.*

When she reached the brow of Westwell Hill, Ned was waiting.

'Great view, isn't it?'

Below them the rooftops of Burford lay nestled together like a huddled flock of sheep. Their moss-covered slates were overshadowed by trees whose leaves were beginning to turn the soft, pale yellow of early autumn. Catriona had lived here for nearly a decade now, but the tranquil beauty of the Cotswolds still took her breath away.

'Let's walk down from here,' she gasped, clutching at her chest like an asthmatic pensioner. 'I read the other day that it's terribly bad for one's knees to run downhill.'

'Bollocks,' said Ned. 'This is the easy bit. You can't wimp out now.' And he was off, bounding down towards the river, leaping over stinging nettles and dock leaves like an over-excited red setter.

Back in the village they parted ways, with Ned turning down Witney Street to run the extra two miles back to

Swinbrook, and Catriona staggering down the twitten towards her house and a much-needed pint of lemon squash.

It was already early evening and the light was beginning to fade. Unlatching the door, Catriona walked straight into the kitchen and stuck her head under the cold tap, revelling in the sensation of cool water against her hot skin. Only when she turned around to grab a glass from one of the top cupboards did she notice the figure lurking in the shadows.

'Jesus Christ!' She jumped a mile, instinctively reaching for the knife drawer. But then a familiar face stepped forward into the light, and she relaxed. 'Stella! You frightened the life out of me. What on earth are you doing here?'

'It's Brett,' sobbed Stella. On closer inspection, Catriona saw that her face was swollen and bloated from crying. Her usually neat-as-a-pin hair was a tangled mess and she had strange red welts across her cheeks.

'What happened?' Catriona asked kindly. She hadn't seen Stella Bayley for more than six months, but she still considered her a friend, despite the fact that Stella remained close to Ivan and Kendall. 'He didn't hit you, did he?'

'No,' sniffed Stella. 'I wish he had. Those kind of bruises heal.' She stumbled into Catriona's arms and cried like a baby. Eventually, after a full minute of wracking sobs, the truth tumbled out. 'He's been having an affair. Brett. My Brett. Can you imagine?'

Catriona, who could easily imagine – Brett Bayley's reputation as a womanizer was legendary, even by music-business standards – mumbled some meaningless words of comfort. She knew what it was like to be the last one to know: the pathetic, trusting wife.

'I know it's awful,' she said, leading Stella into the drawing room and sitting her down on the sofa like a child. 'But try not to panic. It will probably pass. Most of the time these things mean nothing to the men, despite how ghastly they are for us. Brett probably regrets it already.'

Stella laughed bitterly. 'Well, if he does, he's got a funny way of showing it. He's moving back to Los Angeles to be with *her*, this girl. She's only twenty-one, for heaven's sake!'

'Oh dear.' Catriona winced. Brett Bayley was such a cliché.

'And he wasn't even going to have the balls to tell me. Can you believe that? He was planning to sneak off in the night and leave me and poor Miley for dust. The only reason I found out was because I came home early from Pilates this morning and found Jack Messenger in our kitchen.'

At the mention of Jack's name, Catriona's heart rate suddenly shot back up. 'Jack's in England?'

Stella nodded miserably. 'He and Brett were finalizing the paperwork for The Blitz to dump Jester and sign up with JSM. The band are moving back to LA. Poor Jack was mortified when he realized Brett hadn't told me. He assumed I knew.' She broke down again, blowing her nose loudly on Catriona's proffered handkerchief. 'I'm sorry to show up here unannounced. Miley's staying at a friend's house, but I . . . I didn't know where else to go.'

'Don't be silly,' said Catriona, trying not to feel hurt by the fact that Jack was in England and hadn't called her. She should be thinking about poor Stella, not herself. And besides, why *should* he call her? He didn't owe her anything. 'You know you're welcome here any time.'

'Brett said our relationship had "come to a natural end",' Stella went on. 'He said I should accept it and be mature about it and "move on". Like it was nothing! Like he was changing fucking Internet providers or giving away an old shirt.'

Catriona made Stella a mug of hot, sweet tea and forced her to eat some toast and honey. She'd always been slender, but ensconced in Catriona's big, squashy sofa she looked painfully thin, as tiny and fragile and pale as a porcelain doll. After letting her talk and cry and rage for an hour, Catriona sent her upstairs for a bath while she made up the guest bedroom, thanking her lucky stars that both the children were away for the night. Rosie was flexi-boarding at school, and Hector, newly returned from Los Angeles with a tan, a dreadful Loyd Grossman mid-Atlantic accent and an absolute determination to pass Year Nine so he could go back to America next summer, was kipping over at a friend's. Finally, Catriona took a lightning shower herself, then went downstairs to make supper.

'You're very kind.' Stella appeared in the kitchen doorway looking even tinier than usual in a giant fluffy bathrobe of Rosie's and with her wet hair scraped back. 'But I'm not sure I can eat.' Delicious smells of frying onion, olives and anchovy filled the air. Catriona dropped a handful of fresh pasta into a pan of boiling water and returned to chopping sage on the breadboard.

'Try,' she said. 'Just a little. And have a glass of this.'

It felt strange, opening a bottle of Newton Unfiltered Merlot, one of her favourite reds, and pulling only one glass out of the cupboard. But it also felt good, a little inner buzz of confidence: *I can do it.*

'You're not drinking?' said Stella.

'No. But my husband hasn't just swanned off with a twenty-one year old. When he did, I drank, and so should you. Anyway, it's medicinal. You need the iron.'

In the end, the two women had an enjoyable kitchen supper. Too spent to cry any more, Stella found she was hungry after all, wolfing down two bowls of Catriona's delicious *pasta alla puttanesca*. She talked endlessly about Brett, and how she should have seen the writing on the wall.

'I knew he wasn't totally happy in England. I always felt much more settled here, and I think he resented that. Plus, you know, the blog kind of drove him nuts. He started complaining that all I talked about was babies and organic mung beans. That's not true, is it?'

'No,' lied Catriona kindly. 'Of course not.'

'And professionally he's been unhappy for a long time. Since Jack left Jester, the business has gone down the tubes, to be frank with you. Ivan's been totally absent as a manager. Kendall's the only client he cares about, and his TV stuff. Everybody's up in arms about it, not just The Blitz.'

'I see,' said Catriona. This was bad news. Even when she was married to Ivan she'd known next to nothing about the day-to-day workings of the business. Since the divorce, Jester had become little more than a word. Unfortunately, it was a word that paid Rosie's school fees, the whole family's medical insurance and half Catriona's bills. If Ivan went bankrupt, they were all sunk.

'Now Brett's gone to JSM, the floodgates will open. If Jack's been calling Brett, trying to cut a deal, you can bet he's been calling the rest of the Jester list too. I mean, it's no coincidence he's in London now. He knows Ivan's in Paris this week, distracted with Kendall's album. While the cat's away . . .'

'But JSM are doing so well already,' said Catriona, spearing a stray fusilli with her fork. 'Jack doesn't need Jester's clients. After all, they turned their back on him two years ago, and he moved onto bigger and better things. I'm surprised he'd *want* them back.'

Stella looked at her curiously. 'You don't get it, do you? It's not about wanting them back. I'm pretty sure Jack despises Brett, and he'll certainly never trust him again.'

'Then why . . .?'

'Because of Ivan. Jack wants to destroy Ivan, to wipe him out completely. He's obsessed.'

Catriona felt her stomach churn unpleasantly. Was that why Jack had kissed her, and been so kind to her, and so keen to take Hector in? Was it all some twisted way of trying to get back at Ivan? It hadn't felt that way at the time. And yet something about Stella's words rang true.

'I don't think Jack ever fully got over what happened with Kendall,' Stella went on, her every word like a knife in Catriona's heart. 'He cared about that girl. I don't know if deep down he was in love with her, or what it was, but there was some weird dynamic going on there. When Ivan stole Kendall away from him, Jack snapped.'

Catriona thought about the way Jack had defended Kendall to her over dinner that night in LA, the night he'd kissed her and said she was beautiful. How he'd laid all the blame for the affair at Ivan's door. She felt sick.

'It's a sad situation,' said Stella. 'It's obvious Kendall's still in love with Jack.'

'Is it?'

'Sure. But she's too proud to go back and he's too proud to take her. So she digs in with Ivan, and Jack focuses all his energy on getting revenge on Ivan, and nobody wins. Nobody's happy. Not Jack, not Kendall, not Ivan, not the clients. And certainly not me.'

Nor me, thought Catriona miserably.

'My marriage, my life is just collateral damage in all this,' said Stella sadly.The tears welled up again and Catriona changed the subject to Miley, a topic on which Stella could happily talk for hours, even in her current state of distress. When she finally went to bed, at midnight, she seemed a lot happier, or at least less panicked than she had been when she'd arrived.

Up in her own bedroom, Catriona stared out of the window at the full moon, feeling gripped by despair. How foolish she'd been to imagine, even for a second, that Jack Messenger was interested in her. The whole idea was preposterous. Lisa Marie, the Jennifer Garner lookalike, and pouting, perfect, made-for-sex Kendall Bryce: these were the sort of women that Jack was attracted to. That Ivan was attracted to. That all men were attracted to. Not dumpy, middle-aged mothers like her. Even pretty, fit, blonde slips-of-things like Stella Bayley were being traded in for younger models.

'I'm forty years old,' she said out loud to her empty bedroom, 'and I will never be with a man again.'

They were hard words to say and hard words to hear, but she forced herself to believe them. Jack had been in England for a whole week and hadn't bothered to call her. Ivan was never going to leave Kendall. Lying to herself about either of those things wasn't going to help anyone.

Catriona Charles was on her own.

CHAPTER SIXTEEN

Ava Bentley stared out of the window of Ivan's vintage Aston Martin DB 7 wondering when she was going to wake up. Ever since she'd made it past the first round of *Talent Quest* auditions up in York seven months ago, her life had been one long, incredible dream. One minute she was a schoolgirl from Hutton-le-Hole whose only experience of London had been a school trip to Buckingham Palace back in Year Seven. The next she was a national TV star, with her face in the newspapers and perfect strangers calling out her name in the street. And she had Ivan Charles to thank for all of it.

Ava idolized Ivan, and was slavishly grateful for all that he'd done for her. But if truth be told, she was also more than a little afraid of him. He was so forceful and of course he knew *everything* about the music business and media and this strange, fast new world she'd woken up in. These things made him the perfect mentor, but they also made him very, very difficult to say 'no' to.

'Penny for them?' said Ivan, smiling broadly as they turned off Marylebone High Street into George Street. They were headed to the Daniel Galvin salon, stop one on the grand makeover tour that Ivan had insisted Ava go on before next week's quarter-finals.

'Oh nothing,' Ava blushed. 'I'm just thinking how weird I'm gonna look with blonde hair. Me dad always said he'd throttle me if I ever dyed it.'

'Yes, but things are different now,' Ivan said smoothly. 'Your father's a clever man. He understands.'

Privately, Ivan viewed Dave Bentley's mental capacity as little above an amoeba's, but with Ava still only seventeen he knew he needed her parents on-side.

'Besides, you won't be blonde as such. It's only a few highlights.'

Twenty minutes later, Ava was sipping Buck's fizz as Louise Galvin ran expert fingers through her lank, mousy-brown hair. 'So,' Louise asked brightly, 'what are we thinking of doing today?'

'Well, I thought I might get—'

'We don't want anything too drastic,' interrupted Ivan, cutting her off. 'It's vital that she keeps that youthful, innocent look. I was thinking a few honey highlights, maybe some layers. Don't go too short.'

'OK,' Louise nodded.

'I'll be back at two to get her. We've got the beautician after this, then wardrobe, so we need to stay on schedule.'

'No problem. Leave her with me.'

I am here, you know, Ava felt like saying. But she was nowhere near brave enough, and in any case there wasn't time. Ivan left, his phone glued to his ear, and Ava found herself being shuttled from station to station and basin to chair like a pampered sheep being expensively dipped and sheared. Other than 'how's the water temperature?', no one asked her a thing about her hair or what *she* actually wanted.

They did, however, want to know all the inside scoop on *Talent Quest*, firing questions at her about Stacey and Isabella James and all the other contestants, especially Michael Matterson, the fifty-year-old brickie from Sunderland who was considered Ava's biggest competition. By the time Louise Galvin held up the mirror to show her her new look, Ava was almost too tired to care. It did look lovely, though; like a mane of shimmery golden feathers.

'Wow, thank you!' she said sincerely. 'I hardly recognize myself.'

'You looked gorgeous before,' said Louise, 'but it brings out your eyes more and the shape of your face. I'm glad you're pleased.'

Ivan burst in like a whirlwind, pressing a wodge of fifty-pound notes into the hairdresser's hands and practically dragging Ava up out of the chair. 'Thanks darling.' He kissed Louise on the cheek. 'She looks perfect. Gotta run but I'll call you, OK?'

Back in the car, he handed Ava a smoked-salmon sandwich as he sped towards The Berkeley Hotel.

'Oh, I'm all right, thanks Ivan,' Ava said meekly. 'They gave me a salad back at the salon. They had champagne and everything, all free.'

'It's hardly free,' laughed Ivan. 'You could buy a small farm for the amount that place charges for highlights. Anyway, eat up if you can. A salad's not much and we've still got a long day ahead of us.'

He wasn't kidding. Sveva, the beautician at The Berkeley, had a friendly, smiling face that belied the ruthless operator beneath. Ava had no idea that the removal of a few, previously unnoticed hairs could be so teeth-crackingly painful. Worst of all was when, having waxed her eyebrows, Sveva decided the symmetry was not perfect and insisted on plucking away further with tweezers, a process that left Ava feeling as if a blackbird were repeatedly pecking away at her forehead. By the time she emerged onto Knightsbridge, red-faced and blotchy from her facial, every square centimetre of her skin stung as if she'd been dipped in acid.

'Put these on,' commanded Ivan unsympathetically, handing her a pair of oversized Stella McCartney sunglasses and a big YSL scarf as they dived into Harvey Nichols. 'You don't want some nosy punter taking a picture of you looking like that.'

By the time they'd spent two solid hours choosing a new wardrobe with Hillary, the private stylist Ivan had hired and whom he'd used to revamp the images of many of his big-name acts in the past, Ava was ready to drop. She had clothes for day and night, clothes for rehearsals, and outfits for each of the remaining shows before the *Talent Quest* final. She had handbags and sunglasses and scarves and hats and jewellery. She knew she ought to feel happy and lucky and grateful, and she would tomorrow, after twelve hours' sleep. But right now, all she wanted to do was go home to Yorkshire, crawl under the sheets of her own bed in her own room, and never, ever leave.

Ivan drove her back to the hotel in Earls Court where all the *Talent Quest* contestants were staying, checking his watch impatiently as they pulled up outside. He was already late for dinner with Kendall, never a good move, and he still had a couple of phone calls to make on his way home. Still, it had been worth it. Ava looked great – not remotely trashy, but a better, more polished and commercial version of her sweet, innocent self. As getting her image right could mean the difference between Jester surviving or collapsing, today's makeover had been an investment well worth making, even if Kendall did bite his head off about it.

'You must feel like Cinderella,' he said to Ava as she climbed wearily out of the car, still swaddled in her scarf and shades. 'You deserve it, though.'

'Thanks,' said Ava, fighting back tears and grateful for the ready-made disguise. Ivan had never been anything other than kind to her, but somehow she shied away from showing weakness in front of him. Worse still would be to have him think her ungrateful. He must have spent ten thousand pounds on her today, and she knew that in the morning she'd be delighted with the results. But the homesickness that gripped her now was choking, like a vice.

Was this what fame felt like?

'See you in the morning, kiddo.' And with a roar of his exhaust, Ivan Charles was gone.

Lex Abrahams picked up the rubber stress ball on his desk and squeezed it. *Nothing.* How did people get away with selling this junk? Standing up, he paced around his glass-walled office, moving the potted palm from one corner to another, rearranging the photographs on his coffee table and plumping up the cushions on the couch-that-nobody-ever-sits-on. It didn't help. He still felt anxious and restless and, quite frankly, pissed.

What the hell was Jack playing at?

On the other side of the glass, Jack watched JSM's staff scurrying about their business. It was a vibrant, buzzing office, full of light and colour and creativity and ambition and optimism. Lex was MD, and he was only thirty. Most of JSM's employees were in their twenties, barring a few of the senior agents, and an atmosphere of youthful energy pervaded everything about the company. *They're talented too,* thought Lex, *and hard-working. And they're relying on Jack and me to steer their ship safely.* Yet here he was, once again alone at the helm, while Jack swanned off on some ill-conceived 'sting' against Jester in London.

He'd called last night, eight o'clock Lex's time, to announce that he'd 'successfully' poached The Blitz from Ivan and signed them to JSM. Lex was furious.

'What? Why? You never even discussed this with me. What the hell do we want Brett Bayley back on our books for? His US career's in the toilet, he's totally untrustworthy and he's a nightmare to work with. Plus, we already have Land of the Greeks. We don't need The Blitz. Have you considered how those boys are going to react to this news?'

'They'll be fine,' Jack bristled. 'We've just taken on four new agents, remember? There's plenty of room for everyone.'

'It's a mistake,' said Lex.

'I disagree,' said Jack tersely. 'And I've been in this business a lot longer than you have.'

That was the part that really ticked Lex off. Jack had made him an equal partner. God knew he did at least fifty per cent of the work, more like ninety per cent when Jack took off on one of his mystery tours, like the one he was on right now. But whenever it suited him, whenever he wanted to defend some arbitrarily taken decision, he would play the 'experience' card and dismiss Lex's objections out of hand. Deep down there was a part of Jack that still saw Lex as the photographer kid who used to hang around with Kendall. It drove Lex crazy.

The other thing that drove him crazy was Jack's unpredictability. Not only had he taken off to London without so much as a by your leave, just assuming Lex would pick up his clients and workload while he was gone, but he'd given no indication as to when he planned to come back. And why *was* he in London in the first place? Jack swore blind last night that he'd re-signed The Blitz for purely commercial reasons. But Lex hadn't forgotten his bizarre comment at Frankie B's Grammy nomination party, about 'the best revenge' being success. If this was all about revenge, then where would it end? Was Jack going to try and take over all Jester's lame-duck acts, clogging JSM's carefully cherry-picked client list with dross? If he wanted to sacrifice his own life to some vendetta with Ivan, that was up to him. But he had no right to drag the company down with him.

Underlying all of Lex's anger and frustration about Jack's London trip lurked one, specific fear. What if his ultimate goal was to woo back Kendall? Wiping out Jester would be one thing. But re-signing Kendall would surely be the ultimate revenge? She'd become a symbol in Jack's mind, the beautiful Helen of Troy who had unwittingly unleashed years of war and bloodshed, and whom he must win back in order to truly defeat Ivan.

For Lex, however, she was much more than that. The way she'd used him when she was last in LA had wounded him very deeply. Not just because of the selfishness and cruelty of what she'd done. But because it reminded him, beyond any doubt, that he was still hopelessly, helplessly in love with her. Even after all these years and everything that had happened, Kendall touched Lex in a way that no other woman ever had. Or ever would.

Love is not love which alters when it alteration finds . . .

He'd broken up with Leila because he knew he didn't love her, not in the same way he loved Kendall. Yet, at the same time, if Kendall's publicity stunt on the Chateau Marmont balcony had shown him anything, it was that she did not return his feelings. She didn't even care about him as a friend. Friends didn't set friends up like that.

So the thought of Kendall coming back to Los Angeles

and, worse, being managed by JSM, filled Lex with absolute, abject horror. She would be in and out of the office on a daily basis. He would have to see her all the time. For all he knew, she and Jack might even get together romantically. Kendall obviously still had feelings for Jack, and if Jack was planning to steal her from Ivan, why not go the whole hog? The whole thing was a nightmare, a hideous, ghastly nightmare he couldn't bear to think about.

Lisa Marie Evans, Jack's on-off love interest and one of JSM's highest-producing new agents, tapped on Lex's door.

'Hi.' She smiled sweetly. 'I don't suppose you've heard from Jack at all? He's not returning my calls.'

'No,' said Lex. 'I'm just his partner. Why in the hell would he tell me anything?'

'You know he re-signed The Blitz?' Lisa Marie sounded excited. 'I'd love to get that account.'

Lex raised an eyebrow. 'You would?'

'Sure. They're still a great brand, but their sales are in the tank. Whoever turns that around is gonna make a fortune.'

'Hmm. I guess so.'

Maybe he was worrying too much? Overthinking things? If Lisa Marie saw The Blitz as a good signing, perhaps Jack really was basing this on commercial instincts.

'Let me know if you hear from him, OK?' said Lisa Marie, disappearing back to her own office.

'Sure,' Lex called after her retreating back. *Don't hold your breath.*

Catriona switched on the radio and sat down at the kitchen table with a well-earned, and much-needed, cup of tea. Stella Bayley had finally gone home to London yesterday after an emotionally draining three-night stay, and Catriona had spent the morning cleaning the house, sorting out her filing, and generally getting her life back on an even keel. The delight of having the house to herself and sipping a big mug of Earl Grey while Classic FM washed over her was quite extraordinary. From now on, she told herself, she would make sure she enjoyed life's simple pleasures. The garden; spending time with her children; peace, on the rare moments she got it. The romantic side of her life might be over, but she still lived in a beautiful home in a glorious village, she had her photography, her friends (well, Ned), her health. There was so much to be thankful for.

She'd thought briefly about calling Ivan to let him know about The Blitz's defection to JSM. She and Ivan had been getting on much better recently, touching base every few days about the children, and in particular Hector, who was making great progress since his return from LA. But on balance she'd decided against it. They weren't married any more, and it wasn't really her place to get involved with Ivan's business problems. The fact that this particular problem involved Jack would only make it more charged and difficult. Besides, he'd find out for himself soon enough.

A knock on the front door startled her. No one ever used the front door – certainly not the postman, who always came up the twitten to the side entrance like everybody else. Perhaps it was some delivery man from London or Oxford, although she couldn't remember having ordered anything.

'Hang on!' she shouted, putting down her tea and running into the hallway. 'I'm coming.' She was still in her dressing gown and slippers (oh, the decadence of the work-from-home lifestyle) and suddenly found herself hoping that it wasn't the vicar or someone from Hector's school dropping in for a social call. The front door was bolted top and bottom and, as it was never opened, the bolts were stiff. By the time she'd wrenched them free, her cheeks were flushed with exertion and her hair was dishevelled, escaping from its elastic band in strands that stuck out at all angles.

'Sorry,' she panted, opening the door. 'We don't normally use this entrance. I . . .'

The words trailed off mid-sentence. Standing on the doorstep in a quite ridiculous outfit that included a beret, a silk cravat tied at the neck and covering half his face, and a pair of Ray-Ban aviator sunglasses, was Jack Messenger.

'Hello, Cat. Can I come in?'

Numbly, Catriona stepped back into the hallway, letting him inside and closing the door behind them. She had any number of questions to ask him, but the one that came to her lips was, 'What on earth are you wearing?'

'This?' said Jack, admiring himself in the hall mirror. 'It's my disguise. I'm here incognito, you see. I wouldn't want any of the neighbours to see me and alert your dastardly husband.'

He grinned. *Was he joking?* Suddenly Catriona felt herself feeling quite cross.

'Well, you needn't involve me in your games,' she said hotly, walking back into the kitchen. 'I had Stella Bayley here for three nights in absolute pieces about Brett leaving her. She said you've poached him back to LA.'

Jack followed her, frowning. 'It's true I re-signed the Blitz to JSM,' he said defensively. 'But that had nothing to do with Brett leaving Stella. He's having an affair.'

'Yes, with a girl in LA,' said Catriona. 'It would have fizzled out like all the others if you hadn't offered to re-start his career over there.'

She knew she was being unfair, but her anger needed an

outlet, and Stella Bayley's misery was as good a peg to hang it on as anything else.

'Cat,' Jack said gently, touching her arm. 'It's business.'

'Hmm.' Catriona sniffed. 'Bloody backhanded business if you ask me. You only came to London now because you knew Ivan was away in Paris. You're stealing Jester's clients behind his back.'

'Hang on . . .' began Jack, but Catriona was on a roll.

'It's the exact same thing that Ivan did to you with Kendall, but two wrongs don't make a right, you know. Not to mention the fact that if you bankrupt Ivan, you'll be bankrupting me. But I suppose none of that means anything to you, just as long as you end up getting Kendall back.'

'*Kendall?*' Jack looked baffled. 'This has nothing to do with Kendall. She's not even here, she's in Paris with Ivan.'

'I know where she bloody is!' shouted Catriona.

For a moment they both stood there in silence. Jack was too scared to say anything else in case he got his head bitten off, and Cat was on the verge of a nervous breakdown. Ten minutes ago she'd been full of calm positivity. Now she felt as flustered and awkward as a schoolgirl, sitting down, then standing up again, her hands flapping uselessly like the wings of some flightless bird. Catching sight of her reflection in the window, all wild hair and egg-stained dressing gown, she let out a little moan of horror and ran out of the room.

'Make yourself a cup of tea,' she called over her shoulder. 'I'm going to get dressed.'

Upstairs in the bathroom, Catriona stood naked in front of the mirror, shaking like a jelly.

Get a grip, she told herself sternly. *You must get a grip*.

Letting go of the idea of Jack had been easy. Well, relatively easy. But now that she was faced with actual flesh and blood Jack having a cup of tea in her kitchen, her emotions were whipsawing all over the place. Was she angry because of Stella or because of Jack doing the dirty on Ivan? Or was she angry because he'd been in England for a week and hadn't bothered to call? Maybe it wasn't Jack she was furious with at all, but herself, for allowing a ridiculous, childish crush to get the better of her like this.

A crush! At forty years old, on a man I've known more than half my life. It was the very definition of pathetic.

Jumping into the shower, she turned the jets up to full blast and the water onto cold in an attempt to jolt some sense back into herself. Once dry, she dressed in a pair of slim-fitting dark jeans from Next and the chocolate-brown cashmere polo neck that Ned Williams had bought her last year for Christmas but which she'd been far too fat to wear until now. She deliberately did not wear make-up. Jack was an old friend, not a suitor she was trying to impress. But she did brush her tangled blonde hair and tie it back in a neater ponytail, spritzing on a little Chanel 19 because that was what she always did. It wouldn't be right to change her habits just *because* Jack was here, and he'd once kissed her out of pity. *Oh God, stop overthinking it. He's going to think you're a madwoman and run screaming from the house.*

When she came down, Jack was standing in the kitchen looking out over the walled garden. He turned around when he heard her tread. 'I'm sorry if I upset you. I didn't come here to fight about business. I came to visit a dear, old friend.'

Dear. Old. Friend. Catriona repeated the words in her head like a catechism. *That's how he sees me. That's what we are to each other.*

'It's me who should be apologizing,' she said. 'I overreacted. I just felt terribly bad for poor Stella . . . and things.'

Jack looked at his watch. 'It's almost twelve,' he said

brightly. 'Why don't we drive over to The Fox at Oddington for a bite of lunch? My treat.'

Catriona racked her brains for a reason to refuse. It was a bit disloyal to Ivan, especially if what Stella had said about Jack raiding his client list behind his back was true. Then again, Jack *was* an old friend, he *had* worked miracles with Hector. And it was only lunch.

'OK,' she said. 'But only if you promise not to wear that ridiculous hat. You look like Hercule bloody Poirot.'

The Fox was a charming fifteenth-century coaching inn with a bar, snug and formal restaurant in a pretty hamlet near Stow-on-the-Wold. Jack and Catriona took a table in the snug, a cosy room with mellow, uneven flagstone floors covered in tatty Persian rugs, hops hanging in bunches from the beamed ceiling and a huge open stone fireplace in which a pile of pine logs burned and crackled merrily. Too nervous to eat a big meal, Catriona ordered the field mushroom soup and a side salad. Jack had a 'when-in-Rome' moment and opted for steak and kidney pudding and a pint of pale ale.

'You look terrific,' he told Catriona, watching her sip at a Diet Coke. 'You've lost a lot of weight.'

Catriona flushed, half from pleasure and half from embarrassment. 'I've been running,' she admitted. 'And I haven't had a drink since I left LA.'

'That's wonderful. Good for you.' Jack reached across the table and patted her hand. If Catriona needed any more proof that his feelings for her were a hundred per cent platonic, this was it. 'Do you feel better?'

'Yes,' she said truthfully. 'I really do actually. It's as if everything came together at once. Me getting healthy, Hector getting himself back on track, Ivan and I becoming friends again.' Jack frowned, but Catriona continued, oblivious. 'The irony is that it was Hector taking off like that that triggered it all. Not to mention the fact that it brought you back into our lives.'

The food arrived. Jack's pie was delicious, the suet pastry just the right side of stodgy and the meat as succulent and tender as he'd tasted anywhere. 'How is Hector?' he asked. Catriona spent the next fifteen minutes filling him in on the strides his godson was making at school and at home, her face lighting up as she listed each miraculous step forward. Jack listened eagerly, delighting in her happiness and thrilled to think he might have played a small part in bringing it about.

'And of course Ivan's over the moon too. It's been hard for him. Hector still won't talk to him, let alone see him. But we're both hopeful this could be the start of a change there. That eventually there'll be some *rapprochement*.'

Jack pushed aside his empty plate angrily. 'You're too good to him, you know. Too forgiving.'

Catriona looked confused. 'How can one be "too" forgiving?'

Jack couldn't help but laugh. She meant the question quite sincerely.

'Anyway, this isn't really about Ivan, it's about Hector. I love my son, and whatever he might say to me or you or his friends, I know deep down that he loves his father and misses him. They should have a relationship, Jack, if they can. Surely you can see that?'

'Hmmm,' Jack grunted grudgingly. 'Maybe.'

'Is it true you came here to steal Ivan's acts while he's in Paris?' Catriona blurted.

'It's true I timed JSM's deal with The Blitz to coincide with his absence,' said Jack cagily.

'But it's not just The Blitz, is it?' asked Catriona. 'It's all of them. You won't stop till you've destroyed Jester.' She wanted to add *'and got Kendall back'*, but something made her hesitate.

Jack was silent for a moment, considering his next words. 'Do I want Jester to fold? Yes. I do. But am I destroying it? I don't know. I'd say it was destroying itself.'

'What do you mean?'

'You can't *steal* a client, Cat, any more than you can *steal* a wife or a husband. People do what they want to do, what's in their own best interests. Brett Bayley wouldn't have come back to me if Ivan hadn't dropped the ball as his manager. And that applies to everyone else on Ivan's list. They could come to me at JSM or they could go elsewhere. But no one's going to stay where they aren't being taken care of. Everybody knows the only artists your ex cares about are Kendall and the girl Ava from his TV show. If Ivan's chosen to put all his eggs in two baskets, it's nothing to do with me.'

'So this isn't a personal vendetta, then? Is that what you're saying?'

Jack looked awkwardly out of the window through the dangling wisteria, but said nothing.

'He was your friend too, you know,' Catriona said quietly. 'Once.'

Jack turned and looked Catriona in the eye. Something about his expression made her fearful, and when he spoke his voice was a monotone, as cold and unyielding as the grave.

'You can never go back,' he said. 'Never. Not if you want to survive.'

Later that night, after Jack drove back to London, Catriona thought about his words. *Was it true? Could you really never go back?* If so, then there could be no hope for her and Ivan. It was only when Jack said it that she realized a part of her *had* still been hoping, fantasizing, imagining how life might be if Ivan finally tired of Kendall and came home. Especially if Jester really did go under, and Ivan's career hit the skids, she'd pictured herself as his safe haven, the one who took care of him, who put it all right.

'Do you still love Ivan?' she asked herself out loud. But she had no answer. Only Jack Messenger's brutal words in her head.

You can never go back.

CHAPTER SEVENTEEN

Kendall sat at a quiet corner table of Harrods' Ladurée tea rooms, poring over the same *Daily Mail* picture she'd been mentally dissecting for the past twenty minutes.

'May I bring you some more tea, madam?' The poncey waiter with the non-specific Euro accent who'd been hovering around her table like a fly on a turd since she first sat down, was back.

'No,' snapped Kendall. 'I'll ask if I want anything. Actually,' she changed her mind, 'I could go for another pistachio macaroon. One of the big ones.'

It was turning out to be a two-macaroon sort of day. Unfairly, really, because this was the week when Kendall should have been celebrating, dancing on air after a flurry of career triumphs. The French trip with Ivan had been a roaring success, vastly raising and enhancing her profile in Europe's second-largest music market. Meanwhile, two days after her return to London, she'd learned that 'Liar, Liar' was now the most downloaded song in the UK. As if that weren't wonderful enough, on Monday Clairol had called Ivan and offered her a highly lucrative endorsement deal to front their new shampoo line, Temptress. After so long in the wilderness and living on tenterhooks after her last, bombed, album, Kendall was finally firmly back on the up. This was the time to exhale, to enjoy. But of course it had all been ruined.

'Miss Bryce? I'm so s-sorry to bother you. But do you think I could maybe get your autograph?'

Kendall looked up from her newspaper. The boy was about fourteen, and as pale and spotty as a Dalmatian puppy. He was holding up a copy of her 2011 calendar and a marker pen with such an endearing look of hope that Kendall couldn't help but crack a smile.

'Sure.' She wrote her name, followed by the usual hugs and kisses, and the boy skipped away, gushing thanks. Then her second macaroon arrived, an object of such utter, ambrosial deliciousness it was hard not to feel just a teensy bit happier having bitten into it.

But only a teensy bit. The newspaper picture soon brought her back down to earth.

It was a shot of Jack Messenger walking down a rural lane with his arm wrapped around Catriona Charles's waist. Catriona looked marginally less frumpy and enormous than usual. She visibly *had* a waist for Jack to wrap his arm around. Jack looked his usual aloof, handsome, rigid-jawed self. Except that he was smiling, really smiling. As for Catriona, her round, kindly face was practically alight with happiness, beaming back up at Jack like some love-struck moon.

Or was it? Perhaps Kendall *was* reading a lot into one long-lens, more-than-slightly-grainy picture. Stella Bayley certainly thought so, and had said as much in no uncertain terms when they spoke this morning. 'I've just spent the better part of a week with Catriona. If she's sleeping with Jack, I'm a republican, OK? Believe me, there's no way.'

According to Stella, the only reason the picture was considered newsworthy in the first place was because of the media furore surrounding the now publicly announced defection of The Blitz from Jester to JSM. What started out as a gossip piece in the music press soon went mainstream once Jester's other acts started following The Blitz's lead. Suddenly the headlines were everywhere.

Ivan Charles's Rival Strikes Back.

Bayley and Co Bail on Jester.

Jester's Wild: How Jack Messenger Got His Revenge.

So far, in a single week, Ivan had seen almost sixty per cent of Jester's client list defect to his arch rival. Up till now, JSM hadn't had a single classical artist on their books, but that hadn't stopped Jack from opening his corporate arms to welcome Jester's Ned Williams and Joyce Wu. Jack's interest in The Blitz might conceivably have been viewed as legitimately commercial. But his open-door policy towards anyone and everyone who had had so much as a cup of tea at Jester, and the speed with which he was siphoning off Ivan's business, was starting to look more like a personal vendetta. Apparently, JSM's conversations with many of these artists had begun quietly months ago. In fact, the only Jester client with whom Jack Messenger and Lex Abrahams had not spoken was Kendall Bryce.

Stella Bayley seemed confident that this was a temporary state of affairs. 'Jack will call you. Of course he will. You're the point of all of this, honey. Everything else is just foreplay.'

Stella sounded so down, so defeated, Kendall didn't have the heart to question her further about it. Evidently Brett had already packed up and moved in with his mistress in LA, leaving poor Stella stranded. But, as appealing as it was to think that Jack viewed her, Kendall, as the ultimate prize, it didn't ring wholly true. The last time she had seen Jack in person, in The Brentwood restaurant in LA back in the spring, he'd practically looked right through her. As for Lex, he still hadn't forgiven her for the Chateau Marmont photos. Kendall felt terrible about that whole incident, but it was done now, and if it hadn't been done she wouldn't be back on top, riding high with 'Liar, Liar'. It had been a matter of survival.

Still, Jack Messenger's surprise trip to England had left Kendall feeling deeply unhinged. Just the thought that he was in the same country as her, perhaps even the same city, set off a swarm of butterflies in her stomach. It was not a pleasant sensation.

Finishing her macaroon, she folded the paper shut, forcing the cosy image of Catriona and Jack out of her mind. That was one thing Stella Bayley was right about. No way in hell was Jack sexually interested in a frump like Ivan's ex-wife. He probably staged the pictures just to further irritate Ivan, and rub salt in the wound of his stealth attack on Jester. But, even as she had the thought, Kendall realized this was unlikely. Jack might have good reason to hate Ivan, but he wasn't vicious and would never stoop so low as to use Catriona, or any innocent party, for that matter. Maybe there really *was* something between the two of them? It was an idea too awful to contemplate.

As for herself, Kendall clearly no longer fitted into the 'innocent party' category. *Does Jack despise me as much as he despises Ivan?* Kendall wondered. *Or is Stella right? Has he come here to win me back?*

She pushed her plate away, feeling sick to her stomach with a potent mixture of hope and fear, panic and excitement. Clearly this wasn't over. But what would Jack's next move be?

* * *

'You can consider this a formal, verbal warning.'

Don Peters glared at Ivan Charles from across his desk. A big, fat man with ruddy, drink-ravaged cheeks and a bulging paunch pushing his hairy belly through the gaping holes between his shirt buttons, admirers usually referred to Don Peters as 'larger-than-life'. Detractors preferred 'lard-arsed megolamaniac'. Either way, Don was a television heavyweight in every sense of the word, a man capable of making or breaking careers with a nod of his bald head or a wave of his fat, stubby finger.

Only a year ago he'd had high hopes for Ivan Charles. After his disastrous performance in the *Talent Quest* pilot, the telegenic co-founder of Jester had somehow managed to rediscover his confidence. Since then, the public had warmed to him as a judge, particularly since his vocal championing of the little girl from Yorkshire, Ava Bentley. But therein lay the rub. Don and the other *Talent Quest* producers had warned Ivan repeatedly about his closeness to Ava and told him to back off.

'No one contestant can become bigger than the show. Nor can any individual judge. Ava Bentley's contractual relationship is with House of Cards and ITV, not with you. I'm switching her to Stacey Harlow's group. You can take Mike Matterson.'

'The brickie?' Ivan sounded aghast.

'He's got a great voice. Second favourite to win after Ava, as you well know. Anyway, I'm not asking you, I'm telling you.'

Officially, Ivan had accepted his producer's directive. There was not much else he could do. But behind the scenes he'd waged a ruthlessly successful PR campaign in the press, leaking stories about how distraught Ava was to have been forced to switch mentors, making sure that both the media and the public continued to view him and Ava as an inseparable team. In the end a vast Facebook and Twitter campaign led ITV to reverse the producer's decision.

'I'm sorry, Don,' said Mike Grayson, Head of Programming, in a tense phone call to Don Peters. 'It's bad for the network. You'll have to give her back to Ivan Charles.'

Don Peters was livid.

From that point on he'd been actively looking for an excuse to sack Ivan. After weeks of nothing, he'd suddenly been handed three such excuses on a plate. Firstly, Ava Bentley had dropped out of the competition with some mysterious illness. All of a sudden, Ivan's closeness to the show's star began to work against him. Without Ava, viewer approval of Ivan's judging performance dropped through the floor. Secondly, Ivan had spent longer than agreed in France with his girlfriend and protégée, Kendall Bryce, thus for the first time putting himself in material breach of his *Talent Quest* contract. And thirdly, Jester, his once flourishing music-management business, and the reason he'd been hired as a judge in the first place, was very publicly collapsing around his ears.

'For *Talent Quest* to be credible, our panel need to be genuine players within the music business,' Don told Mike Grayson. 'Read the papers, Mike. Ivan Charles is a has-been.'

Ivan kept a poker face when he looked back at Don. *Disgusting, fat fuck. You can 'verbal warning' me all you like, but it's gonna take a lot more than two extra days in Paris for you to work your way out of my contract, chum.*

Aloud he said calmly, 'Understood, Don. Now, if you'll excuse me, I have a lot of work to do.'

Closing the door of Peters' office behind him, Ivan made straight for the Gents, locking himself in a stall and sitting down heavily on the closed loo seat. Loosening his tie and undoing the top two buttons of his shirt, he leaned forward and put his head between his knees.

Calm down. Breathe.

Ivan had always prided himself on his physical fitness. But, in the last few months, and in the last week in particular, stress had really started to take its toll. Right now he could feel his chest tightening and his airways start to constrict. His palms, face and underarms were all sweating profusely, and his head throbbed and ached, as if someone had pumped it full of air and his skull was about to explode with the pressure.

Xanax no longer helped, but he took one anyway, swallowing it dry. He must try not to panic. Tonight he and Kendall would drive up to Yorkshire, ostensibly on a romantic break, but actually so that Ivan could finally get Ava's father, Dave, to sign her contract with Jester. Once Ava was safely and legally under his wing, everything would be fine. Jester would be saved. Ava would print money for whatever record label was lucky enough to land her, and Kendall's new album, *Flame*, looked set to do great things, despite her rocky start at Polydor. With his own and Jester's star once again rising, Don Peters wouldn't be able to get rid of him at *Talent Quest*. And, even if he did, it wouldn't matter. *Talent Quest* had got him Ava and had made him a household name in the UK. In many ways, the show's usefulness to Ivan was on the wane anyway.

It wasn't Don Peters who was making him so anxious. It was his erstwhile friend, Jack bloody Messenger. Though it pained Ivan to admit it, Jack's hostile raid on Jester had been brilliantly planned and meticulously executed. The Blitz's defection to JSM had come as a complete shock, as had the speed with which his other acts, especially his long-standing classical list, had deserted him. But what really scared him was Kendall.

Since the earliest days of their relationship, Ivan had feared that Kendall still harboured romantic feelings for his hated rival. The thought of Kendall wanting Jack sexually drove him to the brink of madness, tormenting him with a jealousy he had never experienced before. She'd assured him countless times that those feelings were over, that he was the only lover she wanted, and the only manager. But Ivan's doubts remained. And now Jack was here, in England, crawling all over every aspect of Ivan's life like a plague of lice. Was Kendall next on Jack's hit list? Ivan could only assume that she was. If Kendall left him, it would wipe him out both professionally and personally. But would she go? Would she really stab him in the back like that, after everything they'd been through together, and how close they'd become over this past summer? The truth was, he didn't know. It was the uncertainty of it all that was slowly killing him.

Nor had today's pictures of Jack and Catriona helped. Ivan knew he had no right to quiz Catriona on her friendships, romantic or otherwise; that he had lost that right long ago. But seeing pictures of her arm in arm with the man who was openly and publicly trying to eviscerate his business had shaken him to the core. It was like watching your mother show up at boarding school and taking your worst enemy, the boy who'd bullied you and stolen your lunch money all term, out for a cream tea. The fact that you had bullied the boy in the past didn't make it any better. It was still a betrayal, and it hurt all the more for being so utterly unexpected. Ivan had never trusted Kendall. She was too like him to be trusted. But Catriona had always been his rock, her loyalty solid and constant and unchanging. Was Jack trying to steal that too?

Ivan opened the stall and splashed cold water on his face. *You'll be fine. You just have to keep your cool.* He had another difficult meeting at four, with Jester's accountants, followed by a string of crisis talks with Jester's remaining acts, such as they were, almost all of whom now wanted to renegotiate the terms of their contracts. *Once your blood's in the water, everyone's a shark*, thought Ivan bitterly.

Later that night, Kendall ordered in dinner for Ivan at the Cheyne Walk flat. She'd made an effort. Lobster linguini was his favourite, followed by panna cotta, coffee and hand-made praline truffles from the new chocolatier on Old Church Street.

'I thought you might need cheering up,' she said thoughtfully. 'You've had a hell of a day.'

'I do need cheering up,' said Ivan, grabbing her quite roughly by the wrist and pulling her onto his lap. Fumbling with the buttons on her blouse, he pulled it open hungrily, unhooking her bra and cupping her incredible breasts in his hands. His thumbs traced slow circles around her nipples as he kissed her, forcing his tongue into her mouth and pressing his stubble hard against her soft cheeks. Instinctively Kendall arched her back, kissing him back and squirming with pleasure. Tonight she needed the release as much as he did.

They staggered into the bedroom, discarding items of clothing as they went, and fell onto the bed, grappling like bear cubs. Kendall had always been aroused by the fight. She liked the feeling of being overcome, and let out little moans of excitement as Ivan flipped her over onto her back, spreading her legs with his knee and pinning her arms back on the bed with the weight of his body.

'Tell me you want me.'

'I want you,' she whispered, obediently and truthfully. 'Please, Ivan, don't play with me. Just fuck me. Now.'

The sex was incredible, wilder and more explosive than it had been in months. As Ivan thrust ever more deeply inside her, Kendall found her thoughts drifting between him and Jack. The idea that Jack might have come back to fight for her, that two such powerful, sexual men were at war over *her*, Kendall Bryce, the girl whose own father hadn't given a shit about her and had walked away without a backward glance, aroused her more than any of Ivan's skilful ministrations.

Afterwards, replete and happy, she lay back on the pillow and said idly, 'I think I might skip the Yorkshire trip if it's OK with you, darling. It's really just a business thing, isn't it, between you and Ava? And I have a hundred and one things to do in London before *Flame*'s launch party.'

Ivan stiffened, like a dog sensing danger. *She's been buttering me up. The meal, the sex. She's arranged to meet Jack this weekend and she wants me out of the way.*

He forced himself to sound calm. 'Actually, baby, I really need you. I'm using the "romantic getaway" thing as cover to meet with Dave Bentley. But it's not just that. I want you there. I need you, Kendall.' Slipping down beneath the covers, he started to lick between her thighs, his expert tongue bringing her to the brink of orgasm almost instantly. But just as she was about to come, he stopped.

'Promise you'll come with me.'

Kendall thrashed her legs in frustration. 'Come on, Ivan. Don't!'

'Promise.'

His moved his mouth over her inner thighs, then up to her lower belly, then down again, always just avoiding the one area she was screaming for him to touch. The truth was Kendall had no plans with Jack. But she *had* wanted to stay in London, just in case he called. The idea that he might reach out for her and she would miss him was unbearable. But not as unbearable as the exquisite torture Ivan was putting her through now.

'OK!' she gasped. 'OK, I'll come.'

Five seconds later, she did.

CHAPTER EIGHTEEN

Hutton-le-Hole is a chocolate-box village of grey stone and brick cottages nestled around a village green in the North York Moors National Park. Sheep wander unchecked through its lanes and pathways, and cross the hilly green to drink from the clear waters of Hutton Beck, the stream that winds its way through the village and down into the valley below. In summer tourists flock to picnic by the crumbling footbridges or stroll through the Ryedale Folk Museum, watching local craftsmen ply their ancient trades of weaving, thatching and basket making. But when Ivan and Kendall arrived, on a rainy October afternoon, the village was all but deserted.

'People live here?' The bucolic, rural idyll did not impress Kendall. 'What the hell do they *do*?'

'Farm. Commute into Pickering or Helmsley. Run tea shops,' said Ivan vaguely. Judging from the bolted doors and darkened windows in many of the cottages, he assumed a lot of property was owned by second-homers. The year-round population of a village like this, with no school, shop or pub must be minute. No wonder Ava was so wide-eyed and awestruck by London. Soon she'd be leaving this cloistered, peaceful world of her childhood for ever. It almost made Ivan feel sad.

Almost.

'Which one's Ava's house?' said Kendall irritably. 'Let's get this over with.' The drive up the A1 had been long and boring, and she hadn't been able to shake the feeling that every passing mile was taking her further and further out of Jack's reach. Not that he'd tried to call, or email. She'd checked her BlackBerry every few minutes but the hateful thing had remained resolutely, mockingly silent for the whole five-hour trip. By the time they checked in to the Black Swan Hotel in Helmsley, Kendall was in a foul mood and felt her old resentment towards Ava bubbling up again. She should have been in London this weekend, hanging out at Mahiki or Soho House, revelling in the success of 'Liar, Liar' and the attentions of her adoring public. Instead, because of sodding Ava Bentley, she was stuck in the rain in Nowheresville, Yorkshire, where none of the locals gave her a second glance.

'The only celebrities round here are pigeons or ferrets,' Ivan joked lamely, but Kendall wasn't in the mood. The warm afterglow of last night's sex had already worn off. Jack Messenger and California were becoming more appealing prospects by the second.

'It's number sixteen Back Lane,' said Ivan, peering at the rows of modest homes through the drizzle. 'Twenty-seven . . . twenty-nine . . . it must be on the other side.'

Kendall followed him across one of the narrow bridges, her New Balance trainers squelching with every step. A couple of teenage girls came running round the corner and stopped dead, screaming with excitement when they saw Kendall.

'Oh my God! Is it actually you? Oh my God, I can't believe it! Janine! Janine, it's her!'

'Can we have your autograph?' asked Janine. 'Oh shit.
I've not got owt to write on. Have you, Lisa?'

'No, but I've got me phone. Can we 'ave a picture with
you, Kendall? Please.'

As ever when she found herself the object of such adoring
attention, Kendall's spirits lifted. 'Of course,' she smiled,
wrapping an arm around each of the girls' waists and tossing
her damp hair back in a suitably starry pose. 'Ivan, honey,
would you do the honours?'

'No,' said Ivan crossly. 'We don't want any pictures, not
here. We're on a private trip.'

The girls' faces fell. Kendall scowled. 'What the hell's the
matter with you? Take the stupid picture.'

Pulling her aside, Ivan hissed in her ear. 'Not here, OK?
We're practically outside Ava's door.'

'So?'

'So if these shots made it into the papers . . . I don't want
Don Peters to smell a rat until the contract's done and
dusted.'

'You're being ridiculous,' snapped Kendall. 'They're kids,
not tabloid hacks. And we're signing the stupid contract in
five minutes, aren't we?' Grabbing Lisa's phone, she held it
out at arm's length and took the shot herself, to both girls'
squealing delight. 'Off you go now,' she said, handing the
phone back, 'before Mr Scrooge here really loses his temper.'

A minute later and a stony-faced Ivan knocked on the
door of number sixteen.

Nothing.

'Maybe they went for a walk?' said Kendall. 'Enjoying
this lovely weather.'

Ivan looked at his watch. 'Maybe,' he brooded. 'But Dave
and I agreed on four o'clock. I'm surprised he'd be late for
something this important.'

'Hmm,' sniffed Kendall. 'Well I don't know about you, but I don't intend to stand out here in the piss waiting for some builder's merchant to come home. Give me the keys. I'll wait in the car.'

Twenty minutes later, Ivan joined her, soaked to the bone and looking deeply unhappy. 'I've tried his mobile, his work number, Ava's mobile, everything. No one's answering. The house is shut up like a clam and Dave hasn't left me any messages.'

Kendall gave an unconcerned shrug. 'So something came up. Maybe they got stuck in traffic, or got a flat, or had some kind of family crisis to deal with. Who knows? You can come back and sort it out tomorrow.'

'He would have left me a message,' said Ivan, grimly starting the engine. 'I've been dealing with this guy for months now and he's straight as an arrow.'

'He probably couldn't get cell reception,' said Kendall reasonably. 'We are out in the boondocks, in case you hadn't noticed.'

This was true. Ivan tried to shake his deep sense of unease. Just because he was tense and wired, he mustn't assume that everybody else felt the same sense of urgency. It could be as simple as Kendall suggested: a flat tyre and no mobile reception.

'Let's go back to the hotel,' she said, pulling her cable-knit cashmere cardigan more tightly around her, 'before I die of fucking hypothermia. Some romantic getaway this is.'

The evening was not pleasant. Billed as Helmsley's most luxurious hotel, The Black Swan, known locally as The Mucky Duck, did not meet Kendall's exacting standards. The rooms were small, the decor dreary and the en suite bathroom distinctly lacking in the usual urban five-star accoutrements such as Jacuzzi, steam room and fluffy Egyptian cotton towels. Unfortunately, when she made these observations to Ivan, she got short shrift. 'Stop being such a fucking prima donna. It's not all about you, you know,' and the night deteriorated from there.

Dinner was uninspiring, roast chicken with peas and potatoes followed by a lacklustre fruit salad. Both Kendall and Ivan took their BlackBerries to the table and spent considerably more time looking at their blank screens than they did talking to each other. Conscious of the other diners looking at them, Ivan made some attempt to lighten the mood and engage Kendall in conversation, but after a volley of monosyllabic responses he gave up and returned to brooding.

Still no word from Dave Bentley. What the hell could he be thinking?

Across the table, Kendall toyed with a strawberry.

Still no word from Jack. I wonder what's going through his mind?

Later, lying in bed next to each other, each consumed by their own, private worries, Ivan reached over and stroked Kendall's hair. It was a tender gesture, something he used to do with Catriona all the time, but never with Kendall. He wasn't even aware he'd done it till Kendall turned over and looked at him strangely, her head cocked to one side.

'What was that for?'

'I don't know,' said Ivan truthfully.

Kendall couldn't put her finger on it, but she suddenly sensed an immense sadness. She wasn't even sure if it was Ivan's sadness or her own. All she knew was that it was there, lying in the bed between them like a big, dark cloud.

She kissed him on the cheek. 'Let's go to sleep.'

*   *   *

After a fitful night, they woke up late. Ivan immediately switched on his phone. No messages. He tried Dave Bentley's numbers again to no avail, before heading grumpily into the shower.

Once she heard the sound of the jets pumping, Kendall drew back the curtains and checked her own BlackBerry. Three new messages! For a second her heart soared, but she soon came back down to earth. Two were from Stella, asking how the weekend away was going, and one was from Fiona, the new publicist at Polydor, forwarding a schedule of promotional events for next week's official release of *Flame*. Nothing from Jack.

Breakfast was fried and enormous. There was no menu, no continental option, just vast, towering plates of bacon, scrambled eggs, mushrooms, grilled tomato, baked beans, fried bread and black pudding. Kendall thought about complaining, but changed her mind once she started eating and realized it was all delicious. Fortified by this calorie bomb and two large pots of coffee, both she and Ivan got into the car in slightly better spirits.

The plan was to make one more trip over to Hutton-le-Hole, just in case there were signs of life at the house, then to head back to London. The Bentleys would make contact eventually. Ava usually called Ivan at least twice a week, so sooner or later he'd get to the bottom of it. In the meantime, Jester, *Flame* and *Talent Quest* all required his urgent attention.

Ava's house was as lifeless and gloomy as it had been the day before. Clearly none of the family had been home overnight. Irritated, but not surprised, Ivan took the scenic route back to the motorway, across the moor and down the steep bank into Rosedale Abbey. Kendall gazed out of the window, more appreciative of the beauty of the landscape now that she was leaving it, heading back to London and life, and getting closer to Jack with each rev of the engine. Or was she? For all she knew, Jack might at this very moment be on a plane back to LA. Perhaps he hadn't come for her after all. Or worse, he had come, but she'd missed him. *Maybe he thinks I've been avoiding him on purpose?* Maybe, maybe, maybe. She had to stop thinking about it all the time, trying to second-guess Jack's motives. She'd drive herself mad.

Ivan switched the radio onto Classic FM. It was a track from Joyce Wu's *Greatest Hits* album. He quickly turned over.

'Oh God, not this,' groaned Kendall, as James Naughtie's familiar Scottish tones filled the car. Radio Four was for intellectuals and old people. It occurred to her that perhaps Ivan fitted into both categories – a depressing thought, but she pushed it quickly aside, flipping over to Radio One where the latest Rihanna track was finishing.

'And in breaking news,' the DJ's voice started in as the vocals faded out, 'very exciting for all you Ava Bentley fans out there . . .'

At the mention of Ava's name, Ivan swerved, almost taking them into a hedge. He righted himself, driving slowly as the DJ went on.

'We've just heard that Ava Bentley has been signed by the top American management company JSM. So all you *Talent Quest* fans who were upset not to see her in the final, you can rest assured you haven't seen the last of Miss Bentley.'

'Isn't JSM run by the guy that used to be Ivan Charles's partner?' a female voice chimed in, presumably one of the DJs sidekicks.

'Jack Messenger, that's right. He's already signed up a lot of the talent from Ivan's own agency, Jester, in the last few weeks. I wonder how Ivan's gonna react to seeing his protégée sign up with his arch rival as well? We'll bring you that reaction as soon as we get it.'

'But in the meantime, well done, Ava!'

Ivan stopped the car. He looked white as a sheet. 'I don't believe it.' All this time he'd been worried about leaving Kendall behind in London, scared Jack would use his absence to worm his way in and steal her back. But it had never been Kendall he was after. It was Ava! Ivan had been played.

He picked up his mobile. No reception.

'Give me your phone,' he barked at Kendall. She looked white too, like a cancer patient who's just been told their tumour isn't operable after all. She gave him her BlackBerry and Ivan punched out a number.

'Will?'

Jester's beleaguered number two, Will Jameson, picked up instantly. 'You've heard, then?'

'Just now. Some idiots on Radio One, but there were no details. What do you know?'

Will Jameson sighed. 'I've been online for the past hour. Ava's saying nothing; they're still going with the line that she's too sick to make a statement.'

'They're using my strategy!' said Ivan furiously. 'They don't want to risk Don Peters suing.'

'Messenger gave a press conference, though, about fifteen minutes ago. I can play you the audio if you like?'

'Go ahead.' Ivan put Kendall's BlackBerry on speaker and propped it up on the dashboard. Kendall wanted to open the door and run, but it was too late. Seconds later, Jack's voice filled the car.

'I'm delighted to announce that Ava Bentley has decided to become part of the JSM family. I've followed Ava's progress with interest since she first appeared on *Talent Quest*. Ivan Charles was quite right to identify her as a major vocal talent, and I believe with the right US platform she has what it takes to become a huge global star. JSM will be able to give her that platform.'

'*Bastard*,' hissed Ivan.

'Like all Ava's fans, I was devastated for her when she had to pull out of the competition due to ill-health. She's still very unwell, but the doctors have assured her she should make a full recovery within the next four to six weeks. Too late for *Talent Quest*, but in this case it turns out that Britain's loss will be America's gain. I knew I would have to move quickly to secure a deal with Ava, but her father Dave and I hit it off immediately. We finalized the paperwork yesterday and my hope is that Ava will move out to Los Angeles to start recording some material after Christmas.'

In the background a reporter could be heard shouting, 'What does Ivan Charles have to say about this? Have you spoken to him? Has Ava?'

'Ava's too sick to speak to anybody right now. And no, Ivan and I haven't spoken, but I'm sure he'll be as delighted for Ava as the rest of her friends are. This is a unique opportunity—'

Kendall reached forward and hung up the phone.

'What did you do that for?' said Ivan.

'Because I can't listen to it any more. And I don't know how you can.' She opened the door and bolted into the lane. It felt strangely incongruous, standing there among the green fields and sheep and centuries-old dry-stone walls, surrounded by peace and beauty while her hopes crumbled to dust.

Jack hadn't come for her. He'd come for Ava.

He didn't want her any more.

Try as she might to stop them, tears started to flow down Kendall's cheeks. She had made her choice, she had chosen

Ivan, and no one was going to come and rescue her from the consequences of that decision. The irony was that by taking Ava, Jack had driven Kendall and Ivan even more closely and irrevocably together. Professionally, Kendall was now all Ivan had left. He needed her. Only a few months ago, that was exactly what Kendall had wanted: that certainty; that security of knowing that Ivan would never leave her, either as a lover or in her career. Now, thanks to Jack, she had it. But instead of triumphant trumpets sounding, all she could hear was the clang of prison doors closing. She was trapped.

Alone inside the car, Ivan felt similar emotions, only his were tinged with rage. Jack had taken everything from him. His business, his reputation, the love and affection of his own son, and now Ava.

Of course he still had Kendall. Sexy, talented, unpredictable Kendall, the one who'd started it all. He watched her pacing in the lane, picking berries off the hedgerows and flinging them furiously into the meadows beyond. She had her back to him, but Ivan could tell from her shaking shoulders that she was crying. *She thought Jack had come back for her*, he thought sadly. He wondered if she would ever stop wanting him, stop yearning for the life she'd left behind? Then again, would he? Now that he and Kendall had been thrown back together, Catriona was farther away from him than ever. He, too, had made his choices. And there was no rescue in sight.

Getting out of the car, he walked up behind Kendall and gently put his arms around her. 'It's OK,' he whispered. 'He's hurt us both. I understand.'

Ivan's unexpected compassion and tenderness was more than Kendall could bear. Turning around, she threw herself into his arms, sobbing and sobbing until she hadn't an ounce of breath left. Eventually she recovered enough to ask plaintively, 'Oh, Ivan. What are we going to do?'

'That's easy,' said Ivan, tightening his grip around her tiny, shivering body. 'We're going to make you the biggest female recording artist on the planet. We're going to wipe the floor with Ava Bentley, JSM and anyone else who gets in our way. And we're going to annihilate Jack fucking Messenger.'

Kendall managed a small laugh. 'Oh we are, are we? Well, that's good to know. Anything else while we're at it? Take over the world, perhaps?'

'As a matter of fact, there is something else,' said Ivan.

'And what's that?'

'We're going to get married.'

CHAPTER NINETEEN

The morning after Jack Messenger told the world that he had signed Ava Bentley to JSM, Kendall Bryce and Ivan Charles announced their engagement. Just as Ivan had hoped, the news was received rapturously by the British press. Every celebrity gossip magazine from *Heat* to *Now* to *OK!* ran pictures of the happy couple on their front covers, and for weeks shots of Kendall smiling and flashing her huge four-carat diamond engagement ring were plastered all over the red-tops. Indeed, so great was the public surge of affection for the couple, particularly in the light of Ivan's recent setbacks, that Polydor brought forward the release of Kendall's new album, *Flame*, which promptly debuted at number five in the UK album charts and number two in France, as well as going gold in every other European market.

Within a week, it was as if Ava Bentley had never existed. And Kendall and Ivan were already on their way back.

Ava's defection to America and Jack Messenger wasn't the only news to get 'buried' by Ivan and Kendall wedding fever. In the weeks preceding the wedding, Ivan was unceremoniously sacked by ITV; and Jester, the once great company to which he'd devoted his entire adult, professional life, was quietly dissolved in a South London courtroom. But no one wanted to read about these doom-and-gloom stories, especially with Christmas just around the corner. They wanted to read about Kendall's dress, who was invited to the star-studded reception, and where the newlyweds would be going on honeymoon. Everybody loved a happy ending.

Meanwhile, back in LA, Jack could do nothing but watch in frustration as Ivan skilfully rebuilt his image, telling television interviewers around the world that he'd decided his time with *Talent Quest* had reached 'a natural end'. 'I want to spend more time at home with my beautiful wife,' he gushed. 'Who wouldn't? I'm so blessed to have Kendall in my life. Family's really my focus now.'

It was galling to come back from England having succeeded in annihilating Jester, only to find that Ivan Charles had already risen phoenix-like from the ashes. But then perhaps Jack should have expected it? Ivan had always been a consummate master of his own image, and a wily and determined competitor. Jack's mood wasn't helped by the fact that Lex Abrahams, and a lot of the other JSM staff, were still furious with him for taking off for a month and for saddling them with a string of unknown British acts (half of them classical, for God's sake!) without consulting a soul.

'What is this?' Lex shouted at him the day he got back, 'a partnership or a dictatorship?' For once, Jack was lost for a comeback. Even Catriona was upset with him for going after Ava. Apparently she considered it 'below the belt', conveniently forgetting that her slippery, two-faced ex-husband had never exactly been big on Queensbury Rules when it came to business – or any kind of rules, for that matter.

The thought of Kendall marrying Ivan made Jack feel physically sick. There was no doubt that in PR terms it was a masterstroke. But the idea that he, Jack, might have brought the thing to pass was more than he could stomach.

So much for the return of the conquering hero.

Two days before the wedding, Catriona raced around the drawing room in Burford, manically plumping up pillows and rearranging photographs on the various side tables.

'Muuum.' Rosie walked in and rolled her eyes. 'For heaven's sake, stop it. Anyone would think the pope was coming over. It's only Dad.'

In black, skintight jeans and the extortionate Balmain leather jacket that Ivan had bought her for her birthday last year, Rosie looked tall and skinny and gorgeous. Gone was the gawky teen of the last few years, replaced almost overnight it seemed by this clear-skinned, willowy, confident young woman with magenta-painted toes and an artfully arranged selection of bangles jangling at her wrists like Christmas bells.

'You look lovely,' Catriona told her, smiling. 'No one'll be looking at the bride when they see you in that bridesmaid's dress.'

This remark earned a second eye-roll, but it was followed by a hug and an offer of a cup of tea. There could be no mistaking her daughter's happiness as she skipped into the kitchen to put the kettle on, and Catriona didn't begrudge her a second of it. For Rosie the wedding was exciting. She'd been over the moon when Ivan had asked her if she'd consider being bridesmaid. After all the poor girl had been through in the difficult early days of their divorce, the pain of seeing her parents at war, finding herself the undeserving target of her brother's anger for the 'crime' of maintaining a relationship with her dad, Rosie deserved a little joy. Catriona and Ivan were 'friends' now, and even Hector had calmed down on the Ivan bashing. Although he drew the line at attending the wedding, he hadn't given Rosie any stick for her decision. Perhaps Rosie felt that an official union between her father and Kendall would draw a line under all the heartache and enable all of them to finally move on?

Perhaps she was right. Catriona herself had mixed feelings about the wedding. It had certainly come as a shock. She'd had no idea Ivan was even thinking of taking such a big step, and had heard the news on television like everybody else. In fairness, Ivan had tried to call her, as she later discovered when she charged her phone and checked the messages. But it was still a bolt from the blue. There was a time when news like this would have been inordinately painful. Now the negative feelings she had fell more into the wistful, regretful, nostalgic category. This was soft-focus pain, of the sort that called for anxious cushion-plumping rather than a bottle and a half of Gordon's. Not drinking definitely helped.

Ivan arrived before Rosie's promised tea. Through the drawing-room window, Catriona saw him park his blue Bentley on the High Street and climb out, brushing lint off his corduroy trousers and smoothing down his hair as he walked round the side of the house. *He's nervous too*, she thought, not without affection. How strange this all was! Catriona hadn't actually seen Ivan in person in well over a month, not since before Stella came to stay. So much had happened in his life in that time, and so little in her own. But she was happy pottering around Burford, tending her garden and taking her photographs. She wondered if he was happy, living his life at warp speed, having his every up and down splashed all over the tabloids for public consumption.

I suppose he must be. He wouldn't do it otherwise. Perhaps Kendall was the wife he needed after all.

'Dad!' Rosie flung open the kitchen door, spilling tea all over the flagstone floor.

'Hello, Rose.' Ivan hugged his daughter tightly. Like Catriona he was astonished by how quickly she seemed to be growing up. 'You look gorgeous as ever. Are you packed?'

'Nearly,' said Rosie, who hadn't even unearthed a suitcase yet. 'I'll just go upstairs and, er, finish off.'

Catriona walked in just as Rosie was leaving. *Bloody hell*, thought Ivan, *she looks good too*. Ever since she got back from California, Cat had been on some health kick, no doubt inspired by St Jack of Brentwood. But, as irritated as he was by Jack's influence, Ivan had to admit that Catriona looked ten years younger as a result. Her skin was clear, her pale-blue eyes bright and shining and her wild blonde hair as thick and lustrous as he remembered it in her twenties. But the biggest change was in her figure. She must have lost two stone at least, none of it from her tits, which seemed fuller and more glorious than ever beneath her tight coral T-shirt. Her legs looked terrific in a pair of slim-fitting cords and sexy riding boots, and Ivan searched in vain for the comforting roll of fat that used to be wrapped around her hips and belly.

'Hello, Ivan.' She kissed him on both cheeks. Ivan noticed that she smelled of violets. 'How are you?'

'Fine,' said Ivan. 'You know. Busy. You?'

'Less busy.' Catriona laughed. Now that he was actually here, she felt her tension easing. 'Nothing much changes around here, you know that. Can I get you some tea?'

They sat in the parlour at the back of the house, overlooking the garden. It was only half past three, but midwinter dusk was already beginning to settle over the frosty ground, giving everything an eerie, silvery feel. Catriona lit a fire and poured piping hot Lapsang into mismatched china cups. 'Shortbread?' She offered a plate to Ivan. 'It's home-made.'

Ivan looked at it longingly. 'I can barely get into my morning suit as it is.'

'Nonsense,' said Catriona. 'You're skinny as a bean. You always were. Go on.'

Ivan gave into temptation. 'What about you?' he mumbled through a mouth full of delicious, buttery biscuit crumbs. 'You look like you haven't had a biscuit in a year.'

Catriona blushed, swatting away the compliment.

'I'm serious,' said Ivan. 'You're looking fantastic. Like a new woman.'

You're marrying a new woman, thought Catriona stupidly. Aloud she said, 'I'm trying to be healthier. Jack sort of got me into it, running and eating protein and whatnot.'

At the mention of Jack's name, all the congeniality drained from Ivan's face. 'You and Jack still thick as thieves, eh?'

'I wouldn't say that,' Catriona bridled. She thought of her last conversation with Jack, where she'd got upset with him about 'stealing' Ava Bentley from Ivan, and they'd actually had rather an unpleasant row. 'We have our differences, but he's an old friend.'

'He looked like more than a friend in those *Daily Mail* pictures,' said Ivan grumpily. 'You were all over each other.' He knew he was being ridiculous. That he had absolutely no right to say anything to Catriona about her friendships, love life, any of it. But he'd never been much good at controlling his emotions, and the jealousy welling up inside him needed an outlet.

Catriona was just about to get to her feet, a *how dare you* already half formed on her lips, when Hector's voice drifted in from the kitchen. 'Mum? Are you home? MUM!'

'In here,' Catriona called back nervously. 'With Dad. He's come to pick up Rosie for the wedding.'

Hector stuck his head round the doorway. Ivan was shocked by how much older he looked. *Christ, he's matured. They're growing up without me.* Blond and blue-eyed like his mother, but with his father's strong jaw and masculine bearing, Hector had recently lost the freckly, *Just William*-ish look of his boyhood and shot up several inches in height. He still needed to fill out a bit, to get past that gangly limbed teenage stage. But you could already see the handsome, intelligent, decent man he was going to become.

He met Ivan's eye without flinching, and nodded a curt 'hello'. Not exactly a warm welcome, but a light year's improvement on his former rabid hostility.

'Hi,' said Ivan warily. He didn't want to jinx the good start. 'I wasn't expecting to see you.'

'I didn't know if I'd make it back in time,' said Hector. 'I wanted to see Rosie before she goes. I've got her a surprise.'

Catriona eyed her son distrustfully. 'What sort of surprise?' Rosie was so excited about the wedding and her trip to London, the last thing she needed was one of her brother's practical jokes. However well intentioned, Hector's 'tricks' had an alarming tendency for getting out of hand.

'A brilliant one,' grinned Hector. 'Come into the garden in five minutes and I'll show you.'

He dashed out of the room, leaving his parents looking at one another with raised eyebrows and an amused look on their faces. The earlier tension between them had evaporated like dew in an unexpected burst of sunshine.

'I was just thinking how grown-up he seemed,' said Ivan with a smile, 'but perhaps I spoke too soon?'

'Do you remember when he was little, his "traps"?' said Catriona. 'In the London house – how he used to drag us out into the garden where he'd tied all the plants and garden implements together with string?'

'Wearing my father's old RAF cap and holding his cap gun? How could I forget?'

They both laughed at the memory. But when the laughter trailed off, the room felt heavy with silence. A million words formed in Ivan's head, most of them beginning with *I'm sorry*, but none of them coming near to conveying the regret that he actually felt. In the end, silence seemed more respectful. Catriona, who'd been fine up until this point, suddenly found herself having to use every ounce of energy not to cry. When Hector called 'Ready!', she shot out of her seat like a racehorse at the sound of the starter's pistol, practically running into the garden.

'What do you think?' Hector looked at his mother expectantly.

'Oh!' Catriona gasped. 'Oh my goodness gracious! He's *lovely*!'

A pathetically small brown and white puppy snuffled and tumbled its way over the cold stone path. It had too much skin for its tiny frame, like a bloodhound or a basset, but the longer legs and wiry coat suggested some sort of terrier. Gambolling over Catriona's flower beds, it threw itself at Ivan's feet, pressing itself into his trouser leg for warmth. Ivan crouched down to pet it, pulling it up onto his lap where it promptly peed.

Utterly charmed, he turned to Hector. 'Where did you get him? He's a cross-breed, I presume?' In the delight of the moment, he had forgotten to edit himself around his son and just asked the question naturally. Hector responded in kind.

'He's from Middle Farm in Icomb. Fifty quid. The bitch is a Jack Russell with a bit of spaniel in her, I think. Maisie, Jonas Lyon's dog.'

'My God,' laughed Ivan. 'I remember that dog. Hasn't Jonas had her since prep school? I'd have thought she was a bit long in the tooth for puppies.'

'That's what the Lyons all thought. They've got no idea who fathered the litter, but I reckon it was a pedigree something. Look at the way Byron holds his head up. He knows he's something special.'

'Byron?' Catriona giggled, watching the scruffy little dog worrying at the sleeve of Ivan's cashmere Aquascutum Jacket. 'As in the poet?'

'As in Lord Byron,' said Hector firmly. 'Was he a poet? I thought he was just a cool dude. Anyway, he's a present for Rosie, a sort of sorry-for-being-such-a-tosser-last-year slash Christmas present. Do you think she'll like him?'

The question was addressed to Catriona, but Ivan answered, with Byron still hanging off his arm, legs flailing and tail wagging wildly. 'She'll love him, mate,' he grinned. 'He's a fucking inspiration.'

'Thanks, Dad,' said Hector. And quite without thinking, the two of them hugged.

Upstairs at her bedroom window, Rosie had watched the whole scene play out. The puppy, her parents' obvious affection, Hector and Ivan laughing and joking with one another, like the old days. It should have made her happy. Everybody getting along at last. But instead she locked her bedroom door, sank down on the bed, put her head in her hands and wept.

Two days before her wedding to Ivan, Kendall booked herself into a suite of rooms at The Connaught Hotel in London. Tucked away in a quiet corner of Mayfair, The Connaught was less flashy and brash than The Dorchester or The Berkeley, yet every bit as exclusive. Downstairs the lobby and formal rooms were decorated in classic English upper-class style, with eighteenth-century portraits and landscapes on the walls, antique but unfussy mahogany furniture and exquisite red and blue Persian rugs thrown over wide, walnut floorboards. Upstairs, Kendall's 'apartment suite' was more sleek and modern in design, a smart mixture of dark blues and greys contrasting with the crisp white linens and gleaming silver fixtures. At over three thousand square feet, the suite was vast, comprising of three bedrooms, each with their own bathroom, a living room, study, library, butler's pantry and two terraces. Rosie, Ivan's daughter, and Stella Bayley, Kendall's bridesmaid and maid of honour respectively, would spend the night before the wedding in the two spare bedrooms. Then, on the morning itself, the reception rooms and terraces would be flooded with stylists, hairdressers, dress designers, make-up artists, florists and the rest of the seemingly never-ending entourage considered essential for a modern celebrity wedding. It would, Kendall told herself, be fun.

So far, since the first heady days of her engagement, there'd been little time for fun. *Flame*'s success, and the furore surrounding her and Ivan's marriage, meant that Kendall had been on a pretty much ceaseless round of publicity. Every day she had at least four 'official' work engagements, CD signings, appearances on TV or radio shows, photoshoots for fashion magazines or for commercial sponsors. But, beyond that, every time she stepped outside her door she was 'on', playing the role of the returning mega-star, or the ecstatic fiancée, smiling till her jaw ached and waving till her wrists felt limp. She had no idea how Kate Middleton did it. As exciting and rewarding as it was to be the centre of so much attention, it could not fairly be categorized as 'fun'.

It also meant that she had almost no time to think about the personal side of what was happening to her. Marrying

Ivan was more than just a wedding. It was a marriage, a commitment to forge a life together, to have children, to grow old. How did she feel about that? She told herself she was happy, that she loved Ivan. If she was confused and anxious, it was because it had all happened so suddenly, the proposal, the media frenzy, the sudden career success. Even so, for someone who'd just been given everything she ever wanted wrapped up in a big red bow, Kendall felt a pronounced lack of elation. For some reason she found herself longing to speak to Lex Abrahams. In past emotional crises he'd always made sense of things for her in a way that no one else since had been able to. Twice since she'd checked in to the Connaught, she'd dialled Lex's number, only to hang up the phone at the first ring.

When the morning of the wedding finally dawned, Kendall woke feeling much brighter. She'd gone to bed early, at Stella and Rosie's insistence, and slept for eleven straight hours thanks to the Ambien that Stella had crushed into her hot chocolate.

After a delicious breakfast of pains au chocolat and almond pancakes, washed down with freshly pressed orange juice and multiple cappuccinos (for some reason she felt ravenously hungry), she jumped in the shower while Stella and Rosie dealt with the arriving army of people.

'Where should I go first?' Emerging from the bathroom in a bathrobe with a white towel tied turban-style around her head and her face scrubbed clean of make-up, Kendall looked incredibly young and vulnerable. As the matron of honour, Stella immediately took control.

'Hair and nails,' she said briskly. 'Anthony's set up in the study.'

'Is my dress back from downstairs?' Kendall asked anxiously. 'I sent it to be pressed last night and I haven't—'

'The dress is fine. Everything's fine,' said Stella, ushering her through to where the hairdresser was waiting.

'Yes, but I didn't see it this morning and the concierge said—'

'Stop worrying,' said Stella firmly, 'and leave everything to me.'

Sometimes, thought Kendall, it paid to have a bossy friend.

No sooner had she sat down in Anthony's styling chair than Rosie wandered in carrying a portable telephone. 'It's your mother.' Kendall opened her mouth to protest. She hadn't spoken to Lorna in months, and what with the whirl-wind of the last few weeks, realized she had forgotten to reply to her last two emails. She couldn't face a haranguing this morning. But Rosie had already thrust the phone into her hand, and before she knew it, Kendall was listening to the familiar voice from five thousand miles across the ocean. Not berating her, as it happened, but wishing her joy.

'I hope my flowers got there in time, honey.' Lorna's voice was loaded with love. 'Coals to Newcastle, I expect, but I wanted you to have something natural and beautiful from all of us at home. We miss you.'

Guilt and homesickness hit Kendall like a double punch to the stomach. She burst into tears. 'I miss you too, Mom, and the twins. Once the promotional tour's over, I promise I'll come out to visit.'

'With your new husband, I hope,' said Lorna. 'You'll have to get used to saying "we" now, not "I". You're about to be a married woman, Kendall.'

Kendall started howling again. 'I knooooow!'

By the time she hung up, her nose was clown-red, her eyes puffy and her cheeks blotched and tear-streaked. Karen, the chief make-up artist, walked in and gasped in horror. 'No more phone calls!' she said imperiously. 'Who gave her this phone?'

'I did,' said Rosie meekly. 'It was her mother and—'

'I don't care if it was Jesus fucking Christ.' Karen glared at Rosie. 'In two hours' time half the world's press are gonna be zooming in for close-ups on that face. Kendall is *not* to be upset, she is *not* to be disturbed, she is *not*—'

'I am here, you know,' said Kendall, winking encouragingly at Rosie, who looked as if she might be about to cry herself. 'Come on, guys. Lighten up.'

'Lighten up?' said Karen and Anthony in horrified unison.

'Sweetie,' Karen explained patiently, 'this is your wedding day. Probably the single biggest PR opportunity of your career. It doesn't get any more serious than this. Now,' she clapped her hands loudly, like Mary Poppins, 'bridesmaid and MOH. I need both of you in the chair right now.'

Bizarrely, everybody else's nerves and stress had a calming effect on Kendall. When Stella and her stylist, Sasha, came in with the dress, carefully helping her into it before slipping on her cream satin Manolo Blahnik heels, she felt happier and more peaceful than she had in days.

'How do I look?' she said, twirling in front of the full-length mirror in the master bedroom. But she already knew the answer. In a clinging silk and lace column from Amanda Wakeley, with her dark hair piled luxuriantly on top of her head and fixed in place with an array of diamond and platinum pins that twinkled like stars when they caught the light, she looked like a goddess of the night. Her make-up was understated, making the most of her luminous skin, with only her extraordinary green cat's eyes played up by a subtle, smoky shadow. As usual, Karen had worked wonders, although with a face as perfectly formed as Kendall's, you could hardly go wrong.

'Daddy's going to die of pride when he sees you,' said Rosie, hugging her before scurrying off to adjust her own dress.

'I just hope Ivan's hard-on doesn't spoil the ceremony,' said Stella once she'd gone. 'No one likes to see a groom with a boner.'

'I do,' grinned Kendall.

'You look amazing honey, truly.' Stella squeezed her hand. 'Now, everybody get out of here and leave the bride alone. She needs a few minutes to herself before the cars arrive.'

The bedroom door closed, and Kendall enjoyed the first minute of absolute quiet since she'd opened her eyes. She twirled and preened in front of the mirror, enjoying her princess moment and drawing strength and confidence from her reflection. She *did* look beautiful. It wasn't vanity. It was an objective fact. The magazines tomorrow would be full of pictures and comments, all of them pronouncing her wedding look a dazzling, triumphant success.

Enjoy it, she told herself. *Just enjoy it.*

When the phone rang beside her bed, she picked it up without thinking. All the nerves of the past few days and hours had gone. No one could bring her down now.

'Hello, this is the bride speaking,' she giggled.

'Hi, Kendall. It's me.'

Lex's voice was like a glass of cold water in the face. Serious. Joyless. Distant. Only last night, she'd been desperate to speak to him. Now she felt her confidence and *joie de vivre* draining away like rainwater in a gutter.

'I can't really talk now, Lexy,' she said nervously. 'Thanks for calling and everything, but I'm about to leave for the ceremony.'

'I know.' He sounded strained, as if he were already regretting the call. 'I should've called earlier but I didn't . . . I wasn't . . .' He cleared his throat. 'I didn't know exactly what to say. So I put it off.'

'Well, "congratulations" is probably the safest option. Traditional, you know,' Kendall joked weakly. 'A lot of people go with that.'

'It's not too late,' Lex blurted.

The words came out so quickly that at first Kendall wasn't sure she'd heard him correctly.

'I'm sorry?'

'You don't have to marry him. You don't have to go through with it.'

Kendall sank down on the bed. She was shaking, frightened and angry at the same time. 'Why are you saying this? What the hell's wrong with you? It's my wedding day.'

'Just because people expect it, just because there are cameras and fans out there waiting, it isn't too late,' Lex pressed on. 'You can still change your mind. That's all I'm saying.'

'And what makes you think I want to change my mind?' said Kendall coldly. How dare Lex call, minutes before the biggest moment of her life, and throw a bomb like this in her lap? Yes, she'd treated him badly in the spring. But she didn't deserve this. No one deserved this. 'Has it ever occurred to you that I might be happy? That I'm marrying Ivan because I love him?'

'No,' said Lex bluntly. 'It hasn't. I know you don't love him.'

'Oh, right,' snapped Kendall. 'What are you now, telepathic?'

'Any more than he loves you,' Lex went on relentlessly. 'This is all about publicity, about business, and you know it.'

320

'Fuck you!'

'You'll regret it, Kendall. Ivan Charles is a monster. He's an opportunist, a womanizer—'

'I don't have to listen to this.'

'. . . a back-stabber, a liar—'

'Back-stabber? And how would you describe Jack's recent actions, your beloved partner? What he did to Jester, then going after Ava like that? I'd call that some pretty fucking A-level back-stabbing, wouldn't you?'

'We're not talking about Jack,' said Lex. 'We're talking about you making the biggest mistake of your life.'

'Yeah, well, not any more we're not,' said Kendall, slamming down the receiver. 'Jerk,' she said out loud. She was still shaking. 'Asshole. Fucking ASSHOLE!'

Stella Bayley came running in. 'Is everything OK?' she asked anxiously. 'What happened?'

'Nothing,' said Kendall grimly. 'Everything's fine.'

Rosie stuck her pretty, smiling head around the door. 'The cars are here. Are you ready?'

'Absolutely,' said Kendall, adrenaline coursing through her veins. *Fuck Lex Abrahams. Fuck Jack. Fuck all of them. I'm going to marry Ivan and we're going to be ecstatically happy.* 'Let's go.'

Across the lobby of a New York Hotel, where they were both staying on business, Jack Messenger saw his partner looking troubled.

'You OK?' he asked Lex.

'Fine.'

'Who was that on the phone just now?'

Lex turned on him furiously. 'None of your damn business, Jack, OK? Jesus. Can't I even make a private call without you breathing down my neck?'

He stalked off. Jack let him go. Today was Kendall and Ivan's wedding in London. Everyone at JSM knew that Lex still held a torch for Kendall Bryce, but no one knew it better than Jack. Poor kid. No wonder he was on edge.

Nay-sayers and would-be malicious gossips were disappointed by the Bryce/Charles nuptials. The least you expected of pop stars and TV talent-show hosts was that their wedding should be brash and vulgar, but Kendall and Ivan's ceremony was exquisite, a triumph of understated good taste. You could practically see the girl from the *Daily Mail* gnashing her teeth at the lack of glitter ponies and Jordan-esque bling. Instead the small, celebrity-packed crowd of around a hundred guests were treated to an intimate, touching ceremony under a marquee at the Chelsea Physic Garden. Discreetly hidden gas heaters kept everyone from freezing as they stepped out of the frosted wonderland into a Victorian Christmas-themed tent, decked simply in boughs of berry-laden holly and scented with oranges, cinnamon and cloves. It was dark by the time Ivan and Kendall said their vows beneath a mistletoe-covered arbor, which lent the service an even more festive and magical air.

Unable to stomach the thought of being given away by a male acquaintance, or worse, an exec from her record company, Kendall decided that she and Ivan would arrive and walk down the aisle together. In the exquisitely simple lace and silk dress, Kendall looked as young and virginal as The Lady of Shalott. Leaning into Ivan, uncharacteristically shy now that the big moment was actually here, she appeared like a little lost lamb, clinging to her shepherd. Ivan, dashingly handsome in a classic Savile Row morning suit, was more than happy to play her protector, guiding her with a firm, loving hand to the temporary 'altar' while the string quartet played Handel in the background.

'Are you OK?' he asked, just audibly, once they'd greeted the minister.

Kendall nodded mutely.

'Try and relax,' said Ivan. 'You look beautiful. You *are* beautiful.'

Kendall smiled and squeezed his hand, to a collective 'Ahhh!' from the guests in the front row. But her unexpected nerves seemed to continue throughout the service. When the minister asked, 'Do you, Kendall Lorna Grace take Ivan Peter St John Charles to be your lawful wedded husband?' Kendall's 'I do' was as faint and tremulous as that of a little girl on her first day at nursery school, answering her teacher's question. And her hands shook visibly as her new husband slipped on the plain Tiffany wedding band.

Ivan, by contrast, spoke clearly and with conviction, especially during the 'forsaking all others' part, when he made a point of looking Kendall deep in the eyes. His 'till death do us part' boomed mellifluously around the marquee like Richard Burton narrating at the Pyramids of Karnak.

'Bloody hell. I think he really means it,' an old friend from Oxford whispered to his wife.

'I think you might be right.'

All in all, it was a touchingly romantic ceremony from a couple everybody knew as a pair of tough-minded careerists. Perhaps the traumas of recent events really had changed them and strengthened their bond as a couple? Kendall certainly seemed gentler, and Ivan mellower and more content than any of their friends could remember them, smiling and laughing as they walked back down the aisle to a standing ovation.

After an extended break for press photographs and interviews, it was finally time for the reception. As the guests sat down to a sumptuous candlelit dinner of smoked salmon parfait, roast goose with all the trimmings and a towering traditional Christmas cake, decorated with silver snowflakes and spun sugar ballet figures dancing *The Nutcracker Suite*, much of the talk was of the bridesmaids, who had both looked ravishing in simple, floor-length midnight-blue gowns. Rosie Charles was a natural beauty, and Stella Bayley, the object of so much public 'pity' (actually gleeful *Schadenfreude*) since her husband left her, positively dazzled in her borrowed Fred Leighton diamonds, smiling and laughing like a woman on a genuine high.

Numerous famous married men openly hit on Stella during the reception, to the relief of the *Daily Mail* journalist who'd been panicking she'd have nothing at all for her feature tomorrow. Sometimes it was tough working for a paper whose motto was the opposite of that of mothers the world over: 'If you can't say something nasty, don't say anything at all.'

But Catriona Charles had been wrong about one thing. Nobody, not even Rosie, had outshone the bride. Not only was Kendall radiantly beautiful, but she and Ivan seemed so in tune with one another, so naturally and obviously in love, it was impossible to do anything other than wish them well. At dinner Kendall talked excitedly about their upcoming honeymoon in St Bart's (thereby helpfully letting the press know where to find them; the innocent lamb from the earlier service was gone now, replaced by the more familiar ballsy pop star the nation knew and loved), while Ivan gave a touching and funny speech about their colourful romantic history together. He finished up by praising his young wife's enormous talent and toasting the success of *Flame*, ending sweetly: 'To the woman who lights up *my* life: *my* flame, *my* passion. To my darling Kendall.'

It wasn't until 2 a.m., when they finally climbed into their chauffeur-driven vintage Jaguar en route to their 'top secret' wedding-night location (a modest hotel in West Sussex, near Gatwick) that the bride and groom had any real time alone together.

'Well done,' said Ivan kissing her. 'You were fabulous, perfect, a work of art. I'm a lucky man.'

'Thanks, honey,' sighed Kendall. She leaned into him, exhausted.

'I can't wait to see the papers tomorrow,' said Ivan. 'Can you? You were the sexiest bride ever. There isn't a hot-blooded male alive who won't rush out and buy *Flame* once they see you in that dress.'

It was the sort of comment that usually wouldn't have bothered Kendall. Indeed, it would have pleased her. This was the way she and Ivan always communicated. But tonight, on her wedding night, Lex's words came back to haunt her.

'This is all about publicity, about business, and you know it.'

Did she know it? During the service it hadn't felt that way. It had felt like something more. But like Lucy stepping back through the wardrobe and leaving the magic of Narnia behind, reality reasserted itself unpleasantly now as the car sped away. Lex was at least partly right. Business was and had always been her and Ivan's glue.

'What's the matter?' said Ivan, seeing her face fall.

'Oh, nothing,' she said quickly. 'I'm just tired I guess. It's been a long day.'

Ivan took her face in his hands and kissed her again, more passionately this time. When he pulled away he asked: 'Are you happy, Kendall?'

She stroked his face with her hand, exploring it the way a blind person might examine a stranger. Even after two years there was a part of Ivan that remained a stranger to her. She wondered if there always would be. But they were together now, man and wife, till death do us part. The die was cast. It was up to her to make it work.

'Yes, Ivan,' she said, a new note of determination creeping into her voice. 'I am happy. Very happy.'

He wrapped his arm around her and they drove on into the night.

PART THREE

CHAPTER TWENTY
Six months later . . .

Ava Bentley sipped her freshly pressed grapefruit juice and stared at her reflection in the mirror. Behind her, Eduardo, probably the top hairstylist in Beverly Hills, picked up strands of her lightly highlighted hair with distaste, as if he were peeling some particularly smelly seaweed off a rock.

'You don't like it?' Ava asked meekly.

Eduardo shrugged. 'When did you last get it cut?'

Ava thought back. No one had touched her hair since Louise Galvin last year, but she was too embarrassed to tell Eduardo that. Instead she admitted vaguely: 'Not for a while.'

'And the colour?'

Ava blushed. 'Probably nine months?'

Her Yorkshire accent was so striking, the smart LA women seated near her all turned to stare.

'So what you want today?' demanded Eduardo. 'You want shorter, yes?'

Ava didn't want shorter, but the record company had insisted on something 'dramatic'. The general consensus in the States was that the makeover Ivan had got for her in the UK, the 'new look' that had felt so radical at the time, was actually pathetically half-hearted. 'You're a rock star, not a dreamy school kid,' Ava was told. 'Let's see some edge.'

Ava relayed this information to Eduardo, simultaneously waving her corporate AmEx card in his general direction.

'Hmmm.' The stylist lifted her head, turning it from one side to the other to get a better view of her jaw line and the strengths and weaknesses of her pretty, elfin face. Finally, unexpectedly, he broke into a broad grin. 'Perfect!' he exclaimed. 'I make you very, very sexy. It's good?'

'I guess so,' giggled Ava. In for a penny, in for a pound. Besides, it wasn't just the record company that she was hoping to please. She had to be 'sexy' if she was ever going to get Lex Abrahams to notice her. Sexy and sophisticated, a young woman, not a child. Tonight a select group of JSM's senior management and some record-company people were hosting a small dinner in her honour at Sushi Roku in West Hollywood. Ava was determined to show up with a new look that would turn heads. One head in particular.

She'd been living in Los Angeles for six months now, away from England and home, and (crucially) away from her father Dave. Ava loved her dad dearly, but Dave Bentley had controlled every aspect of his daughter's life before *Talent Quest*, with Ivan Charles doing the same during the show's run. At eighteen, and with a bright future in front of her, Ava needed to break out from under her father's wing. Had she stayed in London, under Ivan's management, she knew this would never have happened. Dave and Ivan would have been all over her, monitoring her friends, her social life, interfering in all her career decisions. So when Jack Messenger came out of the woodwork offering not only to help her forge a US career, but to provide her with a convenient escape route, Ava grabbed it with both hands. Yes, she was young and sweet and naïve in the ways of business and the world generally. But Ava Bentley was also ambitious and she knew her own mind. She felt sorry for Ivan, who had helped her so much during *Talent Quest*, and for Kendall Bryce who'd been so kind. But the truth was, JSM had made her an offer she couldn't refuse.

It had been the best decision of her life. From the moment she stepped off the plane, Ava adored LA. Up until that point, her only experience of 'abroad' had been family camping holidays in the Dordogne, so California seemed wildly exotic – with its blazing sunshine, its ubiquitous palm trees and its freeways that seemed to stretch wider than the English Channel. Everything about living here was an adventure, from the accents, to the giant plates of food they served in every restaurant, to the cars that were bigger than Ava's family's cottage in Hutton-le-Hole. Because she was still unknown in the US – her days were spent in the studio, recording tracks for her new album – and because both Jack and Lex made it their business to protect her, she had no exposure to the tacky, aggressive, seedy side of Hollywood life. As a result, Ava thought LA quite the friendliest, most pleasant and unfairly maligned city in the world. She couldn't imagine what had possessed Kendall to leave it.

Then again, Kendall was riding high in Europe at the moment, with her album topping the charts from London to Lisbon and Athens to Antibes. Plus she and Ivan had married and, if the gossip magazines were anything to go by, they were blissfully happy. So it had all worked out all right in the end. All Ava needed to do was follow her lead, launch a hit album here in the States and find a love of her own.

Of course, as far as she was concerned she'd already found him. In Ava's eyes, Lex Abrahams was the perfect man. Handsome, dark (she'd never been into blonds), kind, funny and phenomenally successful. He was also older (mature, exciting), and hugely artistically talented in his own right. Basically, he was far too good for her, an unattainable dream. But Ava had chased one of those before, and here she was in Los Angeles, about to launch her debut album. She wouldn't forgive herself if she didn't at least try.

Although Jack was Ava's official manager, and it was Jack who had negotiated her two-album deal with Columbia Records ('That's Columbia as in Celine Dion,' he'd explained to a totally overexcited Ava on the day they signed), day to day she spent most of her time with Lex. This was partly because she couldn't drive and therefore needed regular lifts, which Lex was good-natured enough to provide. He also took an active interest in her image, working closely with Columbia's own photographers and art consultants to try to come up with the right look with which to launch the Ava Bentley brand on an unsuspecting American public. In Britain, the entire country had watched Ava battle her way through the gruelling audition rounds. They knew her family history, her humble background, and were invested in her story. Here in America she was quite literally a nobody. Jack was happy to let Lex step in to help with the artistic side, it had always been his forte, but again it meant that Lex and Ava spent a good number of business hours in one another's company. And finally there was their friendship.

When Jack first signed Ava to JSM, Lex had been livid. To be honest, the entire JSM staff had raised eyebrows at the decision. This wasn't like signing The Blitz, an established group who could be helped to make a US comeback. This was some kid from an obscure English reality show. It made no sense.

But gradually, once they came to hear her sing and saw how adorable and unspoilt and engaging she was, literally the Anti-Kendall, people started to change their minds. By the time Jack landed Ava the Columbia deal, nobody was surprised. The kid's likeability factor was off the charts. And nobody liked her more than Lex Abrahams. Indeed, it hadn't been until Lex started working with Ava that it truly hit him how fucked-up he'd been over Kendall. For the last three years now, his emotional life had seesawed in accordance with Kendall Bryce's actions. Her trip to England, her defection to Polydor, her trip to LA – and using him for those awful pictures, her wedding to Ivan. None of these events had been *about* Lex. The truth was that, for Kendall, his existence barely even registered. Yet Lex had allowed his own happiness to hang on Kendall's every move. No amount of material or professional success, not even finding a beautiful, lovely, understanding girlfriend like Leila had been able to shake him out of this awful, destructive dependence.

But then Ava had come into his life – this funny, chatty, positive little kid, this ball of energy and optimism – and something shifted. He certainly wasn't in love with Ava. Not only was she only eighteen, but she was a young eighteen, as bright-eyed and bushy-tailed as a Labrador puppy. But she was fun. She made him laugh all the time. Working with her was exciting, and being with her was like plugging yourself into a wall of electricity. Despite the age gap, the culture gap, the everything gap, Ava Bentley had snuck up on him and become a real friend. Until he met her, Lex hadn't realized quite how much he'd needed one.

At the hairstylist's, Ava who'd been daydreaming about

exactly how Lex would eventually propose to her (either on the beach in Malibu or back on the village green in Hutton-le-Hole; she hadn't quite pinned down the fantasy yet) when she suddenly glanced back up at the mirror and screamed.

'My hair!'

'What's the matter?' Eduardo asked innocently.

'What's the matter?' Ava shrieked. 'It's gone! It's all bloody gone, that's what's the matter. Oh my God! Columbia are going to go spare.'

'I don't know what that means,' said Eduardo nonchalantly, 'but your hair is not all gone. Look. Here it is.' He ran his hand lovingly through her short pixie cut, spiking it this way and that, like a sculptor thoughtfully moulding clay. 'In any case, I am not feeneeshed. Next, we color. Then, we style. Very, very sexy. You will see.'

It was another two and half hours before Ava did see, two hours during which Eduardo had insisted she also submit to having her eyebrows shaped (thankfully the stylist was gentler than Sveva and used threading rather than the hated tweezers) and her eyelashes dyed to 'complement' her new look. And what a look it was. Ava barely recognized herself.

Her hair was indeed very short, although thanks to some inexplicable, scissor-related magic, it didn't look harsh and masculine as she'd feared, but instead gently licked her face like a soft crown, the layers folded on top of one another like perfectly cut slivers of silk. She couldn't stop touching them. As for the colour, the closest word Ava could think of to describe it was silver. Although more of a blonde than a grey, there was an iridescence to it that illuminated her face, emphasizing cheekbones she never knew she had and bringing out the blueness in her eyes. Or perhaps it was the subtly arched eyebrows that did that, or the inky lashes that

looked ten shades blacker next to the gleaming light-bomb
that was the rest of her hair and face? Either way, the overall
effect was quite stunning. Exotic, otherworldly and yes, she
had to admit it, 'very, very sexy'.

'You like it?' Eduardo asked proudly.

Bouncing out of the chair, Ava flung her diminutive form
into his arms, leaping up at him like a silver-headed Tigger.
'I love it,' she squealed excitedly. 'I totally and completely
love it.'

Lex was the first to arrive at Sushi Roku. Sitting down alone
at the table for eight he ordered a beer and some *edamame*. He
was in roaring spirits. JSM's quarterly figures had come in
that morning. He knew they were going to be good, but
reading them in black and white had been quite a feeling,
an adrenaline rush like he hadn't had since the early, heady
days of forming the company, back when it was just him
and Jack. They now had four really big-hitting acts on their
books: Land of the Greeks, Frankie B, Martina Munoz and
The Blitz who, contrary to Lex's misgivings, had started to
make the agency big money right away, selling out stadiums
across the US with their live tour as if they'd never been
away. True, plenty of the smaller Jester acts that Jack had
snaffled from Ivan had been a waste of time, sinking deal-
less without trace after only a few months. But it wasn't as
if they'd wasted much money promoting them. Plus, they
still had Ava Bentley, who Lex was now convinced would
turn out to be their ace in the hole. He'd spent most of
today discussing locations for the video shoots Ava would
do next week, in the run-up to the August release of her
debut album, *Pure*. Lex hadn't supported the title at first,
arguing vehemently against it to anyone who would listen
at Columbia. He felt it made Ava sound too sickly, too

goody-goody; that it didn't convey the spirited, merry nature that went with her innocence. But again it was Jack who'd changed his mind.

'It's not about her character. It's about her sound. Just listen to the vocals on those tracks. Not a whisper of breath, man.'

He was right. And over time the visual possibilities that went with that title, be it for album cover shots, videos or promotional branding, began to look more and more appealing. The location he'd seen today, a hidden waterfall and natural pool up in the redwood forests of Northern California, was a photographer's dream.

Ava's publicist Jen Gomez was the next to arrive at the restaurant, followed by Liam Haines, the main producer on *Pure* and the rest of the Columbia crew. Jack showed up shortly afterwards with Lisa Marie, whom he was still casually dating, looking almost as happy with life as Lex. After a strained few months, relations between the two JSM partners were almost back to normal. The fact that the company was printing money certainly helped to oil the wheels of reconciliation.

'Where's the guest of honour?' Lisa Marie asked Lex. 'Didn't she come with you?'

'Uh uh. I just flew down from Napa, remember? Awesome location by the way, it's gonna be perfect for *Feel the Rain*.'

'Should we have sent a driver for her?' The most junior member of the Columbia contingent looked nervous. 'I didn't realize.'

'Hi, guys.'

The whole table turned and started open-mouthed at the vision who'd just walked in. She walked like Ava. She talked like Ava. But she looked like nothing on earth. Beneath her iridescent helmet of silver-blonde hair, she'd gone for dark, dramatic kohl-rimmed eyes, highlighted cheekbones and pale lips. She wore tight black leather pants, spiked Louboutin boots and a sexy, off-the-shoulder cotton T-shirt in faded grey from L'Agence. The little girl from Yorkshire was gone, transformed overnight into an ethereal, punk Barbarella.

'What do you think?' She twirled around, enjoying everyone's astonishment but anxious for a sign of approval from Lex. 'More sophisticated?'

Jen Gomez was the first to find her voice. 'You look incredible,' she said truthfully. 'Sexy as all hell. But it's a big departure.'

'Not exactly "pure",' muttered Liam Haines under his breath, but he said it with a whistle of admiration.

Jack stood up and led Ava to her seat. 'You look terrific,' he said encouragingly. A more experienced artist would never have made such a drastic change to their image without clearing it with their stylists and PR people first. But no one could deny that Ava looked ravishing, not to mention extremely commercially appealing. Columbia had been talking for weeks about ways to sex her up. They wouldn't have to talk any more.

'What about you?' Ava turned to Lex. 'Do you like it?'

No, thought Lex. *I hate it. You're just a kid, for God's sake.* The truth was, she looked amazing. Too amazing. He didn't hate the look, he hated himself for the way it made him feel. It wasn't just the hair and make-up, it was the clothes, accentuating a smoking hot body that he had genuinely never noticed before. How was that possible? The Ava he knew had apple cheeks, wore sweatpants and got the giggles in his car quoting *The Simpsons*. He'd seen that Ava only yesterday, but now she was gone, swallowed up by this disturbing, erotic impostor. Why did that bother him so much?

'Lex?'

'You look good,' he said guardedly.

Ava's face fell at his lack of enthusiasm. 'You don't like it.'

'I didn't say that,' said Lex. 'It's a shock, that's all.'

'Let's order,' said Jack, breaking the tension with his bonhomie. 'This is supposed to be a celebration, remember? I for one can't celebrate on an empty stomach.'

Ava put on a brave face, forcing a smile as toast after toast was made in her honour, and thanking all the relevant people for their contributions to *Pure*. But inside she was dying. It had all been for nothing. Sure, it was a relief that Jen and the others approved of her dramatic new style. But the one person she'd really wanted to impress wore an aggrieved frown of grievance on his face, as if she'd just stolen his wallet or run over his cat. As for responding to her sexually, as a woman, Lex showed considerably more interest in his chicken robata than he did in the Burberry trousers that had cost Ava two weeks' wages. *I could strip naked and dance on his sashimi salad, and he still wouldn't notice me.*

Depressed, and with no real appetite, she started knocking back the sake instead. At eighteen, Ava was under the legal drinking age in California, but no one was going to say anything to the guest of honour at so important a table. After forty minutes or so, in which they discussed her upcoming video shoots and appearance singing live on Jay Leno, Ava got up to go to the loo looking distinctly wobbly on her six-inch heels.

'I'll come with you,' said Lisa Marie, grabbing her under the elbow and steering her towards the Ladies. Over her shoulder she mouthed '*coffee*' to Jack.

As soon as Ava was out of earshot, Jack leaned forward excitedly, addressing the table as a whole. 'OK. So I don't want to raise this in front of Ava yet. She's got enough on her plate with *Pure* coming out and I don't want to overstress her. But I had a great meeting with Don Lenner today about next steps.'

The Columbia staffers all pricked up their ears. Don Lenner was the label's CEO. Jack Messenger was basically telling them he'd had a direct dialogue with God.

'We both feel that it makes sense to push Ava internationally the moment she's begun to make an impact here,' Jack went on. 'Obviously the most crucial market to capture would be the UK. Our thought was to have her do a full-on UK PR assault in November, reintroduce her to the British public, then release the album mid-December and shoot for a Christmas number one.'

Jen, Liam and their colleagues all nodded enthusiastically, murmuring assent. It didn't pay to argue with God. Only Lex looked less than happy.

'This was Don Lenner's idea, or yours?' he asked sceptically.

Jack leaned back, folding his arms defensively. 'It came up in conversation. I can't remember who raised it. But we both agreed.'

'Oh really?' said Lex. 'And did you mention to Don that your interest in going back to London has nothing to do with what's best for Ava's career, which is clearly to strengthen her presence in the domestic market, but everything to do with your bullshit personal vendetta against Ivan Charles?'

The Columbia staffers exchanged embarrassed glances. None of them wanted to be present for a JSM domestic. Lex Abraham's tone was overtly hostile and deeply provocative.

'No,' said Jack coolly. 'I didn't. Because what you've just said isn't true. I happen to genuinely believe—'

'Oh spare me,' snapped Lex. 'Tell it to someone who hasn't bought your bullshit before. When is this all gonna end, Jack? I mean, seriously, when? No one cares about Ivan but you.'

'Funny,' said Jack, 'that wasn't the impression I got a few months back when Kendall married him. Back then you seemed to think he was the devil incarnate.'

'Who's the devil?' Ava, still leaning heavily on Lisa Marie for support, weaved her way back to the table. Even in her drunken state, she could see that all was not well. Jack's fists were clenched and his jaw rigid. Lex looked as if he'd just swallowed a wasp.

'No one, honey,' said Jen Gomez soothingly.

'But Jack said—'

'Would anyone like dessert?'

No one, it seemed, was hungry any more, or in the party spirit. Jack asked for the check, and Lex offered to drive Ava home. She wanted to refuse. It was only a couple of blocks to her apartment, and Lex had been so off with her all evening she really should have walked. But the temptation to spend even another few minutes in his company was too great. Ten minutes later she found herself in the familiar passenger seat of Lex's Range Rover, playing nervously with her hair as they headed down Melrose.

'You and Jack were fighting,' she said quietly, as much to break the awful silence as anything.

'No we weren't.'

'Was it about me?'

'I told you,' said Lex curtly. 'We weren't fighting.'

The silence resumed for the rest of the short drive to Ava's building on Alta Loma. Lex pulled over and was about to give her a kiss on the cheek goodbye when he noticed she was crying. 'What's the matter?' he said gently.

'You!' Ava sobbed. 'You're the matter. OK, so you hate my hair. I get it,' she hiccupped. 'But there's no need to be so mean to me and get so angry all the time.'

Lex winced. It was Jack he was mad at, not Ava. 'I don't hate your hair. I was surprised, that's all.'

But Ava had already jumped out of the car, slamming the door behind her. After about four steps she stumbled, twisting her ankle and falling painfully onto her knees in the driveway, prompting renewed sobs. Lex opened the door and walked over to her.

'Leave me alone,' she sniffed.

'No can do, I'm afraid,' he said, scooping her up into his arms. 'I told Jack I'd get you home safely. This isn't safely.'

She let him carry her into the building, too exhausted and emotional to protest. Once they reached her apartment, Lex sat her down gently on the sofa, produced a bag of ice from the freezer which he wrapped in a tea towel and told her to press against her bruised knees, and started brewing some coffee.

'I don't need any coffee.' She hiccupped again, wondering at exactly what point the gods would decide she'd been humiliated enough.

'I do,' said Lex. 'I had too many sakes myself. Plus I have to get all the way back to Malibu after this and I'm exhausted.'

In the end she took the proffered mug without complaint, along with the accompanying slices of toast and peanut butter. After a few bites and gulps of the strong, comforting Colombian blend, she began to feel more herself.

'I made a fool of myself, didn't I?' Ava could hardly bring herself to look at Lex.

'You had a bit too much to drink,' he said kindly. 'It's not like you were taking your clothes off or dancing on tables. Besides, it was your party. Nobody minded.'

'But that isn't what you and Jack were angry about?'

'No.' Scooching along next to her on the sofa, Lex stroked her strange new hair. It was as soft as rabbit's fur and felt oddly erotic. He stopped instantly.

'Well what then?' said Ava. 'And please don't tell me "nothing" again. I'm not a child and I wasn't *that* drunk. I know what I saw.'

'If you must know, it was about Ivan Charles,' said Lex. He didn't want to say anything to her about the UK Christmas number one plan, he still hoped Jack would eventually see sense on that score, but he did owe her some sort of an explanation. 'Jack said something about my reaction to Ivan and Kendall's wedding that ticked me off, OK? It was nothing to do with you.'

'It was to do with Kendall,' said Ava bleakly. 'I understand. You're still in love with her, aren't you?'

'I . . . what? No!' Lex shook his head vehemently. 'Why would you say something like that?'

'It's OK,' Ava went on. She'd drunk enough to lose her inhibitions and watched her hand stroking Lex's thigh as if it belonged to somebody else entirely. 'Kendall's incredibly beautiful. Why wouldn't you be in love with her?'

'I'm not in love with her,' repeated Lex. Ava's hand was making it hard to concentrate. She looked so different tonight, so adult and sensual, so close to him. 'Maybe once, a long time ago, I had feelings for—'

Ava's hand had slipped under his shirt. She nuzzled her face against his neck. 'I could make you happy,' she whispered, her warm breath caressing his skin like a kiss. It felt so good, Lex struggled to suppress a moan of pleasure. 'I'd appreciate you like Kendall never did.'

He tried to pull away, but when he did Ava's dewy eyes were gazing into his, her pupils dilated and pale lips parted in a look of purest desire. Before he knew it, he was kissing her. Pulling off her T-shirt and unfastening her bra, he ran his hands over her beautiful body, the tiny apple breasts and narrow waist. For a second the cold jolted him back to sanity. 'We shouldn't be doing this,' he murmured, as Ava's fingers fumbled with the buttons on his fly.

'Why not?'

His jeans were open now, his erection straining at his Calvin Klein boxer shorts. Ava stroked it gently through the fabric and the last vestiges of Lex's willpower melted away. He couldn't remember why not. Something to do with Kendall, or Jack, or work or . . . *God, that felt good.* Closing his eyes he surrendered to the pleasure of the moment. He was with a girl who wanted him. Really wanted him.

It had been a long time.

Across town in Brentwood, Jack brushed his teeth angrily, scrubbing away till his gums bled. Just thinking about tonight's conversation made him furious. When would *he* let it go? The barefaced cheek of it! When would Lex let it go?, that was the question. Lex was the one who brought everything back to Ivan and, by extension, Kendall. Not him.

Marching into the bedroom in a sulk he picked up Sonya's photograph. It was one of his favourite pictures of his wife, taken on holiday in St Paul de Vence the year they'd got engaged. Technically, it wasn't a great shot. Sonya's face was turned half away from the camera and her hair was blowing everywhere. But somehow it captured her spirit perfectly. Her laugh that lit up her face like a beacon; her easy, natural beauty, the exact opposite of the contrived, high-maintenance perfection of the LA girls; her intelligence, so different to the laboured intellectualism of the women Jack had dated at Oxford.

'It's not fair, Son,' he told the picture. 'When I signed all Jester's acts, everyone said I was crazy, but I proved them all wrong. JSM's more profitable now than ever. So why can't the kid give me a break and let me manage this girl without second-guessing my every decision? Would I like to get back at Ivan? Sure. But that doesn't mean a UK number one wouldn't be the right thing for Ava, does it?'

He stared at Sonya's image, waiting to feel a connection. Not an answer, as such, but a sense of her presence, of companionship, of not being completely alone. In the first year after her death that connection had come so easily. There were times when he closed his eyes that Jack almost felt as if he could touch her, hear her voice, smell her skin. But not now. Now there was nothing but a photo in a frame. Was this what people meant by time being a healer, Jack wondered bitterly? That as the months and years passed, what little you had left of the person you loved would be taken from you too? It struck him forcefully that he could no longer remember the sound of Sonya's voice. She had slipped away from him, slipped to a place he couldn't follow.

Replacing the picture on the dressing table, he sat down on the end of the bed. At first the sadness was overwhelming. But then he had another thought. What if the silence was an answer in itself? What if Sonya was telling him to let go, to move on, to take his comfort from those who *could* still comfort him – from the living?

He thought about Lisa Marie. She'd have spent the night with him tonight if he'd asked her to. They'd been dating casually for over a year now and Jack enjoyed her company. She was smart, perceptive, beautiful and completely undemanding, never suggesting that they go on long vacations together or swap keys to one another's places. It was an easy relationship that never got in the way at work or caused Jack any anxiety. But that was the problem. He wasn't anxious because he wasn't in love. Neither was Lisa Marie. And they never would be. He hadn't asked her home tonight because he knew in his heart she couldn't comfort him, couldn't support him in the way he needed.

The one woman who could was six thousand miles away, fast asleep in her bed in a sleepy Cotswold town, as unreach-able as the stars. Catriona had been so cross with him about signing Ava, he hadn't called for a few months after that. When he did pick up the phone again, the closeness he'd thought had been developing between them last year had gone. She was happy to hear from him, polite, friendly, full of news about Hector and Rosie and village life. But the window for something more between them – if there had ever really been such a window – seemed irrevocably to have closed. Since then work had sucked Jack back into his own life, his own world in LA. And really, what did Catriona know of that world, of the stresses of dealing with a suspi-cious partner whilst trying to butter up the likes of Don Lenner? How could she help him, if he did pick up the phone and call her?

Even so, the urge to hear Catriona's voice was so strong, Jack found himself dialling her number anyway, getting three-quarters of the way through before he finally came to his senses. At last, restless and depressed, he slipped under the bedclothes, turned out the light and went to sleep.

Lex Abrahams woke the next morning with a dry mouth, a pounding head and a sinking feeling in his stomach that he couldn't quite account for. Then he opened his eyes and blearily took in his surroundings. That was definitely not his ceiling. Or his wardrobe. Or his discarded leather trousers lying casually strewn over the chair by the bed.

Oh shit.

Ava slept peacefully beside him, face down and with the duvet pulled up only as far as her waist. Lex stared at her bare back and short, silken crop of hair for a long time. She was beautiful. No doubt about that. And funny and smart and great company. But she was also eighteen and vulnerable and his client. What was Jack gonna say?

In Ava's shower a few minutes later, he scrubbed himself off, as if the Kiehl's lime body wash could make him feel less like a dirty old man. More of last night's events drifted back to him: the restaurant, the sake, Jack's plan for Ava to make a UK comeback this Christmas. What he'd experienced last night as anger now felt more like anxiety. But what was he anxious about? Losing Ava, the way he'd lost Kendall? Certainly the whole concept of 'trips to England' didn't fill him with happiness and confidence.

I'm overthinking it, he told himself, wrapping a pink Victoria's Secret towel around his waist and hunting through Ava's kitchen cupboards for some Alka-Seltzer. This UK trip might never even happen. They'd all have to see what happened with Ava's album here first. In the meantime, would a relationship with Ava really be the worst thing in the world? After all, she'd made all the moves last night. It wasn't as though he'd tried to seduce her, or tricked her into anything she didn't want to do. In Lex's job, with the hours he worked, it was tough to find time to date, period. Being with someone who understood, who operated in the same world, made sense. Jack was dating a colleague, after all. Was Ava really so different?

'There you are.' Swaddled in a fluffy white towelling bathrobe, Ava padded into the bathroom and put her arms around him. 'I thought you'd done a runner.'

'Why would you think that?' Lex hugged her back. 'Get dressed and I'll take you out for breakfast.'

Fuck it. He couldn't stay single and alone for ever. He was tired of pining for Kendall, tired of having nothing else in his life but work. He and Ava might be good for each other.

Really, what was the worst that could happen?

'And . . . action!'

Ava Bentley threw her arms wide as the cameras began to roll, twirling around joyously amid the artificial snow-flakes. Or 'snowfakes', as Lex called them. Thank God he was here. Shooting a Christmas video was a gruelling and thankless task at the best of times. But doing it in LA, surrounded by vacuous Valley-girl runners and swaying palm trees in unseasonably warm eighty-degree sunshine lent the process an even more preposterous, farcical air.

'Hug your shoulders a little bit,' the shoot director shouted into Ava's headset as she mimed along to 'Home', the catchy, upbeat track that her record company planned to release as a European Christmas single, to go head-to-head with Kendall Bryce's festive offering. 'Try to look cold.'

If I were cold, thought Ava, *I'd have put on a sweater and jeans. I wouldn't be cavorting around in distressed silver leather pants and a studded bra.* But she did her best, cosying up to the fur-clad backing dancers as horrid synthetic blobs of white settled in her silver cropped hair. It was harder than it sounded, miming lyrics while performing a dance routine, and trying to appear happy and freezing cold at the same time. One look at Lex's face confirmed her suspicions, that the effort made her look ridiculous.

'I'm sorry,' she said, pulling off her headset to groans from the crew, all of whom were sweltering in the open-air set and longing to go home. 'Can we try something different? This isn't working. It's kitsch as hell and I look like a—'

'I think "ass" is the word she's looking for.' Lex Abrahams got up from his folding beach chair and walked over to the director. He wished he were directing Ava's video himself, but they'd both agreed they needed some distance between their personal and professional lives, and at the time bringing in an outsider had seemed like a good idea.

'She looks great,' the director said defensively. 'It's holiday season, people. It's supposed to be kitsch. Do you know how much money Katy Perry's made out of kitsch music videos?'

'Ava isn't Katy Perry,' said Lex. 'She's never done that whole knowing, tongue-in-cheek thing. She's no good at it.'

'Thanks a lot!' said Ava, cooling herself down in front of an on-set snow blower. But she knew he was right.

'The outfit says sexy, the set says cheesy, the dancers say gay. What message are we trying to send here?'

'Oh would you quit it?' the director snapped. 'Dancers always say gay. That's their job. We already cleared the art direction and the choreography with Columbia, OK. If you don't like the direction we've taken, take it up with them. But for now can we just shoot the damn thing. Ah!' Turning around, he clapped his hands in delight. 'There they are. Perfect!'

Lex looked at Ava. 'You have *got* to be kidding me.' They both burst out laughing. There, being led across the blistering parking lot by a bikini-and-Daisy Duke-clad extra, was a team of four reindeer, complete with jingle bell harnesses and little red bows around their necks.

'Don't tell me,' said Ava, wiping away tears of mirth and hopelessly smearing her eye make-up in the process, 'they have red noses that light up when you push a button?'

The director scowled. 'OK, break time's over, people. Let's

go again, from the top. Reindeer won't come in till the final chorus.'

Ava tried to get a grip on her giggles while the make-up ladies set to work repairing her face. It was funny, but only to a point. What on *earth* were people going to say when they saw this crap back in England? It made Cliff Richard's *Mistletoe and Wine* video seem positively cutting-edge. At this rate, Kendall Bryce was going to wipe the floor with her.

'Help me,' she mouthed to Lex.

Reluctantly, Lex dialled Jack's number. They weren't getting on well at the moment, but he needed to bring in the big guns. If they didn't get the record company to tone down the cheese factor, they all stood to lose money, not to mention end up with serious egg on their faces.

'Don't worry,' he mouthed back to Ava. 'It's all under control.

CHAPTER TWENTY-ONE

London, six months later . . .

Backstage at the world-famous 100 Club on Oxford Street, Kendall shivered in her stage outfit of black PVC hot pants, thigh-high Vivienne Westwood boots and a mesh vest top with an orange silk flame appliquéd across the breasts.

'You'll be fine,' said Ivan, wrapping a cashmere blanket around her shoulders to warm her and passing her a bottle of Evian. 'You'll knock 'em dead.'

'And if I don't?'

'You will.' He leaned into kiss her and Kendall instinctively leaned back. She could already smell the alcohol on his breath and it was only half past seven. A shiver of fear ran through her. *Please don't let him get loaded tonight. Please don't let him lose his temper. Please let me be OK.*

It was November now. Next month, Kendall and Ivan would celebrate their first wedding anniversary. Was it really only one year since that magical, starry night at the Chelsea Physic Garden? So much had happened in that time it felt like a decade ago.

The first six months of marriage had been exciting. Or rather, Kendall's career had been exciting, a nonstop frenzy of travel, performing and promotion that had seen her visit over forty different countries and countless cities. The marriage itself was just something that existed in the background, a part of the Kendall Bryce story to be wheeled out in every interview and feature. Meanwhile *Flame*'s sales spread across the globe like wildfire. Despite achieving only modest success in the US, it was a multi-platinum-selling album, and back in the UK, Kendall's star had risen to an all-time high.

Ivan accompanied his wife on as many trips as possible, occasionally taking breaks to see to business in London or to spend time with his children. Now that they were older, his relationship with both Rosie and Hector had blossomed, with the years of tension between Ivan and his son finally appearing to be over. On paper, everything seemed to be going well. A string of magazines did features on Ivan and Kendall Charles's 'perfect' life together, and speculation was rife as to when the young Mrs Charles would find a window in her schedule to conceive their much-anticipated first child.

It wasn't till the summer that Kendall had first became aware of Ivan's drinking. With hindsight, there had been signs of it much earlier. Every time Ivan returned from spending time with his family, he hit the bottle harder than usual at the endless round of after-parties and promotional events that were his and Kendall's life. But it wasn't until Kendall's record company allowed her a month-long break in August that the scale of the problem truly sank in.

A few things happened in August that didn't help the situation. First, Ava Bentley's debut album, *Pure*, was released in the US to a rapturous critical reception and strong domestic sales. Suddenly an almost unrecognizable Ava was everywhere, her face appearing to mock Ivan from the cover of

Rolling Stone magazine and her rags-to-riches story being trumpeted by all the British gossip rags that remembered her from *Talent Quest* days. Kendall was sanguine about it. *Flame* had outsold *Pure* globally by almost two to one, so Ava's success was no threat to her. But Ivan became obsessed, scouring the Internet for hours each day, looking for pieces on Ava, cutting out articles that made any reference either to her or to JSM. Often during these computer sessions, Kendall would notice a tumbler of whisky by Ivan's side.

Secondly, Hector flew back to LA to do another month's internship with his godfather's company. Ivan felt deeply hurt by this, but on Catriona's advice he bit his tongue. It had taken so long to get back on an even keel with Hector, he didn't want to risk losing him again. Still, the effort of repressing his feelings of betrayal only served to make Ivan more withdrawn. He refused to talk about it with Kendall or anyone, and spent long hours alone in his study, often drinking so much that he would pass out there and wake up in the morning, slumped drooling over his desk.

And thirdly, an entirely erroneous story came out in the press linking Kendall to one of her backing dancers. For a man who barely talked to her, or interacted with her at all once the cameras were switched off, Ivan remained pathologically jealous and possessive, insisting that Kendall fire *all* her male dancers for the upcoming winter tour, and demanding she send him hourly texts when they were apart, confirming her whereabouts.

It wasn't as if he were always drunk, or always withdrawn and unreasonable. The charming, witty, affectionate Ivan was still there and still made cameo appearances in Kendall's life, showing up with a horse-drawn pony and trap on her birthday to take her to a newly opened French restaurant by the river, and presenting her with an exquisite custom-made diamond charm bracelet the day she went on Radio Four's *Desert Island Discs*. The problem was, you never knew which version of Ivan you were going to get. As the weeks went on, and the drinking intensified, Kendall realized with shame that she had become afraid of her husband. She began to dread going home.

Throughout the entire, turbulent eleven months, her saving grace had been Stella Bayley. Stella had bravely decided that she and Miley would stay on in England after Brett left them, but she no longer had the heart to continue her blog after all the smug, hate-filled 'so much for her perfect life' comments that people posted once her marriage collapsed. When Kendall offered her a job as her PA, both women had looked on it as a temporary thing. But Stella had proved so astonishingly efficient, and such a cheerful, sane presence through the madness, that Kendall had begged her to stay, throwing money at the problem until her friend finally caved. Although she and Miley still lived up in Primrose Hill, Stella spent most of her days at Ivan and Kendall's Cheyne Walk apartment, and witnessed Ivan's mood swings and incipient depression first-hand. For some reason she was better at getting through to him in these moods than Kendall was. Stella often found herself diffusing what would otherwise definitely have turned into a nasty marital row between the two of them. Recently, it had reached the point where Kendall dreaded Stella leaving at night and refused to travel abroad with Ivan unless Stella could squeeze the trip into her schedule.

'Remember, it's a small crowd.' Ivan's voice brought Kendall back to reality. 'There's only three hundred people out there, it's not Wembley. Try to keep it intimate and natural. Don't over-project.'

Kendall nodded mutely. She wanted to be alone to calm

her nerves and was relieved when Ivan wandered off. But her spirits sank as she saw him slip onto one of the red velvet stools at the bar. This morning, JSM had announced Ava Bentley's plans for a Christmas comeback in the UK to tremendous fanfare. Ivan had flown into a rage, and spent most of the afternoon locked in a room with his PR people, working out a strategy for a smear campaign to derail his former protégée. Kendall was also worried. Ava being successful in America was one thing, but to have her here, competing head-to-head on home turf, was quite another. Her own new album was set for a Christmas release. Given the history between them, there was no way the press weren't going to turn this into some sort of personal vendetta, some battle to the death between the two of them. When she tried to raise her concerns with her husband, Ivan bit her head off, accusing her of not trusting him (how the hell had he got that?) and stormed out of the flat. Clearly he'd spent the hours between then and now drowning his sorrows in a bottle of Jack Daniel's. How Kendall wished she could do the same! But the crowd were already clapping, calling her name. Taking a last swig of her Evian, she handed it to a runner and walked, smiling, on stage.

'Good evening, London!'

Wild applause lifted her spirits a little. She tried to forget about Ivan at the bar and focus on the fact that she was here, in The 100 Club, on the same stage that had hosted so many of the greats, from The Sex Pistols to The Clash to The Rolling Stones. Best known as a punk and rock venue, it was rare for mainstream pop acts like Kendall to play here. But the crowd could not have been more welcoming and the stage, as ever, felt like home.

The band struck up the first few chords of 'Liar, Liar'. Kendall leaned forward provocatively in her mesh top, blew a kiss to the audience and, ignoring Ivan's advice, started belting out her best-known hit as if she were trying to fill the whole world with sound. The audience loved it, erupting into screams of approval.

The night was going to be a success.

After forty-five minutes, Kendall thanked the fans and took a fifteen-minute break. Though there was no choreographed dancing in her set – the stage at The 100 Club was barely big enough to swing a cat on – but the close atmosphere and punishing heat of the overhead lights had left her feeling dehydrated and exhausted. Normally Ivan would have been the first to congratulate her backstage and to make sure she was getting the fluids and rubdowns she needed, but he'd been mobbed by fans at the bar and had no doubt hung around to press the flesh. Kendall was glad of his absence and the chance to catch her breath alone.

Gulping down weak iced lemon barley water, her drink of choice during concerts, and dabbing the sweat off her forehead with a towel, she tuned in to a conversation going on behind her. One of the runners was talking to Cassie, Kendall's make-up girl.

'Well, that's what I heard,' the runner was saying. 'And it came from a friend who's done tons of music shoots in Los Angeles. She says it's an open secret over there.'

'There's no such thing as an "open" secret,' said Cassie reasonably. 'If Ava were in a serious relationship, the media would have got wind of it by now.'

'Not if her label put a lid on it. Columbia don't want people to think she's attached. Stops them buying records.'

'Yeah, but come on. Everyone knows Ava Bentley's single. And she's still only eighteen. He's way too old for her.'

Kendall's ears pricked up. Who? Who was too old for Ava?

'Besides, wasn't she pictured with Justin Bieber, like, a week ago?'

'PR stunt,' said the runner dismissively. 'I'm telling you, she's with her manager.'

A few feet away, Kendall choked on her drink, spraying lemon squash all over the floorboards. *Jack? Ava and Jack?* No. That wasn't possible. That, categorically, absolutely was not possible.

'That's not possible,' said Cassie, reading her client's mind. 'Jack Messenger may be many things but he isn't a cradle snatcher.'

'Not *Jack!*' The runner burst out laughing. 'Oh my God, no wonder you were so scandalized. No, the other one, the younger guy. His partner.'

'You mean Lex Abrahams?'

'Yes. That's the guy. According to my friend, Lex and Ava have been an item since the summer. He's coming with her to London and apparently she's been pushing for them to "come out" as a couple, but the record company are all over it, like "no way, you can't, the single will bomb," yada yada yada. I'm telling you. You heard it here first.'

'Kendall?'

A tap on her shoulder made Kendall jump a mile. It was Barry, one of the club managers.

'Sorry, sweetheart, didn't mean to scare you. You're on.'

The second half of Kendall's set was an unmitigated disaster. She forgot lyrics halfway through one song, and miserably missed the high note on another. All the rapport she'd built up with the audience earlier seemed to have evaporated, a combination of Kendall's mental absence and the copious amounts of alcohol that the crowd had consumed during the interval. A lacklustre performance of 'Wait For

Me', her latest single, was met with near silence. A stumble in 'Two Steps from Heaven' prompted boos.

Kendall knew she was unravelling, committing the cardinal sin of not giving her fans what they'd paid for. But she couldn't help it. Her body was on stage but her mind was six thousand miles away, repeating the same mantra over and over, willing it not to be true.

Lex and Ava. Ava and Lex.

When she'd first heard the runner say it wasn't Jack, she'd been relieved. But only for a split second. The thought of Lex, *her* Lex, shacking up with Ava Bentley was almost as bad. She didn't know why it should be. But it was.

They're coming to London.

Ava wants them to come out as a couple.

The whole thing was unbearable. Somehow making it through to the end of her set, Kendall practically ran off stage. Her disgruntled fans were already leaving but she barely registered. Suddenly all she wanted was Ivan. She wanted to tell him what she'd heard, to have him hold her and comfort her and tell her it would all be all right. Miraculously, when she reached her dressing room, there he was, looking a lot more sober than when she'd last seen him a couple of hours ago. Leaning against the wall in his dark suit, tall and strong and businesslike and reassuring, he had transformed back into the husband she needed, the one she could rely on.

'I'm sorry,' she sobbed. 'I know I was awful. But I heard something in the interval about Ava and Lex.' Ivan raised one arm, inviting her to come under his wing. Kendall moved gratefully towards him. 'Did you know that they're a couple? Apparently the rumour—'

'You stupid cow!'

Kendall staggered backwards. Putting both hands on her

chest, Ivan had pushed her, more violently than he'd intended to. Too stunned to react, Kendall had slammed into her dressing table. Turning, she lost her footing and slumped to the floor, but not before she'd caught her cheek on the corner of the table, nicking her skin just below the eye. Touching her face she found her fingers were slick with blood.

'You were a fucking dishgrace out there.'

However he might look, Ivan was in fact extremely drunk. The violence of the push he gave Kendall was testament to that, as was the fact that he was slurring his words like a stroke victim. Looking up at him through a haze of blood, Kendall saw that his face bore the heavy, vicious, brooding look of a punch-drunk boxer angrily contemplating his next swing.

'Whaddafuck happened?'

'I told you,' stammered Kendall, answering him because she was too shocked and frightened to do anything else. 'I was upset about Lex and Ava.'

'Ava's a bitch,' slurred Ivan. He was visibly confused, looking around Kendall's dressing room like he had no idea where he was. Then he focused on Kendall and his eyes darkened again. 'You hurt your face.'

'*You* hurt my face, you asshole!' sobbed Kendall.

Ivan ignored her, staggering over to where she lay slumped on the floor. 'Are you cheating on me?' he mumbled. 'R'you fucking around? C'sif you are I swear to God . . .' He raised his hand, whether to hit her or to steady himself, Kendall didn't know, but this time she was too quick for him. Scrambling to her feet she grabbed him by the elbow and simultaneously raised her knee, smashing it into his groin. Ivan let out the most horrendous scream and fell to the floor himself, writhing in agony.

Panicked and in complete shock – Ivan had never laid a finger on her before, never – Kendall grabbed her purse and ran, still in her stage clothes and with blood streaming from the wound under her eye. Ignoring the concerned cries of the club staff, she ran out into Oxford Street and jumped into the back of the first passing black cab.

'A and E?' asked the cabbie, who had also noticed the blood. 'St Mary's is probably the closest.'

'No,' said Kendall. She gave him an address in Primrose Hill.

Stella Bayley opened the door in pink floral White Company pyjamas, looking as clean and wholesome as Kendall looked debauched and bloody. Without saying a word or asking a single question, she paid the cabbie and helped her friend inside.

'I'll run you a bath.'

Kendall was so grateful, not just for the bath and the open door, but for Stella's silent, non-judgmental support, she burst into tears. The salt-water stung her cut face like acid.

'Come on. That's enough of that,' said Stella gently, leading Kendall upstairs the way she would a child.

The bathwater was warm and smelt of geraniums. Washing her face with a flannel was too painful, so Kendall took a deep breath and submerged her whole head instead, emerging clean but sore and with her wet hair clinging to her head like the sleek coat of an otter. Drying herself off, she wrapped one of Stella's fluffy white towels turban-style around her head and slipped into the grey Frette bathrobe and slippers that Stella had laid out for her. She found her friend downstairs in the sitting room, curled up on the sofa with a mug of hot chocolate.

'That one's yours.' Stella gestured to the red spotted Cath Kidston mug on the coffee table. Next to the milky drink was a plate of home-made shortbread biscuits. Kendall started to cry again.

'You don't have to talk about it,' said Stella. 'Only if you want to.'

Suddenly Kendall did want to. Sipping the hot chocolate and taking bites of biscuit in between tearful interludes, she told Stella the whole story. Ivan's drinking, the gig starting well, then hearing about Lex and Ava and coming apart at the seams. When it came to talking about the actual assault in the dressing room, she found herself feeling unaccountably embarrassed, stumbling over her words and skipping over the details, as if she were the perpetrator of a crime and not the victim. Stella noticed but said nothing, waiting patiently for Kendall to finish. If she was shocked, she didn't show it.

Eventually she said, 'Has he ever hit you before?'

Kendall shook her head vehemently. 'No. Never. And he didn't hit me tonight either. He pushed me and I slipped.'

'But you've been scared of him before? When he drinks?'

Kendall bit her lip and gave an imperceptible nod.

'Are you going to press charges?'

Kendall rolled her eyes. 'And have the media camped outside my door like vultures for the next two months, turning me into some sort of victim? No, absolutely not.'

'Are you going to leave him?'

Kendall tried to look out of the window but it was pitch dark outside. Instead of finding distraction, she was ambushed by her own reflection. She winced. Who was that sad, battered girl looking back at her? The cut under her eye had stopped bleeding now, but the whole eye area had begun to swell and livid purple bruises were forming there and on her opposite cheek. She looked as if she'd been in a car accident.

'I don't know,' she said quietly. 'It was sort of an accident. It's complicated.'

She waited for Stella to launch into a rant about how it wasn't complicated at all. How physical violence should never be tolerated and no woman should ever accept living in fear, not for their career or for any other reason. But she didn't. Instead, after a thoughtful pause, Stella asked, 'Do you think you'll ever have children with him?'

Kendall surprised herself by replying instantly and with absolute certainty, 'No. Never.'

'Interesting.' Stella nodded slowly. 'So who *would* you want to have children with, if not with Ivan?'

Again the answer was instant and instinctive. 'Lex.'

Kendall clapped her hand over her mouth. 'Oh my God. I have no idea why I just said that.'

'Maybe because it's true?' offered Stella.

'No. No, no, no. I'm not attracted to Lex, I never have been. We're friends. We *were* friends. I mean, he'd definitely make a good father but . . . no. That's just crazy.'

Stella made no further comment. Clearing away their mugs and plates, she hugged Kendall, taking care not to press against her injured face, and showed her upstairs to the guest bedroom. A simple, whitewashed room next to Miley's room, it smelled faintly of lavender. Everything in Stella's house seemed to smell of something sweet and restful and comforting.

'Sleep as long as you like in the morning,' said Stella. 'If I'm out when you wake, I'll just be running Miley to pre-school, so don't panic.'

'OK,' said Kendall. 'Thanks.'

She didn't think she'd sleep, so frenziedly was her mind racing about Ivan and their future and how the hell she was going to explain away the damage to her face when the world finally saw her next week. But as soon as her head hit the lavender-scented pillow, she was out like a light, sinking instantly into a deep, post-traumatic sleep.

By the time she awoke at noon the next morning, Ivan had already called Stella a total of eleven times.

'I admitted you were here,' said Stella. 'He knew anyway. But I told him I wasn't going to wake you and it would be up to you whether you wanted to see him or not.'

'Any press calls? Do the media know I'm here?'

'Nope,' said Stella. 'And there's been nothing online either, I've been checking all morning. A couple of bitchy reviews about last night's gig, but that's it.'

That much at least was a relief. In a way, so was Ivan calling. They would have to see one another and talk eventually. To be able to do it today, privately and in the safety of Stella's home, was a lot better than any of the other possible scenarios.

'Let Ivan know I'll see him,' said Kendall, brushing her hair back from her face and wincing at the pain as she inadvertently touched her bruises. 'He can come over as soon as I'm dressed.'

'You're sure?'

Kendall nodded. 'You'll be in the house, though, won't you? You don't have to go and pick up Miley or anything?'

'Oh don't worry,' said Stella firmly. 'I'll be here. I wouldn't dream of leaving you alone with him. Besides,' she added meaningfully, 'I have a few things I want to say to your husband myself.'

Unsurprisingly, Ivan turned up looking ashen, miserable, and as remorseful as either Stella or Kendall had ever seen him.

'I feel terrible,' he told Stella in the kitchen, while Kendall finished getting ready upstairs. 'Just terrible.'

'Yeah, well, a hangover'll do that to you,' said Stella unsympathetically, pulling the dead leaves off her potted basil.

Ivan groaned.

'You have a serious drinking problem,' Stella went on. 'You do know that, right?'

'Of course I do,' grumbled Ivan. 'I thought I had it under control, but when I got home last night and she wasn't there . . . when I realized what I'd done . . .' His eyes welled with tears. 'I'm not a violent person.'

'We're all violent people under the right circumstances,' said Stella, slightly more softly. 'And you have a horrific temper.'

'Do you think she'll ever forgive me?'

'I hope not,' said Stella, angrily tearing some healthy basil leaves.

Just then Kendall walked in. She was wearing Stella's clothes, a white chunky-knit sweater over a 'sensible' pair of dark jeans. The outfit completely de-sexualised her. *Perhaps that's the intention*, thought Ivan. It also did nothing to distract attention from the awful swelling on her face.

She looked at Ivan without emotion. 'Hi.'

'Hi.'

Silence hung in the air between them like a wall.

'Thank you for seeing me.'

They went into the sitting room and sat down on opposing sofas, as awkward as two teenagers on a blind date. Clearly the onus was on Ivan to begin, to say something. 'Sorry' was laughably inadequate, yet not to say it was impossible, unforgivable. He cleared his throat nervously.

'I don't know what to say. I'm so sorry, Kendall. I didn't mean to push you so hard. I was just lashing out. I . . . I don't know why I did it.'

'I do,' said Kendall. 'You were angry, you were drunk and you thought you could get away with it.'

Ivan crossed his legs gingerly, jokingly cupping his hands over his crotch. 'Yeah, well. You soon put me right on that last one.' He tried to smile, but Kendall wasn't laughing. 'Sorry,' said Ivan lamely. For almost a full minute he stared down at his shoes. When he looked up he was crying, properly crying, the tears rolling unchecked down his cheeks like a small child who's suddenly lost sight of its mother.

'Are you going to leave me?'

When she walked into the room, Kendall hadn't had an answer to that question. Now, unexpectedly strengthened by his weakness, she found she did.

'No,' she said calmly, 'I'm not going to leave you. I'm going to stay, and we're going to be happy, and if Ava Bentley comes back to Britain, with or without Lex or Jack or any other hangovers she's stolen from *my* old life, we're going to wipe the fucking floor with her.'

Ivan was so happy he could have burst into song. He was convinced it was the stress of Ava's 'comeback' that had finally pushed him over the edge. But not only was Kendall not going to leave him, she was going to fight Ava and JSM with him. She was going to be his team-mate, his best friend, the way that Catriona always used to be.

'Oh, darling,' he gushed, 'I can't tell you how much that means to—'

'Not so fast.' Kendall's tone was icy. 'If I agree to come back I expect things to change.'

'Of course.' Ivan nodded, humbled. 'Whatever you want.'

'You have to quit drinking. Completely.'

'I know. I will. I have, as of this morning.'

'I'm serious, Ivan.' For the first time Kendall's own voice started to break. 'I'm not talking about a few days off because you feel guilty. I need you to stop for good.'

'I know and I will.' Getting up, Ivan came over and sat next to her. 'Catriona was drinking very heavily a year or so ago and she knocked it on the head just like that. I'll talk to her about AA or support groups or—'

'No!' Kendall sat up, physically pushing him away. 'I don't want you talking to Catriona. I don't want her anywhere near us. She's part of the reason you started drinking in the first place.'

Ivan frowned. 'What do you mean?'

I mean that you miss her and your old life. But you can't have it while you're with me, and you don't want to lose me, so you feel like you're being ripped apart and you drink to blot it out.

'Nothing,' said Kendall 'I don't know what I mean. I just . . . I don't want that woman involved in our lives.'

Ivan reached out and stroked her hair. *That woman.* It was the clearest expression of jealousy he'd heard yet from Kendall, and although he knew it shouldn't, it reassured him. If she was jealous of Catriona, she must still care. His own sexual jealousy and paranoia about Kendall being with other men was the glue that kept him with her. That and the fact that they needed one another professionally, now more than ever with Ava Bentley's UK comeback on the horizon.

'I won't talk to Cat,' Ivan assured Kendall. 'Not if you don't want me to.'

'Of course you can talk to her,' said Kendall. 'About the children, or whatever. Just not about drinking or our private lives. And I'd like to be there when you *do* talk to her. I don't want to feel shut out any more. *I'm* family now too, remember?'

'Of course,' said Ivan. 'Of course you are. And I will stop drinking. I promise you, sweetheart. I'll be a model husband from now on. I'll make this up to you.'

'Good,' said Kendall, willing herself to believe him. She still felt angry and humiliated and hurt. But she focused on channelling those feelings away from Ivan and towards Ava. Ava was the threat, not just to Kendall's career and her UK dominance, but to her marriage. It was *Ava*'s betrayal that had pushed Ivan over the edge, *Ava*'s relationship with Lex that had made Kendall fuck up last night's gig, *Ava*'s return to England that had lit the match which ignited an explosion of violence in Kendall's relationship.

Once Ava was out of the picture, things would get better with Ivan.

They had to.

CHAPTER TWENTY-TWO

'Team Ava'– consisting of Ava herself, Lex, Jack, Lisa Marie, Ava's publicist Jen Gomez, and two Columbia gofers who delighted in the names of Chuck and Rusty – landed at Heathrow on 1 December. The next day the biggest snowfall for twenty years dumped itself over London, carpeting the city in a magical blanket of white and bringing services, transport and life in general to a complete, grinding halt.

'This is a disaster!' Jack stared out of the window of his suite at The Dorchester, cell phone in hand. 'Ava's supposed to be filming live in Manchester tonight but all the motorways are kaput, domestic flights have been cancelled and the train services are running a skeleton service, whatever the fuck that means?'

'Helicopter?' suggested Jen Gomez. Sitting at the desk in the office section of Jack's suite, Jen was wading through last week's press clippings on Ava's imminent arrival in Britain. Thanks to a relentless and brutally successful PR campaign being waged by Kendall Bryce's camp, the coverage was wholly negative. Ava had been painted as a traitor who'd turned her back on Britain and her roots and been corrupted

367

by the lure of Hollywood, money and fame. Much had been made of her 'manufactured' new look, which the entire nation apparently loathed. One article even poured scorn on Ava's 'newly adopted American accent', an entirely fictitious creation as Jen Gomez knew only too well. One of Jen's biggest challenges when it came to promoting *Pure* had been trying to make Ava's broad Yorkshire vowels understandable to a US audience. The kid sounded about as American as Gerard Depardieu with a throat infection. But the *Daily Fail* weren't about to let a little thing like facts get in the way of a good, bitchy feature.

'I tried.' Jack threw his arms up in frustration. 'But it looks like every rich banker in London trying to get to Gstaad had the same idea. There's not a chopper to be had. We'll have to cancel.'

Jen groaned. She could see the headlines now. 'Spoilt Brat Bentley "Too Important" For Regional Chat Show.' 'Ava Snubs North To Party With Hollywood Pals In London.' It was terribly unfair. Anyone less starry and self-centred than Ava would be hard to imagine. So far Jen and the team had managed to shield Ava herself from the worst of the bad press. But the truth was they had a mountain to climb if they were going to win back the British public in time to have a shot at being Christmas number one.

Just then Ava stuck her head round the door. In a red woolly hat with a bobble on it, a matching puffa jacket and big, white, fluffy snow boots, she looked like an excited little kid about to go sledging. 'Any news?'

'We're cancelling,' said Jack. 'We've tried, but there's no way to get you there. It can't be done.'

'Oh, that's a shame,' said Ava, grinning from ear to ear. She clearly had no idea how important these first few days of publicity were. All she wanted to do was go outside and play. 'Am I free for lunch then? My dad booked a table at a posh Italian in Knightsbridge. He wants to meet Lex.'

'Yeah, you're free,' said Jen. 'Have fun.'

'And if anyone wants your autograph or asks for a picture, make sure you give them one and make nice,' added Jack. 'You want to make a good impression out there.'

Ava looked at him strangely. 'Of course I'll give people my autograph. Why on earth wouldn't I?' Skipping out through the door, she was gone.

Lex had not wanted to come to London. He had disapproved of the whole exercise from the first, and had kept up his told-you-so grumbling all the way across the Atlantic, much to Jack's irritation. Not only had Ava's own reputation been thoroughly trounced by the notoriously no-holds-barred British media, but her return to London had actually boosted Kendall's own image and profile. Pictures of Kendall and Ivan together looking loved-up and supportive in the face of Ava's 'betrayal' were everywhere. Whereas Ava was the local girl who'd been corrupted by evil Americans, Kendall was the new Kylie, the foreigner who'd abandoned her own country for England and made it her home. The Brits couldn't get enough. If Lex read one more interview about how much Kendall *adored* England, how she loved spending time in the countryside and the north, how her favourite food was steak and kidney pudding and she'd given up vodka in favour of Guinness, he was seriously gonna puke.

But even he was having a tough time being down on London this morning. Ava had leapt out of bed literally shrieking with delight when she saw the snow, and it was hard not to share at least some of her childlike enthusiasm. The city looked unreal, like a scene from a Victorian Christmas card, all snow-topped spires and silent, muffled-white streets.

Walking to Harrods to do some Christmas shopping (there was no other way to get there) he passed rows of grand, white-stucco-fronted houses, whose front gardens had been transformed overnight into perfectly iced wedding cakes. Turning into Hyde Park, a frosted wonderland of majestic oaks, their leaves shocked white like old men's hair, interspersed with dark, shiny green holly bushes, some of them erupting in a profusion of blood-red berries, the thing that struck Lex most was the silence. There wasn't an engine to be heard, only the soft crunch of footfalls in the snowy blanket and the distant peal of church bells. Unlike Oxford Street, Kensington and Chelsea had eschewed gaudy holiday fanfare, decorating their pretty streets instead with greenery. Miniature Christmas trees clung to the top of lampposts, which twinkled in the evenings with merry white lights. But if nature and a Conservative council had restricted the outdoor decorations to a restrained palette of green and white, the explosion of color and richness inside Harrods more than made up for it.

Walking through the Food Hall just moments after it opened, Lex felt like Charlie entering the hallowed gates of Willie Wonka's chocolate factory. Visually it was a work of art, an Aladdin's cave of edible gems in every conceivable shape and colour. There were mountains of candied fruit, iced cabinets full of seafood and vast plates of multicoloured salads. There were chocolates and cheeses and a bakery stuffed with everything from vivid green and pink French macaroons to rustic brown loaves of Irish soda bread. There was coffee from Colombia and juicily trussed joints of beef from Scotland. Finest sushi-grade albacore was being sliced by Japanese chefs just two feet away from blazing pizza ovens, where an Italian man was already doing something wonderful with rosemary and oregano, the scent of which filled the air and made Lex's mouth water. And that was just the ground floor.

Upstairs there was everything from carpets to Christmas cards, modern Danish furniture to priceless, millennia-old fossils. There were dazzling evening dresses and medieval maps and harpsichords and Barbie dolls and diamonds. Nowhere in LA came close to this place. And no store Lex had ever been in, anywhere in the world, could touch Harrods when it came to Christmas spirit. Not even Lex could keep up his Scrooge routine in here.

At twelve-thirty, laden down with shopping bags but considerably lighter in the wallet, Lex re-emerged onto Walton Street. Ava had texted to say the Manchester trip was off and her entire schedule for the next forty-eight hours was 'on hold'. While the country held its collective breath, waiting to see if yet more snow was on its way overnight, Ava's father Dave had booked a table for lunch at Scalini.

Lex had last been to the restaurant a decade ago, as a young photographer touring with Enrique Iglesias. It hadn't changed at all, a good thing in Lex's book, and he tried to relax as he was led to the table. OK, so Dave Bentley had a reputation as being a bit overbearing. But really, how bad could he be over the course of one lunch? Besides, it wasn't as if Lex was about to marry Ava or anything. They'd only been dating for less than a year, so today wasn't going to be some sort of son-in-law interview.

'There you are!' A fat, red-faced Tweedledum of a man in tweed trousers and a garish yellow sweater stood up and literally bellowed across the room, much to the consternation of the other diners. 'You'd better not keep her waiting like this at the altar, eh? EH?' Dave Bentley roared

with laughter at his own joke. Beside him, Ava sat mortified, doing her best to shrink into her chair.

'Alex, in't it?'

Lex had arrived at the table now and bent down to kiss
Ava hello. As he did so, Dave's arm came down like a
metal rod, thwacking him so hard on the back and shoulders he almost fell into Ava's lap. 'Pleased to meet you at
last.'

'You too, sir,' gasped Lex, struggling to get his breath back.

'He goes by Lex, Dad,' said Ava meekly. 'I told you that,
remember?'

'Lex?' Dave boomed. '*Lex?* That's not a name. Not for a
person anyway.'

'*Dad!*'

'Well I'm sorry, but I speak as I find. It's a car isn't it?'
He laughed again. 'No, no, I'll stick to Alex if you don't
mind. I'm not 'aving my daughter marrying a fella who
sounds like a bleedin' Cabriolet. Wine?'

'Er, no thank you, not for me. I never drink in the middle
of the—'

'Oh, go on, 'ave a glass. You're all health nuts aren't you,
you Americans?' Dave filled Lex's glass to the brim. 'Cheers,
Big Ears!'

It was going to be a long, long lunch.

Kendall sat beside Ivan in the helicopter, gazing down at
the winter wonderland below.

'How long till we get to Manchester?' she shouted over
the whirring blades.

'About an hour,' said Ivan smugly. He was picturing Jack
Messenger's face when Kendall appeared on *Good Morning*
tomorrow in Ava's stead. Talk about a coup. By the time
Kendall had finished charming the pants off the audience

and painting Ava as the two-faced little snake that she was, he wouldn't be surprised if Jack gave up the whole misguided Christmas number one campaign and flew back to LA with his tail between his legs.

Kendall stared out of the window. The noise of the chopper gave her a perfect excuse to avoid conversation. These days she found the less she talked to Ivan, the easier it was. Not that there was any hostility between them. In fact all their private interactions were scrupulously, painfully polite. (As opposed to their public encounters, which were gushingly romantic and Brangelina-esque.) Ivan had kept to his word and stopped drinking. He'd also done a spectacular job of orchestrating the smear campaign against Ava and bolstering Kendall's own public image in the run-up to Christmas. But all of the fun, the spark and banter, had gone out of the relationship. The sexual chemistry that had been their one constant since the earliest days seemed to have deserted them, like an exhausted guardian angel. Kendall had forgiven Ivan for what happened that night at The 100 Club. So it was a surprise to find that forgiveness alone was not enough. Something had broken that day, a connection between them had snapped, and nothing either of them did or said could bring it back again.

Kendall knew it. Ivan knew it. But nobody had the desire or the courage to say it out loud, still less to think about what it meant for their future. Especially now with their mutual enemy at the gate.

Kendall wondered briefly about Ava, where she was right now and whether she was with Lex. Closing her eyes, she forced the thought out of her mind. She had trained herself to shut down her emotions when it came to Ivan. As for Jack, last time he was in England she'd been in pieces mentally, but this time she felt nothing at all. She could do the same with Lex. She'd have to if she was going to protect herself, no matter how many loved-up shots of him and Ava arriving hand in hand at Heathrow she was forced to endure.

Flipping open her iPad, she studied her notes on Eamonn Holmes: his interviewing style, preferences, the pitfalls other guests had stumbled into on his show. What was Stella always telling her? *Focus on today. Focus on the now.* Right now all that mattered was acing it on *This Morning* and wiping the floor with Ava Bentley.

That much, at least, Kendall knew how to do.

The next ten days were a nightmare for Lex, whose Christmas spirit proved to be as short-lived as the London snow. From a purely professional perspective, the trip had been a disaster. Ava's press was bad enough before her no-show on *This Morning*. But when Kendall took her place on that couch, looking doe-eyed and vulnerable hand in hand with Ivan, you could practically hear the knives being sharpened. Kendall played the thing perfectly, actually defending Ava when Eamonn Holmes accused her of being spoiled and a diva, but in such a weak way, '*I really don't know what happened. I guess she must have had her reasons*', that she ended up making her look worse.

Ivan played the same game. 'I've always had a soft spot for Ava,' he told the host disingenuously.

'And a hard spot for your wife, I assume?'

Cue awkward audience laughter and a perfectly timed kiss from Kendall.

'Well, yes, that's true,' Ivan smiled. 'But joking aside and despite everything that happened, I still wish Ava all the best. We both do.'

Jack had started screaming at the TV at that point, hurling

abuse at Ivan, Eamonn Holmes, the show's producers, the helicopter charter company and anyone else he could think of to blame for this PR catastrophe. But there could be no getting away from it. A catastrophe was what it was.

After the tsunami came the rescue efforts, a draining round of publicity appearances aimed at damage control and showing Ava in a more positive light. Somebody at Columbia decided that part of this rebrand should involve playing up Lex and Ava as a couple. As a result Lex found himself being dragged from TV studios to radio stations to various staged 'photo opportunities' at restaurants, theatres and even children's homes, thrust wholly unwillingly into the limelight. The fakeness of it all stuck in his craw. Not that he wasn't with Ava. But they were hardly love's young dream, altar-bound. At least that wasn't how Lex perceived them. Some of the comments Ava made live on air had him worrying that perhaps she was starting to believe the hype.

He tried to talk to her privately about it, but it was difficult with her father always there, following them around like a fat shadow. Lex tried hard, but within a few days he had come to loathe Dave Bentley. Not only was the man a bully, bossy, overbearing and opinionated, but he seemed to have conveniently forgotten the fact that he was no longer his daughter's manager, driving both Lex and Jack mad with his constant interference. It was Dave who arranged the visit to the children's hospice in Wolverhampton.

'Everyone loves dying kiddies,' he announced bluntly and without irony. 'Ava should go and sing 'em some Christmas carols. People'll love that.'

Jack complained, Jen Gomez complained, but Dave insisted, and in the end Ava didn't have it in her to say no to her dad. Once again, Lex was dragged along for a horrendously schmaltzy sing-along with the sick children and their families. The next day's papers were uniformly scathing.

'CRASS PUBLICITY STUNT.'

'DESPERATE BENTLEY DOES "A DIANA".'

'CRINGE-MAKING.'

Poor Ava, who'd been genuinely moved by the children's plight and had privately written cheques to a number of the families, was deeply hurt by the coverage. But not as deeply hurt as her record sales. Pre-orders for 'Home', the song with which she hoped to beat off Kendall's 'Sweet Dreamer' to the number one spot on Christmas morning, now less than two weeks away, were embarrassingly low. Two nights ago she'd finally broken down when in bed with Lex, sobbing for a full five minutes before he could get any sense out of her at all.

'Everyone hates me!' she wailed. 'No one's going to give me a chance. But I don't understand what I'm supposed to have done. Since when is moving to America a crime?'

'It isn't,' Lex assured her. 'Everything's being twisted.'

'Yeah, by Kendall,' said Ava bitterly. 'She seemed so nice when I met her. Why is she doing this to me?'

'Because you're threatening her, honey,' said Lex reasonably. 'You must see that. You're bringing out your single in direct competition to hers, in her primary market. Kendall sees that as an act of war. She's fighting back.'

'Oh, so you're on her side,' Ava sobbed. 'My own boyfriend!'

'I'm not on her side. I—'

'You are! Admit it. You're still in love with her, aren't you?'

And they were back to square one.

Nightmare.

The sooner they got out of London, the better.

* * *

On Tuesday morning around ten o'clock, Lex's cell phone rang.

'What are you doing for lunch today?'

It was a woman's voice, American, but Lex didn't recognize it.

'Er, I'm sorry, this is Lex Abrahams. Who is this?'

'It's me!'

He thought for one awful moment she was going to leave it at that. But then she went on.

'It's Stella, Stella Bayley. You represent my dirty rotten pig of an ex-husband, remember?'

'Stella! Of course. Hi,' Lex said awkwardly. He had known Stella socially in the old Jester days, before Jack and Ivan split. The Blitz had all lived in LA then, and Stella and Brett had been regulars on the West Hollywood scene. But they were hardly good friends, and it had been – what – ten years? 'How are you?'

'I'm good thanks,' she trilled. 'No thanks to you and your dirty rotten partner, luring Brett back to California.'

'Hey, that was Jack's idea,' said Lex honestly. 'Nothing to do with me.'

'Oh, that's OK.' Stella laughed. 'I'm only teasing anyway. Jack did me a favour. But look, I knew you were in town and I'm sure you must be having a shitty time of it, so I thought I'd ask you out for lunch.'

Her candour was refreshing. It was a relief not to have to pretend that everything was OK. 'That's very kind of you.'

'No it isn't. It'll be fun,' said Stella. 'How about Daphne's at one-thirty. Can you do it?'

Lex was supposed to be at Capital Radio studios on Leicester Square with Ava at one-thirty, but the lure of a lunchtime escape was too strong. Jen could take Ava this time. After all, she was supposed to be the damn publicist.

'Sure. Sounds wonderful. I'll see you there.'

Stella was seated in a corner table at the back of the restaurant, half hidden behind a pillar and completely safe from any prying lenses that might have followed Lex, hoping for some scandal. She was wearing a blue-and-white striped sweater and fitted white jeans tucked into boots. She looked like an unusually chic French fisherwoman.

'Hi.' Lex kissed her on both cheeks as he sat down. 'This is such a treat. And a surprise! You look incredibly well.'

'Do I?' Stella beamed. 'Thanks. It's been a rough couple of years but I'm actually very happy right now. I think divorce agrees with me.'

'I think divorcing Brett would agree with anyone,' said Lex. 'God knows how you stood it so long.'

Stella ordered the soup and tagliatelle, along with a large glass of rosé. 'I know you're not supposed to drink rosé in winter, but I just love it,' she grinned. Lex thought back to the macrobiotic, clean-living, serious girl he'd known all those years ago and smiled. *Europe's been good for her. Age too. She's finally found her mojo.* He ordered the minute steak and fries and a beer (*What the hell*, Lex thought), and they got down to the serious business of gossiping.

'I should probably warn you before we start that I am on the enemy payroll,' said Stella. 'I've been working as Kendall's PA for almost a year now.'

Lex's face fell. 'Oh.'

'But I'm *not* here in a work capacity, I'm *not* wearing a wire, and I give you my word that I'm not gonna go running back and spilling your juicy secrets. I'm here as a friend.'

She was so open and kind that Lex instantly believed her. 'I don't have any juicy secrets to spill, in any case,' he said, sipping his beer. 'Do you?'

Stella leaned forward. 'Well as it just so happens . . .'

She didn't draw breath for the next hour and half. Lex's salad and steak came and went, as did two more beers and an ill-advised helping of sticky toffee pudding, while Stella continued to regale him hilariously with tales of Jester and JSM clients past and present. She'd always seemed so straight-laced when she was with Brett, but freed from the role of supportive rock star's wife slash super-mommy, she actually had a wicked sense of humour. For the first time since he got to England, Lex was enjoying himself. Before long he found himself opening up about Ava, her dreadful father and the PR machine's obsession with painting him as Romeo to Ava's Juliet.

'Like that's gonna sell more records, you know?'

Stella shrugged. 'It worked for Kendall and Ivan.'

'Yeah, but they're not being followed around by a twenty-stone cupid from Hutton-le-Hole with a beer gut, bad breath and a boiled Yorkshire cabbage where his brain should be, are they?'

'No,' Stella giggled.

'I swear to God, Dave Bentley makes Donald Rumsfeld look sensitive.' Looking away, Lex asked as casually as he could. 'So, how is Kendall?'

Stella eyed him curiously. 'How is she in what way?'

'I don't know, in every way. Personally.' Lex cleared his throat awkwardly. 'Jack and I watched her on *This Morning* last week. She seemed happy.'

'Did she?'

'Well,' Lex backtracked, 'she came across well, let's put it that way. Jack was spitting teeth. It was a bravura performance.'

'You can always rely on Kendall for a good performance,' said Stella cryptically.

Lex raised an eyebrow. 'Are you trying to tell me something?'

Stella leaned back in her chair, pushing her plate to one side. 'Look, I don't just work for Kendall. I consider her a friend. Ivan too, in a way, although that's a bit more complicated. Anyway, there are things I can say and things I can't. But don't be fooled by the "perfect marriage, perfect life" stuff she spouts in the media, that's all. That's image. It's not reality.'

'So she isn't happy?' asked Lex, ashamed by how good that prospect made him feel. Not because he wanted to hurt Kendall, but because he missed her like hell.

'Neither of them are happy,' said Stella. 'That's my opinion. But they're scared to leave each other, scared to admit they made a mistake. I think they would have separated in the fall if it weren't for Ava coming over here.'

Lex put his head in his hands. 'Please don't say that.'

'It's true,' Stella shrugged. 'This race for the Christmas number one is what threw Kendall and Ivan back together. She's worked so hard to rebuild her career over here, you know. She's not going to let that go without a fight.'

'Of course not,' said Lex. 'That's what I've been trying to explain to Ava. Kendall's always put her career before anything else. She'll fight to the death for it.'

Stella looked at him thoughtfully. 'She's changed, you know. Softened. I don't think work is all she cares about any more.' On a whim, she added, 'She misses you.'

It was embarrassing the degree to which Lex's heart leapt when he heard those words. But he stamped down his elation. Stella was probably just trying to be kind, to make peace between her two friends. What did she really know about how Kendall felt?

'Well, when you see her, tell her I wish her all the best,' he said neutrally.

'I will,' said Stella.

Lex waved for the bill.

Catriona stared at her reflection in the restaurant loo. *What am I doing here?*

She was on a date, an actual proper dinner date with a man, her first since . . . she cast her mind back. When *was* the last time?

That's why I feel so awkward, she told herself firmly. *It's not him. It's me. I haven't done this in so long I've got no idea what to do.*

The man in question was Bill Whitely, a divorced dad from Rosie's school. Bill was in his mid-fifties, tall and distinguished-looking with kind eyes and a deep voice. He reminded Cat faintly of her own father, which didn't help. Nor did the fact that he wore Floris aftershave, a scent that would forever remind her of Ivan. Throughout dinner at Lucio's, the new *Zagat*-rated Italian in Stow-on-the-Wold, she tried to focus on the fact that Bill had all the attributes people usually looked for in those dreadful Internet dating websites. He was funny (*GSOH*). He ran a successful printing business (*solvent*). He had the requisite amount of interests (*opera, travel, polo*). He was, as her smattering of girlfriends all told her, a good catch. Apparently it was less likely for a divorced woman of Catriona's age to marry again than it was for her to become CEO of a FTSE 100 company. She ought to be grateful, ecstatic, biting his hand off. And yet . . .

She'd woken up this morning after a disturbingly erotic dream about Jack Messenger, to find her cheeks flushed, her pulse still racing and a lingering feeling of arousal between her legs. All of which was quite ridiculous as she hadn't been thinking about Jack at all. Well, barely at all. She knew he was in England. She'd seen him in the background, standing behind Ava and Lex Abrahams in a photograph in last week's *Daily Mail*. But he hadn't called, and Catriona didn't expect him to. They hadn't so much fallen out as grown apart over the past year. Cat had forgiven him for signing Ivan's *Talent Quest* protégée, and potentially bankrupting her entire family, but she didn't like the fact that he was bringing Ava back to England to flaunt her under Ivan's nose, now that the dust had finally settled. Thanks to Ava's 'comeback', Kendall and Ivan were once again all over the newspapers and on every TV screen, proclaiming their undying love for each other like some poor man's Burton and Taylor. Catriona had Jack to thank for that. Even so, there was a part of her that still jumped whenever the phone rang at Burford, half hoping and half dreading that it might be him.

One thing she knew for sure was that it wouldn't be Ivan. After a year of much-improved relations with her ex, Ivan had called her about six weeks ago and announced that he'd be 'lying low' for a while. Translated, this apparently meant that he would no longer come to Burford to pick up the children but would pay for their train tickets to London instead. From that day on, the friendly phone calls and emails stopped dead. Whenever he did call, he made a big show of letting her know that Kendall was with him. Apparently he needed a chaperone to talk to her these days. What hurt the most was that Catriona had no idea why. With Christmas just around the corner, and Rosie and Hector both increasingly leading their own lives, she felt more alone than ever.

By the time she got back to the table, Bill had already paid. 'You looked a bit tired,' he said, holding out her coat. 'I thought you'd probably want to call it a night.'

Catriona smiled gratefully. How much easier this would be if he were rude or boorish. Then she could reject him guilt-free.

It took over half an hour to drive the nine miles back to Burford. The snow might have melted in London, but out here it still lay thick and deep, and the unlit roads were slick with ice. Bill talked about his business and asked her questions about the children and her photography, tactfully never mentioning Ivan or the Ava/Kendall soap opera being played out in the press. It was amazing how many people *did* still try and pump her for information about her famous ex and his pop-star wife, conveniently forgetting that it was Kendall Bryce who had blown apart Catriona's marriage.

When they finally pulled over outside Catriona's house, Bill leaned over to kiss her. Catriona thought about letting him. It was a perfect, romantic moment. Outside the snow had started to fall again, dusting the window with fat, wet flakes. At the top of Burford Hill, the town Christmas tree stood proudly, its multicoloured lights throwing a cheerful, festive glow over the sleepy, white-roofed cottages. And then there was Bill himself. He'd been terribly charming and thoughtful tonight in the face of Catriona's blind panic. Not to mention that he was solvent with a GSOH and three interests. But as the waft of Floris came closer she baulked, jerking her head to one side just at the wrong moment so he ended up head-butting her cheek, which in turn sent her flying backwards so her skull cracked painfully against the passenger-side window.

'Oh God! I'm so sorry,' he said, mortified. 'Are you all right?'

'I'm fine. Please, don't apologize.' Opening the car door, Catriona literally scrambled out into the cold night air. 'Thank you for a lovely evening. Goodbye!'

She ran inside so fast she almost went flying in the icy twitten and earned herself a second bump on the head. The first was throbbing painfully. Opening the freezer she pulled out a packet of frozen sweetcorn and pressed it to the back of her skull.

'Let me do that for you.'

Catriona screamed and dropped the sweetcorn. Rosie and Hector were both away for the night. The house was supposed to be empty.

'Relax,' said Ivan, stooping to pick up the packet. 'It's only me.' In a dinner jacket and dress trousers, with his bow tie removed and his white shirt unbuttoned at the top, he'd obviously just come from some sort of party. As he handed Catriona back her home-made ice pack, it irritated her that he looked so bloody handsome. Didn't he ever have an off day? And what right did he have, showing up here after six weeks of radio silence, frightening the life out of her.

'What are you doing here?' she said coldly. 'The children are both out. It's not a good time.'

'I can see that,' said Ivan. 'What happened?'

Catriona thought about the bungled kiss. 'I . . . we were . . . Oh look, what does it matter what happened? It's none of your beeswax anyway.'

'Why don't you lie down on the sofa and I'll fetch you a pillow.'

'I don't want to lie down on the sofa!' she said crossly. 'What are you *doing* here, Ivan? You can't just turn up willy-nilly whenever you feel like it and let yourself into my house. Are you drunk?'

'No.' He looked offended. 'I don't drink any more. I've given it up.'

'Oh.' This took Catriona by surprise. 'Have you?'

'Yes,' said Ivan indignantly. 'And you needn't look so astonished. You're not the only person with willpower you know.'

'Fine. So why are you here then?' She did her best to look stern and in control, not an easy look with a packet of frozen vegetables slowly thawing on top of one's head.

'I needed to see you,' said Ivan. 'I know I should have called first but I was scared you'd tell me to sod off.'

'I probably would have.'

'Exactly. Please go and lie down and let me bring you a cushion or something. I can see that lump from here.' He grinned. 'You look like Tom after Jerry's just hit him over the head with an anvil.'

Catriona hesitated, but eventually did as he asked. She was starting to feel dizzy anyway. Ivan ran upstairs and returned with a pillow and a blanket. Gently arranging the frozen bag behind her head, he tucked her in, returning moments later with a mug of hot, sweet tea.

'It's good after a shock,' he said.

'I haven't had a shock,' said Catriona. Although she had an unpleasant feeling she was about to. She wondered what could possibly be going to happen next; why after six weeks of silence he'd bothered to drive all the way down here. Perhaps Kendall was pregnant? With sextuplets? Who'd all be given names beginning with K and who were already represented by Max Clifford? At this point, nothing would surprise her. So, she wondered, why did she feel so nervous? 'What's this all about, Ivan?'

He sighed, pacing round the room like a man awaiting judgement. Just being here, in this room, felt wildly nostalgic. In one corner, a seven-foot Christmas tree was hung with all the gaudy decorations from the old days. There was the papier-mâché angel that Rosie had brought home from school aged six, and the stuffed felt Father Christmas (affectionately known in the family as 'death's-head Santa' because it looked like some hideously sinister voodoo object) that Hector had spent an entire term producing in his first year at St Edmond's. On top of the tree was the same moth-eaten feather angel they'd used every year since they were married. Ivan could remember going to buy it at a long-since-closed department store on Fulham Broadway, how excited he and Cat had both been at the prospect of their first Christmas as man and wife, and how Cat had covered every inch of their grotty basement flat in holly and tinsel till it looked as though one of Santa's elves had broken in and thrown up. What a long time ago it all seemed now.

'It's over with Kendall.'

The words hung in the air between them. Ivan waited for Catriona to respond but she said nothing, lying stock-still, like a shell-shock victim waiting for the next bomb to go off.

'There's no drama. It was a mutual thing. We both agreed on it tonight.'

'You were at a party.' Catriona stared at his dinner jacket. It was a stupid thing to say, utterly pointless and irrelevant, but for some reason those were the words that came out of her mouth.

'Yeah, an awards thing at The Apollo. Kendall was up for Best Female Vocalist. She won it by a mile.'

'That's good,' Catriona said mindlessly.

'She's odds-on favourite for Christmas number one, too. Once that happens we can write our own cheque for her next record deal. I'll easily clear enough to buy back The Rookery.'

'Buy back The Rookery?' Catriona frowned, as if trying

to work out some particularly difficult crossword clue. But that was how it felt. What on earth was Ivan talking about? Christmas singles and awards and buying back their old house. None of it made a shred of sense. 'Why would you want to do that? Is it even for sale?'

'Everything's for sale at the right price,' said Ivan. For a moment, Catriona wondered whether he mentally included her in that sweeping statement.

Sitting down on the edge of the sofa, Ivan took her hand. 'Listen, Cat, I've been an idiot. I made a huge mistake. The biggest. But it's not Kendall I love. It's you.'

'Me?' Unthinking, Cat burst into laughter. 'Oh, no, no, no. Nooooooo.'

'Yes,' said Ivan, deadly serious. 'I love you, Cat. I always have. And I want you back. I want our old life back – you, me, the kids, our house. I've missed you so much.'

Leaning down, he kissed her, so suddenly that Cat didn't have a chance to jerk her head away. It was a bizarre sensation, feeling his lips on hers: strange and yet at the same time totally familiar, like slipping on a comfortable old sweater that you unexpectedly find stuffed down the back of the wardrobe after five years.

'I love you.' He was whispering in her ear, his hands slowly sliding down her body, caressing the fabric of her new Diane von Furstenberg dress, an early Christmas present from the ever-faithful Ned Williams. It was only then that Catriona belatedly came to her senses.

'Have you lost your mind?' she asked, pushing him firmly away. 'You have a row with Kendall, so you think you can drive up here to see me and just, what? Pick up where we left off?'

'No.' Ivan sat up, running a hand through his hair. 'Of course not. I mean, not right away . . .'

'Not *right away*?' echoed Catriona.

'Look, it was more than just a tiff with Kendall. Much more. We're finished, OK, we've been finished for ages.'

'So you thought you'd buy back our old house and move us in and we'd all start playing happy families again?' Cat asked incredulously.

'Why not?' asked Ivan. 'It's better than playing broken families, isn't it? Admit it. There's a part of you that still loves me. I know there is.'

There were tears in his eyes. She knew she shouldn't, but Cat found herself feeling immensely sorry for him. In one way, of course, he was right. There was a part of her that still loved him. That would always love him. He was her first love, her husband and the father of her children. Nothing could change that. But the naiveté of thinking one could just go back, after everything that had happened. Rewind the clock . . . it was heartbreaking. Almost endearing, in a way.

'Look. You can stay here tonight,' she said kindly. Then, seeing Ivan's countenance brighten, clarified quickly 'in the spare room.'

Ivan nodded. 'Of course. Thanks.'

'We'll talk more in the morning, if you want to. It sounds as if we've both had more than enough drama for one night.'

Ivan hesitated. He desperately wanted to talk more now, to batter Catriona into submission the way that he used to, the way that he knew he still could if given half a chance. She *did* still love him, whatever she said. He'd felt it in the days leading up to his wedding, and in countless little affectionate exchanges since. But it wouldn't do to scare her off too soon. Naturally she wanted him to prove himself, to show that he was serious this time; that it really *was* over with Kendall.

'You're right, as usual,' he said, standing up and yawning. 'We should talk tomorrow. Here.' He held out his hand. 'Let me help you upstairs.'

Ten minutes later, alone in her own bed but twitchingly aware of Ivan's presence down the hall, Catriona tried to untangle her raging emotions. There were so many. Nostalgia. Anxiety. Fear. Anger. Although it shamed her to admit it, there was part of her that felt flattered by Ivan's overtures. Another, more worrying part, did wonder what it might be like to be part of a family again, living at The Rookery, reconnecting with all their old friends as a couple, as if the past few dreadful years had been nothing more than a bad dream. Was she pleased that he and Kendall had broken up? There was a time when she would have been. Now she felt little more than a weary numbness. And something else: pity. Perhaps compassion might be a kinder word. She cared about Ivan, about his feelings, despite it all. If tonight's awkward encounter turned out to be the first step in a more genuine and long-lasting friendship between them, surely that must be a good thing?

Down the hall, Ivan was having thoughts of a more practical nature.

He wouldn't announce his and Kendall's separation publicly till after Christmas. She – they – needed that number one if she was going to sign the fat new deal that would set his finances back in order, and enable him to buy back The Rookery. Cat couldn't see it now, because it felt like a pipe dream. But once he took her hand and led her back into that beautiful house, the once happy home that they had built together; and once he showed her how happy he was going to make her again, he felt sure Catriona would want a reconciliation as much as he did.

We were meant to be together, he thought happily, drifting off beneath Cat's freshly laundered, lavender-scented sheets. He was home again at last.

CHAPTER TWENTY-THREE

Jack Messenger wandered through the second floor at Fortnum & Mason's, admiring the decorations. This year his favourite London department store had gone for a 'Victorian Christmas' theme, complete with miniature trees in the windows hung with clove-stuck oranges and a wonderfully intricate hand-painted mural of skaters on the frozen Thames. When Sonya was alive she used to love coming to London or New York for pre-Christmas shopping. LA was beautiful, but there was something about palm trees and sunshine that never felt quite right during the holidays, however brightly dressed and be-ribboned they may be. Walking among the papier-mâché robins, complete with real feathers, and the delicately carved and painted wooden reindeer, Jack missed her. He always missed her, although it was no longer with the furious, raging pain of his early years as a widower. It was more of a dull ache, a flicker of sadness, like a passing storm cloud, but tinged lately with the silver lining of nostalgia. Fortnum's held many happy memories.

Idly he picked up one of the robins and a stack of pretty

Medici cards. It was rare for him to have an afternoon off, and he intended to make the most of it, stocking up on British goodies to take back with him to LA. Lisa Marie had gone back last night. She'd told him before the London trip, in the kindest possible way, that she'd started seeing somebody else, and she'd gone back home to be with him.

'I adore you, Jack, you know that. And I really hope you still wanna work with me. But I'm thirty-eight and I want to have kids. We always knew it couldn't last for ever.'

If only more women were like Lisa Marie. So straightforward and uncomplicated and civilized. He assured her that her job at JSM would be there for as long as she wanted it, as would his friendship. Slightly to his surprise, they'd spent a couple of nights together since they got to London, a sort of farewell to their affair that Jack had thoroughly enjoyed. Nevertheless, he was relieved when she flew back to join her new beau for the holidays, and felt a renewed sense of freedom this afternoon as he strolled the brightly lit streets alone.

'Jack.'

He spun around. Looking tinier than usual in a pair of tight black corduroy pants and a jade-green polo-neck sweater that clung to her matchstick-like arms, Kendall Bryce smiled up at him. It was the smile, more than the coincidence of running into her, that threw him. He found himself blushing and stammering like a schoolboy.

'K . . . Kendall. Wow. This is a surprise. Small world.'

'Actually the world's pretty big. If you'd stuck to your side of it I doubt we'd have run into each other. But . . . here we are.' Her smile broke into a grin. He was relieved to see she was joking. *I guess she can afford to be magnanimous, now that Ava's crashing and burning in the press here and she's a shoo-in for number one.* 'How are you?'

Jack shrugged. 'I'm OK, I guess.' He contemplated making a snide remark about the way she and Ivan had bad-mouthed Ava, but nobody liked a sore loser. If Kendall was prepared to bury the hatchet, with Ava's competing single being officially released tomorrow, the least he could do was return the favour. 'I'm surprised you aren't out on the PR treadmill, this close to the big day.'

'You too,' said Kendall. 'I heard Ava on Capital Radio in the cab on my way over here. Didn't she want her hand held?'

'Lex is with her,' said Jack. Was it his imagination, or did Kendall's face just fall? 'Look, if you're really not busy, d'you want to go and grab a coffee?'

Kendall cocked her head to one side suspiciously. Last time she'd seen Jack he hadn't exactly been in a coffee-buying mood. At least not towards her. 'Really?'

'Only if you want to.'

'I'd love to,' she said quickly. 'We'd better go somewhere private, though. If anyone got a picture of the two of us talking, it'd seriously set the cat amongst the pigeons.'

'You're the Londoner,' said Jack, putting back the Christmas cards. 'Any suggestions?'

Ten minutes later, they were sitting at the back of a nondescript Italian café a stone's throw from The Berkeley.

'They do an amazing coffee cake here,' said Kendall, sitting down at a table in the back facing away from other customers. 'And mince pies, but with Amaretto butter instead of brandy.'

'You like those things?' Jack made a face as if she'd just suggested he order a dog-shit sandwich.

Kendall laughed. 'I do actually. They're an acquired taste.'

She ordered one, along with a pot of delicious freshly

ground Italian coffee for two. Watching her bite into the warm pastry, Jack said, 'From the look of you that's more calories than you've eaten in the last month. You're skin and bone.'

It was the sort of thing he used to say to her in the old days, like a nagging father always worrying about her health. Back then it used to bug her, being treated like a child. Now it felt nice, having someone care enough to notice.

'I eat,' she assured him through a mouthful of crumbs. As if to prove a point, she scooped up a spoonful of Amaretto butter from the whipped heap on the side of the plate and devoured it greedily. 'This is not starvation. It's stress.'

It was a surprisingly honest comment, under the circumstances. Jack responded in kind.

'I don't think you have too much to worry about. You're number one right now. Great song, by the way.'

'Thank you,' said Kendall. 'Sweet Dreamer', her Christmas offering, was a soulful, nostalgic melody with lyrics about separated lovers who rediscover each other at Christmas. It wasn't exactly risky, but it was a strong commercial track with just the right degree of festive schmaltz to hook those elusive seasonal record buyers.

'All you have to do is hang in there for another week,' said Jack. 'If the bookies know what they're talking about, you have this thing in the bag.'

'A week's a long time in pop,' said Kendall philosophically. 'And they haven't heard Ava's single yet. Plus, this is Britain. They love an underdog here. Right now Ava's the underdog.'

'Thanks to your husband,' said Jack. He hadn't intended to say it. The words just slipped out. But to his surprise, Kendall didn't seem angry at the mention of Ivan, just sad. She pushed away the last bite of her mince pie and stared down at the table, fighting back tears.

'Is everything OK?' asked Jack.

She looked up at him and shook her head. Without thinking, Jack reached across the table and took her hand. 'Kendall?'

It was the hand-squeeze that did it. Out of nowhere, the floodgates opened, and Kendall found herself pouring her heart out to Jack. She told him everything. How things had started to go wrong with Ivan very quickly after they married. How he'd started to drink, and only stopped after that awful night at The 100 Club when she'd fallen and badly cut her face. How since then they'd tried to go on, but after last week's awards ceremony they'd both realized that whatever love there might once have been between them had gone.

'There's no bitterness. No anger.' She dabbed at her eyes with a butter-smeared paper napkin. 'In fact, weirdly, since we decided to split, things have been better than ever between us. I thought it might be difficult, putting on a front until after Christmas. But you wouldn't believe how thoughtful and considerate he's being.'

'After physically assaulting you?' seethed Jack. 'Sure I would. He's probably terrified you'll report him to the police. Or, worse from his point of view, the tabloids. Why the hell didn't you?'

Kendall looked him straight in the eye. 'Same reason we aren't divorcing tomorrow. Because we needed a united front to see off the threat from Ava.'

'Oh,' said Jack awkwardly.

'Also, it was an accident. He didn't actually mean for me to fall. You must promise you won't say anything. Not about that, or us splitting up, or any of it. I told you as a friend.'

'I know,' said Jack hesitantly. 'And I appreciate it. But—'

'No buts,' said Kendall, slightly hysterically. 'You have to promise. It's not as if you're blameless in all this, Jack. You bringing Ava back here was what tipped Ivan over the edge with his drinking in the first place.'

Jack's eyes widened. 'You're saying it's *my* fault the bastard hit you?'

'No,' Kendall sighed. 'Of course not. And he didn't hit me. He pushed me.' She was already starting to regret telling him. But it was hard not to open up to Jack, especially when he was being so kind to her again after so long. 'You're focusing too much on one incident. The point isn't what happened at the club that night, it's that we never really loved each other in the first place.'

Now this really was an admission. In Jack's humble opinion it called for something stronger than coffee. He ordered a bottle of Sangiovese, then another. Afternoon turned into night. Coffee and cakes were replaced by *insalata mista* and *cioppino* with crusty bread and olives while Kendall talked him through the last five years as they'd looked from her perspective.

'I was in love with you, you know,' she announced, somewhere between her third and fourth glass of red and with the warm soup and bread sitting heavy in her stomach. 'I can tell you that now 'cause it's not true any more. But at the time I was – and I felt – rejected. You saw me as a child.'

'You were a child,' said Jack.

Kendall shrugged. 'Ivan didn't think so. And you know it was fun in the beginning. Flattering. He can be very charming.'

'Don't I know it,' said Jack.

'And you were so bloody serious all the time, not to mention pig-headed about the money.' She drained her glass and poured herself another. 'You pushed me away.' She smiled, but she was clearly only half joking.

'Perhaps I did,' said Jack quietly. 'I was so angry with Ivan myself at that point, the way he was neglecting the business and messing around on Catriona.'

'You really have a soft spot for Catriona, don't you?' said Kendall archly.

'She's a nice woman,' said Jack. He didn't want to admit, even to himself, how much he had missed Cat in recent months. The business, Ava, and his affair with Lisa Marie had all been distractions. But mentally, Catriona was the mother-ship to which his thoughts always seemed to return. Deep down, he felt guilty about this. As if Catriona were somehow 'pushing Sonya out'. But he hadn't untangled his own feelings yet, and certainly wasn't ready to talk about them.

'Ivan's still in love with her, you realize.'

Kendall's words hit him like a slap in the face.

'He told you that?'

She shook her head. 'He doesn't have to. It's obvious. Every time he'd come back from visiting her and the kids, he'd hit the bottle. Like clockwork. I wouldn't be surprised if they got back together eventually.'

Jack shook his head, as if trying to dislodge such an unpalatable idea. 'Christ, I hope not. That really would be the last straw.'

He's still so attractive, thought Kendall, gazing unsteadily into his blue eyes in the candlelight. They were the only customers left in the café now, and she felt as if they were the only two people on earth. Lex shacking up with Ava had been the last straw for her. But Lex wasn't here. He was probably in bed with Ava somewhere right now, making love to her, telling her not to worry about tomorrow. And she was here, alone, with Jack.

Reaching out for what she thought was Jack's hand she

ended up grabbing the salt-shaker instead. Shit. She must be drunker than she'd thought. Seconds later she felt Jack's warm, dry hands wrap themselves around hers.

'You deserved better, you know,' he said gruffly. 'I knew Ivan was a shit. I should have come back for you when I raided the other Jester acts. Taken you back to LA and talked some sense into you.'

'Why didn't you?' Kendall asked him. She no longer felt bitter about it, but she'd always wondered.

'I don't know. I should have,' said Jack. 'Too angry I suppose. And Lex would have killed me. To lose one partner might be considered a misfortune, but to lose two starts to look like carelessness. I couldn't have gone against his wishes, not when it came to you.'

The Oscar Wilde reference went straight over Kendall's head. All she heard was *Lex didn't want you*. He probably already fancied Ava and had his sights set on her from afar. Not that Kendall could blame him. Ava was a beautiful girl. And if Jack had pushed *her* away, how much harder and more cruelly had she pushed poor Lex away, when she staged those pictures at the Chateau Marmont? It was all such a mess.

Marco, the good-natured manager, came over to the table. 'Sorry, guys, but I really need to close up now.' Jack looked at his watch and saw with horror that it was almost midnight. He had a six o'clock start in the morning, taking Ava to perform live on ITV's new breakfast show, *Sunburst*. But he didn't want Kendall to go, not yet. There was still so much he wanted to ask her, especially about Ivan and Catriona. If she went home now, God knew when he would next get the chance.

'Come back to The Berkeley for coffee,' he blurted out.

Kendall hesitated. She could certainly use a coffee. All

that wine had really gone to her head. But she was staying at Stella's at the moment while Ivan used the flat and she wouldn't score any brownie points by staggering in at four in the morning. On the other hand, finally burying the hatchet with Jack was a big deal. Stella would understand that, wouldn't she?

'OK,' she said eventually. 'One coffee. But I can't stay long.'

Back at the hotel, the lobby was still surprisingly busy. To avoid attention they decided to order coffee in Jack's private suite.

'I feel like Mata Hari,' joked Kendall, looking over her shoulder to check the corridor was empty before slipping in to room 508. 'Like I'm sneaking into enemy territory.'

'You're not sneaking. I invited you. And I'm not the enemy.'

Not any more, thought Kendall happily.

While Jack put the coffee on in the en suite kitchen, Kendall snooped around. Jack's desk was piled high with press releases, schedules and reams and reams of sales figures. Tucked under a stack of correspondence from JSM's other clients, Kendall pulled out two photographs of Ava. They were similar to the cover shot for her Christmas single, 'Home'. As with that picture, Ava was staring straight at the camera with her short, silver-blonde hair swept back and a beach (Malibu?) in the background. But whereas in the official 'Home' image she looked fierce and combative, in these pictures she was laughing. Her short, snub nose was wrinkled, her mouth opened wide, and her eyes had receded into two slits of merriment. It was a totally natural expression, uncontrolled and spontaneous. Because of that, she looked beautiful.

'Did Lex take these shots?' asked Kendall.

Emerging from the kitchen, Jack handed her a mug of strong black coffee, sweetened with enough sugar to kill an elephant. 'Uh huh. They're great, aren't they? We tried to persuade Columbia to use them but they wanted something with more "edge".'

'She looks lovely,' said Kendall wistfully. 'So happy.'

Jack smiled. 'I think she is happy. Lex has been really good for her. They've been good for each other.'

Kendall looked as if she'd just had acid thrown in her face. Mistaking her expression for sadness at her own situation, Jack put his arms around her. 'You'll be happy again too, sweetheart. I know you don't think it now, but you will. You'll find the right guy and it'll all work out for the best.'

'Will it?' Turning her body to face him, Kendall stood up on tiptoes and wrapped her arms around his neck. Lex was gone, lost to her for ever. She must accept it. But in that moment all she wanted was to feel a man's arms around her. Any man's.

Jack stiffened. Her loneliness was palpable and he felt for her. God knew he understood that feeling. But the last thing either of them needed was to fuck up their minutes-old reconciliation with a stupid, drunken fling.

'Come on,' he said, gently disengaging himself from her embrace. 'That's not the answer, is it?'

When Kendall opened her eyes it was still dark outside. Her head ached and her mouth was dry and for a moment she wondered where she was, until she felt the soft cashmere of the sofa blanket laid over her and realized she must have fallen asleep on Jack's couch.

God, how embarrassing. I must have been seriously drunk. Still, she couldn't regret yesterday, running into Jack the way she had, sharing intimacies and apologies over too many bottles of wine. It had been wonderful to see him again, and to rekindle their friendship. Like the closing of a circle.

Pulling the blanket around her like a towel, she padded quietly into the bedroom.

'Jack.' She whispered. '*Jack.*'

'Hmm?' Jack sat up, disorientated. His hair stuck out at a hundred crazy angles, which gave him the look of a bewildered schoolboy. 'Is everything OK?'

'Everything's fine,' she smiled. 'Except my head. I'm heading back to Stella's to sleep it off. I just didn't want to leave without saying goodbye.'

Leaning over the bed to plant a kiss on his cheek, she was startled when the door to the suite suddenly burst open.

'Jack, what the fuck? It's six-fifteen, man, Ava's got *Sunburst* this morning, we gotta . . .'

The words died on Lex's lips. From the door he had a direct line of vision into the bedroom. *No. It couldn't be!*

'It's not what it looks like,' began Jack, rubbing his eyes. 'Nothing happened.'

'He's telling the truth,' Kendall chimed in. 'I came up for some coffee and I passed out cold.'

Lex held up his hand. 'Please. You don't owe me any explanation.' The look on his face could have melted stone. 'It's none of my business.'

Kendall could have wept. *He hates me.*

Turning away, Lex said gruffly, 'The car's downstairs, Jack. We can wait another five minutes, then we're out the door.'

Both Jack and Kendall winced as the door to the room slammed shut behind him.

'He'll be all right,' said Jack. 'I'll talk to him. Explain.'

Kendall said nothing. Her sweet dream of friendship

renewed had just become a nightmare. She wanted the bed to open up and swallow her.

'Are you all right to get home?' Jack was already up, pulling on clothes and grabbing his cell phone from the charger by the bed. 'Do you have somewhere you need to be this morning? Can I get you a car?'

'A meeting with Ivan in the office, but not till eleven.' Kendall's voice was a monotone. This wasn't happening to her. It was all happening to someone else. 'Then promotion all day. I'll go to Stella's now for a sleep. I'll be fine.'

Jack kissed her on the top of the head. 'OK, well, if you're sure. I'm sorry to cut and run, but this is a big day for Ava. For both of you. Here.' He pressed a wodge of notes into her hand. 'For a cab and anything else you need. Take care of yourself, kiddo.'

He was gone.

CHAPTER TWENTY-FOUR

Thankfully, over the next few days, Kendall had no time to brood over what Lex Abrahams might be thinking, still less to analyse her own feelings after her night with Jack. There was work to be done.

Ava's single, 'Home', was a terrific track: catchy, poppy, upbeat and instantly memorable. Without exception the radio stations loved it, shooting it to the top of their playlists. By contrast, Kendall's more thoughtful, melodic 'Sweet Dreamer' began to sound a little dreary. The fact that Kendall's single had already been out for almost two weeks gave 'Home' an additional novelty bounce. This was what Ava's management had been counting on, of course, but it was a risky strategy. There was typically a time-lag between airplay and sales. This was even more pronounced at Christmas, when music bought as gifts tended to be purchased as much as a month in advance. Ava was putting on one hell of a final sprint, but was it too late to catch Kendall?

Two days after the release of 'Home', the *Mail on Sunday* ran a gushingly approving feature spread on Ava. For the first time since she got to England she had free rein to tell her side of the story on the Ivan/*Talent Quest* affair and her defection to America.

'All I ever wanted was to make music, and to learn from the best. America's not my home. England is.'

Lex featured heavily in the picture spreads, striding hand in hand with Ava across a snowy field, raising pints of Guinness with her rosy-cheeked father. Kendall scanned his face for signs of doubt and unhappiness. Not so long ago, photoshoots like this one would have turned Lex's stomach. But his contentment seemed as genuine as his girlfriend's. Kendall felt sick.

'Don't look so horrified,' said Ivan, watching her skim through the piece again a couple of days later. 'It's too little too late. If we're not number one on Friday, I'll eat my way through Philip Treacy's showroom.'

They were sitting in Ivan's office on Sloane Street having a last-ditch strategy meeting. Kendall's publicist Sasha and a posse of minions from Polydor sat together on the oversized Chesterfield sofa. Martin Higgis, the PR guru and Ivan's close friend, was playing table football in the corner, and Ivan stood at his desk, surveying the mass of newspapers in front of him like a general studying maps of the battlefield.

He looks well, thought Kendall. *Energized.* There was nothing Ivan enjoyed more than a good fight, as long as he was winning. As a lover he'd had his pluses and minuses, as a husband he'd been unremittingly awful, but as a manager, Svengali and overall career strategist, he was brilliant, in a class of his own. Both he and Kendall wanted to continue working together after they announced their split in the New Year. Although, of course, if he got back with Catriona, all bets would be off.

The scrupulous politeness that had marked Ivan and Kendall's relationship since they agreed to split extended to a newfound respect for one another's privacy. Kendall hadn't asked what was going on with his ex-wife, just as Ivan had made no enquiries into her love life or social plans. As for her night with Jack, and Lex walking in on them, she had not breathed a word of it to Ivan or anyone else – and she never would.

'It's simple,' said Martin Higgis, looking up from his game. 'Ava's people are hoping that a late boost to her personal popularity will bring them their numbers swing. We have to fight fire with fire.'

'Meaning?' snapped Kendall. Martin was widely considered a PR genius and Ivan loved him, but Kendall had always found his cryptic, soundbite pronouncements to be an irritant. If Ava didn't make UK number one this Christmas, she would no doubt be disappointed and return to LA and her US career with her tail between her legs. But she would still *have* a US career, with potentially decades of life left in it. Kendall had no such safety net. Her whole career was here, now, and her livelihood depended on Friday night's chart.

'Meaning she knows we can't beat her on the song. She has a better song.' Kendall scowled disapprovingly but didn't disagree. 'But we're stronger on personal approval ratings. People have been buying Kendall's record because they like *her*, not necessarily because they like *it*. Ava's making a late bid for some of that action.'

'Too late,' said Ivan confidently.

'Probably. But we can't afford to get complacent. If she's playing the happy couple card with her ugly boyfriend, we need to get you and Kendall out there doing the same.'

'Lex isn't ugly,' Kendall blurted, earning herself a curious look from Ivan.

'Well, he's no Brad Pitt,' said Martin bluntly. 'Ivan's far

more charming, far more photogenic. But we need to make your romance a story again. Reignite the public interest.'

Kendall and Ivan exchanged glances. It wouldn't be easy, going out there and faking happily-ever-after, knowing what was going on behind closed doors. But it had to be done. Walking over to Kendall, Ivan put an arm around her and kissed her.

'We're up for it, aren't we?'

Kendall nodded. 'Absolutely.'

'Just tell us what needs to be done.'

The next three days were a circus. Both Kendall and Ava threw themselves headlong into a firestorm of promotion, each trying to portray herself as the nation's sweetheart and their respective relationships as the ultimate Christmas love story.

Graham Norton's viewers were treated to a nauseating interview with Ava, in which she and Lex pawed one another like lovesick teenagers and declared that they spent twenty-four hours a day in one another's company.

'What, even when you go to the loo?' teased Norton.

'He can come if he wants to,' giggled Ava.

'I'll bet he can.'

Mercifully, Kendall hadn't watched this exchange. She was too busy walking out of Nobu and gasping with prescribed delight at the fifty-piece orchestra in white tie that Ivan had laid on as a 'surprise' for their first wedding anniversary. Uncannily, a fleet of television crews and newspaper photographers just happened to be walking down Park Lane at the time, so were able to catch the happy couple's tears of joy as Ivan danced with his young wife, having first pinned a single white rose in her hair and presented her with a diamond pendant in the shape of a snowflake.

'Christmas is a very special time for us,' he gushed to interviewers afterwards.

'What's the best Christmas present he could give you, Kendall?'

'I don't need presents. Ivan's love is enough. Although it would mean the world to me if 'Sweet Dreamer' made number one. I guess we'll have to see.'

In the days leading up to Christmas Eve, Ivan and Kendall visited Leeds, Manchester, Edinburgh, Bristol and Oxford for CD signings. They were photographed at six different romantic restaurants, guested on eighteen radio stations and made eleven separate television appearances. They streamed a live video of themselves putting up Christmas decorations on YouTube and tweeted with joy after attending the carol service together at the Royal Albert Hall.

Meanwhile, Ava's *Mail on Sunday* effect seemed to be wearing off. Ratings for her chat-show appearances were consistently lacklustre, and she was booed at a shopping centre in Birmingham during a live performance of 'Home', with hecklers shouting, 'Go back to America if you love it so much!'

By the time Christmas Eve morning dawned, Kendall's confidence was soaring. Unfortunately, so was her temperature.

'There's no way she can make the party tonight,' said Stella firmly, elbowing Ivan aside to plump up Kendall's pillows and hand her a steaming mug of Lemsip. 'She has a hundred-and-two-degree fever. She'll collapse.'

'I'll be fine,' croaked Kendall inaudibly.

During the last few days' media blitz she'd moved back into the Cheyne Walk apartment with Ivan, and was sleeping in the master while he bunked in the spare room. So far no one had noticed Kendall's regular sleepovers at Stella's place in Primrose Hill, but now would not be a good time for them to start.

'She doesn't have to stay long,' said Ivan. 'But she must put in some sort of an appearance.' Polydor had laid on a lavish 'Number One' bash at The Box tonight, to celebrate what now looked like certain victory in Kendall's battle with Ava Bentley. Kendall and Ivan were both physically and emotionally exhausted, but it had been worth it.

'You're both crazy,' said Stella crossly. 'What if she passes out? It's possible, you know.'

'She won't,' said Ivan brusquely. 'She can rest up here with you all day, get her strength back. After tonight we can all switch off.'

'What do you mean "here with me"?' Stella's eyes narrowed. 'Where are you going?'

'I have somewhere I need to be.'

'You're not coming to the party?' Kendall's voice was barely a whisper. Ivan had to bend low over the bed to hear her.

'Course I am, sweetheart,' he assured her. 'I just have a few personal things to tie up first. I'll be back here at six and we can go together.'

The estate agent from Jackson-Stops was a roly-poly ball of a woman in a tweed skirt and the sort of worsted horsehair shirt that Ivan thought had stopped being made in the 1940s. Despite being only five foot tall, she had a commanding bearing, glowering at Ivan like a disappointed headmistress. Clearly neither celebrity nor a handsome face impressed her.

'I've told you, Mr Charles, as plainly as I can, that The Rookery is not for sale. I presented your offer to the owners last week, and while they agreed it was very generous, they simply don't wish to move.'

'Then make them wish it,' snarled Ivan. 'I want that house back, and I'm going to have it. Ask them to name their price.'

'This is Burford, Mr Charles,' the agent said witheringly. 'Not Las Vegas.'

'Just ask them. You've got my number.'

At three o'clock, Jack Messenger sat alone in his suite at The Berkeley, listening to Radio One. The UK singles chart was still run in a curiously old-fashioned manner, revealing the week's positions on Reggie Yates's Sunday afternoon show before the OCC (Official Charts Company) had even posted the results on their own website. Apparently, based on combined record sales and download numbers, there was virtually no transparency to the process. If Radio One said you were number one, then number one you were. If they didn't, you weren't, no matter how much independently verifiable sales data you produced to the contrary.

This year, however, in an unprecedented break with tradition, it had been decided to announce the chart on a Friday: Christmas Eve. Kendall and Ava's battle for the top spot had generated so much publicity and much-need revenue for the sector, it was thought to be in everyone's interests to string out the tension as long as possible.

Not that, by this stage, there was much tension left, especially amongst insiders. Everybody knew that Kendall had seen off the would-be pretender to her crown. Ava's download figures might be high, but on the street the wave of affection and loyalty towards the American girl who had 'chosen' England was palpably overwhelming. Don Lenner from Columbia had already been on the phone to Jack, expressing his disappointment and demanding Ava's immediate return to US soil. The label had forked out for a 'celebration party' tonight at Annabel's, to rival Kendall's bash, but everyone knew that once Ava came in at number two it would be more of a wake.

Ava herself had been sanguine in defeat, but announced this morning that she couldn't bear sitting around a radio set listening for the inevitable. Lex had whisked her off to a private viewing at Tate Modern and would take her for a low-key dinner afterwards. Then, after a cursory appearance at Annabel's, Ava would head up north for Christmas with her family and Lex and Jack would catch the next plane home to LA. Both of them dreaded the flight. They'd barely exchanged two syllables since Lex walked in on Jack with Kendall the other morning, but given that they would be side by side on a plane for eleven hours, at some point they'd have to talk about it.

'Merry Christmas, guys, and welcome to the last UK Top Forty of the year!' Reggie Yates's London accent rang out through The Berkeley's Bose speakers. 'As you all know by now, it's all about two beautiful young ladies this week. So which one is going to be having a Merry Christmas, and which one's gonna end up a Christmas turkey, huh?'

Who writes this stuff? thought Jack wearily. Ava wasn't the Christmas turkey. He was, for bringing her here in the first place, for underestimating Kendall and Ivan, for having no one to share this most special of all days with. Kendall's words floated back to him:

'*We're both alone, Jack.*'

'*Ivan's still in love with Catriona. It wouldn't surprise me if they got back together.*'

Pouring himself a Laphroaig from the minibar, he turned up the volume on the sound system to drown out his own thoughts.

* * *

Across town, in the kitchen of Kendall and Ivan's Cheyne Walk flat, Stella Bayley was also tuned to the Reggie Yates show, with the volume turned down low. Kendall was sleeping in the master bedroom and next door in the sitting room little Miley was happily making glitter-paper chains and watching *Frosty the Snowman* on DVD.

Please let her get it, thought Stella. *She needs it so much more than Ava does.*

She turned back to her cinnamon cookies.

'Do you think they've announced it by now?' Ava asked Lex anxiously.

They were at Tate Modern, standing in front of what looked to Lex like a giant wire coat hanger draped in red cloth, entitled *Bloody Murder.* The privately hired curator was filling them in on the sculpture's provenance, but neither Lex nor Ava were listening. *We should have gone to the movies,* thought Lex. *Really distracted ourselves.*

'No,' he replied. 'Not till four. Try not to think about it.'

He might as well have told her to try not to breathe.

In JSM's LA office, Lisa Marie and a smattering of other staffers who'd made it in on Christmas Eve morning sat sipping Starbucks coffees and picking at sunrise muffins while Radio One played live on the Internet.

'Do you think she has a shot?' asked Candice, one of the PAs. Candice liked Ava. Everybody liked Ava.

'Probably not,' said Lisa Marie. 'But it ain't over till it's over.'

She thought about Jack, where he was right now and whether he was OK. Poor guy. He was a great music manager, one of the best, but he'd really fucked up on this one. No one enjoyed looking like an ass.

* * *

'Are you coming, Mum?'

Hector's voice rang out from the front parlour. Catriona, skulking in the kitchen, called back nervously. 'In a minute.'

The kitchen clock said ten to four. In eleven minutes she would know. If Kendall's single was number one, she would sign a huge new deal, which would guarantee financial security for Catriona and the kids. How strange to have one's livelihood depend on the girl who had destroyed one's family. But Catriona wasn't focused on the money. She was focused on her future. Would it be clearer in eleven minutes? Or still a murky, frightening blank?

Since their night together, she and Ivan had spoken on the phone most days, but she hadn't physically seen him. Ivan talked constantly about next year. Buying back The Rookery, taking the kids on holiday to the south of France, remarrying in the tiny church at Widford that had always been one of Catriona's favourite spots in the world. Sometimes she loved to hear him talk this way. It made her feel happy and hopeful, a return to reality, to the normal order of things.

Other times she felt sick.

She hadn't said anything to the children yet, not least because she had no idea what to say. But she sensed they knew, or at least suspected something might be afoot. If they were appalled by the idea of their parents reuniting, neither of them had shown it. Equally, they had tactfully refrained from doing victory dances, asking questions, or pushing their mother for a decision. *It must be hard for them, after all this time. They're probably as confused as I am.*

'Muuum!' Rosie yelled even louder than her brother. 'Come *on*. He's already at number five.'

'All right,' said Catriona. 'I'm coming.'

* * *

Pulled over in a lay-by off the M25, Ivan felt a glow of contentment almost as warm as the air swirling around his Bentley Continental. At long last, it was all coming together.

After tonight's victory, he could begin negotiations on Kendall's new deal, a deal that would make both of them millionaires several times over. Ending their marriage had been remarkably painless. Until now, he'd always thought that 'mutual' divorces were a myth. But Kendall plainly wanted out as much as he did, which was an immense relief. Even so, he felt better walking away knowing that he had left her a seriously rich young woman, and that they would part quite genuinely as friends. It was astonishing how suddenly, and totally, his desire for Kendall had evaporated. As soon as he began to think of her as a friend, an ally in this fight against Ava, the erotic charge that had kept him glued to her side for so long like a miserable barnacle in a storm had fizzled out into nothing.

It was Catriona now who filled him with longing. Catriona, who he'd always loved as a mother and a soul mate and a friend, suddenly appeared in a whole, new light. He could tell this new Catriona was passionate, greedy, wild even. She was the girl he fell in love with twenty years ago and he wanted her back so badly it was like a heroin craving.

Soon, very soon, he would have her.

And, last but not least, there was the prospect at long last of beating Jack Messenger. Publicly, the chart battle had been all about Ava and her 'betrayal' of Ivan as her *Talent Quest* mentor. But, deep down, Ivan bore Ava no ill-will. She'd been offered a better deal and she'd taken it. Simple as that. There was no malice in it, only self-interest, and Ivan Charles was the patron saint of self-interest.

But Jack was different. With Jack it was personal. And business was the least of it. Jack had inveigled his way into

Ivan's family. He had flirted with Catriona's affections and tried to replace Ivan as Hector's father. For that, Ivan would never forgive him.

Everyone dated their bitter rivalry as beginning when Ivan 'stole' Kendall from Jack and broke up Jester. But the truth was it had started far, far earlier than that. Even at university, at the height of their friendship, there'd been an edge to the relationship. 'Competitive' was the nicest word for it. But for Ivan at least it had always run deeper. Somewhere along the way he had learned to hate Jack, for his moral superiority, his 'shyness' that had always seemed to Ivan to have a burning ball of arrogance at its core, for his pride. Everything about Jack seemed to scream at Ivan: *I'm better than you.*

Well, today, Ivan was going to prove to the world once and for all that that was not the case.

Reggie Yates's smooth tones flowed through the Bentley's sound system like warm honey. 'So now's the moment of truth, guys, the result we've all been waiting for. This week's number *two*, the runner-up in one of the hardest-fought battles we've ever seen for a Christmas number one single, *is . . .*'

He paused for dramatic effect.

Ivan savoured the moment. *Fuck you, Jack.*

'"Sweet Dreamer", from Kendall Bryce.'

CHAPTER TWENTY-FIVE

At The Box on Brewer Street, amid the balloons and champagne bottles and streamers, there was total disbelief. Someone turned off the radio. Martin Higgis, who'd stopped by early to check on the party preparations, summed up the mood.

'Fuck. We are totally fucked.'

'Should we cancel?' asked Kendall's publicist, Sasha.

'Definitely not,' said Higgis. 'The worst thing she could do now is come across as a sore loser. We party, we smile, we congratulate Ava and bleat on about what an honour it is to come in second to such a great song. Got it?'

There were a few desultory nods.

'I'll get a statement to the press and try and make sure we still get some decent coverage and the paps don't all fuck off to Annabel's. And you lot,' he turned on Ivan's staffers, 'stop standing around like a bunch of lemmings and start blowing up some more snowflake balloons. And smile, would you? Don't you know it's fucking Christmas?'

*   *   *

Kendall double-checked her appearance in the mirror. It was a long time since she'd got ready for an event this important on her own, but she'd insisted Stella and Miley go home and leave her to it.

'It's Christmas Eve. Miley should be at home, hanging her stocking and putting out carrots or something, not watching TV in our living room.'

'But are you sure you're all right?' said Stella. 'I know it must have been an awful shock, and your fever's only just come down. I don't like leaving you here alone.'

'I'm fine,' Kendall assured her. 'Really. And I won't be alone for long. Ivan said he'd be back by six. We need to talk about things on our own, anyway, before we face the world.'

'But—'

'I'm a big girl, Stella. Go. I'll be fine.'

It was a relief to go through the motions of washing and drying her hair, picking out a dress and doing her make-up. When Stella had broken the news, Kendall felt a short, sharp pang of shock, then nothing. She kept waiting for it to hit her, waiting to cry or yell, waiting to *care* in the way she knew she was supposed to.

She had failed. Ava had beaten her. Ava Bentley was number one.

But the truth was, she felt numb. Her anxiety, such as it was, was entirely focused on Ivan. Not only had he not come home at six as he'd promised, but he hadn't called and his phone was switched off. Nightmare images of him heading for the nearest bar and drinking himself into a stupor haunted Kendall's pounding head. Perhaps she shouldn't care any more, now that they weren't a couple, but she did. Old habits died hard.

Her reflection stared back at her, poised and confident. A perfect disguise. Given how sick she'd been this morning, she scrubbed up pretty well. Her long, dark hair was worn up, pinned in a loose chignon, nothing too formal. She wore a clinging white jersey dress by Alexander McQueen, sexy but understated with a plunging back and a bias cut, floor-length skirt. Her make-up was equally simple but striking. Smoky eyes, a little bronzer to take the edge off her exhausted pallor and a swipe of Elizabeth Arden Eight Hour Cream in lieu of lipstick. After a bit of deliberation she ditched the jewellery, with the exception of her wedding ring. She would have liked to take that off too – it felt like the right time – but it was a big step to take without telling Ivan, and the pale circle of skin beneath it would doubtless have prompted questions that she was in no mood to answer.

The doorbell rang. She ran to the buzzer. 'Ivan?'

'Good evening, Miss Bryce. Your car's here.'

Kendall sighed, throwing her cell phone and keys into her Marc Jacobs clutch. 'OK. I'll be right down.'

Stepping out of the limo twenty minutes later, Kendall was surrounded by a sea of cameras.

'How do you feel, Kendall? It must be a disappointment.'

'How's Ivan taking it?'

'Have you spoken to Ava?'

'Where's Ivan tonight?'

She smiled sweetly at them all but said nothing. Inside, her publicist Sasha whisked her instantly aside. 'You OK?'

Kendall smiled weakly. 'I'd be better if people stopped asking me that every ten seconds.'

'Sorry. Where's Ivan?'

Kendall looked troubled. 'He isn't here?'

'No. No one's heard a word from him.'

'Damn,' said Kendall. 'Neither have I.'

Martin Higgis walked over and pressed a drink into

Kendall's hand. 'I'm sorry,' he said. 'I really thought we'd pulled it off.'

It was a rare admission of weakness on Martin's part and Kendall accepted it graciously. 'Me too. But it's not your fault. At the end of the day she had a better song. I thought I'd stop in at the Annabel's party after this, offer my congratulations in person. What do you think?'

The PR man and the publicist exchanged approving looks. 'I think it's a wonderful idea,' said Martin Higgis. 'Ivan should go with you. Where is he anyway? People have been asking.'

Kendall frowned. 'I have no idea.'

'Kendall, there you are.' Aiden Lomax, the new head of Polydor, sidled up to her. He already had the wild-eyed look of a man who'd overdone the coke in the limo on the way over, and his sunken cheeks glowed red from too much champagne.

'Commiserations, my dear, but well done on a well-fought fight.' He slipped a lecherous hand around Kendall's tiny waist. 'We should talk about next steps at some point. I believe your deal's up for renewal.'

You know it is, prick.

'That's right,' Kendall smiled graciously. 'But if you want to talk business, you really need to speak to my husband.'

'Of course, of course.' Lomax looked around. 'Where is Ivan, by the way? I haven't seen him all night.'

It was going to be a long evening.

Over in Mayfair, the mood at the JSM party was distinctly more celebratory. Annabel's was packed to bursting with celebrity well-wishers, and those of the music business's great and good who hadn't already decamped to Mustique for the holidays.

'I always said me daughter would be a star,' Dave Bentley was loudly and drunkenly proclaiming to a cornered Annie Lennox. 'You watch this space, luv. She'll be the next bloody Celine Dion or I'm not a Yorkshireman.'

A few feet away, Jack was enjoying being schmoozed by the same Columbia Records assholes who only this morning had been tearing a strip off him.

'We always knew she had it in her,' the head of the label's London office was saying, without a hint of irony. 'But it's a funny old market in the UK, especially at Christmas.'

'When can we talk about a European tour?' The head of A&R interjected. 'Obviously we'll have to fit around her US schedule, but I know Lenner wants us to sit down ASAP and work out an integrated, global strategy.'

Does he now? Well Don Lenner can kiss my lily-white ass. 'I'll have to talk to Ava about all that,' said Jack. 'And my partner, of course.'

He glanced over at Lex, who was hovering beside Ava at the bar. The two of them had finally shaken hands this afternoon back at the hotel and made things up. Kendall wasn't mentioned. But Ava's success was a triumph for all of them. Not only did it reopen doors for Ava in the UK, but it raised the very real possibility of JSM expanding to include a London office.

'Who'd run it?' asked Lex.

'Me? You?' Jack beamed. 'Personally I'd be happy on either side of the pond.'

No decision had been made, but they'd have plenty of time to discuss it between now and the New Year. In the light of Ava's unexpected news, both of them had cancelled tomorrow's flights to LA.

Looking at Lex now, Jack was taken aback by how down he looked. You wouldn't think the guy had just scored a major career coup, not to mention that he was here celebrating one of the biggest nights in his girlfriend's life.

A flurry of popping flashbulbs disturbed his train of thought. Turning around, he was astonished to see Kendall, looking tired but stunning in a long white gown, battling her way through the crowd towards him.

'Hey!' His face lit up. 'You're the last person I expected to see tonight.'

She kissed him on the cheek and the flashbulbs went wild. 'I thought I should come and congratulate Ava in person. Let her know there are no hard feelings.'

'Well, now's your chance,' said Jack. Noticing the commotion, Ava had made a beeline for Kendall. She looked at her warily, almost as if she might be an impostor, or had stowed an explosive device in her clutch bag. *Perhaps I can't blame her after such a bitter campaign*, thought Kendall, *but she could act a little more magnanimously in victory.*

'Congratulations.' Kendall stuck out her hand. 'It's an awesome song. You deserve the success.'

'Thanks,' said Ava, blindsided by this spontaneous show of generosity, especially after some of the horrible things Kendall and Ivan had told the press about her in the past few weeks. But her distrustful look had more to do with Kendall's looks than her sincerity, or lack of it. She'd forgotten quite how stunning the girl was close up, like a Greek goddess. Until Kendall walked in, Ava had felt sexy in her black leather trousers and off-the-shoulder top from Current Elliott. Now she felt like Buttons beside Kendall's Cinderella – and this was supposed to be her pantomime, her party, her night. She glanced over her shoulder to see if Lex was drooling over Kendall too, but was gratified to see he had turned away and was busy chatting with her parents. 'It was sweet of you to stop by.'

The two girls hugged, and Ava hurried back to Lex's side.

'That was big of you,' said Jack, wrapping an arm around Kendall's shoulder and giving her a paternal squeeze. 'Not many people would have had the courage to show up here tonight. You look amazing, by the way.'

'Thanks,' said Kendall. Her voice was getting croaky again. 'I feel like shit.'

Across the room, Lex finally gave in to his curiosity and turned to sneak a quick look at Kendall. When he did, his heart sank into the pit of his stomach. She and Jack were all over each other again, arms wrapped around one another like they didn't care who saw them. *Unbelievable. Un-fucking-believable. After all that bullshit Messenger gave me about 'nothing happened'. He's clearly trying it on with her, and she's lapping up every second of it.*

'Would you like some free advice?' Jack asked Kendall.

'If it's about my love life, then no, thanks all the same. I'm becoming a nun and that's an end to it.'

He laughed. 'Now *that* I would pay to see. It's not about your love life. It's purely professional. You should focus more strongly on live performance.'

Kendall blinked. 'What?' This wasn't the advice she'd expected.

'I don't think you and Ivan are seeing the big picture, here. Ava beat you to number one because she had a better song. She has better writers and better producers, not because she's more talented but because she has a huge US label behind her.'

'Tell me something I don't know.'

'So play to your strengths, not your weaknesses. You're twice the live performer she is. If you focused on filling stadiums around the world rather than flogging mediocre singles in your domestic market, you could be up there with Christina and Beyoncé.'

Kendall raised a sceptical eyebrow. 'Since when did you get into flattery?'

'Since never. I'm serious. What happened today was a setback to your UK career, not an end to it. Don't focus on the setback. Focus on the opportunity.' He pulled out a business card and handed it to her. 'This has my new cell and . . .' he scrawled something on the back '. . . private email. I'd like you to think about signing with JSM.'

Kendall shook her head. 'I couldn't do that to Ivan. Not now. I'm really worried about him.'

She told Jack about Ivan's radio silence since the chart was announced and his no-show at their own party earlier.

'Discuss it with him,' said Jack. 'Believe it or not, I'm not doing this to kick the guy when he's down. I care too much about Catriona and his kids for that. But you may find he wants out too.'

This hadn't occurred to Kendall, but she supposed Jack might have a point. Now that her big new UK deal was dead in the water, was it really worth Ivan's while economically to stay on as her manager? If not, and he was serious about making a go of things with Catriona, he might be willing to let her go.

'What about Lex?' She bit her lower lip nervously. 'I thought you said he didn't want me back. That he was dead against it.'

'He was.' Jack glanced over at Lex and Ava, who were chatting to Ava's father, arm in arm. 'But things have changed since then.'

'You really think he'd go for it?' Kendall failed to keep the hope out of her voice.

'Ask him,' said Jack.

'*Ask him*', thought Kendall. *Yeah, right. Like it's that easy. 'Hey, Lexi, have you forgiven me for being a total bitch and trying to ruin your life? You have? Great! How about we work together?'* But despite her misgivings, she found herself inching slowly in Lex's direction. She waited till Ava had wandered off to work the room before tapping him on the shoulder.

'Hi.'

Lex spun around and looked at her. The dress was stunning, and her perfectly made-up face as magnetically beautiful as ever. But beneath the artistry he could see she was tired and drawn. *She's upset she lost today. But I guess now she has Jack to comfort her.* His expression hardened. 'Hello, Kendall.'

Oh dear, thought Kendall. *He's still mad at me for the other day, finding me in Jack's bed. But surely Jack explained? He said he'd cleared everything up, that he and Lex were cool again.*

Desperately nervous all of a sudden, she couldn't think of a single thing to say. Finally she blurted out, 'Do you have any plans for Christmas?'

'No.'

'I suppose you'll have to stick around in Britain for a while, now that Ava's gonna be in such demand.'

'Possibly.'

It was like getting blood from a stone. Kendall took a deep breath.

'Jack and I were just talking about the possibility of me signing on with JSM, maybe even coming back to LA for a while.'

'Of course you were,' said Lex contemptuously. The conversation was not progressing as Kendall had hoped.

'I wouldn't do it if you didn't feel comfortable with it,' she said hurriedly. 'JSM is your company too. I wouldn't dream—'

Lex swatted her words away like an irritating fly. 'I couldn't care less. You and Jack do as you please.' He started looking around for someone to talk to, an escape route. It was unbearable, listening to her lay the groundwork for a romance with Jack, but her pity for his feelings was the last straw.

'If you prefer I didn't come to LA—' began Kendall, but Lex cut her off again.

'It makes no difference to me,' he said brutally. 'In fact, I'll probably be setting up a new London office next year, so our paths need never cross. Johnny!' He waved to an acquaintance like a man flagging down a lifeboat and left Kendall standing there without another word.

She was still standing when Jack came up to her. 'What did he say?'

'Hmmm?' She awoke as if from a dream. 'Oh. He said he was fine with it. He said he'd be running the London office, so if I came to LA our paths wouldn't cross.'

'Did he?' Jack's expression visibly brightened. Lex had seemed totally noncommittal about London earlier, so this was good news indeed.

'You know what? I'm shattered,' said Kendall, who suddenly looked it. 'Do you mind if I cut and run?'

'Of course not,' said Jack, kissing her warmly on the cheek. 'Take care of yourself, Kendall, OK? And think about my offer.'

'I will.'

'Oh, and Kendall?' Jack called after her as she headed for the door.

'Yeah?'

'Merry Christmas.'

* * *

The streets of Mayfair were deserted as Kendall's black cab weaved its way south towards the river.

Christmas Eve, Kendall thought sadly. *Everyone has somewhere to go. Family. Friends. Everyone but me.*

Then she pulled herself together. She had family, albeit scattered and far away. More to the point, she had a friend, a friend she'd be joining for Christmas lunch tomorrow just as soon as she knew that Ivan had turned up somewhere, safe. *Thank God for Stella. Where on earth would I be without her?*

Just then her mobile rang. Kendall leapt on it. 'Ivan?'

'No. It's me.'

Catriona sounded cold and distant. It was years since the two women had spoken, but the pain was still evident in Catriona's voice. Not knowing what to say – what *could* she say to the wife whose husband she'd stolen and whose family she'd destroyed – Kendall said nothing.

Catriona's next words shot through her veins like ice.

'I'm afraid there's been an accident. Kendall? Are you there?'

'Yes,' Kendall croaked. 'I'm here. What happened?'

'Drink-driving. The stupid arse downed the best part of a bottle of Jack Daniel's and wrapped his car round a tree on the Oxford Ring Road.'

Is he . . .?'

'He's alive.'

The relief was so huge that Kendall thought she might vomit. She opened the window of the cab, letting in a blast of freezing night air.

'But we don't know for how long.' Finally Catriona's calm, capable façade slipped. Kendall recognized the terror in her short, sharp intakes of breath. 'He's in Intensive Care at the John Radcliffe. He hasn't regained consciousness.'

The tears flowed freely now. 'I don't know how things stand between you, but you're listed as his next of kin. Oh, Kendall!' Catriona broke down into uncontrollable sobs. 'The doctors are saying he might not last the night.'

CHAPTER TWENTY-SIX

Two months later, Los Angeles

Jack walked along the paths of the St Martin of Tours cemetery, enjoying the crunch of gravel under his feet. It was early, not yet eight, but it was already shaping up to be a beautiful day, the sort of day that only LA could provide in the depths of winter. Above him a pale morning sky was beginning to burn through the mist and filter through the leaves of the giant eucalyptus trees. The air smelled of pine and honeysuckle and newly mown grass. Summer scents. They added to the sense of peace that Jack always felt when he came here. He'd never been a religious man – that was always Sonya's bag. But he had soul enough to appreciate the tranquillity of this church-yard.

Crouching down by Sonya's grave, he swept away some dry leaves with his hands and laid down his flowers. In the early days he'd found it too painful to come here. It was too brutal a reminder of his loss. Later, the feeling became one of awkwardness. What sort of crazy person brought flowers to a dead person? But now, stretching out his long legs on the grass, Jack felt totally relaxed. He found he could talk with an easy sense of companionship, certain somehow that Sonya was there, she was listening. It beat therapy every time.

'I miss her,' he confided. 'I mean, I'm here, I'm with you, it's a beautiful day. I'm not unhappy. But I miss her more than I thought I would.'

The 'her' in question was Catriona Charles. Ivan's car accident had been a terrible shock for all of them, even Jack. Pictures of his totalled Bentley printed in the *Sun* were shocking enough to make strangers wince. The car looked like a crushed Coke can, its entire front section obliterated by the huge tree Ivan had careered into at over eighty miles an hour. No one should have survived that crash, still less done so with their mental faculties intact. But then Ivan Charles always *had* had the luck of the devil.

After six weeks at the John Radcliffe Hospital, with Catriona dutifully visiting him for hours each day, the jammy bastard had made a full recovery. He would still need hours of physio, possibly for the rest of his life, and he was under strict doctor's orders to rest and avoid stress of any kind. Kendall had also made regular visits. The shock of what had happened seemed finally to have cleared the way for forgiveness, and there was no animosity towards her from Catriona or the children. Even Hector had hugged her in the hospital cafeteria, a moment that brought tears to Kendall's eyes.

'I won't be able to manage you any more, you know,' Ivan told her, sipping his favourite orange juice that Catriona had brought in from Huffkins in Burford. 'According to the quacks here, all I'm fit for is knitting.'

Kendall laughed. 'Please! You wouldn't have the patience.'

She didn't say anything to Ivan, because she didn't want to risk upsetting him or precipitating a fight, but the truth was she'd already decided to quit the business. Jack's offer to join JSM was a generous one and kindly meant, but the thought of seeing Lex Abrahams at work every single day was more than Kendall could bear. He and Ava were happy, and she told herself she could be happy for them . . . but only from a distance. In any case, her heart just wasn't in it any more. The music business wasn't about music. It was about business. In the early days with Ivan, she'd enjoyed the fight, the constant battle to stay at the top of one's game. But not any more. She wanted to go home, to see her family, to start again. It was time to close this chapter and open a new one.

Jack had called Catriona a couple of times, but he knew from Kendall how Ivan still felt about her, and he was wary of doing anything that might jeopardize his recovery, or make a difficult situation worse. The times they had spoken, Catriona had sounded strange, agitated, as if she were in a hurry to get him off the phone. Reluctantly, Jack had taken the hint and backed off.

'I spoke to Hugh Storey the other day,' Jack told Sonya. 'You remember Hugh, from Oxford? The rower who looked like John Cleese? Anyway, he said Ivan was living with Catriona again. He ran into him at some lunch party in Woodstock and Ivan said he was happier than he'd been in years. You're going to tell me I should be happy for him, aren't you? Happy for both of them? Well, you're right of course. That's the trouble with you, Son. You're always right.'

At that moment a starling landed right on top of the gravestone. It hopped from foot to foot, observing Jack for a moment with its beady, amber eyes. Then it took off, swooping back up into the trees.

Jack grinned. 'I get it. You wanna change the subject.'

He tried to think about something positive to tell her,

some happy news to share. JSM was going great guns, but Sonya didn't want to hear about business. Eventually he said, 'Lex is coming home today. I'm worried about him, actually. He's supposed to be setting up our new office in London, which he *was* excited about. But every time we've spoken recently he sounds like his cat just died.'

Jack would see Lex tonight at dinner. He hoped his fears were ill-founded, that he'd just been catching his partner at bad moments on the phone. But he couldn't shake the feeling that something was really wrong.

Lex gazed out of the plastic plane window at the familiar sights below. The wide grid of freeways, lined with toy-sized palm trees; the grey circle of smog surrounding the city like a carefully blown smoke ring; the tower blocks of downtown, incongruous in such a low-rise city, and dwarfed by the snow-capped peak of Big Bear behind them. This was LA. This was 'home'. So why did it feel so alien? He'd been desperate to get out of England. But now that he was finally here, it hit him with a jolt that what he was running from could not be escaped with air miles. Geography couldn't fix a broken heart.

'I'm gonna have to ask you to stow your computer, sir,' the pretty stewardess told him politely. 'We've started our descent.'

'Of course. Sorry.' Lex flipped shut his MacBook and handed it over. He'd had the figures open on his lap for the past three hours, but may as well have been staring at a blank screen. *What's happening to me? I can't focus on anything.*

He'd finally done the deed and broken up with Ava last night. He'd assumed that she already knew things weren't right between them. He'd been so down and evasive with her lately, refusing to look at apartments for them to move into in London or to talk about summer vacation plans; barely touching her sexually. He'd given her all the signs. But when he actually sat her down and let her know it was over, she'd gasped and sobbed and wailed like a wounded animal. It was awful, just awful.

Today wouldn't be much better. He'd barely slept a wink on the plane, and tonight he had to face Jack and tell him that he wouldn't be moving to London after all. Someone else would have to oversee JSM's expansion. Lex had only offered to do it in the first place because the alternative was coming back to LA and spending every day with Kendall. But now that she'd turned down Jack's offer and reportedly quit the music business, there was nothing to stop him coming home. London winters were grey and bleak and long and unutterably depressing. One more and he'd end up on suicide watch.

They landed on time and for once Lex made it quickly through Customs and baggage claim. The heat mugged him the moment he stepped outside, the sunlight so bright he instantly began scrambling for his shades. Jumping into a yellow cab, he headed straight to Malibu. Patricia, his lovely Guatemalan housekeeper, was there to greet him, relieving him of his bags in the pristine white kitchen and offering to make him frittatas.

'You look *theeen*, Mr Lex,' she exclaimed disapprovingly. 'You go on a crazy diet?'

It's called unrequited love, thought Lex. *I've been on it for a while*.

'Sit down, please. Eat. I cook.'

He stooped down to kiss her on the cheek. Patricia was so short she could be half-Munchkin. 'Later,' he promised. 'I need to sleep right now. But I have a dinner later, so will you be sure to wake me at six, latest?'

Climbing into his crisp, Egyptian cotton sheets, Lex felt as close to happiness as he had in months. Within minutes he sank into a deep, dreamless sleep.

'Would you like to order now, sir, or are you still waiting on your other party?'

The waitress looked at Jack with a mixture of pity and bewilderment. She clearly thought he'd been stood up by a date, but couldn't imagine how such an elegant, good-looking man would find himself in that position.

Irritated, Jack looked at his watch. Lex was forty minutes late and his cell phone was switched off. *Fuck it.* 'I'll order, please. I'll have the California roll, the salmon hand roll and the snow crab claws.'

'Anything to drink?'

'A beer. Asahi, if you have it.'

As soon as the waitress left, Lex came running over to the table at a jog. 'Sorry. Really sorry. I overslept.'

From the crease marks imprinted on his cheeks, the wildly unkempt hair and the shirt buttoned up wrong, Jack could see he was telling the truth. 'Rough flight?'

'It was OK.' Lex ordered a beer and began attacking what was left of the bowl of *edamame*. Without preamble he announced, 'I can't go back to London.'

Jack sighed. He'd been expecting something like this, but it was still depressing to have his suspicions confirmed. 'You wanna tell me why?'

Lex told Jack about his break-up with Ava and the strain of having to play out their relationship in the public eye. 'I wasn't comfortable with it from the beginning. Here in LA it was easy with me and Ava. But once we got to England and the media got involved and her father . . . it was all too much.'

'I understand,' said Jack. 'But—'

'Look, no "buts", OK?' said Lex harshly. 'My mind's made up. I'm not asking your permission, Jack, I'm telling you. I won't go to London.'

'Fine,' snapped Jack. Well this was rich! If anyone ought to be feeling angry and aggrieved here it was him, not Lex. He was the one being let down, with some half-arsed explanation about Ava Bentley. It made no sense anyway. In all likelihood, Ava would spend at least half her time in LA, maintaining her US career, so it wasn't as if Lex could avoid her.

The sushi arrived and they ate in silence. Jack had lost his appetite but Lex suddenly found himself starving, wolfing down roll after roll. Watching his partner stuff his face with *his* food, Jack finally lost his temper.

'What the fuck is going on with you? If you're mad about something, why don't you just tell me? Because for the life of me I can't think of one reason why you should waltz in here, acting like a spoiled child and giving me the evil eye.'

Lex stopped, mid-mouthful. 'You can't think of one reason?'

'Not a one,' said Jack defiantly.

Now it was Lex's turn to lose it. 'How about you fucking Kendall in London?' he spat, pushing his plate away. 'How about that for a reason?'

For a moment Jack was too flabbergasted to respond.

'How about the pair of you being all over each other at Annabel's on Christmas Eve? Or you trying to lure her back to LA to be with you? You know how I feel about her, Jack. How I've always felt about her.' There were tears in Lex's eyes. 'How could you do that to me?'

'But you were with Ava,' Jack protested.

'I never loved Ava!' Lex was shouting now. 'Just like I

433

never loved Leila, not really.' These were things he'd never said to anyone, never even said to himself out loud. It was as if he needed to throw the words out of his body, to get rid of them like live hand grenades. 'It's always been Kendall. But she always wanted you.'

Jack frowned.

'Maybe I wouldn't even care so much if I thought you really loved her too,' Lex went on. 'But you don't. What happened in London was just sex for you, wasn't it? That's the part I can't forgive.'

'You are way off base,' Jack said calmly.

'Am I?' Lex stood up to go. 'Am I, Jack?'

'Yes, you are,' Jack said more forcefully. 'Now, for God's sake sit down before you make even more of an ass of yourself.'

Lex hesitated, then sat with his head in his hands.

'Do you want the truth?' asked Jack. He took Lex's pained groan for assent. 'Number one, nothing happened between me and Kendall in London. Nothing. I swear on my wife's memory.'

Lex looked up. If ever there was a sacred vow for Jack, that was it. 'Really?'

'Really. We'd both had too much to drink that day. We were talking, catching up till late, and she fell asleep on my couch. Period.'

'So what were you doing in bed together?'

'We weren't in bed "together",' said Jack. 'I was sleeping. Kendall came in to say goodbye. You just caught us at an awkward moment, that's all.'

Lex digested this information. 'But what about afterwards? At the Annabel's party, you offering her a contract, trying to get her to move out here?'

'That was business.'

434

'You had your arm around her.'

'I'm her friend!' said Jack. 'She'd just missed out on Christmas number one, she was devastated. What was I suppose to do? Shake her hand? Wave from a distance? It was brave of her to show up at that party, especially knowing you'd be there.'

Lex looked puzzled. 'Me? What do I have to do with it?'

Jack shook his head. How stupid people were when it came to their own love lives. 'She loves you, you moron. It's not me she wants. It's you. What do you think we spent the whole night talking about when she stayed over at The Berkeley?'

'But she . . . she never said anything.'

'Are you surprised? You were with Ava. Plus you were giving her the major cold shoulder.'

Because I thought she was with you.

'I gotta say, it wasn't just Kendall you had fooled,' said Jack. 'I knew you held a torch for her in the past, but I thought all that was dead and buried after the Chateau Marmont pictures.'

Lex sat in stunned silence, too amazed by what Jack had just told him even to be happy. Was it really true? Did Kendall really love him? Suddenly he felt his whole body tense with fear. What if she *had* loved him, but he'd pushed her away and now it was too late? What if she'd already found someone else?

'She's here you know,' said Jack, guessing at his friend's thoughts. 'She's in LA, staying at her mom's.'

'Hi!' The waitress was back with the rest of Jack's order. 'How's the food so far? Is there anything else I can get you gentlemen?'

Ignoring her, Lex stood up and stumbled out of the restaurant without another word. He hadn't even said goodbye to Jack. It was as if he were sleepwalking.

'Is he OK?' asked the girl, frowning.

'Not really,' said Jack. 'But I'm hoping he will be in about – ' he looked at his watch – 'half an hour. The food's excellent, by the way. Can I take a look at your dessert menu?'

Kendall sat by the fire in her mother's house, poring over old photograph albums with her younger sister Holly.

'Can you believe that's me?' She pointed to a picture of herself standing outside the house on the first day of shooting for her reality show, eight years ago. 'I look so young. And check out those *pants*! Why did none of you stop me?'

'You still look young,' said Holly loyally. 'And with your figure you could get away with those pants. Unlike me.'

'Nonsense. You have a gorgeous figure.' Kendall wrapped an arm around her sister. At twenty-two, Holly was plumper than Kendall had ever been, and her cheerful, round face was pretty rather than sexy. But she was without doubt the kindest creature on the planet. Having barely laid eyes on her for the last four years, Kendall was immensely grateful for the warm, forgiving way that Holly had welcomed her back into her life. Their brother Joe was away working in Houston, and Lorna's social life put Paris Hilton's in the shade, so the two girls had had plenty of time alone to reconnect.

Holly yawned. 'I think I might hit the hay. I have an audition tomorrow morning at ten and I still need to learn half my lines.'

'OK,' Kendall kissed her. 'Goodnight.' Watching her sister walk upstairs, she felt a pang of anxiety. She wished Holly hadn't decided to go into acting. The thought of her kid sister at the mercy of all those Hollywood vipers made Kendall's blood run cold. But she knew she mustn't preach. She'd had her own moment in the spotlight. And, besides,

Holly was so much more grounded than she was – she might even be OK.

The doorbell jolted her out of her reverie. The grandfather clock by the fireplace said five after ten. Who on earth could it be at this time of night, and why had security let them past the front gates? If it was some bozo selling something, she was gonna give them a piece of her mind.

Putting on her slippers she shuffled to the front door. 'I hope this is impor . . .'

She left the sentence hanging. All of a sudden her throat had gone horribly dry.

'It's late. I know. Is it too late? Oh shit, I woke you up, didn't I?' Lex stammered. Only then did it occur to Kendall that she was wearing a pair of Snoopy pyjamas and giant fluffy slippers with dog faces on the end.

'I should have called. I'll come back tomorrow.' He turned to go.

'No!' It was more of a yelp than a word, so great was her panic that he would disappear again, that the magic would come undone. 'It's fine, I was up. Come in.'

She led him into the living room. Her heart was pounding so wildly she could hardly hear herself think. 'Would you like some hot chocolate?' All she wanted was for him to stay. Whatever he'd come to talk to her about, a hot drink would drag it out.

'Er . . . OK,' said Lex. After he left Jack, he'd driven into Beverly Hills like a bat out of hell, desperate to see Kendall with his own eyes, to ask her if what Jack had told him was really true. But now that he was here, opposite her, his courage seemed to have deserted him. Where to begin?

'Jack told me you were staying here. Are you just visiting or is it permanent?'

'I'm looking for a place here,' Kendall said cautiously. 'But I don't really know. I've given up planning for the future. It never works out the way you think it's going to.'

Lex smiled. 'That's true.'

An awful silence descended. He wanted so badly to reach out and touch her, but it was as if he'd lost the use of his limbs as well as his tongue. *Do something! Say something, you idiot.*

'Jack says you're not in love with him any more.'

Not that! Jesus fucking Christ, why did you say that?

'Is it true?'

It was like he had Tourette's. The stream of idiocy just kept coming, spewing out of his mouth like sewage. What a fucking disaster.

'Yes, it's true,' said Kendall. 'I'm in love with someone else now.'

'Oh,' said Lex, crestfallen. But what had he expected? Of course she'd found someone else. Why wouldn't she? He'd missed his window, if there'd ever really been a window. What had possessed him to come here?

'He's all I think about, this guy,' said Kendall. 'But it's hopeless. He's taken.'

Lex stood up, his mind a blur. He couldn't cope with hearing about some new man Kendall had set her sights on, with being her shoulder to cry on yet again. 'I'm sorry,' he blurted. 'I made a mistake. I shouldn't have come here.'

Kendall watched him walk away. She tried to be stoic but her heart cracked.

'Why?' she called after him.

'Kendall, I can't.' To his immense embarrassment, Lex realized he was crying.

'Why can't you? Because of Ava? You're getting married,

438

aren't you?' Kendall sobbed. 'That's why you came here tonight, to tell me. You're engaged.'

Lex turned around and stared at her. 'Engaged? Of course I'm not engaged. Ava and I are finished.'

'Then what . . .?'

The two of them gazed at one another, neither one of them daring to hope. Then somehow, without words, they came together, clasping each other like two shipwreck survivors miraculously washed up on the shore.

Lex found his voice first. 'I love you,' he murmured, kissing Kendall's hair and neck and cheeks. 'I've loved you for so long.'

'Even after Ivan?' asked Kendall, kissing him back.

'Even after Ivan.'

'And the Chateau Marmont?'

'And the Chateau.'

'And—'

Lex stopped her with a kiss. 'Let's not run through the whole laundry list, shall we?'

'OK,' sighed Kendall. She felt replete with happiness, gorged like a nectar-swollen bee.

'I don't have a ring,' said Lex. 'But I don't think I can wait another second. Darling, darling Kendall. Will you marry me?'

She hesitated momentarily. Technically she wasn't divorced from Ivan yet. But this was definitely, categorically, *not* the moment to focus on technicalities.

'Of course I'll marry you, Lexi,' she beamed ecstatically. 'Consider yourself stuck with me till death do us part.'

CHAPTER TWENTY-SEVEN

Jack Messenger walked around the empty office space, trying to visualize the room filled with noise and people and computers and constantly ringing telephones. The best thing about the building was its windows; floor-to-ceiling, arched Georgian sashes giving way to panoramic views across Magdalen Meadow and The Fellows' Garden.

Everyone had told him he was mad to set up JSM's UK offices in Oxford rather than London, but Jack had insisted. If he was going to run the UK office himself and start a new life away from LA, he was damn well going to do it in a place he loved. Staring out at the sparkling, frosted wonderland – a late March cold snap had dusted Oxford with a gossamer-thin blanket of snow – he was sure he'd made the right decision. He and Sonya had been happiest here, amid the mellowed, honey stone buildings and charming cobbled streets. The city was idyllic, accessible and creatively inspiring. And the rents were four times cheaper than central London.

'It's serviced, you say?'

'Fully serviced.' The pretty estate agent adjusted the top buttons on her blouse and thought again how much she would like to fully service Jack Messenger. Most of her firm's clients were fat, balding middle managers in telecoms companies, relocating from Swindon or Slough. Drop-dead gorgeous LA rock managers didn't pass through Oxford all that often. 'If you were able to put down a year's rental in advance, we could offer you a considerable discount.'

'I'll take it.' Jack turned away from the window and smiled. 'But I need to be up and running within a week. Can you do that?'

'I'll try,' said the estate agent, flicking back her glossy auburn hair.

'Don't try,' said Jack. 'Succeed. I'll be staying at The Randolph for the next few days. You can drop all the paperwork off there.'

Strolling idly across Magdalen Bridge, past All Soul's, Brasenose and Exeter Colleges towards the spectacular Ashmolean Museum, Jack felt a warm glow of contentment that insulated him against the biting March wind. He'd found an office, which meant that JSM UK had just moved from being a concept to a reality. There were so many opportunities in the British market and across Europe. Coming here with Ava had opened the door, and her battle with Kendall had been the catalyst. But the possibilities for growth went way beyond broadening the careers of JSM's existing clients. There was a wealth of new, untapped talent in the UK, all of it desperate to sign up with a management company that had genuine global reach. For the first time in a long time, Jack found himself genuinely excited and inspired by the business again. Being back in Oxford was merely the icing on the cake.

He was also looking forward to lunch with his godson. Jack hadn't seen Hector in person since his second internship at JSM last year, and even then their paths had crossed rarely. Sticking to his policy of non-involvement in Charles family life, a policy based in equal parts on respect for Ivan's recovery and self-protection, Jack had made no contact since the accident, so he was surprised and delighted when Hector called him up out of the blue and suggested a lunch date.

'You'll have to pay,' he told Jack cheerfully. 'I'm so broke I owe myself money. But can we please go somewhere with big helpings and decent puddings? I'm trying to make the Burford Rugby Club first fifteen so I need to bulk up.'

Jack had chosen Carlo's, a cheap and cheerful Italian that had been around since his own student days and that still served the best spaghetti vongole and tiramisu in town. Hector was already at the table, attacking the bread basket, when he walked in.

'I'm not late, am I?' said Jack, looking at his watch.

'Nope. I was early,' said Hector through a mouthful of crumbs. 'I thought if I sat here for fifteen minutes they'd be bound to feed me something. And they did!' He flashed his godfather a cheeky grin. It was uncanny how much he looked like Ivan.

'So how are things?' asked Jack, sitting down and ordering a salad and chicken paillard. Hector went for the vongole to start, another creamy pasta dish as a main and a side of rosemary roast potatoes, all washed down with full-fat Coke.

'Great,' said Hector, and proceeded to talk about rugby and his love life for the next twenty minutes. Jack listened attentively. It was a relief not to have to hear how blissfully happy Ivan and Catriona were together, although inevitably that conversation was to come. As it turned out, Hector didn't mention either of his parents till he was halfway through his first course.

'Dad's been to a couple of my matches,' he said, wolfing down his roast potatoes one after the other like a dog swallowing treats. 'It's incredible how quickly he's recovered, not just physically but mentally. He's even started a new TV production company and got Jeremy Clarkson and Adrian Gill to back him. So much for retirement.'

'That's great,' said Jack. Despite everything, he couldn't help but feel a sneaking admiration for Ivan's irrepressible energy and ambition. He didn't doubt that the new company would be a success and would put Ivan back on top. He was the ultimate comeback kid.

'Mum always said it would never last, the whole "taking it easy" thing. But I don't think even she imagined he'd be back in the saddle quite this fast.'

Desperate to move the conversation away from Catriona (Jack wished her happiness with Ivan but he wasn't ready to hear about it and wasn't sure he ever would be), he asked Hector about his sister.

'And how's Rosie doing? Did she get into Exeter?'

'Of course she did. Straight As in her exams. Rosie never fails at anything.' It was said with an eye-roll but no real bitterness.

'She must be pleased to have your father back home,' said Jack.

Hector looked at him strangely. 'She's pleased he's better. We all are. But he's not living at Mum's any more.'

Jack put down his knife and fork slowly. 'What do you mean?'

'I mean he's got his own place in Chipping Campden. It's only rented. I'm sure he'll end up back in London eventually.'

'So . . . so . . .' Jack struggled to stop himself from trembling. 'He and your mother aren't back together?'

'Back together?!' Hector burst out laughing, spraying Coke all over the table. 'Jesus Christ, no! Mum wouldn't have Dad back if he were the last man on earth. And, actually, Dad knows deep down it would never work out between them. He likes excitement and Mum likes, well, gardening. She only took him in because he was so ill and had nowhere else to go. She's such a soft touch. Not that I'm complaining,' he grinned. 'Sometimes it pays to have a saint for a mother.'

'So, er . . . are either of your parents, you know, seeing anyone?' Jack asked nervously.

Hector shrugged, as unconcerned with his parents' romantic lives as only a sixteen-year-old boy could be. 'No idea. Dad's probably got some bimbo on the go somewhere. I don't think Mum's really interested in all that stuff. Anyway, she's far too old to get remarried now.'

'Nonsense,' said Jack sternly. 'Your mother could marry anyone she wanted to. She's gorgeous.'

Hector raised an alarmed eyebrow. 'Rosie Huntington-Whiteley's gorgeous, Uncle Jack. Mum's . . . Well, she's just Mum, isn't she? She never changes.'

'No,' said Jack wistfully. 'She never does.'

In Burford, Catriona crouched down in her walled garden, half hidden behind a holly bush and with an ancient 1970s Nikon camera perched on her knee. Three feet in front of her a puff-chested robin was stabbing away at the frozen ground with its beak, determined to unearth a worm. It was an old bird, with worn, frayed feathers and certain stiffness to its movements that lent it a sort of pathetic charm. *Like me*, thought Cat, keeping as still as she could as she snapped away. The robin started at the first click of the shutter, but was too hungry to give up and fly away. At last he prised the worm free, turning direct to camera triumphantly with the thing dangling in his beak before finally hopping away.

Cat stood up, gratified, and stretched her aching legs. That was a perfect shot. She'd begun turning her hand to nature photography recently, bored by the portrait work that had become her bread and butter. Ivan's accident had taught her a lot of things, but one of the main ones was that life was both short and fragile. Rosie had told her an old Inuit saying over Christmas. *'Yesterday is ashes. Tomorrow wood. Only today does the fire burn brightly.'* From now on Catriona was going to be all about today.

Coming inside she put down her camera and threw another pair of logs into the wood-burner. The combination of crisp winter's air and wood smoke never failed to delight her, and she smiled as she warmed her hands over the flames. Her thoughts turned briefly to Hector. He'd planned to have lunch with Jack Messenger in Oxford today, and she wondered if the meeting had actually happened. But she forced her curiosity aside. Thinking about Jack did not make her happy. Her New Year's resolution was to stop doing things that did not make her happy, be it big things like dwelling on the past, or little ones like taking the wrong sort of photographs. Besides, Jack clearly wasn't thinking about her. She hadn't heard a peep from him since Christmas, and only knew he was in Oxford because the children had mentioned it.

Yesterday is ashes. Time to move on.

When Jack first saw her through the parlour window, she was sitting in an armchair by the wood-burning stove, doing *The Times* crossword. With a pair of reading glasses perched halfway down her nose, a pencil in her mouth and a thoughtful frown on her un-made-up, slightly charcoal-smeared face, it was true that she was no Rosie Huntington-Whiteley. But Jack wouldn't have traded Catriona's earthy beauty for all the supermodels ever to grace the pages of *Sports Illustrated*, or her corduroy gardening trousers and holey Guernsey sweater for all the couture gowns in the world.

He stood outside for a long time, staring. By the time some sixth sense made Catriona look up, he was so cold his nose and ears were glowing red and his breath was escaping in smoky plumes in front of him.

'Hi,' he mouthed, waving lamely.

Catriona jumped out of her seat. Her hands flew despairingly to her hair (*greasy, tied up with knickers*) her face (*haggard and bare*) and her clothes (*tramp*). *Why?* Surely there should be some sort of guidebook, some compulsory reading for men, that taught them it was completely unacceptable to appear at a woman's house unannounced, when the woman in question may very well be looking like a dog's breakfast?

You're being vain, she told herself sternly, pulling the knickers out of her hair and stuffing them under a cushion as she got up to let Jack in. *Vain and ridiculous. He doesn't see you in that way anyway.*

Opening the door, she tried to smile. 'Jack. What a nice surprise.'

Jack stood in the doorway, hopping from foot to foot like a nervous teenager. When Hector had told him it was over between Cat and Ivan – more than that; that it had never really even begun, he'd paid the bill at Carlo's, jumped in a taxi and driven straight out to Burford. It wasn't even a choice. It was as if some magnetic force had pulled him here. But now that he *was* here, and the magnetic force was right in front of him being sweet and polite and, *Oh God*, totally uninterested, he had no idea what to do.

'Please, come in,' said Cat. 'You must be freezing.'

Jack dutifully stepped inside.

'Would you like some tea and cake?'

Oh Jesus. Shoot me. She'll start asking me about the weather next.

'Thanks. That'd be nice.'

Jack perched awkwardly on the sofa while Catriona faffed around in the kitchen. When she returned with a tray laden with fruitcake, tea and home-made biscuits, he noticed that she'd wiped the black charcoal smear off her cheek, powdered her nose and sprayed on some sort of perfume.

'I saw Hector today,' he began. 'He came into the city for lunch.'

'I know,' said Cat, trying not to focus on how long and lean his legs looked in those jeans or how the shadows under his eyes somehow managed to make him look even more preposterously handsome. 'How was he?'

'Fine,' said Jack. 'He talked about rugby mostly.'

Cat smiled. 'Ah yes. His new love. I'm afraid he's a little bit obsessed.'

'And Ivan,' said Jack. 'He told me the two of you . . . that Ivan wasn't living here any more.'

'That's true,' said Cat. 'He's much better now and living in Chipping Campden. He can cope on his own.'

'I can't,' said Jack.

Catriona looked up, confused.

'I can't cope on my own. Without you. I just can't. I thought I could, but that's when I thought you and Ivan were back together. As a couple I mean.'

'A *couple*?'

'Yes. Hugh Storey told me—'

'Hugh Storey?' said Catriona crossly. 'What on earth would Hugh Storey know about it? What did he say?'

'Well, come to think of it, all he actually said was that Ivan was living with you and that he was happy. I suppose I put two and two together and made five.'

'Why didn't you call?' asked Catriona, not yet quite brave enough to meet Jack's eye. 'You could have asked me yourself, but I haven't heard from you in months. You just disappeared.'

'I was giving you some space! I thought you were rebuilding your marriage.'

'I don't believe this.' Catriona shook her head. At last she looked up at him. When she did there were tears in her eyes. 'And what if I *had* got back together with Ivan?' She was angry now, although she didn't know why. 'What then? Would that have made it OK for you to drop me as a friend? Do you know how much it hurt, hearing that you were in Oxford of all places, from bloody Rosie?'

Jack stood up and walked to the window. 'I'm sorry. But if you had got back with Ivan, the answer is no. I couldn't have been your friend. I *can't be* your friend, Cat, don't you see?' He turned to look at her. 'I love you.'

Glued to the chair, Catriona felt as if she'd been shot with a stun gun. *He loves me. He loves me!* She knew he was waiting for her to react, to say or do something, anything, but every one of her faculties seemed to have deserted her.

The silence went on forever. Jack felt his hopes die. Fighting back tears, he looked out of the window again. Outside people were milling up and down the hill, shopping and chatting to one another, getting on with their lives as if the world hadn't just ended. *Fools.*

'I don't expect you to feel the same way,' he said bleakly. 'I know everybody says I'm arrogant, but I'm not that arrogant. Why should you want me? I've been distant, and childish about this feud with Ivan, and I daresay you have plenty of reasons not to love a stubborn, workaholic widower who . . .'

He stopped. Catriona was behind him, her arms wrapped

around his waist, her soft, womanly body pressed against the hard wall of his back. She still hadn't said anything. But she pulled at him gently, urging him to turn around. When he did, he saw she was crying. Crying, and smiling. And moving towards him, her face tilted upwards, her beautiful, full, sexy lips parting in what could only be an invitation, an affirmation, a reciprocation of the love that was threatening to burst out of him like water through a dam.

And then it did burst. It was more of an explosion than a kiss, a bomb erupting between them the moment their lips made contact, fusing them together like two atoms in a nuclear reactor. It went on for a long, long time. And when it finished it began again, in a delicious, slow series of aftershocks. By the time they finally surfaced for air, still locked in one another's arms, a small crowd had formed on the pavement outside. Somebody started clapping. Soon the whole street seemed to have joined in, whooping and cheering as if Jack and Catriona had just won the doubles at Wimbledon.

Jack laughed. 'That's community spirit for you. I think I'm going to like living here.'

Blushing, Catriona closed the curtains.

'Living here? I thought you said you weren't that arrogant! Don't you think that's a little presumptuous, after one kiss?'

'You're right,' said Jack, scooping her off her feet and into his arms and marching upstairs to the bedroom. 'One kiss doesn't cut it, does it? But by the time I'm finished with you, Catriona Charles, believe me: you're going to be begging me to stay.'

Catriona did believe him.

She would never doubt him again.

EPILOGUE

The wedding of Kendall Bryce to Lex Abrahams was the music-business event of the year. Rock stars, managers, producers and record-company moguls all waited eagerly to hear whether they would be among the favoured few attending the service itself, held in a small chapel in Montecito, or merely making up the numbers at the lavish, star-studded reception at the famous San Ysidro Ranch.

It was Vernon Bryce, Kendall's long-absent movie-producer father who'd insisted on the San Ysidro.

'It's the best, and my daughter deserves the best. Vivien Leigh and Laurence Olivier were married there. You could hardly ask for a better omen than that.'

'Couldn't you?' said Lex. 'She was a manic depressive who would berate her husband so violently she used to pass out afterwards, then cheated on him, divorced him and died of TB.'

Kendall giggled.

'Well, what about Gwyneth Paltrow and Chris Martin, then?' Vernon countered. 'They got married here. And they're still together.'

'Great. We could have kids called Banana and Peaches and write songs that make people wanna slit their wrists.'

But Vernon had prevailed, largely because of Kendall's desire to keep the peace. Also because she wouldn't have cared if she'd married Lex in a lay-by off the 405. All that mattered was that they were getting married. The rest was for other people. A *lot* of other people.

The service went off beautifully, with both the bride and groom visibly glowing with love in front of their close friends and respective families. But the reception was the main event, with over five hundred people, many of them world-famous celebrities, milling around the hotel's famous wedding garden, while paparazzi helicopters swarmed overhead. There was a vodka ice fountain that proved very popular with many of JSM's acts, especially The Blitz's Brett Bayley, who was so drunk by the cutting of the cake he had to be carried out on a stretcher.

'Do you think it's because of Stella and you-know-who?' Martina Munoz asked Ben Braemar, the lead singer of Land of the Greeks, as Brett was carried away.

'I doubt it,' said Ben. 'I think it's probably because he's a raging alkie. You're totally hot, by the way. D'you have a boyfriend?'

The big gossip of the reception so far had been Ivan Charles, Kendall's ex-husband, turning up arm in arm with Stella Bayley, one of her closest friends.

'Can you believe Stella and Ivan are dating?' Lex asked Kendall, incredulous. 'Isn't that, like, insanely incestuous?'

'Insanely,' Kendall agreed. In a simple Alice Temperley gypsy-style wedding dress and bare feet, she looked more radiantly beautiful than even Lex had ever known her. Every time he looked at her he was torn between the urge to rip her clothes off and the urge to take a picture. That sort of perfection deserved to be immortalized. And it was all his.

Sometimes, most of the time, he still had to pinch himself to believe it.

'You're not upset, are you?'

'Upset?' She beamed at him, physically unable to emerge from her happiness cloud, even for a second. 'Of course not. Why would I be? Stella's an angel, and she knows all his faults. If anyone can keep him on the straight and narrow, she can.'

Catriona agreed. Stella was already proving to be a good influence on Ivan if his civility towards Jack today was anything to go by. With half the world's press on standby for fireworks between the old Jester partners and well-known rivals, Cat had been nervous about attending the wedding. But Jack had insisted – 'we've got nothing to hide' – and in the end it had been a wonderful day, a party full of love and laughter and old friends, and Ivan on his very best, most charming behaviour.

'You're much nicer than you were when we were married,' Catriona teased him good-naturedly.

'Hitler was much nicer than I was when we were married,' joked Ivan. 'And *you're* about twenty times more gorgeous now that you're with Jack. What's that about?'

Catriona grinned. 'Love, I guess. We're very happy.'

At the bar, watching her chatting with her ex, Jack felt a painful stab of jealousy. He and Catriona weren't married. They'd both agreed that at their age, and having known one another so long, they had no need of the formality. But when he saw her around other men, especially Ivan, the fear that he might lose her easily transformed into full-blown panic. When she left Ivan and headed straight for the ladies loo instead of coming to find him, his head filled with ridiculous thoughts. *She's going to text him. She's sending him a private number. Seeing him with Stella has made her question everything.* By the time Catriona finally emerged, smiling from ear to ear, Jack was in a paroxysm of self-doubt, paranoia and outright terror.

'You took your time,' he snapped at her.

Catriona's smile faded. 'I didn't realize it was a race. I was in the loo.'

'Doing what?'

'Jack! What on earth's got into you?' she frowned. 'I was having a pee. What did you think I was doing, snorting cocaine?'

'Of course not. Don't be ridiculous.'

'You're the one being ridiculous,' she told him crossly. 'What's all this about?'

'Oh, God. Nothing. I'm sorry.' Jack pulled her into his arms. In a pale-yellow empire-line dress with white roses sewn along the bust, she looked like a Jane Austen heroine, pure and lovely and timelessly elegant. Just looking at her made his heart crack. 'I'm an idiot. Forgive me?'

'Yes, well,' she kissed him. 'You *are* an idiot. But I suppose we'll have to forgive you.'

She looked up at him knowingly. It took Jack a few seconds to register the 'we'. And quite a few more seconds to process the implications of that innocuous-sounding two-letter word.

'You aren't . . .?'

Pulling him to one side, Catriona pulled the pregnancy test out of her bag and showed him the two pink lines.

'What do you think?' she smiled nervously. 'I know it's unexpected, and we're both a bit long in the tooth for nappy changing. But it's good news . . . isn't it?'

Tears of happiness rolled down Jack's cheeks. *Good news?*
It was the best news ever.

Also by Tilly Bagshawe:
SCANDALOUS

If you loved *Friends and Rivals*, come and immerse yourself
in a story of revenge, love and betrayal, played out among
the ivory towers of Cambridge.

Sasha Miller comes to Cambridge with a dream,
but she soon falls for the lies and charms of her
Director of Studies, Theo Dexter.

She leaves betrayed and humiliated.

Years later, Sasha emerges from Harvard Business School
with a plan for vengeance.

Meanwhile, Theo's long-suffering
wife Theresa also finds herself
betrayed – she is cast aside for
a younger and prettier model.

One night Sasha turns up at
Theresa's door. She wants
revenge at any cost, but will
Theresa help her?

From the deepest betrayal
comes a shocking alliance.

Two vengeful women,
one very unlucky man …

Tilly
Bagshawe

SCANDALOUS

'Total escapist, self-indulgent pleasure'
Sophie Kinsella

Also by Tilly Bagshawe:

FAME

A must-read, glamorous blockbuster

Plucked from obscurity at the age of seventeen, Sabrina Leon is
the new darling of the film scene, bagging lead roles in the hottest
Hollywood movies. But a YouTube scandal on the web is about
to destroy everything she's fought for …

Hotshot movie producer Dorian Rasmirez has struggles of his own.
After a bitter feud with a rival, Dorian has the plug pulled on every
project he goes near. Casting the disgraced Hollywood diva
Sabrina Leon in *Wuthering Heights* is a risk that might turn
his losing streak around, or destroy what remains of his career.

Newcomer Viorel Hudson has
scored the role that every A-lister
in Hollywood auditioned for –
Heathcliff in Dorian Rasmirez's
Wuthering Heights. But is he ready
for his latest role? For a five
million pound pay cheque, it's a
risk he's willing to take.

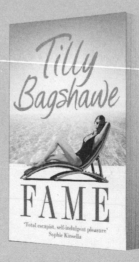

Set against the backdrop of a
sumptuous English country house,
the filmmakers are desperate for
some on-screen chemistry – but it's
off-camera that the sparks are
really going to fly …